T0031954

The **Spy**
and **I**

The Spy and I

TIANA SMITH

BERKLEY ROMANCE

New York

BERKLEY ROMANCE
Published by Berkley
An imprint of Penguin Random House LLC
penguinrandomhouse.com

Copyright © 2024 by Tiana Smith
Excerpt from *Mr. Nice Spy* copyright © 2024 by Tiana Smith
Penguin Random House supports copyright. Copyright fuels creativity,
encourages diverse voices, promotes free speech, and creates a vibrant culture.
Thank you for buying an authorized edition of this book and for complying
with copyright laws by not reproducing, scanning, or distributing any part
of it in any form without permission. You are supporting writers and allowing
Penguin Random House to continue to publish books for every reader.

BERKLEY and the BERKLEY & B colophon are
registered trademarks of Penguin Random House LLC.

Library of Congress Cataloging-in-Publication Data

Names: Smith, Tiana, author.
Title: The spy and I / Tiana Smith.
Description: First edition. | New York: Berkley Romance, 2024.
Identifiers: LCCN 2023031112 (print) | LCCN 2023031113 (ebook) |
ISBN 9780593550304 (trade paperback) | ISBN 9780593550311 (ebook)
Subjects: LCGFT: Romance fiction. | Spy fiction. | Novels.
Classification: LCC PS3619.M59524 S69 2024 (print) |
LCC PS3619.M59524 (ebook) | DDC 813/.6—dc23/eng/20230928
LC record available at https://lccn.loc.gov/2023031112
LC ebook record available at https://lccn.loc.gov/2023031113

First Edition: February 2024

Printed in the United States of America
1st Printing

Book design by Ashley Tucker

This is a work of fiction. Names, characters, places, and incidents
either are the product of the author's imagination or are used
fictitiously, and any resemblance to actual persons, living or dead,
business establishments, events, or locales is entirely coincidental.

To my siblings:
You're all so obnoxiously amazing, it
gives me a complex. So thanks for that.
You know I love you anyway.

The Spy and I

Chapter One

· · · · · · · · · ·

IF YOU GAVE ME FOUR MINUTES, I COULD GIVE YOU THE world. Okay, so maybe it's more like I could hack into any secure network and give you all the private data stored there. But when that data included someone's credit cards, Social Security number, or complete medical history, it may as well have been the world.

I had my limits. I'd never hacked into the Pentagon or tried my hand at the FBI's firewalls. I was good, but I wasn't stupid. And yes, if I was being completely honest, some sites definitely took longer. A lot longer. But going off averages, four minutes was more than enough time to ruin someone's good day.

Earbuds in, "I Did Something Bad" by Taylor Swift began playing and the stopwatch in my head started ticking down.

I inserted the USB drive into the server, which uploaded the code embedded there and created a back door into the system. Ten seconds down.

To my right, my own laptop rested, its cursor blinking incessantly, the only real light in this dark room stacked full of computer towers and cords. I sat cross-legged on the cold linoleum floor of Enderlake Enterprises' mechanical room with my back to the wall and eyes on the door.

Thirty seconds. I pulled my laptop over. No time for games; I needed to steal the CEO's cookies. Not the edible kind—though I could really go for a snack right about now—no, what I needed were cookies of the digital variety. I needed to make a fake admin account.

That took almost a minute, the stopwatch in my head steadily ticking louder with each passing second. The perfectly timed song playing in my ears had passed the chorus, letting me know I was slightly behind.

I grabbed the session token by sniffing the traffic, then I brute-forced the password list. A bead of sweat wound down my neck as my fingers flew over the keyboard, inputting a string of code. Two scripts later, I was finally in. A minute and a half down.

Then the real work began. I booted up IceWeasel, generated a target list, and started a Metasploit listener, all with a few practiced keystrokes, the various screens barely having a chance to pop up before I'd moved on to the next task. Three minutes.

One by one I copied the vulnerabilities from the server to my own laptop, the red highlight from the screen reflecting onto my face. A strand of hair fell in front of my eyes, but I couldn't slow my typing to brush it out of the way. Moving on from the red vulnerabilities, I started on the orange.

My automated software covered everything from SSL/TLS layers to basic CGI vulnerabilities and more, so I let it do its thing while I stole a glance at the clock.

Four minutes. My time was up, the stopwatch now ringing in my mind, Taylor's song coming to a close. But I'd already succeeded.

The door to the mechanical room opened, the light spilling from the hallway to my hiding place. Standing in the doorway was the vice president of Enderlake Enterprises—who just so happened to be my old college roommate and a good friend.

"Do you always work in the dark like a criminal?" Nyah flipped on the overhead light, her textured curls silhouetted like a halo around her face. I squinted against the sudden glare and shaded my eyes with a hand. I removed my earbuds and shot her a grin.

"Working like a criminal helps me think like them." I turned my computer around so she could see everything I'd documented. "Bad news is, your network isn't as secure as you'd hoped. Good news is, I did everything on a modified admin account and recorded all my actions so you can easily see how to fix the flaws."

Though my job was honest, it didn't make me a lot of friends. No one liked knowing I could bring down their company with just my pinky finger. It paid well though, and besides some late nights, I couldn't really complain. Companies paid me to find their security flaws, and I obliged, like a modern-day Robin Hood but without the potential for jail time.

Nyah groaned. "When you said you could hack us in four minutes, I was really hoping you were bluffing." Despite her dress slacks, she settled beside me on the floor and took my laptop to scroll through my color-coded cheat sheet.

For the next half hour, I walked Nyah through the vulnerabilities of her network and the steps she'd need to take to fix them. When I could see her eyes glazing over, I started packing up my things.

"I'll do a more detailed analysis over the next couple of weeks, put everything in writing, and send you the documentation for your developers." I slid my laptop into my bag. "I want to make sure I don't miss anything, so that will take more time."

"Thanks, Dove." She stood up and brushed the dirt from her pants. "You're the best."

I shrugged. "Just doing my job."

"Your job of proving to the world that blond girls have brains?" Nyah smiled. "Or that a twenty-seven-year-old can take out one of the oldest tech firms in all of DC?"

I laughed. "Well, I'm only a blond because of a very talented hairdresser, so I'm not sure I can take credit for that one."

My phone buzzed, my sister's face lighting up my screen. My shoulders tensed.

Nyah waved her hand. "Go ahead and take that." She looked down at her watch before glancing back up at me. "I'm supposed to be in a meeting soon anyway. I'll catch up with you later when you send me all the data. You know the way out?"

I nodded, already bringing the phone up to my ear and accepting Madison's call. Nyah was out the door in a cloud of perfume.

In the two seconds it took my phone to connect, my stomach swooped at least three times. Working on this project for Nyah had allowed me to forget real life for a second. When I was coding, it was easy to feel confident. Powerful. But when I was back in reality? I was just me again. Still single. Still disturbingly average and second best to everyone. Including my sister, who had it all and succeeded in everything she tried.

She knew what she was doing in life. I didn't even know what I was doing for dinner.

"Hey, Mads, what's up?" I zipped my bag and slung it over my shoulder.

"You'd better have plans tonight." Her voice was playful—

the fun ribbing of a sister who most likely knew my "plans" consisted of a bubble bath and maybe a scented scrub if I was feeling fancy.

"Sorry to disappoint." I exited the mechanical room and made my way toward the elevators.

"No, you're not."

She was right. A homebody by nature, I found most social outings either stressful, boring, or a brain-bleeding combination of the two. Especially lately, when all I really wanted to do was stay home and drown my sorrows in ice cream. My sister, on the other hand, was one of those pesky people-person types. The never-take-no-for-an-answer type. She could seamlessly fit into any group and make even the most reclusive person feel at ease in her presence. It was a gift.

One that I did not have.

"It's Friday," she continued when I stayed silent. "You promised you'd get a date for this weekend." My big sister. Always looking out for me. Or always judging—take your pick.

She was one to talk though. It wasn't like she was happily married or anything. But, to give her credit, she was a whole lot better than me at relationships. She'd once dated a guy long-distance for three years. I mean, who does that? Superheroes like Madison, that's who. I, on the other hand, rarely made it to the second date, whether they lived in the same city or not.

"I have an interview in an hour with a journalist," I replied. "He's doing a story on women in tech. Does that count as a date?"

"Not unless the journalist happens to be single and has the build of a Hemsworth brother."

I pushed the button outside the elevator and watched the light illuminate each floor number on its rise to where I was waiting.

"We've been kind of flirty over Messenger for the last, oh, week or so as we set up this appointment."

It had to count for something. I was trying. That was all she could ask of me. And I had to admit, I was curious about this man who managed to flirt despite never having met me in person. He'd ask me random questions and I'd reply with something coy, all the while hinting that he was trying to get out of meeting in real life by doing the interview over Messenger. Then he'd respond how he'd never dream of it and ask me something else that would bring me slowly out of my shell. I blushed, then remembered my sister was waiting for me to continue.

"It's a 'top 30 under 30 in the DC area' kind of story," I added. Hopefully that would be enough to get her off my back. I was just fine putting my career before guys, but Madison seemed to think my chances of becoming a spinster cat lady increased exponentially with every month I was still single. I didn't even have a cat. I pushed the elevator button again, like that would make it move faster. "You should be proud."

She sighed. "Of course I'm proud. But I'd be prouder if you left your apartment once in a while."

"I'm out of my apartment now."

"For work, I'm guessing." She didn't sound mad. Just resigned. She'd taken on the mother role a long time ago, and old habits were hard to break. Even now that we were both grown and out of the foster system, she always checked up on me. It was nice. And also annoying.

"Yes, but in my defense, I also saw an old college friend. So, two birds, one stone, and all that jazz."

She paused, and I knew I wouldn't like whatever she was about to say next. It was the reason I'd dreaded picking up her call.

"Dove, Everett broke up with you two years ago. It's time to move on."

I sucked in a breath. It was just like her to judge me when I was already at rock bottom. I stepped into the elevator and jabbed the button for the lobby with more force than was probably necessary.

Perfect people shouldn't get an opinion on other people's lives. Madison always fit into all her clothes without dieting or watching calories. She dated successful models and important business executives. When it was time to move on, *she* was the one who called things off. Unlike me, who, as much as I hated to admit it, had had my fair share of humiliating dumpings. Like with Everett—who I didn't want to think about right now. Point was, she shouldn't get to have a say.

"Hey, I'll have you know," my throat was closing up and my voice came out strangled, "I went on a blind date last week."

Only because a girl in my apartment building badgered me into going out with her cousin. But hey, it totally counted. And it'd hopefully move the topic away from Everett.

"Really? How'd it go?" Madison sounded way too excited for someone whose wardrobe consisted mainly of cocktail black. I thought back to the date in question and cringed.

"Not well." I chewed on my lip and debated how best to answer. I lowered my voice, even though there wasn't anyone in the elevator with me. "He thought I was an . . . an *escort*, Mads." Even now, almost a week later, the embarrassment stained my cheeks red.

Madison paused, the phone line crackling with static as the elevator descended. There were four seconds of total silence before she spoke again.

"You told him you were a penetration tester, didn't you?" She was barely holding back laughter and I had to stop myself from glaring at the empty air.

"It's the truth!" My voice broke and I took three deep breaths.

Madison's sigh was weighty, loaded with accusations. "*Honest hacker*, Dove. That's the term you should use for people who don't know any better."

I snorted, but she talked over me. "Then you explain that you're basically a glorified computer nerd that hacks into systems for a living and companies pay you to point out their security flaws. There's no need for proper titles." Her voice dripped with disapproval. If she'd been here in the elevator with me, her frown would have made me pause. The expression "if looks could kill" was practically made for Madison.

"If he's going to make assumptions before I've even had a chance to go over the official terminology of my occupation," I said, "he doesn't deserve the explanation in the first place. His reaction told me everything I needed to know about him."

She didn't argue with me there. Honestly, that was a good thing, because I didn't feel like arguing. I felt like crawling into a hole and staying there for the better part of a century.

"I think I'm done with the dating scene for a while," I said. Which was a big understatement. I didn't plan on going on another date for at least a year. If ever. Men were overrated.

"Okay, so no date tonight. But you have to get out of your apartment."

I hummed in noncommittal agreement, because really, it wasn't like she'd find out. As a travel photographer, Madison was *out* of town more often than she was *in* it, and what she didn't know wouldn't hurt her. That was probably half the reason she tried so hard to play matchmaker. She didn't want me to be alone so much. Truth was, I didn't mind the solitude.

I stepped off the elevator and into the lobby, an airy space decorated with plush chairs and an oversized entry desk that was trying too hard to look stately. I placed my guest pass on the counter and gave a small wave to the receptionist as I left.

Over the phone, Madison sighed. "I guess we'll just have to do something together." The hint of humor was back in her voice, her big reveal no doubt meant to capture my attention.

"You're in town? When'd you get back?" And why hadn't she told me before now?

"Only just, and I'll be leaving again in the morning. So, this is a limited-time offer. How about Brock's? I'll pay."

I frowned. "Not fair. You know I can't resist their chocolate mousse."

"You know what they say: all's fair in love and war." I could tell from her tone that she thought she'd already won. But I wasn't about to go down so easily. Oh no, not even the promise of chocolate mousse was enough to make me forget my bubble bath and audiobook.

"I'm not going to get all gussied up just so you can leave me at the bar the second someone attractive starts paying you attention. I'd only get to hang out with you for approximately ten seconds."

When it came to wrapping men and women around her finger, Madison was a pro. I think it came with the whole people-person thing, because even though we looked a lot alike, practically identical, I never got half as much interest as she did. Granted, my dating pool was smaller—that, or I radiated "geek," which was also a distinct possibility.

She laughed. "Way to suck the fun out of it. You know, sometimes you can be a real liability." She tsked, making it clear she was joking, but I couldn't let an insult like that stand.

"A liability?" I huffed. "I'll have you know, I'm an asset. A hot piece of asset, thank you very much. You'd be lucky to have me as your wingwoman. Now," I cleared my throat like I meant business, "I'm waiting for your promise."

"Of course." She chuckled. "I'm only in town for a few hours. You think I want to spend them with some random fling instead of the best sister in the whole wide world?"

I smiled, her approval making me feel warm and fuzzy. "Well, when you put it like that, how can I say no? How about six o'clock? My interview should definitely be over by then."

"Let's make it eight." I heard rustling in the background of the call as I stepped out the doors and headed toward the closest metro station. The noise of the city surrounded me, and I raised my voice to compensate.

"Why so late?" Hunger and I didn't exactly mix. I'd be gnawing on the furniture if I waited that long.

"I have a work thing I need to do before."

I grumbled in response. "All the tables will be gone. How about I show up early to snag us a seat?" And maybe eat an appetizer or two. Perhaps dessert first, because we only live once, and I deserved it.

"You don't have to do that." Her voice was clipped and sharp, causing me to stop short. A woman bumped into me from behind and cursed, navigating around me while muttering and giving me a dirty look. Ah, Washington, DC, don't ever change.

"I'm offering to do something nice," I said into the phone. I ignored the DO NOT CROSS signal and jogged across the street. "You're acting like I kicked a puppy."

Madison huffed. "I just don't want you waiting there all alone when there's no need."

"It's no trouble. And I like being by myself, remember? That's part of my loner charm."

"Dove, don't be a hero. Just show up at eight and we can find seats at the bar." Madison's tone was firm, with no room for negotiation. But I was the youngest child. I was never one to follow authority.

"I'll be there as early as I want." I might as well have stuck out my tongue for how mature I was behaving, but in my defense, Madison was acting out of character too.

Madison sighed in response. "Fine. Be stubborn." She paused, then snapped her fingers. "Oh! How about we try that new burger place by your apartment complex instead? We do Brock's too much."

I glared at my phone, even though she couldn't see it. "Why are you being like this?" I turned the corner and saw the sign for the metro station up ahead. "You promised me chocolate mousse, remember? You can't weasel out of it now." I shook my head. "We're going to Brock's. I'm getting on the metro now, so I'm going to lose service. See you tonight. I'll save us a table." I hung up the phone before she could argue any further.

Chapter Two

· · · · · · · · · ·

SILENTLY, I THANKED MADISON FOR TEMPTING FATE AND asking whether the journalist interviewing me had the build of a Hemsworth brother.

Because the man in front of me was every bit as good-looking as I could have hoped, meaning at least this interview shouldn't be hard to get through. I was already socially awkward enough. The least the universe could do was throw me a handsome guy with broad shoulders to make this experience easier.

He met me in the lobby of the *Journal*, holding his hand out to shake mine.

"Dove Barkley? I'm Sam Olsen."

His black hair curled around the edges of his ears, and he had a five o'clock shadow that fit with his reporter vibe. I pictured him working on an article so late he couldn't be bothered with such a pesky thing as shaving. It somehow made him look simultaneously dangerous and sensual, like one of those guys who modeled expensive watches or cologne. His skin was darker than mine, hinting at a mixed heritage, and his smile was easy and relaxed.

No wonder he was so confident over Messenger. A guy with his looks didn't have to worry about rejection.

"Hi," I said.

Super eloquent. Yep, that was me. Maybe this interview would go downhill faster than I thought.

"Nice shirt," he said, holding open the door that separated the lobby from the interior offices.

I looked down and winced. "Oh." Interviews were not the time to wear graphic tees. Especially ones that read *Code-Blooded*. I'd planned on changing but had spent more time at Enderlake Enterprises than I'd anticipated and couldn't go home first. I made a mental note to change before meeting Madison, or she'd never let me hear the end of it.

"Yeah, uh, thanks?" I didn't know whether Sam was being sarcastic or not. His smile was friendly, but I didn't know him well enough to read him.

"Let's go to my office." He motioned for me to join him in walking past an empty desk and down the hallway. I'd never been in a newspaper's office before, but there wasn't anything special to it. It was modern enough, with glass doors and chrome fixtures, though I guess I'd been expecting more people, noise, and hubbub. More "Stop the presses!" type of running around, with frenzied writers typing away while ranting about deadlines and whatnot.

There wasn't any of that. People quietly worked at their desks, a few of them talking over cubicle walls or milling around in common areas. We walked past an actual water cooler, and I smiled. I'd been a freelancer for so long I almost forgot what an office was like. Usually I worked from home, in my pajamas, on my couch, with an enormous mug of tea to keep me company. I only went in for jobs when the client wanted information about what security flaws were in their internal systems, like I did for Nyah at Enderlake Enterprises.

We went around the perimeter of the cubicles, toward the back of the building, until we approached the end of the hall. I walked a step or so behind Sam, admiring the view. Maybe I didn't want a boyfriend, but that didn't mean I couldn't at least look.

"Two thirty-one. This is it." Sam read the number on the office door, like he had to remind himself. He turned to face me, then pulled on the key fob attached to his belt and swiped it at the pad that was now behind him.

I moved forward to follow him, but that was where I ran into a problem. Literally. Because Sam didn't turn around to enter the office. His key fob blinked red, signaling it didn't work, but by that point I had too much momentum to stop. I collided with him—and my hand? Yeah, that happened to land in a . . . less than ideal, *private* area.

I jerked back immediately, my mouth open like a fish. I was a malfunctioning robot, sparks heating up my face.

"This isn't that kind of interview," Sam said, a hint of a grin playing out on his expression.

"Oh. Myyy—" My mouth couldn't form sentences. Was it possible to die from embarrassment? Because I was pretty sure my heart had stopped beating. "I am *so* sorry." My words came out in a rush. "So so sorry. I didn't mean, I mean, I, of course I didn't mean to, but I didn't, ugh, I just . . ." I trailed off, completely at a loss for how to save this moment and completely aware of how my blathering wasn't making things any better. Did I always have to be so awkward? It was like my soul and body had disconnected, and I was watching myself behave like an idiot from afar. This couldn't be happening. Sam was going to write an article about me, and I'd just touched him. *There.* Who knew what he'd write now?

"Forget about it." Sam's grin was one second away from busting up into a full-on laugh, which kicked my heartbeat back into high gear. This man was so beautiful. Simply looking at him was enough to bring a dead woman back to life. I bit my lip and put my hands behind my back, still at a loss for words. Of course I had to embarrass myself in front of someone who looked like a movie star. Forget Everett—I was ready to build a future with Sam and I'd only just met him. He was *that* good-looking.

Sam swiped his key fob again, and this time the sensor blinked green, unlatching the door. I looked away and waited for him to enter before following at a safe distance, putting a good six feet between us.

The office was generic and small, a fake plant in the corner and a few chairs facing a desk. Sam saw me assessing it and shrugged like he knew it wasn't much.

"I typically work from a cubicle. This is a shared office for when one of us needs to do an interview."

Hence why he'd seemed to need the room number to find it. And why there weren't any knickknacks or framed pictures. But how was I supposed to know if Sam was single?

"Oh." I wasn't sure what else to say. If I didn't figure out how to speak around this man, and soon, this interview would go up in flames.

"So, Dove." He motioned for me to take a seat while he walked around to the other side of the desk. "Tell me about your job in tech."

"You mean my job as a penetration tester." I was practically daring him to comment as I settled into the chair. Might as well get the uncomfortable part of this dialogue over with. Besides, his reaction would tell me all I needed to know.

Sam pressed his lips together and raised one eyebrow.

"Yes, as a penetration tester." He folded his arms across his chest and smirked. The expression really worked for him. "So, you . . . make sure the hardware is firm?"

I choked back a laugh and hoped my ears weren't turning pink. I probably shouldn't have been surprised at the direction this interview was going. I'd already groped him accidentally, so I wasn't one to talk.

"Something like that," I managed to get out between coughs.

Sam listened and took notes with a notepad and pen while I described my job. Old-school, but I liked it. We discussed coding, hacking, and computers for almost half an hour before Sam branched out to other topics. I was surprised at how fast the time was going, because as much as I hated to admit it, I bored people easily whenever I talked shop. But Sam never acted disinterested. Then again, he was being paid to talk to me.

"What about your family?" Sam flipped the page on his notepad, his forearm flexing ever so slightly with the movement. Even his forearm was corded with muscles, and I had to pry my eyes away so I wouldn't be caught staring.

"Your sister, Madison? Are you close?" he asked.

I leaned back in surprise.

Sam inclined his head slightly. "I, uh, may have looked up a few details before our interview." His blush was adorable. Like he was embarrassed to have checked my online profiles, even though he was a journalist and that was literally part of his job description. I didn't have that excuse, but for some reason, the truth came out anyway.

"I looked you up too, but you don't have any social media

profiles. You know who else can say that? Grandparents and serial killers."

The only thing I'd found were articles with his name, since he'd messaged me from a generic work account. There wasn't even a picture to accompany it. Maybe if he'd had that, I would have been more prepared for the tall, dark, and brooding man before me. Especially when he smiled the way he was now.

He paused, considering his answer. "Work in my profession long enough and you realize that information is power."

I raised an eyebrow, skeptical. "They have privacy settings."

"You, of all people, should know how easy it is to get around those."

This made me smile, and I inclined my head. "Touché."

Just because Sam was right didn't mean I had to like it. There was still so much I wanted to know about him, but this interview was only supposed to go one way, and asking *him* the questions burning me from the inside might be frowned upon. The longer I sat in Sam's presence though, the more I found myself wondering whether he was a morning person or if he needed coffee to function. Did he like rom-coms the way I did, or was he more into action movies? Did Sam respect his mother? Maybe he was a mama's boy, like Everett.

Everett. My thoughts stopped cold, and the smile disappeared from my face.

The baggage from that relationship may have been a few years old, but it still circled around the conveyor belt even now. Just because I'd moved on didn't mean I wanted to invite someone new into my life to mess everything up again. I felt like a mom who was tired of picking up after her kids. *I barely got this place clean. Let's not play this game right now.*

Everett was the reason, the *only* reason, I needed to stop

whatever this was with Sam. Sure, we'd flirted over Messenger, and he was acting interested during this interview. And okay, when Sam's shirt pulled across his shoulders, like it was doing now, it made my breath catch. But I never wanted to experience that kind of hurt again. It might feel good in the beginning, but it never ended well.

Sam seemed nice, but even nice boys could break your heart. *Especially* nice boys.

"My sister and I are very close," I said, returning my focus to the interview. Where it should be. Not on Sam's shoulders, or the way the limits of his short sleeves were tested whenever he happened to flex. "She's the only real family I have."

"Right." Sam seemed unruffled by my sudden pivot. "So, your parents . . . ?" he trailed off.

"Haven't been in the picture since I was thirteen."

I didn't elaborate. Those details weren't something I wanted to see in an article attached to my name.

Maybe there was something different in my tone, because Sam paused, and his expression turned soft. "I'm sorry. For what it's worth, I know what it's like to lose someone close to you."

He didn't give details, but I could tell the topic was raw for him by the way he swallowed. He sucked in a shaky breath and leaned back in his chair as we sat there in a moment of shared silence.

He glanced down at his notepad and cleared his throat, a hint of red appearing on his cheeks. "So, your sister and you are close. When did you last see her? What do you like to do when you hang out?"

My mouth scrunched to the side as I tried to remember. "I don't know, maybe two weeks ago? No, more like three. We went to an outdoor concert at the Merriweather Post Pavilion."

Where she'd left me without a car when she "had something come up"—aka someone had probably asked her out. It was always the same story with her. She was the poster child for crossing all her t's and dotting her i's though, so before she'd left, she'd gotten me an Uber. Like I wouldn't have been responsible enough to think of that on my own.

Sam nodded. "Right, the Vamps concert."

I stared at him, mouth agape. We had a lot of bands come through Washington, DC. How he knew that one was almost eerie.

"You found that out from researching me too?" I asked. This guy really got into his job. That, or he was . . . interested? I shouldn't have felt flattered by that. I'd posted a picture from the concert on my main feed after all, so it wasn't hard to find. But there it was all the same, a warmth at the thought that maybe Sam had scrolled a bit longer on my feed than his job required. That maybe he liked to look at me the way I liked looking at him.

"Oh, I wrote an article about it," he said, bursting my bubble. I smiled weakly and brushed my hair off my shoulder. I was failing abysmally at this interview. I needed to keep things on track, not be mooning over some guy who probably wasn't even single. Not with his face. Nothing good ever came from someone with his looks. Everett was exhibit A.

Sam tapped his pen against the edge of the desk. "Okay, next question."

I folded my hands in my lap and nodded, not quite trusting my voice yet.

"Would you say your sister influences your work?"

I almost laughed at the question, because it was obvious Sam wanted a safe topic.

"No, she's not really involved with my work at all." I crossed one leg over the other while I considered what to say. "She doesn't understand it, so she pretty much ignores it. Much like I do with her photography. Her photos are impressive, but I'd be hard-pressed to tell you how her style differs from any other photographer out there." I snapped my mouth shut and prayed he wouldn't use that in the article. I could only imagine Madison's response when she read that.

Sam watched me for a beat, scrutinizing my reaction, probably analyzing why I was so bad at simply interacting with another human being. Then he nodded, writing something on his paper. I resisted the urge to lean over and see what it was. He hadn't written much about the technical aspects of my job, but his pen had barely left the paper since talking of my personal life. The pen was small in his hands, and I briefly allowed myself to daydream about how they'd feel on my skin. There'd be a strength there, even as he tried to be gentle.

I had to remind myself he wasn't interested. Plus, I didn't care. If I had to repeat that to myself a thousand times before the hour was up, I'd do it. It didn't matter that Sam was genuinely nice, hotter than Hades, and had a sense of humor. Those were things that got me in trouble, not things I should find appealing.

"So, you've never done a job at your sister's request?" Sam's eyes were on his paper, only looking up when I took too long to answer.

I pursed my lips while I considered. "Is this an interview about me or my sister?" I laughed, but Sam shifted in his seat, and I worried maybe I'd made him uncomfortable, yet again. I was so good at this whole "be social" thing. No wonder Madison said I needed to get out more. I licked my lips and refocused.

"I mean, it's not like a travel photographer really needs a hacker all that much, am I right?"

My response only made Sam smile, and I tried, unsuccessfully, not to be dazzled.

"You'd be surprised," he said, "at the number of distant relatives who call on me for favors. I thought it might be the same for you, but in a different way, of course. Maybe yours just want you to fix their computer or retrieve data they accidentally deleted." He shook his head. "I have a cousin three times removed who thinks I somehow know the secret inner workings of the government or can put them in contact with the president or something."

I scrunched my forehead and frowned, waiting for him to explain. Sam registered the confusion on my face and blinked.

"Oh, I, uh, used to be a reporter on the presidential campaign trail." He looked down at his notes, clearly not wanting me to press him for more details.

A guy who didn't like to brag. That was a first.

Not interested. Not interested. I had to get back on topic.

"In college, Madison asked me to hack into the system to change her English grade." I blurted it out like I was in some kind of confessional, so eager to please. I was hopeless.

Sam leaned his elbows against the table, his shirt pulling wherever his muscles moved. I averted my gaze.

"Scandalous." His eyes crinkled at the corners, and I pretended not to like it, or the way his voice had sounded a little husky when he said the word *scandalous*. Like maybe he was thinking of something else.

"And did you?" he asked, bringing me back to the present.

"You think I'd admit to anything shady in something that'll be published for the whole world to see?" I grinned, then shook my head. "No, immediately after Madison asked, she took it back and said it wouldn't be fair to cheat the system. Rules and order have always been important to her."

Sam sat back and considered my answer, a smile touching his lips. "But not to you?"

Part of me wanted to pretend to be the devil-may-care rebellious and dangerous type, just to impress him. But my true colors were more of the subdued variety, and I couldn't help the laugh that escaped. "I may be a hacker, but we have a moral code." I paused. "Well, those of us who aren't black-hat. I'd say we have to be even more disciplined than most to stay on the right side of the law when it'd be so easy to go to the dark side."

He smirked and mimicked a Yoda accent. "Fear is the path to the dark side."

Okay, the fact that this guy just quoted *Star Wars* meant he was sexy, smart, and maybe a little geeky, and I wasn't sure if my ovaries could handle that combination.

Sam laughed and steepled his fingers on top of the table. "But would you have done it? For Madison?"

I didn't even have to think about my answer. Yes. There wasn't a whole lot I wouldn't do for my sister. But I didn't say that out loud. Instead, what I said was, "If we were playing Never Have I Ever, I could honestly say I've never broken the law or even been tempted to."

He smiled, and something in his expression hinted at genuine surprise. "Well, that's refreshing."

"Are you saying you haven't broken the law either?" I raised an eyebrow.

Sam looked me directly in the eyes and grinned. "I definitely didn't say that."

Be still my heart. I resisted the urge to fan myself, but couldn't help but appreciate the way his mouth curved.

For the next half hour or so, Sam questioned me on how I got into my line of work, what I did for fun, and if I'd ever run into a computer problem I couldn't fix.

"It's bound to happen sometime," I replied, earning a laugh from Sam that made me feel like I was somehow floating. It was like champagne was flowing through my veins or eating one of those desserts that melts on the tongue.

Sam shook his head. "I'm trying to figure out what your flaw is. Girls like you aren't single."

As if he hadn't seen fifty reasons why in our meeting so far. I blushed from head to toe and couldn't think of a response.

He smiled and leaned back in his chair, arms folded across his chest. "What's your big secret? Are you a criminal or something?"

I laughed. "Well, I am a penetration tester. Most guys have their own theories about what that means."

"I'd think they'd consider that a benefit." He said it with a cheeky grin and raised eyebrow that were simultaneously endearing and roguish. He put his hands on the desk. "Okay, okay, my reserved time for this room is almost up." He started to gather his notes. I pulled my bag from the floor and slung it over my shoulder, standing up on somewhat shaky legs when Sam pushed away from the desk.

"Last question." His eyes locked on mine and he smiled. "Do you like spicy food?"

I hesitated. "Why?" I couldn't imagine how that would fit into the article. But I wasn't a writer, so what did I know?

"Because I'd like to take you to this amazing Thai place downtown. You free tonight?"

I blinked, brought back to reality. Flirting had consequences—consequences I wasn't ready to face. A blind date was one thing, but saying yes to someone when there was actual chemistry? That wasn't bound to end well.

"I—" I swallowed, already hating myself for what I was about to do, but also knowing I only had enough willpower to stop things now, before they had a chance to go any further. "I'm meeting my sister for dinner at Brock's tonight. Sorry." I didn't elaborate. Didn't offer up another time that would work with my schedule. Didn't touch his arm in a coy manner. I clamped my jaw shut and thrust my hands deep into my pockets. Well, not that deep, because women's pockets are a joke and my hands stuck out halfway, adding to the awkwardness of the situation.

Sam nodded slowly, taking a moment before speaking again. "Maybe I can call you later this week?"

Not if I could help it. I wasn't ready for this roller coaster to start back up. But my hand didn't get the memo and I gave him my unlocked phone so he could add himself as a contact. What harm could it do? He already had *my* number from when we'd set up this interview over Messenger. At least this way I'd know who was calling. I told myself I'd screen his calls, but I also knew I was weak and pathetically lonely, so I only half believed myself.

We smiled, I said thank you, and then I got out of there as fast as I could.

He'd asked me out. And for the first time in a long time . . . I'd wanted to say yes.

Chapter Three

· · · · · · · · · ·

"TWO, PLEASE?" I SAID TO THE HOSTESS. MADISON still wouldn't be here for about half an hour, but I needed carbs, pronto.

The hostess looked down at her tablet and picked up two menus, hesitating when she saw I was standing alone.

"My sister will be here soon, but can I sit down?" We came here often enough that the hostess was familiar with me, and I was confident she'd recognize Madison when she came in. Sometimes it helped to look like twins.

"Sure, I can seat you now." She turned, and I followed her messy ponytail down the aisle, trying not to stumble on anyone's outstretched legs.

Brock's was packed tonight. I was starving, and I was super glad we'd gotten a table. If I'd waited until eight like Madison had suggested, we would have had to go someplace else. I suppressed a surge of pride. How was that for adult planning? I'd been more responsible than Madison, just this once. I'd even remembered to go home and change first. Knowing she would have something to say about my graphic tee, I now wore stilettos and a short skirt. Madison couldn't claim I was acting spinsterly with an outfit like this, and I might as well curb her complaining before she even got here. I didn't mind waiting, as long as there was food involved. The complimentary bread would be long gone before she arrived, but that was her loss. I wasn't even sorry.

Brock's was a hole-in-the-wall restaurant that sometimes acted more like a bar. They served an eclectic range of food that made no sense to anyone, except maybe the owner when he was drunk. You could order the greasiest of onion rings alongside five-star crème brûlée that'd knock the socks off any visiting French diplomat. Not that many politicians or diplomats frequented Brock's. They stuck to the fancier side of DC, where a hamburger cost you thirty bucks, french fries were called *pommes frites,* and the parking was strictly valet.

Brock's was the antithesis of all that. Other parts of DC catered to the red-soled-Louboutin people looking to climb up in the world, but Brock's had the beat-up work boots and the I-got-these-for-half-off crowd. My kind of people.

We passed a server handing the check to another patron and I smiled. The last time I was here with Madison, I'd forgotten my credit card. Of course, Madison offered to pay, but not before lecturing me on being a responsible adult and how I was too scatterbrained and impulsive, blah, blah, blah. Spare me. Our server that night knew me well enough that she offered to let me pay later that evening. But instead of taking either of them up on their offers, I bussed tables until midnight just to prove to Madison I *was* a responsible adult, even if we approached things differently. If our personalities could be pared down to one story, that'd probably be it.

We edged our way around a large group and passed the manager, who nodded in greeting. The hostess sat me at a table in the back, where I tried to sit gracefully without letting my skirt ride too far up my legs. Forget being single, this skirt had been a bad idea. Now that I was sitting by myself though, Madison had a point about how awkward it was being here without her. I pulled out my purse to get my phone. Maybe if I was staring at a screen, I wouldn't feel so uncomfortable. Even loners had their limits, after all.

But my phone wasn't there.

I tipped my bag over, and a pack of gum, a tube of lip gloss, and a handful of flash drives and computer adapter cords fell out. I didn't need to carry those around with me, but at this point they felt more like a security blanket than anything. Still no phone. One by one, I put everything back in, just in case I missed it, my blood pressure rising as the table cleared. Mentally, I retraced my steps. I'd had my phone when Madison called as I exited Nyah's work. Had I left it on the metro? No, I'd had it at the interview. I'd handed it to Sam so he could give me his number. But then I'd hightailed it out of there like the building was on fire, simply because he'd asked me out. Did I have it after that? No. No, I distinctly remembered leaving it in Sam's large hands, too afraid to touch him to even reclaim my own property.

Annoying that he hadn't called after me to give it back. Had he wanted to snoop on my phone for his article? Good luck. It was all kinds of password protected. I doubted Sam had the skills or tools to jailbreak it.

I was being paranoid though. He seemed like a genuinely nice guy. I didn't think he'd stoop to that kind of thing, all for a measly article. This wasn't that serious.

Now I'd have to see Sam to get it back. I shouldn't have felt excited by that idea, but my pulse sped up regardless. Stupid pulse. Who needed one anyway?

Then the dread kicked in. I wasn't sure I could handle seeing Sam again. Not this soon. Not when his flirting was still fresh and I was still so hopelessly unprepared for his level of attractiveness.

The server placed a bread basket on the table, and I wasted no time before stress eating. Maybe if I had enough carbs in my system, I'd magically get the backbone I so desperately needed. My mouth was full when a pasty white man I'd never seen before sat down opposite me.

He didn't fit in at Brock's. His jacket was too boxy and his hairstyle too mature. He carried a briefcase and wore the kind of glasses that aged him by a good ten years. But most disconcerting of all was the fact that he didn't seem embarrassed by sitting at the wrong table. Nervous, sure. He kept smoothing his coat and opening his mouth like he was some kind of fish. Not exactly an attractive habit. But he made no move to leave and stared right into my eyes.

I swallowed the bread.

"Let's see, where were we?" he asked, snapping his mouth shut with an audible click of his teeth. There was something different about him. I couldn't place his accent. European? Russian? Accents were common enough here in DC though, so that wasn't what was making me pause. But then I realized he wasn't blinking. He stared intently at my face, like he expected me to break into song or dance at any moment. Well. I wasn't about to disappoint him.

"Oh yes, in the pit of despair." I winked, answering his question by quoting *The Princess Bride*. Because even if he didn't know it, he'd given me the perfect opening and I couldn't resist. He'd said the exact line from the movie. It was Madison's and my favorite—the only movie that made us laugh growing up, even when our family was breaking apart. A movie that promised happy endings and true love conquering all.

I waited for him to realize his mistake and make a hasty retreat to his own table, which was surely right around the corner or in a similar-looking section. But beyond a small nod of his head, the man didn't move. His fingers tapped out a rhythm on the handle of his briefcase, which he put on the table between us like some sort of peace offering.

"Miss Barkley?" His voice had a note of hesitation.

I froze. How he knew my name was a mystery—one I wasn't exactly eager to solve. This man was sweatier than a glass of iced tea sitting out in the sun, and that was saying something. He hastily wiped his forehead with his coat sleeve. Gross.

"Yes?" No doubt, I sounded equally unsure.

"You're late. And you, uh, you look a little different from your picture."

My eyebrows rose into my hairline. "I dyed my hair last week."

Honestly, I thought the blond looked pretty good, and his reaction took a little wind out of my sails. But then it hit me. He knew my name, and he had my picture. A sense of dread settled deep in my stomach.

Madison had set me up. Literally. On yet another blind date. She knew I'd planned on coming early, so rather than have me wait by myself, she'd sent . . . him.

Who knew if she was even planning on coming tonight? She probably considered this her good deed of the day, helping two complete strangers find love. And now I was obligated to sit through it, simply because I didn't have the heart to send this guy packing when he'd only just arrived.

How could Madison do this to me? She knew I lacked the social skills to successfully navigate myself out of this situation.

Then again, that was probably why she'd done it like this.

Inwardly, I fumed at my sister, plotting how I'd get her back and whether she'd notice if I put hair dye in her shampoo. Getting into her apartment would be a problem. She kept that place locked up better than Fort Knox. Maybe I'd bake her cookies using salt instead of sugar . . . She deserved far, far worse.

I sighed, knowing I'd never follow through on any of my fantasies of revenge. Sure, sometimes I wanted to strangle my sister, but she was the only person in the world I trusted with my life. The one who beat up my middle school boyfriend when he told everyone I stuffed my bra. She always had my back. And if she thought I'd get along with this guy, the least I could do was give him a chance.

"I'm not that photogenic." I took another bite of bread and hoped he'd move on to another topic.

He tilted his head to the side, considering me. "Did you get a nose job?"

I choked on the bread. What was it with guys asking inappropriate questions on the first date? Didn't they know there were rules for this kind of thing? Even if he wasn't American, surely there were certain universal standards.

I chugged water, nearly spilling the glass in my haste to get it to my lips.

Deep breaths, I reminded myself. Madison obviously saw something in the guy. Maybe he was secretly a millionaire. Or he was next in line for some foreign throne. I could live with that.

Or maybe he really was just as weird as he seemed. Sure, I was socially awkward, but this guy took it to a whole new level.

"I had to have surgery because I broke it a couple of months ago." I set my glass down and picked up the last roll, tearing it into little pieces with more force than was necessary. "The guy had a killer left hook."

And that was the last time I ever went to a boxing class with my sister.

Despite my vague answer, he nodded like this was a perfectly logical explanation and pushed the briefcase across the table to me. My fingers stopped their movement as I stared at the offending piece of luggage. It was bad enough he carried one, but what did he expect me to do with it? It didn't exactly go with my outfit.

"The code is two four seven six. Inside you'll find information on Holt, as well as a new fake ID to get to Prague. Of course, I used the old photo of you, but the people at customs shouldn't give you a hard time."

I still hadn't moved. This date had started off weird and only gone downhill from there. If I had to guess what was going on, my bet would be that an alien had invaded his body or something. Soon I'd be beamed up too, a blessed end to my night.

But then a light bulb went off in my mind and I leaned back in my chair. This guy must be into role-playing. He probably liked it when girls wore wigs, acted like they were only in town for one night before jetting off to faraway lands like Prague, and pretended he was someone else. Honestly, if I looked like him, I'd want to pretend to be someone else too. The question was why he'd choose a name like Holt, when he obviously was more of a Melvin, or maybe an Elmer. Holt was too masculine for him. Then again, maybe that's why he'd chosen it. This information on Holt that he claimed was in the briefcase was probably a rundown on the character he wanted to play.

"Listen." I gently placed the bread down and patted his hand. "We don't know each other well, and—"

He nudged the briefcase again and motioned for me to open it. I didn't want to. Who knew what I'd find in there. Fuzzy handcuffs? Blindfolds? If my sister had been the one to plan this, it could be anything. Or if this man was being serious, maybe this outfit was too skanky, and I was giving people the wrong impression.

My fingers were slow as I adjusted the combination, my brain whirling along with it, trying to find a way out of this that didn't involve escaping out a window. The briefcase opened with a click. Thankfully, there were only papers inside, and I breathed a sigh of relief. There was some foreign-looking money, which, yes, was a little concerning because my last date had thought I was an escort and Madison might be making some kind of joke about that, but I chose not to dwell on it. I had bigger things to worry about. Like the fact that there was a passport nestled on top of the papers, and it looked anything but fake. This wasn't some phony role-playing document; this was the real deal. The texture was the same as my passport at home, the paper inside just as thick as I shuffled through to find the picture. Then my breath caught.

My sister's picture stared back at me. Instead of saying her name was Madison Barkley, it said Courtney Miller, with all her specifics filled out. Brown hair, brown eyes, five foot eight inches. Truth, truth, truth. But everything about this passport was a lie.

Someone at the front of the restaurant screamed, breaking my inspection. Now, Brock's was normally pretty noisy. Yelling wasn't exactly scarce here. Loud parties, laughing, boisterous drinking games, sure. But this scream was different. It pierced the air and filled the room with terror. As if on cue, everyone turned to the front.

Two burly white men stood by the front doors, their bulk nearly taking up the entire frame. One had short dark hair and the other was bald, but both wore matching hard expressions. The bald man had a gun pointed at the hostess, who looked like she would pass out at any second. I didn't blame her.

"Do something!" the man at my table hissed under his breath.

"Like what?" I whispered back. And hello, why was this *my* problem? He was the guy. I was small, even for a woman. The only reason I looked tall was because of my four-inch stilettos, and it wasn't like they were much of a weapon.

"You're the agent!" he said.

Agent? Just who did he think I was?

Time seemed to slow down, and the answer came in a whoosh of realization. My sister. He thought I was my sister. And he thought she was an agent. Hence the weird conversation and fake ID. I replayed everything he'd told me like a movie in reverse. He wasn't trying to hit on me after all. He'd sat at the table expecting someone else. He had her picture. He'd given a code phrase from a movie that I'd unknowingly answered. The information on Holt wasn't about him, but about someone else altogether. All of that finally clicked into place, but the thing that kept circulating in my mind was that he thought Madison was a special agent.

The idea was laughable. My sister, the travel photographer, a spy? Right. Sure, she had catlike reflexes and she looked good dressed in black, but that was where the similarities ended.

"I think there's been some kind of miscommunication." I closed the briefcase with a click and pushed it toward him. He pushed it right back.

The men with guns started walking in our direction.

Not good. Not good at all. What had I gotten myself into? Correction: What had my *sister* gotten herself into?

A bullet went into the ceiling and more people screamed. Another shot zinged past my ear, and I threw myself to the floor behind the table. It didn't matter what Madison had gotten into. Right now, all I cared about was getting *out* of it.

"You're the only one who has this information." The sweaty man shoved the briefcase into my arms. "You need to get it to—"

But I didn't get to hear who the information needed to get to. Because in that moment, a bullet hit the man in the head, knocking him back from the table and killing him instantly. There was more screaming. I was pretty sure most of it came from me.

I didn't stop to think. I simply grabbed the briefcase and ran. Behind me, I heard someone wrestling with the two burly men, but I didn't turn to look. I didn't want to know who was winning.

I barreled through the back door and into the narrow street. The door slammed behind me, muffling the sounds of chaos I'd left behind. A few cars were scattered along the curb, but my eyes zeroed in on something closer. Something faster. Something infinitely sexier.

Five feet from the door, a man straddled a motorcycle, his helmet casually held against his side as he studied something in his hand. He glanced up when I crashed through the door, and if it weren't for the adrenaline pounding through my veins, my heart might have stopped beating.

Sam. Sam from the interview was here.

He looked good too. He wore black like he owned the color and the rest of us should be paying rent. And while I wouldn't have pegged him for a motorcycle guy, seeing him now made me realize just how much the look worked for him.

I had no idea what he was doing here. All I knew was that he was a gift from heaven. He was right where I needed him, and best of all, he had a bullet bike.

He held up the object, its glow illuminating the small space around his hand. "Thought you might need this. I remembered you saying you'd be here and—"

I didn't let him finish. There wasn't time. I grabbed my phone and shoved it into my bag, already moving toward the back of his bike and hooking the briefcase there.

"Can you get me away from here?" My voice shook as I worked the straps. Maybe I should have been more cautious. I didn't really know him, after all. I didn't know his birthday, his taste in books, or whether he called his mother on Mother's Day. All I knew was that there were guys with guns behind me, and between my options, this one seemed like my best bet.

He grinned and passed back his helmet. I straddled the seat. "Hold on tight."

Chapter Four

. . . .

MY BRAIN WAS GOING INTO A FULL-BLOWN MELTDOWN. Any second now the panic attack would take over and I'd lose all ability to form coherent sentences. But I'd be lying if I didn't admit that there was a small part of me that was distracted by how nice Sam's body felt next to mine now that I was sitting behind him, or how he smelled like leather and soap. And safety.

He kicked his bike into gear just as the back door to the restaurant opened again, the two men from earlier framed in the entryway.

"Friends of yours?" He revved the engine.

"Oh, you know," I said, slightly out of breath, "keep your friends close and your enemies closer. Or so they say." I wrapped my arms around Sam's body, squeezing so he'd know to go fast.

He looked back and grinned as we roared away from the curb.

Should I have been concerned with his response? Probably. He didn't seem to be worried at all, like he ran on pure ego and testosterone. But right now, I was just grateful he took it as a challenge, rather than, say, leaving me in the gutter. I was also really hoping he'd keep this part out of the article, but I knew better.

We turned the corner and I saw the men climb into a car that had been parked along the alleyway. The headlights turned on and I swore under my breath. It might have been their car. But even if it wasn't, if they were the kind of criminals who brought firearms into a restaurant, they probably didn't have high moral standards about hot-wiring and stealing a car. The headlights swerved after us and I squeezed Sam in front of me.

"They're following us!" I shouted.

He turned his head to look but didn't say anything as he accelerated. For how calm and collected he seemed, you would have thought he did this kind of thing every day. Maybe he just liked going fast. Or maybe he had a death wish. Maybe he'd been a reporter in war-torn countries and this was nothing to him.

I had so many questions.

Sirens wailed in the distance, but they'd get here too late to catch the men. They were already on our tail, racing along the street like our vehicles were the only ones on it. Cars honked when we cut them off, the bike's tires screeching on the pavement. I tried to tuck my head against Sam's back, but the helmet was too bulky to allow for that. Instead, I stared ahead and counted all the ways this could end badly.

I'd never been on a motorcycle before. And bullet bikes were *fast*. If my adrenaline hadn't already spiked from the shooting, it was on full alert now, blood coursing through my ears as I held on for dear life. Each turn tilted the bike beneath us to the point where I wondered if I'd traded a bullet wound for becoming

roadkill. The freezing wind on my bare legs was the only reminder I needed that I wasn't protected by an airbag or a metal
frame. If we crashed, I'd have road rash over half my body.

If I'd had a second to regroup, I would have called Madison.
I didn't even know if she was okay. That man in the restaurant—
he'd been murdered. He'd thought I was my sister, and then he'd
been shot. Without warning. What if Madison hadn't come to
the restaurant . . . because she *couldn't?* Somehow, she'd gotten
caught up in all this, but surely she was just as clueless as I was.
Because there was no way my sister was a spy, no matter what
that man had said. Yes, she traveled a lot. But she was a travel
photographer. That was kind of part of her job description. And
maybe she was especially good at martial arts and boxing. But
she had a thing for fitness. That didn't mean anything.

With every justification, I could feel myself spiraling out of
control. Denial wasn't helping my mental state. Because the
truth was, there were two guys with guns after me, and that type
of thing didn't normally happen unless there was a reason. A
reason like maybe my sister really was a spy.

We ran a red light, and I closed my eyes, bracing for an impact that never came. Horns blared as we streaked through the
intersection, but soon we were on the other side, and I could
breathe again. Traffic in DC was always bad, but that was the
nice thing about the bike. We could race past any cars and maneuver ourselves into openings in a way our pursuers couldn't.

We rounded a corner going three times the recommended
speed limit and ended up on an unfamiliar side street. Sam
hopped the sidewalk a few times to avoid cars, and while I could
have stressed over the legality of such an action, to be honest, I
was more concerned about staying alive. His earlier claim of
breaking the law made a whole lot more sense now, knowing

how he'd reacted tonight. But everything else he'd said during the interview made even less sense. Because it didn't add up that a journalist would be this capable during a car chase. How did a reporter learn how to maneuver a motorcycle like this?

Who knew why our followers hadn't shot at us. Maybe their guns hadn't made it out of the restaurant with them. Or maybe the police had cut them off. I couldn't see their car anymore. They'd been caught at the last light, and we'd taken approximately thirty turns since then. I'd lived in DC most of my life, but even I was lost. This street wasn't familiar to me, and as we turned into a covered parking garage, I couldn't see any street signs to give me my bearings. We eased to a stop in a parking stall, and I slowly unclenched my arms and stood on shaky legs. My stomach didn't want to stay put and kept trying to come up through my throat. My hair was sure to be spectacular, but I took the helmet off anyway, handing it back to Sam, who in turn placed it on the handlebars of his bike.

I took stock of my night. I'd been shot at, watched a man die, and now I was in a deserted parking garage with a man I only kind of knew. I didn't know where my sister was, and I hadn't heard from her in hours. For all I knew, she was bleeding out in some alley, having been shot by the same men who came to the restaurant.

"The police," I said. "We need to go to the police." Goose bumps erupted on my arms, and I hastily tried to rub them away. My breath came in shallow gasps, and I felt cold all over. What were the symptoms of shock? Because I was pretty sure I had it. My thoughts weren't exactly clear.

Sam stood and placed his hands on my shoulders. "Breathe. You're okay. You're safe."

I breathed in while Sam counted to ten, then exhaled, repeating the exercise a couple of times even though it didn't do any good.

"Tell me what happened." Sam's eyes bored into mine, open and full of sincerity. I could trust him. A journalist should be able to help me put together the pieces from tonight. He was used to finding the story from a smattering of facts. He could help me figure out what had happened to Madison. He could help me know what to tell the cops so she wouldn't get in trouble. Well, any *more* trouble. There was something about the way he held himself that was so confident and reassuring. It made me believe it would all be okay. *He* would make it all be okay.

A small part of my brain wondered how he was in the right place at the right time, and how he'd learned to drive like that. But those were questions for another day. Right now, I needed to focus on finding Madison.

I told Sam everything and he listened intently, only interrupting twice to ask questions. When I'd finished, he leaned back on his bike, digesting everything he'd just heard. I ran my hand through my hair and tried unsuccessfully not to panic.

Sam shook his head. "I can see why the man at your table got confused," he said. "You look just like your sister."

He stood up from his bike, seemingly unaware of how he'd just caused my heart to stop beating. I hesitated, trying to find the right words, and he started unhooking the briefcase from the back of his motorcycle. He placed it on the seat and tilted his head while looking at me.

"Well, that's not true. You're prettier than your sister."

I didn't register the compliment. I could only mutter a routine response while my mind was whirring in a different direction with a thousand other questions—because Sam was involved, which made him dangerous.

"We're practically identical," I muttered, still trying to catch up.

Even the man at the restaurant had thought so. The man who was now dead.

"There are differences. Her features are . . . harsher. Maybe that's not the right word."

I knew what he meant. The foster system had changed my sister. Now she questioned everyone's motives, drank her coffee scalding hot, and boxed as a form of "relaxation." She had edges, while I was still bright-eyed and optimistic. That was because of her—she'd always shielded me from the realities of the world. Protecting me even then.

But she wasn't here to protect me now.

I was silent for a long time before I worked up the courage to ask the biggest question now taking up the space between us.

"How do you know Madison?" I finally asked. The more important question was, what was he going to do with me now? Or maybe, did I have a chance to escape? But I wasn't about to ask those questions out loud yet. Maybe he'd only seen her picture online and was basing things off that.

I knew that wasn't true though—Madison only used social media to post her art.

He noticed my expression and his own face softened. "Hey, it's okay. She's my partner. Sorry, I should have started with that." He said it simply. Like he didn't just cause my world to tilt off its axis, yet again.

Partner.

Earlier in the day, he'd been charming and flirtatious. I'd been comfortable in his presence. He hadn't seemed dangerous. But the guy in front of me now? He was dressed head to toe in black, and the way he held his body left no doubt he hit the gym. Hard. His stubble was enough to make him look edgy and dangerous, while also giving him an air of casual sophistication. Like he'd be equally at home at a black-tie diplomatic dinner or dealing with drug lords and arms dealers. I'd already seen how he could blend in with the journalists, then become one with the night. He had spy written all over him. I'd just been too naive to see it.

"The interview?" I asked.

"My cover," he said, confirming my fears. "We had to see what you knew."

I gave him a hollow laugh, because the answer was not a lot.

"We? So, you work for . . ." I trailed off, hoping he'd fill in the blanks for me and I wouldn't have to look so hopelessly clueless. Because I still felt like I was playing catch-up, in what could easily be one of the most important conversations of my life. I wrapped my arms around my middle and tried to hold everything together.

"The CIA."

And there it was.

I suppose it could have been worse. At least they were the good guys.

"And my sister?" I was pretty sure I knew the answer to this question already, but I needed to hear him say it.

"Her too."

My sister really was a spy. And she hadn't told me.

I swallowed, forcing the bitter thoughts down. So what? It didn't change anything. Not anything that mattered anyway. She was still the only family I had in this world. It didn't change who she was as a person, just her occupation.

Sam leaned against his bike and propped his boot against the side, so casually cool while I personally felt like throwing up. Madison might be walking into Brock's completely unaware of what had just happened, and if Sam was her partner, he wasn't protecting her either. She could be hurt or on the run, while the government and Sam did nothing.

A thought dawned on me. "Your name isn't really Sam Olsen, is it?" I shook my head at my own stupidity. That was why his articles never had an accompanying picture. Sam Olsen wasn't real. Sam Olsen was a fake persona this man adopted whenever he wanted to fool unsuspecting people. The thought made me curl my hands into fists, my nails biting into my palms.

"What's your real name?" I demanded.

I *should* have been asking where I was. Or what was going on. But, you know, important things first. Or, at least, things that wouldn't cause a full-blown panic attack.

He crossed his arms as he leaned on his bike, his black hair catching the dim glimmer of the parking garage lights.

"Mendez."

I nodded. "And your first name?"

One half of his mouth quirked up in a grin.

"That's on a need-to-know basis."

Well, okay then.

Here I was in a deserted parking garage with a man whose first name I couldn't begin to guess, and the only thing I actually knew was that my sister might be in trouble and everything I thought I knew was a lie. Deep breaths.

Suddenly, it was all too much for me to handle. I stepped back and stumbled.

Sam—no, *Mendez*—reached out to steady me, his hand supporting my elbow. My purse swung from my arm, reminding me of one very important detail I'd forgotten earlier. I had a cell phone.

"I need to call Madison." Maybe she'd be able to answer her

phone. She'd tell me this was all part of her plan, because she always had a plan, and for once, that thought brought me peace instead of frustration. I searched through my purse until I found my phone and pulled it out.

But before I could even place the call, Mendez had whipped out some kind of pocketknife multitool and taken my phone from me. Then he used the tools to remove the front glass.

"What do you think you're doing?" I tried to snatch it back, but he held it out of my reach. I stretched up to grab it, trying to angle my way around all his muscles.

"Do you have any idea how many people will track you once they know you're involved?" His voice was still calm and collected, even though he didn't budge an inch. We didn't say anything for a good minute or two. It felt like eternity. When he spoke again, he was quiet, and his face was concerned.

"You can't call the police because this isn't their jurisdiction. Trust me, we have people working on this. You can't call Madison because Holt might be tracing your calls. Right now, you need to lie low. I'll keep you safe."

He waited for me to drop my hand and step away before bringing the phone back to waist level. He continued to take it apart and I continued to worry. About this guy named Holt. About why he'd be interested in my phone calls.

"The man in the restaurant," I said. "He mentioned Holt's name too. Who is he?"

"A very bad man on the CIA's most wanted list," Mendez said. "That's all you need to know."

Well, that was just peachy. Somehow, I'd been operating under the impression that all this would be like a bad dream, and I'd go back to my normal life once it was all over. Sooner rather than later. But Mendez had destroyed that dream. Because according to him, now I was involved, whether I wanted to be or not.

Spoiler: I did not.

And no matter how nice *Sam* had been, I couldn't trust anything *Mendez* said. Was he really a government agent? Did he really know my sister? The biggest question was one I hesitated to ask, even in my mind.

Was I safe with Mendez?

"Name one of Madison's pet peeves," I demanded.

Mendez gave me a quizzical look as he continued to disassemble my phone.

"So I can make sure you're really her partner. Tell me one of her pet peeves. If you know Madison, that should be easy." She had a lot. Like people being late, or even worse, not showing up at all. Or that disgusted look she gave whenever I chewed on a fingernail. The thought brought a pang of emotion with it now.

Mendez held the pocketknife in his mouth while he pried the battery out of my phone. He finished his work and put the pocketknife away, then handed back my now destroyed phone, may it rest in pieces.

"She hates it when people take multiple days to respond to a text."

True.

"What's she afraid of?" I pressed.

"Nothing."

Also true. As far as I knew.

"Her favorite flavor of ice cream?"

"She's lactose intolerant."

With every answer, I felt both reassured and anxious. Because it meant I could trust Mendez, but it also meant my sister was involved in some really heavy stuff. And now, so was I.

"Does she have any tattoos?" I pushed.

"A couple that I know of. She has a small flame. On her wrist."

Memories floated to the surface. Madison and me, sitting on her bed in the group foster home, her arm around me as I desperately tried to stop crying. Sometimes it all became too much, and I missed our parents. Our home. Our *life*. She'd stroked my hair and told me everything was going to be all right in the end.

"You're the flint, and I'm the steel," she'd said, eyes burning with their intensity. "Together, we're all we need to survive. You and me, forever. Got it?" It had become our own personal code. One she'd reiterate anytime I struggled. When I'd turned eighteen, we'd gotten the matching fire tattoos.

I lightly touched my tattoo and looked up at Mendez, who was watching me with an expression I couldn't name.

"Fine," I said, throat tight. "You're her partner. Can *you* call Madison, then?" I crossed my arms in front of my chest, hoping to appear more confident than I felt.

"She's gone off-grid."

"What do you mean, she's gone off-grid? You're her partner. Don't you have some secret satellite phone or something that works on a secure network?"

He looked away. "Yes. And she's not answering." He paused, letting that sink in. The fear began to sink in with it. Because my sister hadn't gone to the restaurant, and now she wasn't answering her phone.

I wasn't a spy, but even I knew that couldn't be good.

"How do you know she's not hurt, then? Or . . . or . . ." I trailed off, refusing to voice the worry that had plagued me since this night of horrors began. I had a lot of questions about the interview he'd given me, but now wasn't the time. Now I had to make sure Madison was safe.

"The people after your sister want answers. They can't get those if she's dead."

Okay, but torture was a thing. Just because she wasn't dead didn't mean she wasn't in trouble. But Mendez seemed to know where my thoughts were going, because he shook his head.

"Dove." He turned me so he was looking directly into my eyes. "I can't tell you more than that. You're going to have to trust me. Madison hasn't checked in for a few weeks, but we know she's fine. She's in hiding, but not hurt."

A few weeks? That didn't seem fine. Still, I nodded, swallowing the lump that had formed in my throat. If Madison was safe, that was all the information I needed for now. Maybe things weren't that serious if she'd risked calling me earlier today.

Mendez lifted the briefcase off his bike and walked toward the stairwell, motioning for me to follow. I did, because what other choice did I have? It was either follow Mendez or put myself at the mercy of the men with guns.

Mendez turned to me with a smirk, still walking. "Now, let's get upstairs and take a look at those briefs."

Chapter Five

· · · · · · · · · ·

I STARED AT HIM, MOUTH AGAPE, BUT THEN HE TAPPED the briefcase by way of explanation, and my mouth snapped shut. He didn't say anything else as we walked up two flights of stairs, turned down a narrow hallway, and stopped at a door that looked exactly the same as every other one we'd passed. We were in some kind of apartment complex, though I hadn't seen anyone else around. It was eerily quiet. Like we'd walked into an alternate universe where we were the only two people who existed.

One part of my brain was saying how stupid it'd be of me to enter this apartment with a man I didn't really know, especially since no one knew where I was and I had no way of getting out.

But see, here's the thing. *I had no way of getting out.* I had no phone and no method of transportation. It wasn't like I could request an Uber and make it back to my apartment in time for the nightly news. Besides, the other part of my brain? That part liked the idea of going into this apartment, alone, with Mendez. Maybe it wasn't smart, but it was the truth.

He pulled keys out of his pocket and opened the door, motioning for me to enter first. I hesitated, my breath catching while I weighed the pros and cons. I was pretty sure I could trust the guy. After all, he did kind of save my life. Plus, I wasn't likely to get answers standing here in the hall.

I squared my shoulders and stepped over the threshold.

If I was hoping for some insight into what made Mendez tick, I was left wanting. The apartment was plain and non-descript, with beige walls and no artwork. A single couch sat in front of a television, and the kitchen held a table with four matching chairs. Nothing on the kitchen counters. No dishes, no cute little canisters of sugar and flour. No anything.

"It's very . . . clean," I said, searching my mind for a word that wouldn't offend. Mendez grunted.

"It's a safe house, what did you expect?" He closed the door, following me into the kitchen, where he placed the briefcase on the table.

Oh. That made more sense. Of course Mendez wouldn't have taken me to *his* apartment. I placed my purse on the kitchen counter and heaved myself onto one of the barstools at the is-land, sighing as I did so. This day had been a thousand years long. I crossed my arms and rested my head on them. Mendez sat at the table and opened the briefcase. It was only then I real-ized the code hadn't been adjusted since I'd entered it.

He looked so out of place in this kitchen. He needed clean, modern styles and stainless-steel finishes. This man was all chrome and charisma. Not antiqued wood and outdated appli-ances. Still, there was something charming about the way he chewed on the end of his pen. He was still human.

While I was tempted to read over his shoulder as he perused the documents, something told me that wasn't the smartest idea. Spies and their secrets, and all that. So, I settled for watching and waiting, hoping that maybe he could end this madness and I'd be able to get back to my regularly scheduled programming. I didn't have high hopes. After all, if even my sister was missing in action . . .

Mendez studied the papers while I got lost in my own thoughts. Maybe I shouldn't have shared the papers with Mendez. Maybe I should have kept them to myself. Top secret. Confidential. But that guy at the restaurant had said it was important, and honestly, I had no one else to turn to. What if someone else died, all because I'd squirreled away information and didn't trust the right people? But for that matter, what if someone died because I'd trusted the *wrong* people?

I snuck a glance at Mendez. He was bent over the table, his brow furrowed in concentration. Every once in a while, he took a picture of the documents with his phone and sent them to someone. Presumably his superiors. He placed his phone on the table and picked up the next document. One hand held the paper while the other palmed the back of his neck. Stressed. Would he be so concerned if he was one of the bad guys? True, he knew all that stuff about Madison, but he could have done research on her too. Maybe there was some kind of dossier that included all her tattoos and health information, like her being lactose intolerant. My questions earlier had only proven that he knew things about her. Not that he actually worked for the government.

"Do you have a badge or something that lets me know you're legit?" I asked. The real question was, what would I do if he didn't? Because I had no good answer for that.

Why was it that every guy who entered my life brought more questions with him?

This was why I had trust issues.

Mendez's smile was lazy and sanguine as he reached into his pocket and withdrew a wallet. He flipped it open and passed it to me.

I had no way of knowing whether his identification was real. It wasn't like I regularly saw them in my line of work. I dealt with computers, not espionage. The best I could do was compare it to the ones I'd seen on TV shows, which didn't give me a whole lot of confidence, honestly.

It seemed real enough. My gaze zeroed in on a few details. An official seal was next to his picture, with a gold badge nestled next to the card that read *CIA*. Those were the things I focused on, my brain still too fuzzy to know what else to look for. It seemed like a strange thing to carry around just in case he needed to fabricate a story on the spot. It wasn't likely he'd impersonate a spy on a daily basis.

I passed the wallet back, feigning nonchalance. Okay, so Mendez was legit. This whole situation was real, and I was in so far over my head. No biggie. My heartbeat was a little erratic as I padded over to the cupboards and searched for a glass. After I found one, I filled it at the sink and took big gulps, nearly choking approximately twenty times before I managed to drain the glass.

Behind me, I heard Mendez take a call, his voice hushed as he spoke. After a minute, it became clear he was speaking with his superior. He kept saying "yes, sir," and occasionally supplying information about the night's events. I recognized the name Holt as being the same as the one the guy in the restaurant had used in reference to the information in the briefcase, but nothing else made much sense. I drank another glass of water and half listened as Mendez disagreed with whatever plan his superior was recommending, which wasn't giving me a boost of confidence.

"She's a civilian, Tobias," Mendez said, casting a furtive glance in my direction. I swallowed. Whatever it was, I was already pretty sure I wasn't going to like it.

"She may look like her sister, but she's not. She can't do this." He got up from the table and walked to one of the bedrooms. He closed the door behind him and left me alone in the kitchen.

Pride warred with common sense. I wanted to prove Mendez wrong. Prove I was as competent as my sister. But the logical part of my brain knew he was probably right, especially if they were discussing some kind of spy plan. Computers? Sure, I could handle those. Murder, guns, and running for my life? Not so much.

He must have a pretty good relationship with his superior—Tobias?—to challenge his authority like that. I could only hope whatever they were discussing wouldn't put me in the hospital.

I counted the minutes until he returned. Seven whole minutes of leaving me in agony. When he came back, he didn't say anything. He just sat at the table and resumed flipping through pages.

Forget bad guys. The silence would be what killed me.

I placed the glass in the sink, then walked over to the table and tapped the edge of the briefcase.

"So, how long do you think this will take? Just wondering. Because I have a life I'd like to get back to, and, you know, work. Which I don't exactly *want* to get back to but probably should." I was babbling. I should stop talking and let him get back to reading the important spy documents. But I had to know. What had his superior wanted me to do? And could that, pretty please, be "go home and wallow for a bit before returning to life as normal"?

Because I could do that.

"Can you call in sick? Tell your clients you had a personal emergency?" He flipped through a few more papers, not bothering to hide them from me.

Since my phone was now in pieces, I was guessing he had another option tucked away in those nice-fitting black jeans of his. The secure line he'd mentioned earlier, something that couldn't be traced. Something that made him even more secretive.

"I only have a couple active clients right now, and nothing due soon, so I can take a few days if needed, I guess. But do you think this will take that long?" Good thing it was the weekend. Though, to be honest, now that I'd decided to trust him, I was debating whether spending a few days alone with Mendez would really be so bad.

No comment, just a raised eyebrow. More shuffling of papers.

"Do you have a roommate you need to check in with?" he asked.

I shook my head.

"A dog to feed?"

Another shake.

"A boyfriend?"

First Madison grilled me about my love life, and now Mendez? I crossed my arms. "I think you know the answer to that."

He grinned in a way that clearly showed he was aware of the effect he had on women.

"Wow, you're the life of the party, aren't you?" he asked, and I bristled.

"Hey, I have . . . plants. They'll miss me." I sounded pathetic, and even I knew it. But it wasn't a fair comparison, pitting my life against the glamorous life of a spy.

Mendez looked at me over the top of the paper he was holding. "They'll miss water, you mean."

Same difference.

I gave him my best cold stare. Mendez didn't seem to be affected. "Look," I said. "You're one to talk. I bet you don't have any of those things either."

"I'm a special operative. My job requires me not to have those kinds of ties."

Okay, so he had me there. Still, it wasn't like I could admit that. I kept silent, pulling a chair away from the table and sitting in it stiffly. Mendez watched me with humor in his eyes.

"To answer your question, I don't know how long this will take." Mendez put the paper down. "I'm more concerned about staying alive at the moment. I'm taking each hour as it comes."

Taking each hour as it comes—that sounded eerily like what Everett had told me the day before he'd called things off for good. Not a great omen of what was to come from tonight. I waited for the stab of pain that usually accompanied thoughts of Everett, but I guess I'd had my fair share of painful experiences that night, because I found I was too tired to work up the proper emotion.

Mendez returned to studying the documents and we lapsed into silence. A clock ticked away the seconds somewhere in the distance, its sound muted and faint. I tapped my fingers on the table with its rhythm. It was amazing how long a minute took when you didn't have a phone to distract you. No games, no scrolling through hacker forums. Just Mendez and me, sitting here saying nothing.

Eventually I couldn't take it anymore. "What do you know so far? Anything I can do to help?" What I wanted to know was what his superior had told him on the phone, but I couldn't come right out and ask it. "I mean, I know I don't have security clearance or anything, but, uh, I'm a good listener?"

I was pathetic, that's what I was. But how could this man be so content in his silence? So moody and monosyllabic? So different from the journalist he'd pretended to be only a few hours earlier?

He put his elbows on the table and looked directly at me.

"The less you know, the better."

That was debatable. I was the type of person who didn't take no for an answer, and I wasn't all that patient. If he didn't clue me in soon, I'd probably resort to finding things out on my own. I wasn't proud of this fact, but it was true nonetheless. I knew the code for the briefcase, and Mendez could only stay awake for so long. It was just a matter of time before my curiosity got the better of me. Maybe I hadn't hacked into the CIA database before, but I hadn't been motivated to either.

Perhaps he sensed that, because I watched as he drew in a breath and slowly released it. "Here's what I can tell you. The CIA's heard chatter about a man named Holt. We know he's up to something. Problem is, we don't know what. Madison was working on his case, and now she's on his radar." Mendez ran a hand through his hair, then cupped the back of his neck. "This isn't our first run-in with Holt either. I work with an elite subsection of the CIA, and Holt has sort of been our special project."

An elite subsection of the CIA, eh? I couldn't tell if he was bragging or simply stating a fact. He always looked so controlled and stern.

"Are you like Jason Bourne?" I asked. "If I called Langley, would they pretend they didn't know you existed?" I meant for it to sound teasing, but Mendez's answering expression made me pause. This guy probably had a license to kill in at least eighteen different countries, so maybe teasing wasn't something I should be doing. He didn't look annoyed per se, but he wasn't amused either.

His voice was dry when he said, "Something like that."

I wasn't sure how to answer, so I stayed silent. Eventually, Mendez reached into the briefcase, pulled out a picture of a white man who was probably in his fifties, and passed it to me. "That's Holt."

I studied the picture. Sandy hair, wide nose, flat features that made him look like he'd somehow been squashed in one of those car compactors. For all I knew, maybe he had been. He had a thick neck and even thicker eyebrows that took up a large portion of his face. All in all, not exactly someone I'd picture on the front of a magazine. Maybe there was a reason he'd turned to a life of crime; that was all I was saying. If I'd met him in a dark alley, I would have steered clear, even without knowing the things I did now.

I nodded. "So, what happens next? How are we supposed to get more information about Holt's plans?"

Mendez let out a breath. "That's the part you might not like." He crossed his arms, causing his muscles to flex in a very nice way. "I need to go to Holt's head of operations. And that's in Prague."

I didn't like the idea of staying alone in a safe house, without any idea of what was going on, but if it meant someone was actually going after the bad guys and helping Madison in some way, I could get on board with that plan. I nodded.

Mendez hesitated.

"And you're coming with me."

Chapter Six

· · · · · · · · · ·

I HEARD THE WORDS, BUT THEY DIDN'T MAKE SENSE. I couldn't go after the bad guys. I'd only get in the way. I belonged here, with Madison.

Well, when I figured out where she was.

"You want me to go to Prague," I repeated dumbly. "Why?"

A muscle in Mendez's jaw clenched and I narrowed my eyes.

"There's something you're not telling me." I crossed my arms. "What is it?"

He hesitated and ran a hand through his hair. "Madison was supposed to meet someone there." He leaned forward and placed his hands on the table. "A weapons supplier for Holt was finally ready to talk to the CIA. We were hoping he'd lead us to Holt if we followed him long enough. Madison was his handler."

I waited, saying nothing.

Mendez cleared his throat. "With Madison in hiding, she won't be able to make the meeting, and we need you to step in."

I burst out laughing before realizing he was serious. My laugh sputtered to a cough.

When I could control myself again, I held my hand in front

of me, stalling Mendez from saying anything else. My place was with computers. Not people. Or potential danger.

"No can do." I got up from the table. I had no idea where I was going, but it wasn't like I could go far. A small hallway led away from the kitchen, so I turned in that direction, flicking on the light when I reached it.

"Don't you have trained operatives for that kind of thing?" I asked. "Why me?"

Mendez was right behind me. "Because he'll only meet with Madison."

I turned on him, pushing a finger into his chest. "I'm. Not. Madison." I'd lived my whole life being compared to her. I always came up lacking. It wasn't a good idea to test my limits when death was on the line.

He grabbed my hand, holding it there. His eyes bored into mine. "But you look like her." He released my hand, and I rubbed my palms on my thigh, taking a shaky step back.

Mendez glanced away, then returned his gaze to mine. "By the time he got close enough to recognize the difference, we'd already have a tail on him. That's all we need. You don't even need to talk to the guy."

He sighed. "Look. I don't like it either. But we can't think of anything better if we want to get Madison out of hiding. Our number one priority will be to keep you safe."

With a jolt, I recognized that this was probably what he'd been talking about with his superior back when he'd left the room. So, despite how easy he claimed this would be, even Mendez didn't honestly think I could do it. I paced in front of him.

"How would this get her out of hiding?" I asked.

He palmed the back of his neck. "Following this man will lead us to Holt. The sooner we track down Holt, the sooner we can take care of him. That removes the target on Madison's back. I'm not authorized to tell you more than that."

I let out a grunt. "Isn't it against the rules to involve non-superhero people like me?"

"Civilians?"

"Yeah," I said, following the hallway. "Aren't you supposed to, I don't know, keep me far *away* from the danger?" My hands were moving wildly in the air, and I accidentally whacked him in the chest. I wasn't sorry about it. "You're not supposed to put me directly in harm's way, I know that much." Out of words, I walked away.

A bathroom branched off to the right, two bedrooms were to the left. I turned and started back the way I came, not wanting to be stuck in a room with this man who had so casually asked me to risk my life. One shoot-out was enough for me, thank you very much.

"There wouldn't be any danger. Holt doesn't know about the meeting. And yes, there are protocols about involving civilians." Mendez crossed his arms and leaned against the wall, watching me as I crossed in front of him. "But desperate times call for desperate measures. There's no one else who could pull it off."

"See, that's the thing," I said. "Maybe I don't want to pull it off. This is something that has *bad idea* written all over it. And I *don't want to do it.*"

I was the kind of girl who played things safe. I hid behind computer screens. I stopped drinking coffee after two p.m. My idea of a good time was more likely to include a sugar rush than a rush of adrenaline. This, however, was danger on steroids. I'd already been shot at once. I wasn't about to willingly walk into another situation that could end up being the end of me.

Even ignoring the physical danger, pretending to be Madison would be a breach of trust. True, when we were younger, some people thought we were twins and we sometimes played along. We'd style my hair like hers or have her wear the necklace with my name on it as we'd try to confuse the new teacher at school. But this was different. This was putting my life in danger, something I was pretty sure my sister would frown upon.

I was too tired to pace anymore. All this excitement and gunfire really took it out of a gal. I leaned against the wall and took my heels off, sighing with contentment as blood returned to my toes and the arches of my feet flattened against the carpet. "That's better," I said.

Mendez's brow furrowed. "If you hate heels that much, why do you wear them?"

Ah, the ignorance of men. It was kind of cute, how he assumed any of us actually liked wearing the devil contraptions. His naive comment brought out his boyish charm, reminding me more of the journalist he'd pretended to be, instead of the hardened spy. I liked that guy. I wasn't sure how to get him back. The one who put me at ease, smiled, and flirted like nothing was wrong.

"Because my ex said they make my legs look killer," I said, suggestively tilting my head in his direction to catch his reaction. He didn't disappoint. Mendez's gaze was long and slow, traveling from my ankles to hips, taking in all my bare skin. Maybe this skirt hadn't been a mistake after all. Not if it got Mendez to look at me with that expression. Something flickered behind his eyes, a decision he made in a split second.

"You don't need the heels for that." His voice had a husky edge to it that made me burn with pleasure. For a second, I got caught up in the feeling. Then I remembered he was a professional spy, and they probably had training for things like this.

Seduction. Ways to make someone do something they otherwise wouldn't do. That was probably the expression I'd recognized. Mendez seeing an opportunity.

"I'm still not going to impersonate my sister," I said. "No matter how much you compliment my legs." I might have been willing to do other things though, if push came to shove.

Mendez took a step toward me, and despite my resolve not to fall for his games, my breath caught. He was almost unbearably attractive. It really wasn't fair. I had no defenses for someone on his level.

"You want to help Madison?" he asked. "This is how." Another step. I hated to admit it, but he had my full attention now, and not just for the way his eyes smoldered when he looked at me. I'd always be there for Madison, and if she really needed my help, I'd at least listen to what Mendez had to say.

"How would this help Madison?" I asked, narrowing my eyes.

"As long as Holt is calling the shots, Madison has to stay in hiding. If you do this, we're one step closer to finding her."

My pulse raced as fast as my thoughts. Would this actually help my sister? I was a bit fuzzy on the details, but I figured Mendez knew more than me. If true, I didn't see another option, even if it meant using myself as bait.

"I won't let anything happen to you. I know how to take care of a woman." His words were laced with double entendre as he took yet another step. The hallway wasn't that big to begin with, and with Mendez now standing directly in front of me, I was finding it hard to think. Very, very hard.

"All you need to do is stand there and look irresistible." He was up close and personal, invading my bubble with his manly smelling cologne and sexy stubble. "That mission is already accomplished."

I didn't know I was such a sucker for flattery. But here we were. Me, backed up against the wall and trying not to let my knees buckle. My brain knew it wasn't real, but that didn't stop my body from reacting. I hadn't been in a relationship since the breakup with Everett. Maybe it was pent-up need, or all the leftover adrenaline from the night, but I was having a hard time keeping my reactions in check. Of course, I knew that wasn't a good reason to get involved with someone, but I was pretty good at lying to myself. I guess I shouldn't have been surprised I'd be so quick to justify the leap.

I already knew I was attracted to Mendez. The question now was whether I trusted him with my safety for this task. The answer was both yes and no. Helping Madison was enough to get me to agree, but it wasn't enough to make me forget the danger. Right now, I needed a little help forgetting, and if that meant letting Mendez take the edge off . . .

He put an arm to either side of me, effectively trapping me against the wall, his body pressed against mine. His breath was warm against my neck, the scent of his cologne filling the space around us.

There was one thing I knew for sure. If the situation were reversed, Madison wouldn't hesitate if it meant helping me. It didn't matter if there was danger involved. Rain or shine, my big sister had my back.

"I'm willing to be convinced." I said it without meaning to, not sure if I was agreeing to the mission or whatever might happen between Mendez and me right now. I was aware of the risks of both, but my logic was pretty fuzzy at the moment, like I'd had one too many drinks when all I'd had was an extra dose of Mendez.

During our interview, I'd known I couldn't let my guard

down with him. Because something like this would happen sooner than I was ready for. Some clarity returned with that thought, because I knew I still wasn't.

"Does that make me stupid?" I bit my lip, drawing Mendez's gaze there, his eyes burning with an emotion I was all too familiar with in that moment. I was pretty sure agreeing to a secret spy rendezvous meant I'd officially lost it. As for Mendez . . . I wasn't a trained spy, conditioned to stand up to torture. I had no self-control. I couldn't even think of resisting. The only thing I could think about was how Mendez was leaning in, his face so close to mine.

A small part of my brain knew I was being manipulated, but truth be told, I still enjoyed it. A lot.

It was a shame I'd have to start hitting the brakes soon. But would it be such a bad thing if I didn't?

True, eventually I'd have to think this whole thing through. But with my sister in trouble, was there really anything to think about? I might as well get something out of the bum deal.

"I don't think you're stupid." Mendez brought one hand forward, fiddling with a strand of my hair. "Maybe a little blond." He smiled, liquefying my insides and turning my legs to jelly. "But I've always had a thing for blondes."

"Good to know." My voice came out all wispy, but I barely even noticed. I was hit with a sudden realization, momentarily breaking the spell I was under. "Would I have to change my hair to look more like Madison?"

Box dye was not my friend. I'd tried dying my hair myself when I was younger, and the results had been . . . well . . . catastrophic was putting it mildly. I was not about to relive that experience, even if Mendez was now trailing a hand up my arm, to my neck, and into the hair in question.

He twirled a strand between his fingers, brushing my neck with feather-light pressure. Every fiber of my being was electrified, burning at his touch. Oh, what did I care? I'd shave my head if Mendez asked, and he probably knew it. If it'd help Madison too? I might as well wear a clown wig.

"Blond hair makes you look like you're undercover," he said, voice husky. "If you dye it back to brown, it still wouldn't look like her natural shade. This is better. It's sexy."

His breath was hot on my neck, and I almost melted into a puddle then and there. This man didn't need professional seduction training. He could bring a woman to her knees simply by being in the same room. Simply by existing. He hadn't even kissed me yet, but the anticipation was enough to power a city.

"Tell me exactly what I'd need to do." The words took effort. I couldn't hold out much longer. I put my hands on his chest, keeping a little distance between us. I needed to think. *Madison* needed me to think. And that was pretty hard to do when Mendez had removed his hand from my hair and put it at my waist, trying to pull me closer. His fingers spread across my hips, applying the lightest of pressure, tugging me into him.

"We'd fly to Prague on a private jet."

Not going to lie, that part sounded pretty good. His lips were close to my neck, and I almost passed out from just the thought of what they'd feel like on my skin. I could envision it all too well. Soft, yet strong and demanding. Moving with precision and hitting all the right spots to make me melt.

It was dangerous to let my thoughts wander down that path, but I told myself it was okay to fantasize. As long as I didn't let things go too far. That line kept drifting further away though, and I wasn't sure if that was a good thing. Because now I'd convinced myself that letting Mendez have his way with me would be helping Madison too.

"You'd pretend to be your sister at a rendezvous point. No danger involved. The weapons supplier won't even talk to you once he realizes you're not Madison. Our team will take it from there." My skin burned beneath his touch. "That's it. Believe me, I want to keep every inch of you safe."

His voice was raspy and low as he pushed his weight against me. Mendez started kissing the sensitive skin at the base of my throat, and my hands on his chest stopped pushing him away and started pulling him closer. I had no control over them. I couldn't be trusted with anything right now. I wasn't in my right mind.

I murmured my agreement, not saying anything else for a minute while I appreciated the feel of his lips against my skin. It was everything I'd imagined. Slow and sure. Barely restrained. Hinting at something intense and fierce behind closed doors. He left a trail of kisses along my clavicle, then up the side of my neck where my pulse picked up its rhythm. Each kiss was warm and velvety, fogging my brain with promises of more to come. I could feel my control slipping further away. I was like a teenager being pulled from bed, begging for five more minutes. The real question was whether the bed would win.

"If the meeting is with Madison, won't she be there?" I asked, but Mendez was already shaking his head.

He answered between kisses, accentuating each word with the slightest pressure against my neck. "She won't be anywhere close now that she's in hiding."

I had a lot of questions about that. Who was Madison hiding from? Holt? Had I ruined everything when I'd shown up at the restaurant? The questions were indistinct and vague though, barely forming before Mendez kissed them away. Maybe the CIA didn't want me knowing more, or maybe he was bad at sharing details. But I could think of at least one thing he was good at. Very, very good.

I attempted to gather some of my wits. It took way too much effort. "And if I don't do the meeting?"

I liked the idea of staying here. With a lock on the door. And a bed. Maybe with Mendez in it.

"Then Madison stays in danger."

I didn't like that. But I did like the way Mendez's touch awakened every nerve ending in my skin as he trailed his fingers along my bare waist, between my skirt and top.

But I couldn't stand by if it meant Madison had to stand down. There wasn't really another option. I already knew I'd agree to this if it meant Madison would be safe. No matter the danger to me.

"I'm still scared," I said. It almost hurt to say aloud. I didn't want to keep talking about my sister, spy rendezvous points, or any kind of plans. I wanted to do something else. Something I very well could regret in the morning. Something I knew I probably *would* regret in the morning. Something I really should put a stop to now if I knew what was best for me.

"You're handling this better than many other civilians would," Mendez said, bringing his gaze level with mine. "That tells me you're braver than you know." His pupils dilated. "But if you're still worried, I know ways to make you forget you're scared."

Oh, I was sure he did, and I wouldn't mind one bit. I was also sure that after he was through with me, I'd be his puppet on a string, following along like a lost puppy dog. He'd have the upper hand in every way, and I wouldn't even care. That's what a man like Mendez could do to a woman like me if I wasn't careful.

I knew how this would all go down. It wasn't like we'd walk off into the sunset together. Once Mendez got what he wanted, he'd be gone. Like every other guy in my life. My longest relationship had lasted a whopping eight months. Men never stuck around. I'd learned that firsthand from my own father, and more recently with Everett. If my own dad couldn't love me enough to stay, what hope did I have for a relationship?

I was trying to remember all my reasons, my facts on why it was a bad idea to give in. Now was the time to be strong. If I could. Honestly, I didn't know anymore if that was even an option, because Mendez's lips were moving along my jaw, inching closer to my mouth, and my body was responding whether I wanted it to or not.

Now or never, Dove. You can do this. You can reject this beautiful man who is quite possibly the most physically fit human you've ever encountered. Opportunities like this come around . . . once in a lifetime, probably. My fingers clenched, not wanting to agree with my head or my reasons, but I forced them to cooperate.

"I don't do one-night stands." I gently pushed Mendez away, keeping him at arm's length. There. I'd done it. In addition to saving me from myself, I'd also told him the truth. Because the fact of the matter was, I couldn't help but get involved emotionally if I got involved physically. I knew that about myself, so I'd created these rules. Sometimes I hated myself for them, like now, when there was nothing I wanted more than to find a bedroom and pull Mendez into it. But they were rules for a reason.

Rules were meant to be broken, a voice in my head whispered. A voice I usually listened to when something fun came along. I ignored it this time. Without Mendez's lips at my skin, it was easier to do the responsible thing. Okay, so that was a lie. But it was a lie I could swallow.

Mendez looked down at me, all smolder and sex appeal. Then his expression clouded over, and he took a step back.

He sighed. "I don't do commitment."

Relief and regret swirled around in my stomach simultaneously, mixing like cement. After everything else that had happened that day, my emotions were about done. Stick a fork in me. All I wanted was a shower and a soft bed. I'd like to know my sister was safe, but something told me that was pushing my luck. I exhaled as Mendez took another step back, dropping his hands to his sides.

"I'll do the rendezvous," I said, picking up my heels from where I'd dropped them. "Because it's the right thing to do and Madison needs me." And because I wasn't sure there was any other way for this series of nightmares to end. "But don't pretend with me like that again. I don't like being manipulated, and I don't like it when people play dirty."

Mendez's smile was slow. His words echoed in my head long after he walked away.

"Who said I was pretending?"

Chapter Seven

· · · · · · · · ·

HAVING NEVER BEEN ON A PRIVATE JET, I COULDN'T have said whether this one was anything special. But it certainly seemed like it to me. I'd never seen so much white on a plane before, with cream upholstery and snowy walls taking up most of the space. If I'd decorated this way, there wouldn't be any furniture left unscathed by scuffs and stains. Mendez seemed unaffected, however, as he settled into a chair and motioned for me to take the seat across from him. Good thing too, because with the whole cabin to ourselves, I didn't exactly know the protocol for choosing a seat. Plus, after last night, I didn't know if he'd rather I sit in the corner, to lick my wounds and pretend I was unaffected by his presence.

The pilot's voice came over the speakers, alerting us to our imminent takeoff. Mendez and I stayed silent while adjusting our seat belts and waiting for this to somehow be less awkward. Then we were off, the pressure pushing me back into my seat while a different kind of pressure made me unable to speak.

I couldn't tell if the swoop in my stomach was from lifting into the air or the thought of what I was about to do. Flying to a foreign country and putting myself directly in harm's way wasn't something on my bucket list. The travel part, sure, but the danger part, not so much. Especially when paired with the thought that the man sitting across from me was a complete mystery . . . well, it was no wonder my stomach was doing flips.

When he wasn't looking, I studied Mendez's features. His expression was brooding as he stared out the window, his hand rubbing the stubble that had formed along his jaw. I remembered how it felt to have that stubble trace along my neck and collarbone. My cheeks flamed and I looked away.

Mendez was like a chameleon: easygoing and flirtatious in one moment, only to turn grave and serious at others. I had no way of knowing which persona was the real him. Maybe he was both, like two sides of a coin. Maybe neither, and he was pretending to be someone he wasn't, even now.

Flashbacks to our first meeting played out in my memory, now tainted by my knowledge that Mendez was a spy. Every flirty line, every grin, every subtle shift in his weight to position his body toward mine—it had seemed so genuine. He'd laughed at my jokes. He'd seemed disappointed when I turned him down for dinner. Last night, he'd been the one to turn things physical. Had he been instructed to do that? Or was getting involved with civilians going against orders? How come the longer I spent in his presence, the more questions I had?

"The things you said during our interview. How much was a lie?" I asked, unable to keep the question buried any longer.

To his credit, though he looked startled, Mendez didn't ask me what I meant. He ran a hand through his hair and sat back, carefully collecting his thoughts. Or preparing his lies. I wasn't sure which.

I studied him intently, watching for the slightest change in his expression. Some hint that he was about to deceive me again. His eyes regarded mine, accepting my judgment but still holding something back.

"The best cover stories stick close to the truth. Easier to maintain that way." He looked at his fingernails, like his response somehow put an end to our discussion.

"That answers—hmmm, let's see—nothing." I crossed my arms and fixed him with a solid stare. Frustration welled up in my chest. I was tired of the games men played. Like Everett, who, even though we'd broken up, texted whenever he got lonely. He liked messing with my head. I still couldn't wear my favorite black dress, because whenever I pulled it off the hanger, all I could think of was the last time I'd worn it. With him. Men on dating apps were more of the same. They'd say anything if they thought it was what I wanted to hear. If I was going to put my life on the line, the least Mendez could do was tell me the truth.

This time when he looked at me, Mendez's expression softened. "The setup was . . ." His eyes winced, but maybe I was imagining it. "Artificial."

I could tell Mendez wasn't accustomed to letting people see behind the curtain. He wasn't the type to let people in. But he was trying. Because I asked. And that had to count for something. I wasn't sure who I was trying to convince of that fact—myself or him.

Still. Hearing him admit it out loud sent a pang through me. He didn't say his feelings were real. Kind of the opposite, in fact. Everything about that interview had been a setup. He'd probably worn that specific T-shirt on purpose, knowing it'd make me appreciate how it stretched across his chest.

Mendez took in a quiet breath, so faint I almost didn't catch it. "I still revealed too much." He shook his head and one side of his mouth quirked up in a smile. "Sometimes I'm not the best actor."

Could have fooled me. Could have, and did. My neck still burned from his kisses, and I reached a hand up to hide the blush blooming across my chest. I remembered the way he'd pushed me against the wall, and I had to clear my throat.

"So, when you said you'd experienced losing someone close to you?"

He inhaled, then let it go. "Truth."

Mendez didn't elaborate, and I didn't ask him to. With his line of work, I didn't think I'd want the specifics.

"Your flirting?"

I almost didn't ask it. I wasn't sure I'd believe him, no matter what answer he gave. It felt too real to be fake, but too good to be true. This man was literally trained in the art of deception, so I didn't know if I could gauge professionals on his level. Maybe if I had a polygraph test monitoring his every heartbeat and registering the rise and fall of his chest—but then again, I wasn't sure I'd even believe that. Weren't spies trained to trick polygraph tests?

I had only myself to trust.

Or blame.

Mendez hesitated for a minute, debating his answer. His expression was unreadable as he watched the horizon out the window. Finally, he turned back to face me.

"My instructions were to get close to you. It's a necessary evil of my job."

Even though the plane's course stayed smooth, my stomach plummeted. Mendez had been the one safe thing among all this chaos, but even that had been a lie. I tried not to let my disappointment show on my face, but I wasn't the one trained in acting. I was sure it was written there for the world to see.

Mendez grinned then, his expression turning devious. "But some days I *really* like my job."

How was I supposed to interpret that? I supposed I should be happy he didn't give me another monosyllabic answer, but somehow his longer explanation didn't make things any clearer. I stayed silent, weighing his words against the feelings they stirred up in me.

I almost let myself hope. But spies don't do commitment.

And I knew better than to get involved. I was just another assignment. He couldn't have been more direct about that. It was time my heart got on board.

I nodded slowly, working through the knot of emotions in my chest. "And the article?" I said, needing a change of topic. "Why investigate me at all? Why all the to-do?" It wasn't like I expected him to spill all the CIA's secrets, but now that he was actually talking, it wouldn't hurt to get some clarity on things. Clarity was good. Even if it created a hole in the center of my chest.

Mendez idly scratched his arm as he considered his answer. "The CIA has a partnership with many media outlets," he finally said. "The *Journal* is one of them. We have access to their building and can reserve rooms, like the one we met in. We've found that people are more eager to answer our questions if they believe it's for their personal benefit and if they don't know they're speaking with a member of the agency."

I remembered how he'd seemed unfamiliar with the building layout and gave a short, self-deprecating chuckle. They really were master manipulators. And I'd been an easy target.

Mendez shook his head. "The key card they gave me wasn't programmed right away and my team had to scramble to fix it." He grinned. "That led to—"

I blushed and hurried to interrupt him. "Our unfortunate encounter. I remember." My cheeks would permanently be stained red if I stayed in Mendez's presence. I watched a flock of geese off in the distance before returning my attention to the only man in the cabin.

His smile was slow and wide. "I wouldn't call it unfortunate."

I cleared my throat and looked out the window again. It was like I'd left all my common sense on the tarmac, with my thoughts scattered in the wind. Unsure of how to respond, I fidgeted with my seat belt, adjusting the length and messing with the locking mechanism. Eventually I told myself to get over it. Mendez had this way of turning the conversation around so I was always playing defense, but I still had questions I wanted resolved. If I couldn't have his genuine interest, at least I could have answers.

I squared my shoulders and faced him. "And why were you investigating me in the first place?" I raised an eyebrow.

He pursed his lips and sighed. "We thought you might know where Madison was. With her in hiding, we weren't leaving any stone unturned." He shifted in his chair. "We wanted to make sure she was safe, and we didn't know if you were involved in any way."

"And now I *am* involved, somehow." I narrowed my eyes at him. "Are you sure the CIA didn't meddle to make that happen?"

"Well, you're on a CIA jet, so . . ." he trailed off.

"I know it's because of the CIA that I'm going to Prague," I clarified. "I mean back at the restaurant. The men with guns. Was that all a setup too, so you could have your little savior moment and I'd fall at your feet, thankful to be alive?"

Mendez shook his head. "We still don't know who those men were exactly or how they found you there. We're looking into it. I'm simply glad we had some men inside the restaurant, or the gunmen could have gotten to you before you made it outside. Though I am sorry the hitmen slipped through their fingers."

I considered his answer, vaguely remembering people standing up to the gunmen. I supposed I was grateful for them too.

"So, if it wasn't the CIA meddling, what would you have done about the article you were supposedly writing? What if I never met you outside the back of the restaurant? I can't imagine you writing a hard-hitting journalistic piece now that I know who you really are. Who really writes the articles by Sam Olsen?"

"I have many skills." Mendez smiled and folded his arms across his chest. "Are you implying I couldn't write an article and successfully navigate my real occupation at the same time?"

I shot him a skeptical look. Not because I really doubted his abilities. The man was like Hercules. I bet if he wanted to cure cancer and fly to the moon, he'd find some way to make that happen. Probably while filming a hair commercial. But something told me Mendez wasn't the type to sit behind a desk while other people took on the risks.

He chuckled and inclined his head in agreement. "One of the interns at the paper would have tackled it. Sam Olsen is a lot of different writers working under a pseudonym."

I felt cheated but couldn't put my finger on the reason why. "Glad to see my tax dollars hard at work," I said dryly. "Deceiving people." I sniffed, but didn't know what else to say, so I looked around the cabin and let the conversation lull for a bit.

I recognized the need for all the secrets and subterfuge, but frankly, I didn't know what to believe anymore. For all my life, I'd thought the government was supposed to protect me. Have my best interests at heart. Now I knew the lines got blurred when protecting an individual came at the expense of the greater good. Good guys, bad guys, it didn't really matter. Everyone was the hero in their own story. But now, the stakes were higher, and everyone had guns.

Everyone except me.

The fact of the matter was that I had to pick a side. I'd teamed up with Mendez, mainly because I thought it was what Madison would want me to do. He seemed like the safer option—if a bad boy could be considered safe. It wasn't like I could go back and question those thugs who'd shot at me at the restaurant, and I didn't want to. I just wanted to feel like I had my feet on solid ground.

Madison would know what to do. And I needed to go to this meeting in Prague so she could come out of hiding. I was stuck with Mendez for now. At least I knew there was an end in sight. Mendez worked for the CIA. They were all about "eliminating the risk," right? So it wasn't like I'd be blackmailed into some kind of long-lasting agreement where I'd constantly be putting my life in danger.

Although for a man like Mendez, I had to say, I didn't exactly mind. He had this kind of quiet strength, like he could weather any type of storm without getting his feathers ruffled. He was solid. And I wasn't just talking about his muscles, which, yes, were more solid than any alibi.

Okay, fine. In another reality, I could have liked Mendez.

It wasn't exactly reciprocated, or healthy, so I was working on that. But at least I was fairly certain of one thing. I could trust him. I had to.

"Get some rest," Mendez said. "It's a long flight to Prague."

Prague. Why did the city's name look like *plague*? Maybe it was a bad omen of things to come. I adjusted my chair. Even the novelty of being able to fully recline my seat wasn't enough to put the possibility of death far from my mind.

Chapter Eight

· · · · · · · · · ·

YOU WOULD THINK THAT PRIVATE JETS WOULD MAKE JET lag a thing of the past, but you'd be wrong. Despite the plush plane and the copious amounts of melatonin I'd consumed, I still arrived in Prague haggard and sleep-deprived. I blamed the stress. This weekend was proving to have a lot of firsts for me, and I continuously felt like I was a step behind. First time riding a motorcycle. First time on a private jet. First time in the Czech Republic. First time trying to ignore the sexual magnetism of the man opening the back car door for me as we left the tarmac en route to yet another safe house.

The chauffeur didn't say much, so we rode in silence. Red roofs littered the skyline, quaint old buildings that looked like they were straight out of a postcard. DC sometimes felt old—well, at least when you compared it to the rest of the United States. But next to Europe, our buildings were babies. We didn't build them like this either—all regal and iconic. It was as if I'd entered a fantasy world. A swath of tan walls with random bursts of color filled my vision, tall spires of cathedrals jutting out in the distance. But despite the beauty, my eyes were almost too heavy to stay open.

In the car, I leaned on Mendez's shoulder, and he didn't pull away. It was probably for our driver's benefit, so he wouldn't question why the two of us had flown in on a private jet all alone if we weren't a couple.

I closed my eyes and let the movement of the car rock me.

"You're not so good at burning both ends of the candle, are you?" Mendez's voice was light.

"Even burning one end is too much for me. My candle is for decoration only."

This made him chuckle, his body rumbling underneath my cheek. "If you're this comatose after a private flight, I'd hate to see how you'd do in commercial."

"Good thing you won't have to see that." I didn't bother to open my eyes.

Mendez gave a short laugh. "This was an extreme condition." His shoulder moved with the motion of the car, and he re-adjusted so I could continue to lean against him. "We're trying to keep you off the radar until after the meeting. Our way back will likely be on a commercial flight." He spoke softly so our driver wouldn't hear, but the whispering only lulled me to sleep more. I murmured something in response, and the next thing I knew, Mendez was shaking me awake and telling me we were there.

Rubbing sleep from my eyes, I stepped out of the car and waited on the sidewalk while Mendez took our bags out of the trunk. We didn't have much since this safe house was supposed to be fully stocked. But we had a laptop and a bag each for our clothes and shoes. Mendez had a whole separate container for his weapons. I still wasn't sure what to think of that, or the fact that I was traveling with a guy like him who had a separate suit-case for his guns. I guess everyone had to have their thing.

I had new clothes as well. Clothes that were supposed to make me look like a spy, although Mendez said they didn't use that term for themselves. They preferred the title of *officers* or *operatives*. He said a spy was someone who turned on their own side, whereas operatives were loyal to their country. But I couldn't help myself, or the years of indoctrination that had happened through movies and books. To me, Mendez was, and always would be, a spy.

In addition to the clothes, Mendez also wanted me to wear a gun since Madison would have worn one. But, uh, that seemed like a really bad idea. Like, really, really bad. I'd pointed out the problems with his plan and how the bad guys could in turn point the gun at *me*, and eventually we'd settled on a tranquil-izer gun. It'd still look pretty realistic, but if someone used it against me, the worst thing that would happen was I would go nighty night for a bit. Was there a possibility that they would have their own guns? Yes. Was I trying not to think of that? Also yes.

"It's up this way." Mendez motioned with his chin. "I had the driver drop us off around the block in case we were being fol-lowed."

What a pleasant thought.

"I hate to ask this," he said, "but would you carry the regular bags?" He adjusted the Glock at his back. "They're not heavy, and I'd rather have at least one hand free. Just in case."

"Good thing I'm not wearing heels." I lifted the laptop bag and settled the strap over my shoulder. Mendez smiled.

"I don't know; I kind of miss them." He waggled his eye-brows. "And the short skirt."

I blushed, picking up the other two bags and leaving the weapons case to Mendez. It was heavy enough to have been a weapon in and of itself, so I was grateful he'd take that one. Right now, I was also grateful for the black jeans and boots. But maybe heels later . . . ? No. I shook my head. Those types of thoughts were off-limits, now and forever. Even if the memory of Mendez pushing me against the wall would forever be burned in my brain.

We made it to the safe house—or, rather, apartment—without any incidents and I flopped onto the couch in exhaustion. Here I was in Prague for the first time, and I could barely muster up enough energy to care. How pathetic.

"Don't get too comfortable." Mendez placed the weapons case on the table and opened it up. "Your meeting with the weapons supplier is in a couple of hours."

Dread pooled in my stomach. A day ago, the only thing I was worried about was how long I could go without doing another load of laundry. Now here I was wondering whether I'd be alive tomorrow. I knew I'd chosen this, that I could be back in the States, safely sequestered away in that apartment in DC. But that didn't help the fear that settled into my skin, and it wouldn't help Madison either. She needed me right now, and I needed to pull myself together. For my sister's sake.

"What else do I need to know?" I stood up. "What if he doesn't walk away and he comes to talk to me instead? I know you told me the less I know, the better, but if I'm putting my life on the line, I kind of feel I need to know more than 'less.'"

I'd read some of the papers on the plane. The papers Mendez *let* me read. But there was still a very large part of me that felt inadequate to this task. Like a mouse staring down a lion—one misstep and I would be cat food.

"You know all you need to." Mendez took one of the guns out of the case and slipped it into the holster at his hip. He walked over to me with a wicked gleam in his eye, holding a black strip of cloth he'd picked up from the table. "Now lift up your shirt."

"Excuse me?" I didn't know what to think about the turn this conversation had just taken, but I was pretty sure I hadn't misheard him. I replayed his words in my mind, just in case. Mendez grinned and finished crossing the room, coming to a stop directly in front of me.

"I said, lift up your shirt."

It was loud and clear that time, no room for misinterpretation. I crossed my arms over my chest and stared him down, which only made Mendez laugh.

"This is a belly band. We'll strap your tranq gun to your waist so you can carry concealed. It's the way Madison usually wears her gun."

I grumbled as I lifted the bottom portion of my shirt, leaving my bra covered. "You could have said so earlier."

"Where's the fun in that?" Mendez strapped the band to my waist and I tried not to notice his fingers touching my skin. Easier said than done. Instead, I focused on keeping my breathing regular, because okay, maybe I was sucking in a little. That's just what you do when a man is looking at, and feeling, your stomach. So sue me.

Mendez finished securing me into the band and pulled my shirt back down, his fingers gently tracing my hips. He didn't step back, and I wasn't sure what to think of that.

He placed his hands on my shoulders and looked into my eyes. "In order to get Madison out of hiding, we need you to do this, Dove. Are you sure you can? You could still stay here. In fact, I'd like nothing more."

Right. This had all been his supervisor's idea. Mendez didn't think I could do it. The thought made me straighten my spine a bit, even though my knees still felt weak. When this was all over, I was going to ream Madison out for getting me involved. Well, if she was alive. Tears pricked at my eyes, and I blinked them back. Mendez didn't need to see how worried and scared I truly was. He already thought I wasn't up to the task. But how could I be, when there was still so much I didn't know? There was something Mendez wasn't telling me. I could feel it. But sometimes you had to trust the people around you. Right?

I started to sweat under the belly band. A small voice in my head was saying, *Sure, but do you have to trust them with your life?* I didn't have an answer for that voice, because honestly, it kind of had a point.

"I bet you miss Madison right now, huh?" I asked. She'd be brave in this situation. She'd know what to do. Unlike me. "You wouldn't have to hold her hand and tell her everything's going to be all right."

Mendez smiled. "I don't know, I kind of like that you're so innocent about all this. It's refreshing. Reminds me why I'm doing it in the first place. Who I'm trying to protect." He dropped his grip from my shoulders to my hands, where his thumbs made slow circles. I let myself be momentarily distracted until he applied light pressure, reminding me I still hadn't answered his original question. My throat was dry now though.

"Yes, I can do this." I swallowed hard. If Mendez did it to protect innocent people . . . well, I could too. Probably.

He moved his hands to my waist again, his fingers finding the bare skin there. Fire raced along every nerve ending I had, and I swallowed again, this time for a different reason. The last time he'd touched me like this he was only pretending. Trying to persuade me to fly with him to Prague. What was his agenda this time? *Or*, my nerves raced with the thought, *was this real?* He hooked his fingers into my belt loops, drawing me closer. Then his hands were gone. It only took me a second to realize he was taking off his belt.

"What are you doing?" Yes, my voice sounded slightly panicked. Because no matter how hard I was trying to remain calm, the fact of the matter was, *Mendez was taking off his belt.*

"Relax," he said. Which was *so* not the right thing to say. How was I supposed to relax when *this* was happening? Mendez smiled, the kind of smile that was full of charisma and confidence. Not a concern in the world for him. His belt was fully off now, and his hands were once again at my waist. But he didn't kiss me, or pull me close, or any of the other things I expected.

No, Mendez started threading his belt through my belt loops.

"Wha . . . what?" I stammered, my brain trying to catch up with what was happening.

"This is a belt transmitter." His fingers worked around my side, until his arms wrapped around my back. I hated to admit it, but I swooned just a little bit. This close, his scent was intoxicating, and I could feel the way his muscles bunched up next to my skin.

"Like a body wire, just more discreet. If they do approach you and search you, they won't think twice about it. This way I can keep you safe and listen to your conversation once you're at the rendezvous point. Don't worry though, they won't likely have a conversation with you." He added that last part after I shot him a worried look. If there was talking involved, I was destined to fail. He'd seen how much I'd bungled our interview, and that was regarding a topic I knew about in advance and had all the information on. This would be a complete disaster.

"The antenna goes down the length of the belt," he continued, not leaving me any space to dwell on dark possibilities. "That's so it can transmit long-distance. Be careful not to twist it. The downside of this model over a traditional wire is that there's no tracking device. Since I'll have eyes on you, that shouldn't be a problem." He'd finished wrapping it around my waist and was turning the buckle to show me the inside. "Move this microswitch here to turn it on or off."

"Why would I turn it off?" Call me mad, but it seemed like a good idea to keep Mendez in the loop.

He raised his eyebrows. "If you need to go to the bathroom."

"Oh." I fumbled with the buckle, turning it on and off a few times until Mendez was satisfied I knew how to use it. I left it on, then did the clasp.

He took a step back and picked up one of the bags we'd brought with us. Then he disappeared into the back room. When he emerged a few minutes later, he looked like a completely different person. Large glasses took up half his face and his hair was touched with gray at the sides. The clothes he'd worn on the plane were replaced with a European ensemble that easily could have been purchased at the local boutique down the street. Even his shoes were different. What surprised me the most though was that he carried himself differently. Like he'd transformed into a tired business executive in the blink of an eye.

Who was this man, really? Which persona was I supposed to believe? The journalist, the agent, the local—he looked equally comfortable in all these characters, shedding identities as easily as a snake sheds its skin.

He pulled a wallet from the bag and flipped through it before pocketing it and a pack of cigarettes. I raised my eyebrows.

I'd been with Mendez for a few days now and hadn't seen him go for a smoke break once.

"Pocket litter," he explained. "To support my cover."

Now that he mentioned it, I noticed his clothes smelled faintly of smoke. I shook my head, unsure whether to be impressed or anxious over this level of detail.

He'd said it'd be easy. I'd sit on a bench and that'd be it.

Riiiiight.

This was what I got for believing the government.

Mendez strapped a gun to a holster hidden beneath his jacket, then handed me the tranq gun to put in the band wrapped around my stomach. I stared at it. The gun was cold in my hands, heavy and unforgiving.

"So, this is really happening, huh?" I shuddered. Despite the long plane ride and new clothes, it hadn't quite hit me until this moment. Sooner than I'd like, I was going to a spy meeting where I'd need a tranquilizer gun strapped to my stomach and a wire wrapped around my waist. All those things pointed to one hard, cold reality I hadn't been ready to face before now.

This was dangerous.

Mendez didn't answer, but his eyes questioned me. I swallowed and nodded once to show him that I was ready. I knew the truth though. There was no way I'd ever be ready.

Chapter Nine

· · · · · · · · ·

I WAS EARLY TO THE RENDEZVOUS POINT. GIVEN THE circumstances, I thought punctuality was overrated. Not that I had a choice in the matter. Mendez had checked in with the CIA, and then we were off to see the wizard. I kept hearing Mendez mutter things into his earpiece like "all eyes are up" and "target is inbound," but I was too petrified to ask him what they meant. Then, before I had a chance to change my mind, he disappeared into the crowd, and I was all alone in the world.

The tram depot was dirty and old. So, basically like the metro back home. The biggest difference was I couldn't read any of the signs and my heartbeat was loud in my ears. Oh, and the smell. Like someone had died but left their stench behind. Somehow, I'd pictured the spy life being more glamorous.

People milled all around me, none of them saying anything I could understand. Their vowels rolled together like a continuous wave, but every once in a while their consonants jutted out and took over. The conversations were all muted though, like I was wearing earplugs. Or maybe they simply operated at a lower decibel than the Americans I was used to. Maybe we actually were as loud and obnoxious as everyone said.

No one bothered me, and most ignored me, which was a good thing because I didn't know how to act like a spy. I was pretty sure they didn't wander aimlessly around a tram depot, but I wasn't going to sit on the bench yet if I could help it. That bench had cooties. That bench was already sending me bad vibes, and nothing had even happened yet. All I was supposed to do was sit there, but if I did, I'd no longer be in control of what happened next.

I glanced over my shoulder and caught a glimpse of Mendez, who blended in seamlessly with the other people mingling by the tram's entry spots. I straightened my spine and tried to act more like him. Detached. Unconcerned. Like I had a calm and cool center. Ah, who was I kidding? I was terrified Jell-O on the inside.

A loud bang to my left made me jump and my heartbeat went into overdrive. Without thinking, I hid behind a rack of magazines, earning a few concerned glances and skeptical looks. *Smooth, Dove. Super smooth.*

It was only a tourist dropping her suitcase, but that didn't stop the nausea from clawing its way up my throat. I bit my lower lip and swallowed. My hands started to shake, and I knew I had to pull myself together.

Simply knowing I was nervous didn't change anything. My mind still came up with every worst-case scenario. My stomach roiled, but more urgently, I had to pee. I wasn't sure if that was a symptom of being anxious or just my bladder choosing the worst possible time to act up, but there was no denying it was a problem. The weapons supplier was supposed to arrive in five minutes; however, I wasn't going to make it that long unless I found a bathroom first.

There was one down the walkway, and I hastily made my way toward it. At least, I was hoping it was the restroom. It was hard to tell without being able to read Czech.

"I'm going to the bathroom," I said to no one in particular. A woman looked at me and hurried her child away like she worried whatever illness I had might be contagious. My bad. I didn't have an earpiece to hear Mendez's response to my statement, but I could feel his eye roll on my back as I opened the door and ducked inside.

It was a bathroom. There were two stalls, and thankfully only one was occupied. I flipped the switch to my belt and did my business. All was right again with the world. That was, until a piece of paper slipped under my stall, causing my heartbeat to stutter. I leaned over to read it. The paper had one short sentence on it.

Are you wired?

Around me, it was like time slowed down. Each drip of the sink faucet reverberated in the space, and the flickering of the light cast shadows in my stall like cold tendrils of dread reaching out for me. Dimly, I could hear the toilet next to me flush, and the woman walked out to wash her hands. I stayed where I was, debating my options.

One: I could stay here forever, pretending my cover hadn't been blown and that Holt or one of his minions hadn't found me in this dirty bathroom. Problem with that was I knew the reality of my situation. An ostrich with its head in the sand was still a dead bird.

Two: I could pull up my pants and be a big girl.

I didn't want to be brave. I wasn't made for it. I was made for sweatpants and movie nights, not murder. But honestly, if I *was* going to die, I *really* didn't want to die with my pants down. So, I took care of that first, then bent to pick up the slip of paper.

It hadn't come from the stall next to me. It'd come from the front. Looking through the crack, I couldn't see any shoes or anything that might give me any indication of who I was dealing with here. When I'd entered, I hadn't seen anyone besides the woman in the stall next to me. She finished washing her hands and left. Judging from the sound of the door banging on the wall and the brief moment where noise from outside carried into the bathroom, I was alone now. Just me and the person who'd given me this note, who'd entered like a phantom.

Nowhere to run, nowhere to hide.

My hand holding the note started to shake and the words became illegible. Then my mind caught on one small detail. The *e*'s. The *e*'s were familiar. I'd seen this handwriting before.

I gasped and hastily opened the stall with shaky fingers, coming face-to-face with the one person I wasn't sure I'd ever see again.

"Mads?" My voice broke, and I threw myself into my sister's arms. Her gun pressed against me, which was a new experience, for sure. She didn't wear her typical yoga pants and messy bun; no, this time Madison was dressed to kill. Okay, probably literally. The thought almost made me pull back, but I was too happy to see her to care that her jacket had all kinds of pockets with hard metal things inside. Mendez had done a good job making me dress like her, though I'd never seen her in clothes like these. With us side by side, I could have almost mistaken us for twins, aside from the fact that her hair was now a deep shade of red.

Madison was still stiff, like she might run away at any moment, and I'd be left wondering if it'd all been my imagination. Then I remembered her note. "No, my wire's off." Relief bloomed in my chest. I wouldn't have to do this rendezvous after all, and

Madison could take it from here. Obviously, she could come out of hiding now. My part was done.

I could feel the moment her shoulders relaxed, and she returned my embrace. Like the sun shining through after a storm. I was safe. She was safe. That was all that mattered.

"I'm so glad you're okay—" I started to say, until she cut me off.

"We don't have a lot of time," she said, bringing me back to the present. The danger. The fact that we were hugging in a tram depot bathroom in Prague, five thousand miles away from home.

"Love your hair." I flicked her red braid over her shoulder.

She smiled wanly. "I didn't want to be blond and have someone think I was you." Her voice was soft. "I never wanted you to be involved. The man at the restaurant was supposed to leave if I was late, and he never should have met you." She swallowed. "Our meeting was for five thirty. If he had followed the plan and left, you wouldn't be in danger. I'm so sorry, Dove. I shouldn't have called you about dinner in the first place, but I thought I might not get another chance to see you again. Not for a very long time. You deserved to know why. I thought staying away would make you safe, not leave you defenseless."

I could always tell when my sister was lying. And right now, I knew she meant every word.

"Well." I gave a small laugh. "I'm involved now, so I guess it's a little too late for that."

Madison shook her head. "No, it's not. I'm sure you have a lot of questions, and I promise I'll answer them. Later. You need to get out of here. You need to go to this address in Prague." She stuffed a piece of paper into my pocket. Hello, personal boundaries. "And you need to stay there. I'll come as soon as I can, but it might take me a few days. There's food and everything you'll need. Don't leave until I get there. It's not safe."

Yeah, no duh. I'd already been shot at, chased, and had to fly halfway across the world with a complete stranger. I kind of already figured out it wasn't safe.

"Don't worry, Mendez has been taking care of me. He has this whole—" I waved my hands in the air, then gave up. "Plan," I finished weakly. I didn't get into specifics, because . . . well . . . he hadn't gone into specifics with me.

"Mendez?" Madison's eyes shot to mine. "I saw you outside and came to talk to you right away. But Mendez is here too?" Her words implied she was surprised, but her face betrayed no emotion.

"Just outside. The weapons supplier should be there soon too, so we should probably—"

"You need to lose him." She gripped my shoulders. "Can you do that?"

"Holt's weapons supplier?" I was used to feeling one step behind with Madison. But I wasn't used to the time crunch. Panic was starting to creep around my vision, tightening my throat and making it hard to breathe again.

"Mendez." She lifted up the edge of her shirt, took out a gun, and cocked it. Unlike mine, hers was definitely real. It looked like the one Mendez wore—our government's money hard at work.

"Why do I need to lose Mendez? Don't you trust your partner?" My voice was rising, my hands starting to flutter in the air. Why did it all have to be happening so fast? Time was slipping through my fingers, each second accelerating faster than the last.

But then Madison practically made time stop. Her words seemed to fill up the small bathroom.

"Mendez isn't my partner."

Chapter Ten

. . . .

I WAS STILL REELING FROM HER REVELATION WHEN MAD-
ison roughly turned me toward the door, whispering instructions into my ear.

"Walk calmly to the bench and sit down. Don't lose Mendez
here at the depot because he probably has a tracker in your wire.
Continue with his plan as if nothing's changed. Wait until tonight, ditch the tracker, then strike out on your own. Take the ID
you got from the man in the restaurant, just in case you need to
leave the country. You look enough like me that it'll work. He
gave you that, right?"

She waited for me to confirm. I nodded, still dazed.

Her hug was tight and fierce. It felt final. "I'll meet up with
you when this is all over."

That couldn't be it. There were holes in her plan. Big, gaping
black holes. The kind that sucked entire solar systems into them.
I could feel myself spiraling. "What am I supposed to do when I
reach the bench? What am I supposed to do between now and
tonight?" My voice was tinged with hysteria, but I kept talking.

"What if Mendez finds out you were here? Is he CIA? Are you? What should I say to Mendez?"

Mendez. Even his name caused my heartbeat to spike. There were so many questions, but he was the biggest one. Who was Mendez? What did he want? Why did he involve me in all this?

Madison didn't answer any of my questions. Because when it came down to it, big sisters never told you the stuff you really wanted to know.

"Mendez will get suspicious if you're in here too long. Go to that address. Stay put." She pulled open the door and pushed me through it. I couldn't go back inside because Mendez had already seen me, his eyes latching on to mine the second I stepped out of the bathroom. He tapped his ear. With everything else competing for head space, it took me a full three seconds to realize he was signaling me to turn on my wire. I fumbled with my belt, pretending to do up my zipper in case the man meeting me was already watching. What a creepy thought.

I flipped the switch and looked over at Mendez, but he gave no perceptible sign that my wire was once again active. He returned to surveilling the area, his gaze sweeping the tram depot as he merged once more with the crowd.

I watched the back of his head as I made my way to the bench. I'd thought he was a mystery before, and probably dangerous as well . . . at least to the bad guys. I'd had no idea he could be dangerous to me.

My knees gave out as I collapsed on the bench, my muscles somehow simultaneously weak yet stretched tight. With jerky movements, I dragged the palms of my hands across my thighs, trying to wipe away the sweat. Had Madison made it out of the bathroom yet? I didn't dare risk looking and giving away her position, but worry clouded my thoughts.

I scanned the crowd, looking for someone fitting the description provided in the documents. He'd be a white man wearing a gray jacket, jeans, and glasses, carrying a phone in his left hand. The timer in my head was going off, telling me my five minutes were up. The man could be here any second. He'd take a closer look at me, then he'd be gone, and the hidden CIA operatives—if that's who they were—would be on his tail. Everything would go according to plan.

A scream rang out across the platform. My head whipped around to the noise, terror clawing up my throat. The crowd was scattering, though a few of them gathered around . . . something on the ground. I couldn't see what, but dread pooled in my stomach. More people started yelling. This situation was already bad enough, but the fact that I didn't speak Czech wasn't exactly helping things. I had no idea what was happening. Some people ran to the left, while others ran to the right. I hesitated, halfway between standing up and sitting down on the bench. Madison hadn't given me a rule book for this kind of thing. Maybe I should make a run for it now.

Then Mendez was at my side, holding my arm and leading me toward the platform on the left. Toward the screaming and noise. That couldn't be good.

A small throng of people grouped in one area, and Mendez pushed his way into the crowd. Through the tangle of arms and legs I could finally see what had caused all the commotion. A body lay on the ground, unmoving, blood everywhere. I brought a hand up to my mouth, stifling the cry before it had a chance to escape.

"Jsem doktor." Mendez pushed someone out of his way. *"Jsem doktor!"* People shifted so we were finally able to get through. There was a broken man lying still on the pavement before us. Blood soaked the front of his shirt and pooled on the ground beneath him, darker than I would have imagined. His right arm was twisted at an unnatural angle beneath him, his legs stretched out straight. He looked like a Picasso painting. Of course, the blood was the first thing I saw, but my brain soon latched on to other details, like the fact that the man was wearing jeans and a gray jacket. His glasses were on the ground, about a foot away from where we were standing.

He was the man I was supposed to meet, and now he was dead.

Mendez checked for a pulse, gave a slight shake of his head, and then his hands moved down the man's throat to his shirt, ripping it open and exposing what I presumed to be a bullet-proof vest. Obviously the vest hadn't done a very good job.

"Cop killers," Mendez hissed. I looked at him in confusion, my eyes surely showing the panic building up inside me.

"Armor-piercing bullets," he explained. He kept his voice low so only I could hear. "Teflon rounds that shoot right through bulletproof glass, metal, and vests. Most likely government issued, but then again, Holt is an arms dealer."

I kept my face neutral, though my mind was reeling. Too many thoughts competed for space, and I felt light-headed. Mendez snatched up a cell phone I hadn't noticed on the ground and stood up. He saw my face and instantly reached an arm out to steady me. I hadn't even realized I'd been wobbly. How was it I'd gone my whole life without seeing a dead body, only to have witnessed two deaths in the same number of days?

Sweat broke out on my brow and I swiped at it. Had it always been so hot outside? Mendez looked into my eyes, and I was momentarily distracted from my thoughts.

"We have to get you out of here." He took hold of my arm and ushered me away from all the people. A few strangers asked him questions in Czech. He didn't answer. I kept walking, because honestly, what else was I supposed to do? I'd just witnessed my second murder. Yes, he was a weapons supplier. But he had been alive, and now he was dead. *Dead.*

And this time? I was pretty sure it was my sister who'd done it.

Chapter Eleven

· · · · · · · · ·

I HAD TO GET AWAY FROM MENDEZ. THAT'S WHAT MADI-son had said, and I believed her. Even growing up, she'd never lied to me. Not when it mattered. I had no reason to think she couldn't be trusted. It was Mendez who kept secrets and manipulated me to get what he wanted. Each moment I stayed in his company felt like a ticking bomb, counting down the seconds until only catastrophe was left. The bodies were lining up and I didn't want to be next. But now that we'd returned to the safe house, I wasn't sure how to get back out.

How does one trick a spy? Because there was no doubt in my mind Mendez was still a spy, even though I knew he wasn't my sister's partner. He'd had the documentation, the safe houses, the official equipment, and even the CIA private jet. Most likely he was some kind of double agent, and that didn't bode well for me.

Mendez set a house alarm the minute we got inside, effectively locking us in. I didn't have that code, so sneaking out at night wasn't going to happen. I was a sitting duck, and the desperation fogging my mind wasn't helping matters.

Mendez went to the back room to unload his gear, and I

quickly retrieved Madison's fake passport and some of the money, shoving them into the pockets of my jacket. It was enough money to get me to the address Madison had provided, but hopefully not enough to draw attention. The question was, would Mendez notice if I took off the belt? Earlier, Mendez had said there wasn't a tracking device there, but if I couldn't trust him about being my sister's partner, it wasn't like I could trust him about that either.

He'd told me to leave it on in case we got separated, so it was still wrapped around me. He'd taken my tranq gun when we'd reached the car, which was a shame, because I could have used that on him now. Part of me wondered if that'd been intentional—leaving the tracker and taking the tranq gun. He had to be suspicious that Madison was around. When I'd asked him who he thought had killed the man, he'd only given me a look and said something about that information being classified.

Mendez walked back into the room, and I casually leaned against the wall and fumbled with my hands, attempting nonchalance.

"What is it?" Mendez asked, his eyes alert. He was too astute by half.

"Nothing." I bit my lip when the word came out too fast. Mendez's brow furrowed and his eyes narrowed. He didn't say anything as he strode over to the table though. The same table that had the briefcase on it. The briefcase that was missing the passport and money. I was going to be caught before I could even take one step. How pathetic. I held my breath as Mendez reached the table, but he didn't open the briefcase. Instead, he brought over the laptop and woke it up.

"Debriefing with Tobias, the deputy director, in a few minutes." He tapped keys on the computer. "You can listen to the beginning if you want."

How gracious of him, considering I'd been the one putting my life in danger. His eyes lingered on me for a moment, unreadable. "I know you probably have questions about what happened back there. If you want to talk, I'm here, but I'm sorry, it'll have to wait until after the debriefing." His attention returned to the computer, and I wondered why it felt like there was something else he wasn't saying. Probably a lot of things. Like the fact that he was a bad guy.

"Actually," I said, easing my way to the door, "I think I'll take a walk. Clear my head."

He looked up, expression sharp. "No."

That was it, just one word. But it caused my heart to skip a beat. Because Mendez didn't look like he was fooling around. His face was all lines and hard angles, his eyes never leaving mine for a second.

I scrambled for an answer. "I, uh, have to go to the store." The words were out before I could think them through.

"Tell me something." A sarcastic grin slowly overtook Mendez's features. "Do you think I'm stupid?"

I recognized our conversation from earlier, when I'd asked him whether he thought I was stupid for deciding to come to Prague, but it didn't put me at ease. Maybe because he wasn't leaning close this time. Or maybe because I knew he'd lied all along. That knowledge was like a cold rock in my stomach, weighing me down anytime I gave it any thought. He'd used me. I was so sick of being used by men who couldn't care less about me. Even Everett had been a better choice. And Everett quoted *Die Hard* at least twice a day and wouldn't let me borrow his sweatshirts, so the bar was already low.

"Listen," I said with more confidence than I felt. I *had* to convince Mendez to let me go. If he was distracted with his debriefing, there was a chance I could get farther away. Like to Madison's safe house. Or even the airport and my own bed in the United States. How long did debriefings take? "It's that time of the month for me. If I don't get supplies, it'll be a bloodbath."

The muscle in his jaw twitched at my poor joke. He ran a hand through his hair and looked back at the laptop for a moment before returning his focus to me. "Can't it wait? In half an hour, I could go for you."

I'd finally found a man who was willing to buy me tampons in public. It was just my luck he happened to be a spy and a liar. And probably a bunch of other bad things.

"I don't have half an hour." I placed a hand over my lower abdomen like I was experiencing cramps. I was counting on the fact that periods made most men uncomfortable, and he'd seen me take several minutes in the bathroom at the tram depot.

"No one even knows I'm here," I said when he still hadn't responded. "There's a store down the street. I can be in and out in just a few minutes. I'll be perfectly safe."

A small head start. Was that so much to ask?

He kept his gaze steady, obviously weighing his options. I found myself biting the inside of my cheek and watching as his eyes traveled my body, going up from my boots and landing on my belt.

There was definitely a tracker in there. I could tell from the way he drew in a breath and released it slowly, like he was reassuring himself that he had everything under control.

"Take cash." He turned toward the briefcase. I lunged for it, taking it out of his hands before he could open it.

"Good idea." I opened it at an angle so he couldn't see inside. Mendez arched an eyebrow while I made a show of taking out some of the cash and shoving it into my pocket. I now had more than I'd originally intended to take. Oh well. Less for him to use in whatever nefarious scheme he was a part of. I closed the briefcase and left it on the couch, away from where he'd be doing his meeting. Hopefully.

He didn't say anything as he deactivated the alarm on the door. I wasn't sure if he bought my story. In fact, I was pretty sure he didn't. But maybe he thought if he let me go, I'd never get far.

Alarm deactivated, I stepped forward to leave. Mendez put one hand to the side of me, halting my access to the door. He leaned forward.

"Be careful." His voice was low. He stared deep into my eyes, and I swallowed. His face was unreadable. Dark eyes, dark manner, dark expression. Goose bumps erupted on my arms and my skin flushed. For a second I wondered if I was making a mistake. The way Mendez was looking at me turned my insides to liquid. Like he was genuinely concerned. Like he *cared*. My heartbeat thrummed loudly in my ears.

"I will be." My voice shook. Sometimes it was hard to remember this man was a professional liar.

He pushed a strand of my hair behind my ear, his fingers trailing along the sensitive skin at my neck. My lips parted, almost against my will. But then Mendez's expression closed off, he opened the door, and I slipped outside.

Freedom. Who knew it would feel so bittersweet?

I KEPT MY pace even. If Mendez was watching from the window, I didn't want him to see me running. I turned the corner, out of his line of sight, and had the belt off my body in seconds, though I kept the wire turned on in case he was listening. But now what was I supposed to do with it?

There wasn't room for error. I had to be smart about this, because once Mendez's debriefing was over, he'd be on the hunt. Maybe sooner? I wrapped the belt in a circle, making it as small as possible without twisting it.

Ahead of me, a woman sat on a park bench, her dog at her side. She was gathering her things, getting ready to leave. I quickened my pace. I reached her before she'd had the chance to depart.

"Can I pet your dog?" I asked. She looked at me blankly, not understanding my English. I pointed to her dachshund and mimicked petting his head, and the woman smiled.

"*Samozřejmě!*" She motioned for me to go ahead.

I crouched in front of her, using my body to shield the actions of my left hand, which I was using to place the belt in the bag at her feet, shoving it down under the scarf she had on top. With my right, I pet the dog, who wriggled in delight and tried to climb up on my lap. I made the appropriate cooing noises and excited exclamations. All the while, my head was reeling with what-ifs.

I thanked the woman and stood up, brushing my hands on my pants. She smiled and picked up her things. If her bag felt heavier, she gave no indication as she stood up, waved, and went on her way. I breathed a sigh of relief to see she was going right, the same direction as the store I'd noticed earlier, but I didn't stay to watch. I had other things to do.

Like run.

I took off down the street, taking the left turn that would bring me to the main road I'd noticed earlier. Once there, I raised my arm to hail a taxi, all the while walking briskly along the street, always traveling farther from the safe house. Despite the cool temperature, sweat built up on the back of my neck and my breath came in ragged gasps. Jet lag was beginning to catch up to me, even with the adrenaline coursing through my veins. I struggled to keep going but promised myself I could sleep as long as I wanted—once I got out of here.

Finally, a taxi pulled to a stop beside me, and I yanked open the back door. "This address?" I passed him the paper and prayed that this man, with his receding hairline and stumpy cigarette, understood English.

"American?" His accent was strong as he turned to face me. "I take Czech koruna. No euros. No dollars."

"I have koruna!" I slid into the back seat and pulled the door closed behind me, resisting the urge to check over my shoulder. Oh, who was I kidding? I totally looked over my shoulder. I sagged with relief when I saw no one there.

"Please?" I said, when the driver still hadn't pulled away from the curb. He started the meter and finally, finally left, nosing his car into traffic. My heartbeat thundered loudly in my ears, going a thousand miles per hour. A car horn blared and I braced for impact. It never came. The driver kept looking back at me through his mirror, muttering under his breath in Czech. It didn't stop me from bouncing my knee and checking the windows for anything suspicious. Black cars with tinted windows. Mendez dressed as a Catholic nun in disguise—though I would have paid good money to see that.

My heartbeat still hadn't slowed down by the time we made it to a nondescript neighborhood still in the city. My driver brought his car to a stop. I checked the meter, then passed him enough koruna to cover the cost, plus tip, and stepped onto the sidewalk.

Outside the taxi, I suddenly felt exposed. The car had given me walls, speed, and the illusion of safety. Now I stood on the concrete, the wind whipping my hair across my eyes, the people speaking a language I didn't understand. The fake passport was burning a hole in my pocket, not to mention my conscience. I tried to appear confident as I walked up to the door in question.

Was I just supposed to open it or . . .

I looked for a key but didn't find one. I tried the handle and it turned easily in my hand.

"Super secure, sis," I muttered. Then again, she knew I was coming. She'd probably sent someone to unlock it or had come herself, knowing I'd need a way in.

As soon as I entered, I locked it behind me, then leaned on the door for support.

I was safe. I'd made it. Soon, I'd be reunited with Madison, and this whole nightmare would be behind me.

For now, I could let the more experienced professionals handle the scary stuff, like spy rendezvous and chasing down international arms dealers, while I focused on more important matters. Like binge-watching Netflix and getting Oreo crumbs on the couch. If this was Madison's place, she'd have some. Maybe I'd even let loose and eat the whole sleeve of Oreos. I deserved it.

My relief was so palpable it might as well have been another person in the room. But I still wasn't expecting the little drop of sadness and regret that swooped in and made me question whether I'd made the right choice.

I blamed Mendez for that. Mendez with his charming smile and killer abs. Sure, I hadn't seen them, but I knew they were there.

With a sigh, I pushed off from the door and trotted off to explore my sister's house. It was probably another safe house, rather than a place where she actually lived. It lacked the personal details of her home in DC. It was one story, with an old-fashioned fireplace in the corner of the living room. There was an outdated but clean kitchen with white appliances. I used the bathroom, taking my time to regroup and freshen up from my mad dash through Prague. As the younger sister, it was my duty to root through my sister's things and use her beauty products. Plus, I felt better now that I had a new coat of makeup to cover my insecurities. I noticed the shower had her favorite shampoo and conditioner, so I was in the right place.

The house was small. But it muffled the sounds of the city outside, and it made me feel secure.

Until I turned the corner back into the living room.

And came face-to-face with Mendez.

Chapter Twelve

· · · · · · · · ·

HE WAS LEANING CASUALLY AGAINST THE WALL LIKE he was a model who'd shown up too early for a cover shoot. Hands in his pockets, ankles crossed—everything about him suggested he wasn't a threat.

But I knew better.

I stopped in my tracks. "What are you doing here?" Sure, I could run. But where? This guy kept popping up like a jack-in-the-box.

One corner of his mouth lifted up. "I could ask you the same thing."

I crossed my arms. "I found other accommodations."

"With Madison." It wasn't a question.

I opened my mouth, but nothing came out.

Mendez pushed off the wall and came toward me. I backtracked until I was in the kitchen and Mendez held his hands up in surrender, stopping his forward momentum. "Do you want to tell me what's going on?" he asked. "I've had women ghost me before, but I can usually sense it coming."

"You have not had women ghost you before," I scoffed, which actually made Mendez laugh.

"Becka Nash. My last week at The Farm."

It took me a second to realize he was talking about the CIA training camp and not some actual farm with pigs and cows. Momentarily sidetracked, I had to shake my head. "Okay, but the fact that you can only name one means I have zero sympathy for you."

I bet no one swiped left on him. Actually, who was I kidding? The man wasn't on dating apps.

He pointed to the kitchen table. "Can we talk?" he asked.

I analyzed my options. Namely, that I didn't have any. Somehow he'd managed to find me, even when I'd done everything in my power to shake the guy.

Well done, Dove. You took your only escape route and watched it go up in flames.

I pursed my lips and nodded, pulling out a chair and sitting gingerly on the seat.

I had to get ahead of this conversation. Before Mendez could pull me back into his web of lies.

"Why should I trust anything you say?" I folded my arms on top of the table like I was the one in charge. Might as well pretend. Denial was not just a river in Egypt—it was a force of nature.

Mendez took the chair opposite me, swinging a backpack I hadn't noticed earlier from his shoulder and settling it onto the floor beside the table. "Well, I did just save your life."

I waved my hand in the air like an unconcerned heiress. "The restaurant shoot-out was so yesterday. I've forgotten it already, dah-ling."

This made Mendez smile, and he reached over and pulled his laptop from the backpack at his feet. With a few clicks of the keyboard, he'd pulled up a video feed from a doorbell camera. I recognized it as the outside of Madison's house. Here. This street. It was slightly off-center, the feed coming from a nearby house I didn't remember getting a good look at, but I couldn't argue its authenticity. Because five seconds after Mendez hit enter, the recording showed me exiting the taxi to look around the front porch for a key. I disappeared into the house a moment later.

Then my smile froze. The two men from the restaurant shooting entered the screen from the left, their faces instantly familiar to me. They didn't search for a key though. Their intentions were obvious. The bald one pointed a gun at the lock just as Mendez appeared out of nowhere, going all *Kung Fu Panda* on the both of them and masterfully evading their weapons. A neighbor came from across the street to intervene, but it was over before he could even make it to the first step.

Both the bad guys had been knocked out on Madison's porch while I hadn't even heard a sound. Mendez flashed his badge to the neighbor, who in turn pulled out his phone, punching buttons. It took me a moment to realize he was probably sending his house's camera footage to Mendez, which we were now watching. I had a *Twilight Zone* moment, where I half expected the screen to spontaneously combust.

A nondescript van pulled up, taking the men away like the whole thing had been a bad dream. The entire time I'd just been poking around the bathroom like a sucker.

"That's a CIA team stationed here in Prague," Mendez said, pointing to the van. "They're not working Holt's case, but they agreed to take the men in for questioning. They also took the suspects' weapons, since we couldn't very well leave them lying on the streets, and I didn't think you'd appreciate me coming in here with them."

As if he hadn't just demonstrated the damage he could do with his bare hands. I'd blinked and the men had been taken out. Now you see me, now you don't.

I was grateful, don't get me wrong, but it was disconcerting to think I was safe and then have that bubble popped all in the span of a minute.

I stared at the screen without saying anything.

Mendez leaned back in his chair. "They're keeping an eye on things outside while we talk."

I nodded, but being the stubborn person I was, I still refused to believe he didn't have ulterior motives. "Just because you beat up a couple of bad guys doesn't mean I have to trust you," I said.

"Why *don't* you trust me?" Mendez leaned forward on his elbows, resting his chin on his joined hands.

I debated lying. But if I really wanted the truth, lying kind of defeated the purpose. He had my attention, but now I wanted answers, so I didn't mince words. "Madison said you weren't her partner." My words hung in the air for a minute, the accusation ringing loudly in my ears. Mendez swore softly. But he didn't say anything else as he looked at me. His brown eyes never broke contact.

"Is it true?" I asked.

I waited for him to deny it. One more lie and I was out of here. Of course, I didn't know where I'd go. Or how I'd get there. Minor details.

Maybe I'd catch a flight back to the States, or if that failed, I'd wade out into the ocean and hope a passing boat would take pity on me. People swam the English Channel all the time. How much bigger could the Atlantic Ocean be, really?

Mendez sucked in a breath, then released it with a sigh. "Yes," he finally said. "It's true." His jaw clenched, but other than that, he gave nothing away. Eventually, he seemed to come to a decision.

"I'll tell you everything, and if you don't like what I have to say, you can leave." His voice was low. "I won't stop you, and this time I won't follow. I give you my word." He placed his hands on the table like he was bracing for impact. "But in return, you have to promise me you'll listen to everything. No shutting me down when you don't like what I have to say. Understood?"

I wasn't sure I could believe anything he said. All I knew was *someone* was finally offering answers, and I couldn't pass up the opportunity.

Against my better judgment, I nodded, though I vowed to change into Madison's clothes if I left. Just in case he happened to have any other trackers he wasn't telling me about.

Mendez reached into his bag and pulled out a black electronic box, placing it in the middle of the table. He pushed a button and a garbled white noise filled the space, sounding like a handful of seagulls trying to have a conversation with an entire coffee shop of people.

"That's pleasant." I raised my voice a little to be heard over the din. "You listen to that to go to sleep?"

"This is a Rabbler," he said. "It's so Madison can't record anything we say even if she has bugs in here, and anyone trying to listen nearby won't be able to tune in to the frequency without getting a disrupted signal." He shrugged. "It's the only way I can tell you classified information. Unless you want to come back to the safe house with me."

He'd certainly come prepared. He was probably a Boy Scout. Wasn't that their motto?

"I'm good, thanks." I motioned to the Rabbler. "I actually kind of like it. It's soothing."

It wasn't. But it was easy enough to tune out if it meant I was here on my own terms.

Mendez placed a privacy screen over the computer. Presumably that was to keep any cameras from recording whatever he was about to show me. He flipped the laptop back around so the screen was facing me. A picture of Holt filled the monitor. Not a pretty sight.

"Holt is a powerful arms dealer, with his hands in many different areas of foreign affairs." Mendez pointed to some statistics at the bottom, showing me things like countries that had tried—and failed—to bring him to justice.

I grunted in annoyance. "I don't care about Holt. I want to know why *you* claimed to be my sister's partner, and what *you* are doing now." I tried to sound decisive, but it was clear from Mendez's expression he found my interrogation skills lacking.

His eyes slid over to mine. "I'm getting there. Patience."

Patience. I didn't have a lot of that. I folded my arms and leaned back. When Mendez remained silent, I motioned for him to continue.

He tapped his computer screen. "Holt has been on the CIA's radar for almost a decade, but he keeps his hands clean. Sting operations haven't been successful, and any evidence we get mysteriously disappears."

"He's tricky," I said. "I get it."

"No." Mendez corrected me. "Not just tricky. Holt's a ghost. The closer we get, the more we discover how far away we really are. His enterprise spans continents, with hundreds of people in his employ, but he uses isolated circles. No one on the inside knows more than a handful of names, so bringing his operation down is practically impossible. But lately Holt has been making a play for more direct power. He's been quietly dismantling the CIA from the inside out, taking control by turning agents and corrupting the people in power."

His face was still, his expression grave. I shifted in my chair.

"You probably don't need me to tell you," Mendez continued, "but if Holt succeeds in controlling the CIA, it could have disastrous consequences for our entire nation. His success would impact national security for decades to come."

"Not to be dramatic or anything," I said, prompting Mendez to give me a tight-lipped smile.

"The intelligence we got from the man in the restaurant was the biggest lead we've had in half a decade. That man was in Holt's employ as a cobbler—someone who forges documents like that passport you stole. He was using this information to defect to America, trading the intelligence in exchange for clemency."

Okay, it made sense that Holt would send his goons to kill the sweaty guy in the restaurant. And that the cobbler was meeting with my sister if she was the one collecting the intelligence. But why hadn't Madison made the meeting? She could have been done with it before I'd even arrived, as long as she'd kept things quick.

I gasped with realization but tried to mask it as a cough. Madison had to miss the meeting because I'd insisted on showing up early to stuff my face with bread. She'd wanted to meet at eight, but I'd shown up at seven. She said the meeting was at five thirty and he was supposed to have left if she was late. But the cobbler hadn't followed the plan. He'd stayed at the restaurant for a full hour and a half past the original meeting start time, allowing Holt's men to catch up with him. Rather than risk her meeting with him going long and getting me involved, she'd tried to make him leave, but he hadn't played by the rules and I'd gotten involved anyway.

I shook my head, then leaned forward, placing my elbows on the table so I could more easily rub my temples. A migraine was blooming there.

Mendez paused his explanation and went into the kitchen. He rooted around the cupboards for a minute before he returned with aspirin and a glass of water. He placed them in front of me without a word and waited for me to drink before continuing, then pointed to a new screen he'd opened up on the computer.

"This is an internal order explaining the agency's response to the threat of Holt, prior to the new intelligence we received from the cobbler in the restaurant. The CIA appointed a dedicated team to handle everything Holt-related. Remember when I told you I was part of a special team? This was a multipronged effort, with analysts, agents, and executives devoting their entire existence to finding this one man. All the resources and manpower usually stretched across a variety of threats were reserved solely for interrupting Holt's plans."

"Okay?" While it was interesting, none of this information seemed to apply to Mendez, me, or my sister.

"The most ambitious part of this project was the undercover agents the CIA sent to infiltrate Holt's organization." Mendez clicked another button and a page popped up with a man's picture in the left-hand corner. His information covered the screen.

"We wanted someone on the inside," Mendez said, "who could be there long-term, mitigating the worst of Holt's threats and reporting on his actions."

"Long-term?" I interrupted. "Why not send an assassin? Take care of the problem once and for all?"

Was I being morbid? Probably. Did I care? Not after the day I'd just had.

"Because taking out Holt wouldn't take out the threat. Someone could pick up the pieces of his organization and become just as dangerous without our knowing. We'd be back where we started. The CIA needed someone who could gather enough evidence to put Holt behind bars and also figure out his inner circles, deliver names, locations, associations. Someone who could dismantle the entire enterprise. Those things take time."

I still wasn't sure if this was the truth or another story he'd spun to keep me cooperative. How was I supposed to know the difference? I stared at the screen, one of the many official CIA documents that I vowed to read in full after I'd heard Mendez's side.

"Three inside agents," he continued, his gaze shifting to the computer. "The first one didn't even last a week before his allegiance was discovered and Holt killed him."

I had a bad feeling about where this conversation was headed, and I bit the inside of my cheek.

Mendez clicked another button. "Our second agent didn't even make it an hour. As he stepped off the plane, a sharpshooter took him out along with the team that transferred here as a point of operation. Two women, three men, and one Labrador retriever."

"Holt killed a dog?" I interrupted.

What. A. Monster.

Then another thought struck me. "Why was there a dog on a CIA team?" I asked.

"The dog and the canine handlers were specially equipped for sniffing out shell casings, explosive materials, and firearms. Can you think of a better way to track down an arms dealer?"

I didn't answer. Mendez changed the screen again. I looked at the picture and choked. The water burned my throat as it tried to rise back up. I placed the glass back on the table and pulled the laptop closer with shaky fingers.

Madison's picture stared back at me, her usually warm expression stoic and grave, her eyes serious. It looked like an official CIA headshot, with Madison facing the camera straight on, wearing a black suit and pressed collar, her brown hair pulled back into a low ponytail. This wasn't the Madison I knew. But with all the revelations of this past week, it was still a Madison I recognized.

"Officer Barkley was the third operative the CIA attempted to place inside Holt's ranks." Mendez sat back in his chair.

I sucked in a breath, the reality of everything beginning to sink in.

"So now she's on the run?" I asked. "Holt's men discovered she was a double agent and want to kill her, like they did the other two agents?" The pieces of the story were starting to fall into place, but I didn't like the picture they created. Or the fact that the CIA had willfully paraded me around if they thought someone was trying to kill my sister. Not cool, guys. Not cool.

The air was heavy with Mendez's silence. The hair on the back of my neck stood up and a shudder raced down my spine. Slowly, Mendez shook his head, the movement almost undetectable if I hadn't been watching his every move.

"Check the date in the upper right-hand corner." His voice was still low. "Madison began her assignment three years ago, making her the first agent successful at infiltrating Holt's organization."

I released a breath. Of course she'd been successful. This was Madison we were talking about. She suffered from oldest child syndrome—the need to be perfect at everything she did. She made everyone else look like a failure simply for trying.

But this version of events also left a lot of questions unanswered. Because if Madison was successful, why was Holt still a threat? Why was I involved at all? Dread had taken up a permanent residence in my gut, seeping into my bones until I felt the chill all the way to my fingertips. It didn't help that Mendez was looking at me with a hollow expression in his eyes, as if he didn't like what he was about to say either.

"I have my theories about what happened at the tram depot." Mendez leaned forward. "But I want to know your side of the story." His eyes bored into mine, his expression serious.

I glared at him before choking down the rest of my water. "You're the one spilling secrets right now." It took all my courage to keep my gaze steady. It was time for answers. *His* answers, not mine. After a minute, he crossed his arms.

"My hypothesis is that Madison made an appearance sometime between the safe house and the meeting. The bathroom at the depot?"

My expression took on an edge as I stared him down, saying nothing. Mendez watched me with a critical eye, and I focused on breathing regularly.

Eventually Mendez sat back with a sigh. "I don't know what she told you. But here's the truth. Madison has stopped reporting to the CIA."

Mendez's words hit me like a wrecking ball.

"In industry terms, that's what we call going rogue. We can only assume she's working for Holt. She's turned."

He sat forward in his chair and inspected me, clasping his hands together on top of the table. I tried to keep my expression neutral, but something told me I wasn't all that successful. Mendez reached out and put a hand over mine. I could feel his calluses on the backs of my knuckles, his fingertips warm as he applied slight pressure. I pulled away.

"The evidence of her switching sides is also detailed in the paperwork we obtained at the restaurant. That was the information Holt's cobbler was trying to sell us for clemency. The man must not have known who she was when the CIA set up the meeting, which was why he gave Madison a passport that would get her past airport security without alerting Holt. The man wanted Madison to take care of the double agent in Prague so that they couldn't take him out if he defected. *She* was the double agent he was giving us for his clemency. As a cobbler he never worked on site with Holt, and he'd never have had cause to do any forgeries for Madison before, since the CIA would have handled her paperwork. He had no clue who she was."

I guess that explained why there was a passport with her picture, but not why Mendez was so convinced Madison was the double agent in question and not some other agent on the special forces team. Unless the paperwork referred to her by name. But then it didn't make sense why the man would be okay with the CIA setting up a meeting for him with Madison Barkley.

As if reading my thoughts, Mendez continued. "He only had her code name. You'll find his paperwork only refers to her as Steel."

I inhaled sharply. Flint and Steel. I shuddered and remained silent. My finger traced the wood pattern on the table, aware of Mendez's eyes on me as I did so. I turned my wrist so the flame tattoo wasn't visible, but I felt it there like it actually burned my skin. Mendez waited for me to explain my reaction.

I didn't. Instead, I got up, heading to the cabinets and opening them one by one.

"What are you looking for?" he asked.

I opened another cabinet, then closed it with a bang. "Oreos. I think all this deserves cookies, don't you?"

Before he'd barged in here, I was planning on eating an entire sleeve. Now—screw it—I figured the whole package might not be enough.

Really, I just didn't want to have to look at him when he was telling me this.

Mendez let me continue my search for comfort food while he kept talking.

"You can read through it all. It's on our CIA database, which I'll let you access with my credentials if you come back to the safe house with me." He gave a short, low laugh. "But I'll have to monitor your usage, given your occupation and professional talents. I don't want you hacking into the government's most secure network when, for all I know, you might be working with Madison."

How generous of him. I slammed another cupboard. My search for Oreos felt as futile as trying to get concert tickets without any convenience fees, and I bit back a sarcastic comment.

Mendez looked down for a brief second. "That's why I didn't tell you before. Why I lied and said she was on the run from Holt when she's really hiding from the CIA. Why we were investigating you. I'm sorry. I should have told you all this earlier, but I couldn't be sure. Even now, I'm just going with my gut. I could be wrong." He looked back up and his eyes were questioning. "About you."

Too many thoughts jumbled in my head for me to respond. My mouth was dry anyway, and I swallowed, closing the final cupboard. "There aren't any Oreos," I finally said when it was clear he was waiting for me to respond. My voice quivered, but hey, it didn't break, so I was counting that as a win.

Mendez furrowed his brows. "Were you listening to anything I just said?"

"Yep," I said. "Just processing. Oreos help me process."

This seemed to mollify Mendez, who nodded and placed his hands on his knees. I still didn't join him at the table though.

Mendez cleared his throat. "There's one more thing you should know." Mendez's voice was hesitant. "The reason I claimed to be your sister's partner." He sucked in a breath. "When Madison stopped reporting in, the CIA assigned an agent to find her."

I knew what was coming next even without him saying it. Everything was somehow blurry and clear at once, like a kaleidoscope of colors that endlessly rotated, the sharp edges becoming more and more broken with every turn. The reason Mendez kept me close, even when he didn't know whether he could trust me or not. The reason he lied. Why he let me go, then followed me.

"You're the agent." My voice sounded dull, even to my own ears.

"My assignment is to find Madison. That's why I was really there at the restaurant that night."

"That's why you knew things about her. You've studied her."

"We were on the same task force. The same team. At first we were just concerned about bringing her out of the cold and hearing her side, but now that there's even more evidence . . . My guess is she was going to intercept the data so it couldn't get into the CIA's hands, but then everything went sideways and we have the files. Holt's men killed the cobbler when she probably only intended to destroy the evidence that pointed to her specifically so she could continue her charade. But she can't explain things away now. She can't pretend she's still loyal to our government when we have this documentation. She's the double agent, Dove."

Mendez ran a hand through his hair. "That's why I thought she wouldn't be at the meeting in Prague too, and we could follow the weapons supplier if he thought you were her initially. Now that the CIA knew about the meeting with Holt's supplier from the information in the briefcase, I thought Madison would consider the risk too high to be in the vicinity. But I guess not."

And now Holt's men were after me. I'd taken the briefcase and gotten involved. Because of Madison.

Looking at the pieces, I could see why Mendez would think Madison was guilty. But Madison wasn't capable of that kind of betrayal. My sister always had my back—she wouldn't put a knife in it.

When I was thirteen and she was fifteen, we'd been put in the foster care system. We'd bounced from house to house, only staying in one place for about a month before the families grew tired of us. I didn't blame them. Eventually we were put in a group home, where we stayed until Madison aged out of the system.

As soon as she turned eighteen, Madison rented a small one-bedroom apartment that had more issues than a magazine. She worked full time as an executive assistant to some know-it-all hoity-toity defense lawyer while taking night classes at the local college. But despite everything, she applied for parental rights so I could live with her. It meant sleeping on a couch in a bad part of town, but there was never any hesitation on my part when my social worker asked my preference. Madison was my best friend, my support system, my only family.

When this whole mess started, I worried that my sister had been taken by the bad guys. But this was a thousand times worse.

The CIA thought she was one of them.

Maybe someone was setting her up, or maybe she was in too deep and needed help. I couldn't be sure.

There were only two things I knew.

One: Madison couldn't protect me anymore if the men who'd shown up on her doorstep were any indication.

Two: I was literally the only one who believed in my sister's innocence.

The only hope she had of clearing her name was if she had someone fighting for her on the inside. Maybe I could get her out of a sticky situation simply because I was in the right place at the right time. She'd need someone to warn her if the noose was about to close around her neck or they were laying a trap. I couldn't do that if I wasn't working with the CIA. She'd been there for me, and now it was my turn to be there for her.

I had to go back with Mendez.

Chapter Thirteen

· · · · · · · · ·

SAFE HOUSES WERE SUPPOSED TO FEEL SAFE. I JUST felt like a used tissue.

Mendez closed the door behind us, then locked us in and set the alarm system.

Once again, I was back at square one. Sure, I wasn't dead. That was a definite plus. But I also was back with Mendez, the man who'd lied to me and flown me halfway across the world to use me as bait for my sister. So, there was that.

I didn't blame him for thinking she was the double agent—he didn't know her like I did—but I also had no idea how to change his mind. And now that I knew he wasn't a *bad* guy, I really wanted my sister and him on the same side.

Madison wanted me to get away from Mendez because he was trying to bring her in, and I could respect that. But just because I respected my sister didn't mean I always agreed with her. Meaning, I felt like I could trust Mendez.

He was just doing his job. It was *my* job to make him see Madison wasn't a threat.

Mendez strode over to the table, where he opened the laptop

and began pulling up the video surveillance feeds of the surrounding area, even though he'd doubled back approximately a bazillion times on the way here to make sure we weren't followed. He watched the feed for a few minutes without saying anything. When he was convinced we were secure, he turned to face me, his expression strangely soft. He leaned back against the table, his hands gripping the edge.

"I don't think I said it before, but I'm glad you're safe." His eyes searched my face, like he was making sure what he said was true. He ran a hand through his hair, mussing it up. Not that I noticed or anything, but the look worked for him, which was kind of too bad. I wanted him to see me as aloof and sophisticated, not as a lovestruck groupie. I refocused on his face, watching as he figured out what words to say.

"I didn't want anything to happen to you." He took a breath. "Not on my watch."

There was obviously a story there. I didn't say anything, waiting not-so-patiently for him to elaborate as I stood awkwardly by the couch. Mendez was normally so tight-lipped, even this small admission felt like a victory.

He sighed, and for the first time since I'd met him, it was as if he had a hard time meeting my eyes. "Three years ago, a civilian under my protection died." His jaw clenched and his gaze dropped. "I made a judgment call, and it turned out to be a bad one." He looked up, his eyes haunted. "That civilian was . . . close to me."

Like a puzzle, pieces of Mendez snapped into place. The reason it seemed like he *was* his job. The way he kept his emotions at bay. His expression when he'd pulled away after Brock's, only kissing my neck and not my lips. Why he said he didn't do commitment.

"I'm sorry." I couldn't think of anything else to say.

He let out a breath. "I'm just . . ." he trailed off, his eyes finding mine and drinking me in. "I'm glad I found you before those men did."

He'd closed off again, crossing his arms in front of his chest like a barrier. I could tell I wouldn't get more information about that tonight. If he ever retired from being a spy, he had a real shot at being one of those guards who stood outside Buckingham Palace and refused to crack even when tourists told the most inappropriate jokes.

"How did you find me?" I asked. "I got rid of the belt you gave me."

One side of his mouth quirked up in a grin. He took a minute to answer, clearly debating whether he wanted to say anything.

"You promised you'd tell me everything," I reminded him.

He pursed his lips as his eyes took in my expression. "I already told you everything you need to know," he said.

"Nuh-uh," I countered. "I am not playing this game. You said *everything*. From here on out, you're not going to keep me in the dark. That ship has sailed into the sunset."

Mendez tugged playfully on my sleeve, pulling me a little closer in the process.

"Tracker," he said at last. "In your boot."

I gasped and attempted to look at the bottom of my boot, hopping first on one foot, then switching to the other. The only thing that accomplished was making Mendez laugh. I tore the boots off, the socks stuck inside, and threw them one by one at Mendez, who didn't even flinch when one knocked into his arm. The other sailed harmlessly over his shoulder, landing on the other side of the table. I stood there barefoot, attempting to torch him with my glare. Mendez kept chuckling, his laugh contagious until I, at last, cracked a smile.

"Okay, okay." I tried to appear serious. Composing my face and crossing my arms, I stared Mendez down. His lips twitched at my attempt, and I eventually gave up. "I guess I'm glad you had a tracker. Even though I totally could have handled those guys."

Mendez bit his lip, but at least he didn't burst my bubble by negating my claim.

"Speaking of trackers." There was still laughter in Mendez's eyes when he turned to face me. "There were several minutes you were alone with an enemy operative in the tram bathroom, and even longer that you were out of my sight while you went on your little adventure, so if you don't mind, we need to make sure Madison didn't put a listening device or tracker on you somewhere before you get too comfortable here."

Earlier he'd told me his first priority was getting me somewhere safe. Apparently my time was up and now he had a protocol to follow.

"I can check my clothes myself."

"Yeah." He chuckled. "Because you did such a good job of that before." He pointedly looked at my boots and socks, still strewn about the room. I glowered at him but didn't respond. I held my shirt in front of me, then checked over my shoulders, lifting the edge of my jacket and inspecting the collar. Next, I felt inside my pockets and patted around the rest of my body.

"Looks good to me," I said, voice shaking slightly, because it didn't take my college degree to see where this was going. And okay, it wasn't a full TSA pat down or anything, but it was good enough.

He raised an eyebrow. "I'm going to have to do a more thorough search than that. *Much* more thorough."

Mendez grinned, like he was going to enjoy feeling every inch of my body. Against my will, I shivered slightly, imagining what it'd be like to feel his hands at my hips, his fingers tracing the edges of my clothing. Mendez took two steps forward so he was standing directly in front of me, then reached his arms around my waist. His fingers felt along the inch of skin that was exposed there, and I sucked in a breath.

His hand burned at my waist, a reminder of everything we hadn't done. Everything we *could* do.

Somehow the thought of Mendez putting his hands all over me made me simultaneously giddy and terrified. I debated my options. Then my resolve kicked in. I wasn't going to let him win that easily. Maybe he knew how to manipulate me and make me feel attracted to him, but he'd already admitted he wasn't immune to me either. He did say some days he loved his job.

He wanted to play? Fine. Two could play at that game.

I kept steady eye contact with Mendez while I began stripping. First came the jacket, which I thrust into his arms along with the tranquilizer's belly band I still wore from our earlier trip to the tram depot. Then, I lifted my shirt over my head and started on my pants. His expression turned hungry, but he didn't say anything as I shoved more clothes at him. Finally, I stood there in my bra and underwear and fixed him with a solid stare.

"I don't think she could have put a tracker anywhere else without me noticing." I deserved points for how steady I kept my tone. "Satisfied?" I let the word hang there, daring him to respond.

His eyes roamed over my body. He made no effort to hide the raw desire there, and a surge of pleasure traveled through me.

He cleared his throat. "Not nearly," he said, voice low.

Pretending his words had no effect on me, I walked away without a word.

MENDEZ MADE ME sleep before accessing the files on Madison, which, honestly, was probably a good thing. My under-eye bags were big enough to go shopping on their own.

I slept for fourteen hours. It might as well have been an hour, because when I woke up, I still felt no closer to knowing how to get my sister out of this mess.

Finally, I got to read all the files on the CIA database pertaining to Madison. It took most of the day, with Mendez bringing me food while I scrolled through all the data. He routinely checked in with his supervisor, Tobias, while I read file after file on my sister. Apparently, the deputy director didn't like me having access to the database and wanted regular check-ins like I was some kind of criminal.

A few things were above even Mendez's clearance level, and when he went to get some water from the kitchen, my fingers flew across the keyboard to sniff the traffic and grab the session token. I installed a Remote Access Trojan while I was at it, just in case I ever needed to access this computer without his permission. RATs weren't exactly white-hat, but what Mendez and his superior didn't know wouldn't hurt them.

Maybe the deputy director had a point.

Mendez was only gone half a minute. That was all it took for me to save the string of code that would let me duplicate his user credentials and log on later. I wouldn't be able to hack anything now with him watching over my shoulder like a helicopter parent. But this computer and I had a date later. Yep, that was about as scintillating as my dates got these days. At least a computer couldn't let me down.

Not like the men in my life.

The more I read, the higher the odds seemed stacked against proving Madison was on the right side of the law.

When she'd first gone missing in action, the CIA had sent an officer to bring her in and she'd put the guy in the hospital. Which, on one hand, was pretty impressive considering he was a trained operative twice her size. On the other hand, it didn't exactly make her look so innocent either. The CIA claimed there was clear intent to kill, which was irrefutable evidence she'd gone to the dark side, à la Anakin Skywalker. That was when they'd sent in the big guns, or rather, Mendez, and he'd come across the briefcase with evidence of her working with Holt.

But there had to be more to the story. I could feel it. Like indigestion.

Images flipped through my mind like a reel. Documents on the computer detailing her supposed betrayal. The dead man at the tram depot she'd shot, his dark red blood pooling around him. Her cryptic warnings about Mendez that only put me in worse danger. All bad things.

But that slideshow contained other images too—like the time she'd taught me how to braid my hair, her fingers combing through my tangled mess and creating something beautiful from it. Or her face when I told her I was moving out of the foster home and into her apartment. The way her eyes lit up and she lunged forward to hold me in the tightest hug I've ever gotten, even to this day. How once every couple of months she'd excuse me from class just so we could eat pie together at the diner across from the high school.

Good things.

Things that were just as real to me as the evidence in the CIA file.

I had to get some space. Air. Mendez was being understanding about this whole situation, but I felt a bit like a fish in a bowl, with him tapping on the glass.

I stood up from the table and excused myself, escaping to my room. This safe house wasn't much different from the one back in the States. This one had three rooms in addition to the living area that connected to the kitchen. The rooms were cramped and smelled slightly of mold. A small gas fireplace stood in front of my twin-size bed, and the closet was barely big enough to warrant the name.

The clothes provided by the CIA were still mostly packed in the duffel by the side of my bed, so to distract myself, I started hanging them up, as if organizing my shirts could somehow magically organize my life. When I was finished, I sat on the edge of my bed and watched the flames dance hypnotically behind the barrier of my fireplace. Anything to keep from thinking about how much of a colossal failure I was. Here I was with access to the CIA at my fingertips and I couldn't even think of a way to bring my sister home.

Of course, flames made me think of Madison too.

You're the flint and I'm the steel. Together, we're all we need to survive. You and me forever. Got it?

A tear slid down my cheek and I angrily swiped it away. She was out there, alone and probably scared, despite putting on a brave face, and there was nothing I could do to help.

All the files said one thing, and it was my word against the CIA's.

I stared at the tattoo on my wrist, the small flame warm and golden in the light of the actual fire in front of me. I covered the design with my other hand as another tear escaped. It had hurt getting it—the tattoo. But it hurt even more now. Sisters were supposed to help each other, and I only managed to keep getting in the way and making things worse. Two people had died, and I didn't even know what I was supposed to do next.

This feeling of helplessness was a thousand times more painful than even the fear of sitting on the bench in the tram depot, knowing people with guns might come for me at any moment.

I'd do that a million times over if it meant Madison could come home again.

I shifted to get more comfortable and something crinkled in my pocket.

The address. Madison's safe house. I'd transferred it to this jacket pocket to keep it safe. I pulled the paper out and stared at the writing, the slanted *e*'s making my heart ache.

This paper was worthless now. I didn't know how to contact her, or when I'd see her again. I didn't know how to help her, or if she even *wanted* my help.

I threw the paper in the fire and watched as the last connection I had with my sister went up in smoke.

Chapter Fourteen

. . . .

I DIDN'T REALIZE I'D LEFT THE DOOR OPEN UNTIL I HEARD Mendez speaking from the doorway.

"I know all this has to come as a shock." He ran a hand through his hair. "Learning your sister betrayed her country and is wanted by the CIA can't be easy to hear." He pushed his hands into his pockets. "I understand if you need some time to process everything, but uh, I also thought maybe you might want some Oreos."

I swiveled so I could look him in the eyes.

"We don't have any Oreos in the apartment. I know. I looked."

I decided I'd let his accusation against Madison slide. For now. Until I had proof to back up my claims of her innocence, maybe it was better that he believe . . . whatever he wanted to believe. If he thought I believed the CIA, he'd let his guard down and I'd be able to get the information I needed. There had to be something past those firewalls even Mendez couldn't access.

I didn't think it was possible for Mendez to look embarrassed. But the way his cheeks reddened ever so slightly and the way he looked down at his feet was probably the most adorable thing I'd ever seen. And that was including the interview where Chris Evans was surrounded by puppies, so my bar was already pretty high.

"We don't," he agreed. "But I checked the ingredients in the kitchen against a recipe I found online, and if you're okay with helping me make them, I figured we could try our hand at the homemade kind. I know they won't taste the same, but you seemed rather upset when you couldn't find any earlier, and I thought—"

"That you could sweeten me up and make me forget that you lied?"

"No, I—"

"Chill, Wonder Boy, I'm just kidding." I kicked the now-empty duffel bag under the bed. "It actually is kind of sweet." I smiled and made an "after you" gesture with my hands. "Lead the way."

His shoulders finally relaxed and one side of his mouth quirked up in a grin. "Great." He let go of my door and turned down the hall. "We'll have to make some substitutions since I couldn't find any cream cheese for the filling. Most safe houses don't keep those kinds of perishables on hand. But we do have vegetable shortening and margarine, which some recipes said we could add sugar to, and that might work. How good are you with improvising?"

I shot him a dubious look. "I work with code, which should tell you something. Everything has to be exact." *Or a misplaced semicolon could ruin your day.*

We entered the kitchen and he motioned to the ingredients he'd set out on the counter.

"Good thing you're cooking with a covert operative. If you're not flexible, you're dead." He nudged me with his elbow. "And I'm very flexible." He raised his eyebrows to make sure I'd caught his double entendre, then gave a short bark of a laugh when I rolled my eyes.

I pulled a mixing bowl over to where I stood behind the counter. "It's okay that you're doing this right now?" I asked. "You don't have to, I don't know, save the world or something?"

Mendez opened his computer and a recipe popped up on his screen. "Not while we wait for the other team to question the men we apprehended. Sometimes espionage is a game of hurry up and wait. Until we figure out our next steps, I'm all yours."

That shouldn't have made shivers run all along my arms, but it did. I rubbed them away and tried to mask the action by reaching for a whisk.

"How standard is it for safe houses to have all these utensils and this many ingredients?" I nodded to the flour. "I can't imagine many spies have the time to bake."

Mendez hunched over the laptop, reading the first paragraph of instructions. "There are immediate-need safe houses that are kept vacant for whenever a situation arises, and then there are better-equipped long-term units for when the CIA needs to station its operatives in the area for an unknown period of time. We're in the latter. Are you implying agents can't have hobbies or that you think the Central Intelligence Agency doesn't know how to stock a kitchen?"

"Well, they didn't get cream cheese, so . . ." I trailed off, and Mendez slid the flour across the counter to me.

"Just for that, you get to do the first step."

Joke was on him, because the first step didn't call for any improvisation. But the second step called for butter. I wasn't sure if we were supposed to use margarine in the same quantity or if we had to make some kind of adjustment for that. It would be just my luck if Mendez saw me fail this early in the game.

I put my hands on my hips. "I think you just don't want to admit you don't know how to bake." I patted him on the arm. "Don't worry, I can take it from here."

I could not, in fact, take it from here. We hadn't even preheated the oven and already my back was beginning to sweat from nerves.

He swiped the mixing bowl from me. "I'll have you know, I am quite comfortable in the kitchen." He measured out the margarine and put it in a separate bowl, adding the sugar. "Watch and learn, grasshopper."

I pulled out a barstool and took a seat, silently watching as he plugged in the hand mixer.

It was like the man from the 30 under 30 interview was back, and I wasn't sure what to make of it. If he was the spy, I was the private detective trying to put the pieces together. Earlier I'd thought it'd all been an act—that Mendez had been pretending with each outfit he'd put on. But maybe a hardened CIA operative was allowed to have a soft side.

"I wish we had an apron for you to wear," I said. "One with lots of ruffles."

His laugh was deep and unworried. "Done that before for a part. My masculinity isn't so fragile it'd be shattered by some lace."

"Were you undercover?" I asked, leaning forward and placing my chin on my fist. If I kept him talking long enough, chances were good he might not notice he was on step three and I wasn't so much as lifting a finger.

He shook his head. "I was a theater kid in high school." He poured the dry ingredients into the bowl with the mixed margarine and sugar. "That's actually how the CIA recruited me. It's not like I set out to become an operative."

I raised my eyebrows. "Okay, first of all, I was in stage crew, so if we'd gone to high school together there would have been a chance we'd run in the same circles; and second of all, you didn't always want to be an agent?"

Mendez only gave me a wry smile, keeping silent while he mixed the ingredients together.

"What did you want to be when you grew up?" I pressed.

He bit his lip and shook his head again.

I came around the counter and took the mixing bowl away from him. "The batter needs to be chilled for a bit. So if you think I'm going to let this go, you're sorely mistaken. We've got time on our hands."

Mendez crossed his arms and leaned back on the counter while I covered the bowl and placed it in the fridge.

I turned around and fixed him with a stare. He simply grinned in response.

"It's too embarrassing," he replied. "Besides, I already gave you a huge hint."

I thought back to what he'd said while I returned to the barstool I'd vacated. "You said you were a theater kid," I mused, sitting down and tapping my fingers on the edge of the counter. "So does that mean you wanted to go into acting?"

Mendez winced and I sat up.

"That's it, isn't it?" I said. "You wanted to be an actor."

"Not just an actor," he clarified. "I wanted to be famous. That was actually the one character trait of mine that gave the CIA pause in the interviewing process." He ducked his head and a lock of hair fell in front of his eye.

"You may not have noticed," he continued, "but most CIA

officers don't exactly seek out the limelight. The fact that I wanted public approval wasn't a good look. Luckily, they chalked that up to the innocence of youth."

Mendez picked up one of the beaters covered in chocolate cookie batter, holding the other out for me.

"You're not worried about salmonella poisoning?" I asked. I licked my beater before hearing his answer, because, hello, it was chocolate.

He watched me without saying a word, pupils dilating. I honestly couldn't think of what might make his gaze turn hungry like that, so I ignored him. I was getting better at doing that every day.

He cleared his throat as I took another lick.

"No," he said, voice strained. "With my profession, I figure there are other ways to die. Like watching you with that."

I grinned, realization dawning on me. This time, I was deliberate about it, licking the beater slowly up one side while keeping direct eye contact.

Mendez swore and dropped his beater into the bowl. "I need to clean the dishes," he muttered. "Before we get to the cream filling and you really do me in."

I laughed and got off the barstool. "I get to do the dishes since you did most of the first steps. It's only fair."

He raised his eyebrows. "You think you're getting out of the rest of it? We still have to roll them out and do the filling."

I picked up a towel and handed it to him. "Fine. I'll wash, you dry. And while you're doing that, you can tell me all about how the CIA recruited you straight out of high school. How'd they even know you existed?".

Mendez didn't answer my question until the first bowl was already washed and dried, clearly trying to figure out the best way to word his response. I elbowed him in the ribs and he finally caved.

"I won a lot of state acting awards in high school." He set aside another bowl. "The CIA has recruiting offices in each state that follow the high school acting circuits, and they keep tabs on promising students."

I turned to face him, my mouth open. "No way."

He nudged my mouth closed and took the soapy rubber spatula from my hand. "True story." He shrugged.

I took the spatula back so I could rinse it off. Then I lightly smacked him in the arm with it.

"Why didn't you want to say anything?" I asked. "If it were me, I'd be bragging about that to anyone who would listen."

"Oh yes," he said, sarcasm evident. "I always like to brag about how good of an actor I am so that no one ever believes anything I say."

I waved his worries aside. "I've got you figured out now. You're like an open book."

"Yes, well." He chuckled. "That's why I like spending time with you. I don't have to pretend. It's more like the theater days, when things weren't as heavy."

"That's because I was a techie," I said. "Our stage crew knew how to party."

"Let me guess," he said. "You did lights and sound, didn't you?"

"Good job, Sherlock." I placed the now clean dishes back on the counter, organizing them in the order we'd need them for the next steps. "Then again, since you were an actor you'd know it was the only thing done with computers."

I took a peek at the first step of the cream filling instructions and saw that they required butter again. I nonchalantly passed the bowl to Mendez so he could measure that out, because of course I hadn't been paying attention to how he'd adapted the recipe for margarine.

"You do step one while I measure the powdered sugar and vanilla," I said.

He smirked like he knew what I was up to but didn't call me out on it as he mixed the margarine and shortening together.

"So, if you were a theater kid, you must like movies, yes?" I asked, hoping the change in subject would keep him from noticing my abilities—or lack thereof—in adapting a recipe. Because if I let him stop to think about it, I was pretty sure he'd have something to say about it as well.

He made a sound in the back of his throat that made it clear he thought my question was on par with asking whether it rained much in England.

I held up my hands in surrender. "What? It's not like I'd expect you to have a whole lot of time to catch the latest *Fast and Furious Twenty-Three: We Don't Know When to Stop* in between parachuting off skyscrapers and infiltrating foreign embassies."

He cracked a smile. "You really think operatives don't have lives, don't you? Even when I'm on active duty, like now, I'm usually holed up in a hotel or safe house, with nothing to do but wait for orders. I don't always have such a pleasant roommate to share my time with, so I read books or watch movies while I twiddle my thumbs."

I bit my lip to hold back a smile. "How was I supposed to know? You didn't exactly open up before this."

He placed the bowl to the side and leaned over me, pushing the button on the oven that would turn it on. My pulse picked up in response and my breathing became irregular. Not my fault.

"That was before I promised to tell you everything." He set

the temperature, taking his sweet time. "Now you can ask me any question."

My brain was like scrambled eggs. His scent, this close—it was like he was doing it on purpose. Sneaky spy stuff, level ten.

I was short-circuiting. Soon, I wouldn't be able to form complete sentences. *Me Jane, you Tarzan.* If he did this for too much longer, my question was going to be *Will you take your shirt off?*

"What's your favorite movie?" I blurted out.

He raised his eyebrows. "I tell you to ask me anything, and that's what you lead with?" He leaned on the counter, trapping me there.

"Seemed safe." I was practically panting. "Besides, you can tell a lot about a person by the type of movies they like."

"Oh," he said. "So, you're going to judge my movie preferences."

I shrugged. "Of course."

He finally leaned back and my heartbeat took a solid minute to recover. Mendez smiled like he knew exactly what he was doing, which, of course, he did.

"I only get one? How's that fair?" he asked.

I escaped from around him and picked up a spatula. We were done with the filling, but I placed the spatula in the bowl. "What can I say, I fight dirty."

Then I pulled the spatula out and wiped a small amount of the cream filling on his cheek.

With a shout, I jumped away before he could counterattack and held up my arms in the universal gesture of surrender. Laughing so hard I may as well have been a hyena, I took in Mendez's expression.

I expected surprise or even frustration.

I didn't expect . . . delight.

He picked up the spatula from where I'd dropped it on the counter. One side was wiped clean from where I'd left my mark, still present on Mendez's cheek. The other was full of cream, white and fluffy, yet somehow still threatening.

"You realize I know seven different ways to take you out with just an eggbeater." He advanced slowly, holding the spatula in front of him.

"You wouldn't dare." I put the barstool in between us, shrieking when he somehow managed to reach around the left side and tickle me at the waist. I dodged to the right and ended up with cream on my nose.

"Mercy!" I was in his arms, gasping for air as he tickled the sensitive skin that had become exposed when my shirt lifted up. It didn't even take much to make me squirm. I'd always been a lightweight, unable to handle one second of tickling.

Eventually he relented and I regained my breath, wiping hair from my face while I leaned on his chest for support. The rumble of his laughter was contagious, and it was at least three minutes before either of us were able to speak again.

"Thanks," I said, voice slightly muffled by his shirt. "I needed this."

He wrapped both his arms around me, resting his chin on top of my head. When he answered, his voice was soft like a caress.

"It was the least I could do."

Chapter Fifteen

· · · · · · · · · ·

M Y MISSION WAS SIMPLE: OBTAIN MORE COOKIES without Mendez finding out.

I'd already eaten three. I didn't need him seeing just how much of a glutton I truly was if I could help it.

Now that it was two in the morning and the jet lag had gotten the better of me, I could finally make my move. I crept down the hall on the pads of my feet.

The light from the fridge wasn't exactly stealthy, bathing the entire kitchen in a warm glow that might as well have broadcast my presence like a search beam. But I silently grabbed a cookie from the top shelf—the cream made it so they had to be refrigerated—and debated whether a glass of milk would push my luck.

"*You* stole the cookie from the cookie jar." A singsong voice startled me, and I turned with my heartbeat in my throat.

"Mendez," I choked out, hurriedly shoving the cookie behind my back. "You scared me half to death."

"No, no," he gently teased. "The correct line is, *Who me?* and I'm supposed to answer back, *Yes, you*, and we're supposed to go round and round on an infinite loop until one of us eventually dies."

He reached around me and grabbed a cookie for himself before taking a bite. Taking that as permission, I begrudgingly brought my own cookie out, silently daring him to say anything. But he only reached around me again, lifting the milk out of the refrigerator door. Holding the cookie in his mouth, he got glasses from a cabinet and poured one for each of us, then carried them to the coffee table in the living room so we could sit on the couch.

"It's two a.m.," he said, clicking on the floor lamp. "Why are you up?" He settled into the cushions, motioning for me to sit down.

I eyed the spot next to him on the couch, debating how much I trusted myself when it came to soft surfaces, my own sleep deprivation, and Mendez.

Eventually I gave in, because I was lazy and didn't want to hold my glass of milk when there was a perfectly respectable coffee table to do it for me.

"Jet lag," I answered. "What about you?"

"Heard you were up." He took another bite. "I'm a light sleeper. Occupational hazard."

That was when I noticed he was actually wearing pajamas. Just sweatpants and a T-shirt, but it was one of the few times I'd seen him in something other than his standard uniform of black-wash jeans and a leather jacket. He looked soft. Comfortable. I wanted to curl up next to his side and drape his arm over me.

I blinked. Shook my head. This. *This* was the reason I shouldn't be sitting on the couch next to Mendez at two a.m. I shoved the rest of the cookie into my mouth and focused on chewing. That way I wouldn't think about his biceps or how they tested the boundaries of his sleeves.

I swallowed my cookie and washed it down with some milk. "Usually I hack late at night," I babbled. "When I can't sleep." Mendez dunked his cookie, holding it in the glass for so long I thought for sure it'd fall off and become mush. But he brought it out at the last minute, capturing it in his mouth like he'd practiced this maneuver a thousand times.

I debated getting another cookie. But I didn't. Because I was all about the self-control these days.

I'd only eaten one cookie when I could have had two. Pretty sure that made me a life coach now.

"How long does it usually take you to hack one of your corporate jobs?" he asked after he'd finished chewing.

"About four minutes," I answered. "I listen to the same song to time myself."

He looked impressed. "What song?"

I pursed my lips. "Let's play Name That Tune," I said. "Do you have a music streaming service on your computer?"

Mendez rubbed his hands together and opened the laptop next to him on the couch. He handed it to me and I turned the screen away from him while I pulled up "I Did Something Bad" and hit play.

He knew it within ten seconds. "Taylor Swift. That was too easy." He pulled the computer back onto his lap. "My turn."

I raised my eyebrows. "That was fast. It didn't even get to the chorus."

"Please." He rolled his eyes. "I have sisters."

I pulled my legs up on the couch. "You do?"

"Two. The same ones who made me listen to this one a thousand times."

He hit a button and strings came through the speakers. But then it was the unmistakable voice of Steven Tyler from Aerosmith, and I bounced excitedly on my cushion. "'I Don't Want to Miss a Thing,'" I cried out. "From that movie where Ben Affleck blew up the asteroid."

"*Armageddon*," Mendez said. "That's a good one."

"Agreed. Now tell me about your sisters." I took the computer back, already searching for my next song, but from the corner of my eye I caught Mendez smiling.

"I'm the oldest," he said. "The older of my two sisters is married with a baby, and the younger one is single and living in California. I also have approximately nine hundred cousins, so please don't ask me about them all."

I let out a small sigh. Most of my life, my support system had consisted of one individual. I couldn't even fathom being surrounded by so many people rooting for my success. Part of me ached for a family that wasn't even mine and that I'd never meet. Because if they were anything like Mendez, I was pretty sure they were amazing too.

Before I could get too emotional, I hit play on my song, picking one that was heavy on the drums just to counteract the mood in the room.

Mendez furrowed his brows in concentration, but eventually he shrugged, admitting defeat.

"You don't know them? That's criminal." I paused dramatically. "That's a hint, by the way. The band's name is CRMNL. Actually, I'm not surprised, they're not that well-known. But they should be."

He smiled. "You'd like my sister," he said. "The one who's married. You have the same taste in music."

I passed the laptop back to Mendez, swallowing the lump in my throat as I did so. "Yeah?" I asked. "Does she know what you do for a living?"

He pulled the computer onto his lap, nodding. "I can't tell her all the details of my missions, obviously. But she knows I work for the CIA. She keeps buying me crystals, thinking they're going to protect me. She bought me these lucky socks."

He held out a foot, which I only now noticed was covered in four-leaf clovers.

"Well, they're definitely not getting you lucky tonight," I said with a laugh. Secretly though? Okay, that was pretty adorable. Because they were a gift from his sister, and hideous or not, that he was wearing them showed he cared.

He started playing another song and a smile broke out on my face.

"That's Bon Jovi." I finished off the rest of my milk like we were doing shots, slamming it down on the coffee table with my proclamation. "'You Give Love a Bad Name.'"

He laughed and gave me the computer, clearly enjoying our game.

I had to do something ridiculous next. Like that song from *High School Musical* where Zac Efron sang on the golf course or the Spice Girls' "Wannabe." Something that would make Mendez laugh. I really wanted that.

But as I thought about it, I realized there was something I wanted more. "Can I ask you another question?" I placed my fingers on the keyboard but didn't play another song.

Mendez tilted his head. "I told you I'd answer anything." He pulled one leg up on the couch, tucking his foot under his thigh.

"And you'll tell me the truth?" I pressed.

He nudged my knee with his. "I think I proved that already when I told you everything about this case, even when it meant telling you I lied about being Madison's partner."

I sucked in a breath. Then I decided to go for it. "What are you supposed to do when you find Madison?"

Mendez went still.

I set the computer on the table, but Mendez still didn't answer.

"You promised you'd tell me the truth," I reminded him.

He cleared his throat. "My orders," he said slowly, "are to shoot on sight. After what happened to the agent she put in the hospital, the CIA thinks she's too dangerous to attempt to bring in."

I stared at him uncomprehendingly. Mendez placed a hand on my knee and I flinched back as his words started to sink in.

"But, Dove—"

I held up a hand, lurching from the couch. My face flushed and the walls spun around me.

Before I could break down completely, I escaped to my room.

Chapter Sixteen

· · · · · · · · · ·

MENDEZ KNOCKED ON MY DOOR A SECOND LATER.
I didn't bother answering.

I sat on the floor in front of the fireplace, but considering all that had happened, I was giving myself kudos simply for sitting upright rather than lying curled in the fetal position.

I'd have to find a way to warn Madison. To keep her away from Mendez.

I swiped at an angry tear. It was more for my own stupidity than anything. Of course I didn't have a future with Mendez. Because when all this was over, I'd go my own way and he'd go his. If I wanted Madison in my life, there'd be no room for a man intent on hunting her down.

Mendez knocked again, a little louder.

"I don't feel like talking," I called.

"Well, I do," he replied. He tried the handle, but I'd locked it. How he expected anything else was a mystery of Nancy Drew proportions.

"Dove?" he called through the door. I stayed silent, not wanting to explain to this seasoned actor how I had fallen for his good-guy shtick yet again.

Perhaps I should have expected it when he picked the lock and poked his head in, expression strained. His face relaxed ever so slightly when he saw me, still sitting on the ground in my pajamas. Of course, my pajamas consisted of an oversized shirt that hung so loose it slipped off one shoulder and barely covered the cotton shorts I wore with it, so I wasn't sure the word fit. The CIA hadn't put much thought into my pajama selection—i.e., they'd forgotten it entirely—so I went with what I could put together from the pieces they'd provided.

Right now though, I wished it was armor, complete with sword and shield.

I stretched my fingers into the carpet, the only new thing in this entire apartment. Each fiber left a velvety sensation on my fingertips.

Everything else was so hard and cold lately, it was nice to know some things were still what I expected.

I thought Mendez would close the door and leave me in peace once he'd verified I hadn't run away like before. But he came to where I was sitting and settled himself next to me, crossing his long legs and leaning against the foot of the bed like he hadn't just dropped a bombshell on me.

When I still didn't say anything, he grunted in annoyance. "Please don't stop talking to me," he said. "This is all a miscommunication."

I felt it when Mendez angled his upper body so he was facing me, but I still didn't look in his direction.

"I said those were my orders. I didn't say I'd chosen to follow them." His voice was pitched low, but I heard every word.

This time, I looked up.

His face was so open and honest. The firelight reflected in his eyes as he watched my face for my reaction.

"Dove." He placed a hand on my knee. "I already decided I'd bring her in. She deserves to be able to defend her actions herself."

I tried to keep my face blank, but the smile crept up on me anyway, like the sun cresting over the horizon. "You promise?" I asked.

He smiled too, and once again I was struck by how beautiful this man was.

"I promise." He held out his pinky, which I took in my own.

A pinky promise not to kill my sister—who would have thought it'd come to this? We dropped our hands, but our fingers stayed intertwined, causing my heart to beat erratically in my rib cage. It happened so frequently around him, I wondered whether I needed to set up a doctor's appointment.

It was at least a minute before I could trust my voice again.

"You'd disobey orders?" I finally asked. "Why?"

His gaze was soft as he responded. "For you."

They were such simple words, and yet there was nothing simple about them. Mendez was a trained operative of the Central Intelligence Agency for the government of the United States of America. For him to willingly disobey direct orders, for me, was a big deal.

His eyes locked on mine and shivers erupted on my arms.

I couldn't help it. I'd wanted to kiss him for so long and had always stopped myself. But now I leaned forward until my lips touched his. Soft at first. Until he responded, pulling me closer and kissing me back.

The thrill of victory burned through my veins, and I placed the palm of my hand on Mendez's chest. His heartbeat thrummed beneath the pads of my fingertips, but his kiss was slow, promising all the time in the world. I wasn't sure he could make that promise—not with his line of work—but I let myself sink into it anyway. In the kiss, I felt . . . not the reporter or the hardened spy, but the person I was beginning to recognize as the genuine Mendez. Caring, protective, all quiet strength and calculated risks.

I'd forever associate the taste of chocolate with Mendez now. I'd never be able to have another Oreo without thinking of him. But I didn't want to either. Mendez's fingers reached into my hair and my messy bun came undone, my hair falling to my shoulders. I couldn't believe this was actually happening. That Mendez would kiss me back, even when he had every reason not to trust me. He believed my sister was working for the enemy, but Mendez only pulled me closer.

I felt along his jawline, his stubble catching on the palms of my hands. I'd wanted to do that since I first met him, and the touch kindled something in me. Mendez deepened the kiss and I eagerly reciprocated.

I'd never experienced anything like this before. He kissed me like I was something special, to be cherished and cared for. It wasn't needy or selfish. It was an offering. Each of us holding out our heart and asking the other to take care of it.

By the time Mendez pulled away, I was out of breath and out of excuses. I was falling for this man, whether I wanted to admit it or not. He rested his forehead against mine and we sat there in silence for a moment, breathing the same air and listening to the fire crackling a few feet away.

"I should let you sleep," Mendez said.

As if I could sleep now. After he'd kissed me senseless and opened up a host of emotions I didn't know how to manage.

Now, when I was questioning what it all meant and whether Mendez was truly acting on his own or at his superior's direction. I didn't want to think about that part. I just wanted to bask in the afterglow of kissing someone for the first time and everything that entailed.

I couldn't possibly sleep. But I understood that Mendez probably had emotions to sort out also. As stoic as he sometimes acted, I knew the real Mendez felt things. Deeply.

He leaned forward once again, and this time he left a soft kiss on my forehead. It was feather light and only there for a second before he stood up and moved toward the door. Somehow that forehead kiss meant more to me than all the kisses he'd applied to my neck back in DC. It was tender and didn't ask for anything in return, but because of it, I would have given him anything he'd asked for.

Mendez hesitated, his hand on the doorknob as he turned to face me. "Sweet dreams," he said, a whisper of a smile on his lips.

Then he was gone, and I was left alone with my thoughts.

Chapter Seventeen

· · · · · · · · · ·

WHEN I WOKE UP THE NEXT MORNING, THERE WAS A
stranger in our apartment. It was curious that I considered it that—our apartment. I hadn't been here long and already
I was staking a claim to the space. And inviting someone new
into it—well, that felt . . . not great. Too many new things had
been happening recently, and most of them were bad. The jury
was still out about last night, because I had no idea what any of
it meant. I tried not to focus on that and instead studied the
stranger.

He was Asian American, tall, and well-built, with a square
jawline and short, dark hair. He sat at the table with Mendez,
both of them hunched over a folder and speaking in quiet tones.
Papers littered the table, haphazardly strewn about with no
rhyme or reason. It looked like I was late to the party.

I cleared my throat and Mendez looked up. The stranger
noticed Mendez move and jerked back a little in surprise when
he saw me standing there. My entrance hadn't exactly been subtle though. Maybe he'd been in the zone.

"Hi," I said, stepping fully into the room. I didn't offer my name because I wasn't sure if I was supposed to. Stranger danger and all that jazz.

Mendez's eyes softened at the corners as he watched me, and I smiled hesitantly, unsure what to think now that it was a new day. As if the sun had illuminated our obstacles, it was only now that things seemed uncertain, thrown into sharp contrast. He was a spy. I was a civilian. He had a license to kill. I killed my plants and felt bad about it. He said he didn't do commitment. Not only that, but a traitorous part of me still wondered whether Mendez's interest was genuine or if he was stringing me along, keeping me close so he could get the information he wanted. After all, if he wanted to catch Madison, his best hope was that she'd contact me. I was blond, not stupid.

He smiled, a genuine smile, and the knots around my chest loosened ever so slightly. I pushed my worries aside.

"Dove, this is Chan. Chan, this is Dove." Mendez stood and crossed into the kitchen, keeping a distance between us as he opened the fridge. I narrowed my eyes, trying to interpret what it meant.

"You hungry?" he asked.

Okay, maybe he was just being considerate and I needed to chill out. Maybe. Still, the memory of our kiss brought red to my cheeks, and I tried unsuccessfully to appear disinterested. Calm. Cool in the center like a medium-rare steak. Not needy and desperate at all—nope, not me.

"Sure," I said, and sat at the table next to Chan. It was the only word I could trust out of my lips because it was just one syllable. Inwardly, I was doing cartwheels. Mendez was cooking me breakfast. That had to mean something, right? Even if I'd been the one to initiate the kiss last night, he was still making me breakfast this morning. Mendez removed a couple of eggs from the fridge and a carton of milk. While he moved around the kitchen, I turned to Chan.

"Chan is your last name?"

What was it with CIA operatives going by their surnames? Did they think it added to the mystery? Or was it some athletic thing, like they'd all been on the same football team growing up and they'd gotten used to taking orders that way?

Maybe it was military-related. Maybe I'd never know.

I chuckled. *Maybe she's born with it. Maybe it's Maybelline.*

I shook my head, bringing myself back to the present. Briefly I wondered whether I'd ever figure out Mendez's first name.

It was ridiculous how often my thoughts circled back to him, and my cheeks grew hot even as I couldn't help but watch him move around the kitchen. The way his shirt pulled at his shoulders and his sleeves were rolled up, exposing his forearm muscles—like he'd woken up this morning and decided to torture me.

Chan nodded and it took me a second to remember my question.

"First name's Jackie," he said.

"So," I hedged. "Your name is . . . Jackie . . . Chan? Like the martial arts actor?"

Chan's expression was deadpan for a full ten seconds before he snorted and slapped the table. "No, it's Adam, but I had you going, didn't I?"

I shook my head in embarrassment. With Chan's contagious smile, it was hard to stay embarrassed long though, and eventually I found myself laughing too. "You work with Mendez?" I asked, nodding toward all the papers on the desk.

Chan chuckled. "As much as anyone could claim to work with him." He leaned back in his chair and crossed his arms.

"Mendez is what we at the CIA call a lone wolf. Sure, he works with a team when he needs to, but because he's in the field so much, no one gets that close." His eyes glanced over me, appraising. "You've probably spent more time with him lately than most. Maybe you've managed to get past those walls?" He said this in a conspiratorial way, lowering his voice and raising an eyebrow. I blushed so hard Mendez could have fried the eggs on my skin.

I didn't know what to make of Chan. I was used to a special operative acting like Mendez, all business and stoicism. Chan was something else altogether. He smiled and gossiped, acting like we were already close friends. The nerdy introvert in me liked the ease of it. Carrying on a regular conversation was hard enough, but someone like Chan could shoulder that load for me—if I could trust him, which was still under review.

"Uh," I said. My eyes darted to Mendez, appraising whether he'd heard Chan's remarks. Mendez cracked an egg on the side of a skillet, his attention seemingly focused there. But I knew he was a good actor, and I wasn't about to show my hand when Mendez hadn't shown his.

"You sure do get personal fast, don't you?" I asked Chan, keeping my voice low. He angled his body so his ear was closer to me. It was only then I saw a thin, clear line reaching over it and recognized it as a hearing aid. Well, that explained why he hadn't heard me come in.

Chan saw me looking and shrugged. "In our line of work, things change fast." He tapped his ear. "One minute you can hear, the next you get too close to an explosion and you're relegated to a desk for the rest of your life." He nodded toward Mendez. "So, you learn to ask the personal questions first and ask forgiveness later."

"Do you miss being a field agent?" I ignored his fishing for information in favor of fishing myself.

Chan smiled. "To be honest, most CIA work is done from a desk anyway. We gather information. Very few operatives are in the field as much as Mendez. Most officers don't even carry a gun regularly."

I found this hard to believe but didn't say so. Chan saw my skepticism and one side of his mouth quirked up in response. "Seriously, it's not like the shows." He leaned forward and rested his elbows on the table. "We're just regular people, doing a job. We're not Olympic athletes. We're not models. We need to blend in, so that kind of defeats the purpose."

Chan was selling himself short, because I was sure he turned plenty of heads. But we'd only just met and I didn't want to give him the wrong idea or make him uncomfortable. So I looked pointedly at Mendez, who could clearly model for any fashion house in the world. He was beautiful by anyone's standards, even as he scrambled eggs in an outdated kitchen in Prague. My heartbeat picked up as I remembered the feel of his lips against mine. How his hands had felt on my back. How if Chan weren't here right now . . .

"Mendez is a unique case," Chan said with a chuckle. "Of course the CIA needs a honeypot now and then."

I swallowed hard and my hands stilled on the table. I'd seen enough spy movies to recognize the term: someone attractive who got the information they needed by flirting with the target. Someone who could act like a journalist, ask out some poor, unsuspecting newbie, and get the job done. Mendez had already admitted to that much when questioned, so the real question was whether he was still doing that, even now. Was I being honey-potted? Was that even a real term? I didn't have an answer to either question.

Last night had been a bright spot in a sea of black. Now that light looked more and more like that of a firefly, sparkling briefly before disappearing forever. Beautiful while it lasted, but untouchable and ultimately too dim to illuminate the darkness.

Chan scratched his cheek. "Of course, it helps that his skills as a honeypot are only surpassed by his hand-to-hand combat, which, if you're lucky, you'll never get to see firsthand." He leaned back in his chair. "Which makes him ideal for fieldwork." Chan chuckled and shook his head. "Really, it's wildly unfair. Couldn't he leave some talent for the rest of us?"

He didn't seem upset, but there was an undercurrent to his words that carried a hint of truth. I recognized the bitterness in myself, in the ways I compared myself to my sister. Who did that help, really?

Chan and I were silent for a moment while Mendez transferred the cooked eggs to a plate. He removed a banana from a bunch on the counter and placed it beside the eggs. Chan appraised me, watching me watch Mendez, and he grinned like he knew a secret. I averted my eyes.

"What are you two whispering about?" Mendez came over to the table and slid the plate in front of me. I tried to read his expression. How his eyebrows dipped down when he studied the distance between Chan's chair and mine. I wanted so badly to interpret it as jealousy. But that was probably—no, definitely—wishful thinking.

"Nothing," I said before shoveling eggs into my mouth. If I couldn't talk, I couldn't answer questions, from either Mendez or Chan. Mendez smiled like he saw right through me, which only made me wonder what he'd told Chan about us. Maybe there was a reason Chan got so personal so fast. Or maybe they both had so much training in reading body language, I might as well have put a sign across my forehead that broadcast my feelings.

Mendez stood too close, his hand resting on the back of my chair, and Chan's eyebrows raised suggestively. But then Mendez moved away, taking the chair on the other side of Chan. I sighed and took another bite, wondering at the games people played. I'd never keep up with these two. They were experienced in espionage and subterfuge. I, on the other hand, couldn't even beat my sister in a game of Clue. I'd always be playing catch-up, so I might as well get used to it. Maybe it was time to surrender now, tell them both I was helplessly falling for Mendez so at least I could stop pretending otherwise.

"Chan is in Prague for a different case, but he's transferring. Our op takes precedence," Mendez explained. "He's in logistics primarily, which means he's a brilliant strategist. This way we don't have to sneak anyone past Holt's airport surveillance, because he's already here and past the jet lag. He was on the team of operatives who ran surveillance at the tram depot. They also helped handle the men at Madison's house the other day."

At Madison's safe house Mendez had told me how an entire team had been taken out just after disembarking from the plane, and I briefly wondered how we'd made it ourselves. Then I replayed the covert red-eye flight in my mind and remembered how Mendez had insisted our plane not be on any official flight plans or records. Apparently, the CIA had figured out a way to bribe the employees in the control towers at the private tarmac since that disastrous mission.

"Right now, we're trying to determine Holt's location." Mendez pulled some papers toward him and started reading them.

As if he hadn't read them fifty times already. Honestly, I admired his patience. Because I knew with the certainty of a thousand suns that I would have torn those papers up by now. The only thing I could repeatedly read like that was code, and only because I knew if I stared at it long enough, things would eventually make sense.

As much as I was grateful that Mendez had let me read the documents, I was even more grateful he had someone else to help him now. Strength in numbers and all that. More help meant finding my sister faster. I could get her out of Holt's clutches, clear her name, and return to the States with her in tow.

The downside was, with Chan here, I couldn't pull Mendez close, or take his hand, or do any of the other things I wanted to do. Like kissing. Lots and lots of kissing. Sure, Chan's presence would keep us focused, but I didn't exactly want to be focused. Unless I could focus on Mendez.

His forearms flexed when he turned a page, like he couldn't resist showing off. Then again, he didn't have to try. His Henley pulled across his shoulders, and I imagined what it'd feel like to have those muscles under my fingertips. I'd always been a shoulders gal, and Mendez sure had nice ones. But it was the memory of our kiss that made me swallow as heat rushed to my cheeks. I wanted him to push me against the wall and kiss me all over. Well, once we got rid of Chan.

"Not sure how much help I'll be," Chan said, bringing my attention back to the conversation. He picked up a paper, then dropped it back on the table a second later. "So far there's nothing here. Holt's operation seems to be ears only."

I wasn't sure if he was referring to a term used by those who were hard of hearing or some spy phrase I didn't know, so I turned to Mendez, who filled me in.

"Holt doesn't put much in writing. They only use spoken orders, so there's no paper trail for us to follow."

"Ah." I'd finished my breakfast, so I placed my hands in my lap and tried to look like I belonged. The last thing I wanted was to be sent to my room like a child with an early bedtime, forced to stare at the ceiling while the grown-ups did all the real work. If Mendez could focus on the greater good right now, so could I. Probably.

I stood up and took my plate over to the sink, determined to pull my weight where I could. As I scrubbed my dishes, I thought about my options. I wasn't a special operative trained in analyzing the data, nor was I knowledgeable in tracking arms dealers. My strengths lay with computers. But I doubted Mendez would let me insert myself into his operation, even if he did trust me. And I wasn't really sure he did. But Madison was still out there, and she needed my help now more than ever.

I wiped my hands on a towel, then turned around and leaned back against the counter, plastering an innocent expression on my face.

"Can I use one of the laptops?" I looked at Mendez. "I'd like to catch up on some work while we're sitting ducks. If that's okay?" I laced my voice with as much honey as I could muster without tipping him off. I'd seen the files on Madison already, but I wanted to see if there was anything else. Anything hidden behind higher clearances or firewalls that the CIA thought I might not notice because they'd passed me a few breadcrumbs.

He shook his head. "We can't have anyone tracking you—"

"I'll use a VPN," I interrupted. "And Tor, of course. No one will trace me."

I wasn't sure if he'd told Chan what I did for a living, so I gave him a look heavy with meaning. "I know what I'm doing."

This made him smile, and he eyed me slowly, taking me in from head to toe. Okay, I'll admit it. I might have taken a little extra time getting ready this morning. But the way Mendez was looking at me now made all that worth it.

"Yeah, you do."

I bit my lip and blushed all the way into my hairline. I very carefully did *not* look at Chan, who I was sure had his . . . opinions . . . about this exchange. I didn't look at Mendez either. I just stared at the ceiling like it had all the answers to life's mysteries.

Mendez laughed, then pushed one of the laptops to the edge of the table toward me. It wasn't the one he'd let me use to access his CIA account yesterday, but that didn't matter. I had the RAT installed on his computer, which I could access from anywhere. Well, if he didn't use his computer at the same time. And since he was busy looking over the physical paperwork with Chan, I had a small window of opportunity I intended to take advantage of.

I nonchalantly grabbed the laptop, then settled myself in on the couch several feet away, where I could make sure I'd have at least a three-second warning before anyone else would be able to see my screen. As long as I executed a kill command, no one would have to know what I was up to. I downloaded the VPN client and tapped my fingers on the keyboard while I waited to sign in. It took extra time, but I made sure I had everything for my own work displayed on my screen, easily brought to the front should I need it.

Then the real work began.

Access the RAT. Check. Clone Mendez's profile. Check. Bestow the fake profile with higher clearance. That one took a good fifteen minutes to figure out, but then I was in, and the CIA database was mine.

I almost chuckled at how easy it was. But then I remembered that none of this would have been possible to do on my own without Mendez's login to start. The thought took me down a peg, and I navigated the site carefully. One wrong move would implicate Mendez, and that was the last thing I wanted.

Every few minutes I said things like, "Mind if I download IceWeasel so I can work on this client?" or "Can I save documents to this computer?" so Mendez and Chan thought I was working. All the while I was reading files on Holt. Not just the files I'd seen earlier about Madison. *Everything*. Known associates, locations, medical history—all of it was available to me now. Everything that Mendez knew, I knew, plus a few things that were above his clearance. Honestly, there wasn't much, and I had to fight the desperation clawing its way up my chest.

Holt was a heavy drinker, which didn't surprise me. And he had a daughter, which did. She was around my age—though the CIA didn't know her exact birth year, or her whereabouts either. No college or public schooling of any kind. No medical records with her name attached.

The more I read, the more frustrated I got, because none of this was helping. File after file. Nothing. I sighed in irritation and leaned back into the couch, glaring at the laptop. Usually there wasn't a computer I couldn't win over. I was the snake charmer of laptops. But every once in a while I encountered a problem that made me want to take a blowtorch to the thing and throw it off the edge of a cliff. This was one of those times.

We were missing something. All of us.

Well, nothing the CIA knew was helping. So maybe I needed to look at what they didn't know. Rather than focus on the facts, I needed to gather the holes, the spaces in information where secrets liked to hide. That was sometimes how it was with code—it wasn't the actual code that displayed the problem but rather the string of code that was missing.

I started with the tip line. None of this data was verified, but it was still worth investigating. Sorting the tips by credibility, I began at the top, dismissing each one that didn't fit in the puzzle I'd been putting together. No, Holt wasn't in the US, so the "sighting" yesterday in a Wyoming gas station wasn't accurate. Mendez had some old information in this channel too—that Madison would be in Washington, DC, meeting her sister, Dove Barkley, at Brock's. Time unknown, but after six o'clock. That file had been updated with information about the shoot-out and my subsequent involvement in the case. I clicked on my name and a wealth of information popped up beside my picture.

```
KNOWN ASSOCIATES: MADISON BARKLEY, SISTER
AGE: 27
SEX: FEMALE
HEIGHT: 5'6"
HAIR: BROWN, CURRENTLY DYED BLOND
EYES: BROWN
TATTOOS: SMALL FLAME ON WRIST
OCCUPATION: DIGITAL PENETRATION TESTER, CYBER
SECURITY EXPERT. EXTREMELY QUALIFIED.
```

Well, they certainly had that right. I chuckled under my breath, then clicked back to the tip channel. My eyes caught on the name of the person who had submitted the least-credible tip, which was at the bottom of the list because it had already been deemed inaccurate. Madison Barkley had submitted it. I kept seeing her name throughout this investigation, but upon finding it there on the CIA's side, rather than implicated with Holt's . . . my eyes misted up and I blinked furiously.

That was where her name belonged. Problem was, even the people who once considered her trustworthy now thought she was a piranha.

If the CIA thought it wasn't credible, there probably wasn't much use in opening the file, but I did it anyway.

The file loaded on my screen.

I took one look at it and gasped out loud.

Chapter Eighteen

· · · · · · · · · ·

MENDEZ GLANCED UP AND I HIT THE KILL COMMAND, automatically closing the CIA database and deleting every trace I'd been there. My work files were already populating to the front of my screen by the time he stood up. Chan watched us both silently, the paper in his hand forgotten.

"What'd you find?" Mendez strode to where I was settled on the couch and sat beside me, pulling the laptop toward him. In the process, his fingers brushed against my legs and my heart jumped in my rib cage. *It's because of the anxiety of almost getting caught*, I told myself. *Not because he touched you*. The flush on my cheeks disagreed. He sat so close, I could feel every muscle in his upper arm as he pulled the computer onto his lap.

Mendez let out an exasperated breath and turned the screen toward me. "Bring it back."

"What?" My voice only shook a little. I was getting much better at this whole espionage thing. Normally I wouldn't have considered lying a skill I needed to perfect, but there was a first time for everything. "That's what I was working on. Sorry if I alarmed you. There was just a nasty Trojan in their system, and it startled me."

Okay, if I was going to become a professional liar, I had to do a better job of not sounding like some formal robot. *Sorry if I alarmed you? It startled me?* Who spoke like that? Liars, that's who.

Liar, liar, pants on fire, I chanted to myself.

I focused on a string from the hem of my shirt that was coming undone and wound it around my fingers, being very careful not to look in his direction.

Mendez was having none of it. I felt his fingers gently grasp my chin and turn my face toward his. My skin burned at his touch, and I swallowed hard. He didn't remove his hand, and my eyes snaked over to Chan to see his reaction. Chan leaned back in his chair, his arms folded across his chest as he watched us. I rolled my eyes, then focused my attention back on Mendez, who finally dropped his hand. He pushed the laptop back over to me, taking my hand and placing it on the keyboard.

"Dove," he said, his expression patient. "We all know that's not what you were doing over here, so there's no use pretending otherwise."

I sputtered. "I was working on—"

"The CIA database," Mendez interrupted. "There's a mirror behind you. I could see your screen the whole time."

I jerked back and craned my neck to see whether Mendez was telling the truth, then immediately turned back around and smacked him in the arm. And here I thought I'd been so sneaky. Apparently not. I felt my cheeks go hot and I pursed my lips together, shaking my head as Mendez chuckled.

Well, at least he was laughing. He could have been mad. Or disappointed. Or he could have put me in prison for the rest of my life.

Chan joined in, snorting at my expression, which I was sure was a mix of horror and mortification.

"Why didn't you say anything?" I threw up my hands. "Why didn't you stop me?"

"Plausible deniability." One side of Mendez's mouth quirked up in a grin and he reached up to grab my fluttering hands, bringing them back to my lap and keeping his on top. Once again, my eyes darted to Chan, who pointedly looked at the ceiling. Plausible deniability, ha. Apparently that was a spy skill they all liked to use whenever it suited them.

"I'm not authorized to bring you on the case in an official capacity," Mendez said. "But that doesn't mean I won't utilize all the resources at my disposal."

Which meant . . . Mendez trusted me. Like, he *actually* trusted me. More than he was supposed to, and more than the CIA wanted him to. A heady feeling came over me, delicious and warm at the same time. It was like being wrapped in a blanket, clean and fresh from the dryer.

I wasn't sure what my face looked like in that moment, but Chan cleared his throat and deliberately turned away, putting his back toward us so we could have some privacy. Well, as much as we could have with him sitting ten feet away. So, not a lot. But it was the thought that counted. Mendez interlocked his fingers with mine and I bit my lip.

If I was a mark, I sure was an easy one.

"Why now?" I asked, voice quiet. "Earlier you wouldn't let me access your computer without hovering over my shoulder."

He smiled, but it was a wicked grin laced with meaning. "Hovering over your shoulder has other advantages." His gaze dipped down to my chest, and I shook my head, a small chuckle escaping.

Mendez stroked my hand with his thumb, considering his answer. He lowered his voice. "Because earlier I hadn't fully decided." He shrugged. "Now I've decided."

That glowy feeling was back and I almost checked the mirror to see if it was visible. How was it possible to be so confused about a relationship yet still so sure at the same time?

Mendez nudged me with his shoulder. "Will you *please* show me what you were looking at?"

After everything, how could I refuse now? I reluctantly let go of Mendez's hand and pulled the laptop closer. My fingers flew across the keyboard. It took me some time to access everything again, but Mendez was patient, sitting silently while I worked. By the time I navigated back to the page with Madison's discredited tip, Chan had wandered over to sit on my other side. The page opened on my screen and they both leaned in, squeezing me like a marshmallow.

Chan read it aloud: "Received intelligence from Agent Madison Barkley of Holt's intentions to assassinate COO/CIA, date and location determined by inaugural CIA patrons gala. Source: HUMINT."

There were a lot of words in there I didn't understand, but one word had stood out, causing me to gasp: *assassinate*. Holt was going to kill someone in the CIA and Madison knew about it.

On the other hand, this tip had already been discredited, so I probably should have let it go. But Madison had told them something, and they were just going to ignore it? That didn't seem right.

Chan stood up and began pacing the small room, but Mendez stayed where he was, crossing his arms while he thought.

"It means Holt is going to kill somebody, right? In the CIA?"

I asked. Neither of them had said anything yet, and I hated the silence. Silence left too many possibilities. Either they didn't agree with me and were thinking of how to soften the blow, or worse, they did agree, and now we had another problem on our hands. Mendez leaned over and pointed at the screen, his finger hovering over each word as he explained it to me.

"*COO/CIA* means the chief operating officer of the Central Intelligence Agency. I'm not sure when the inaugural CIA patrons gala is. We'd have to look it up, though I believe it's being hosted at the Smithsonian in Washington, DC. That's the assassin's intended opening. And *HUMINT* means human intelligence. We have nothing to back this up besides Madison's word. That's why it's been discredited." He pointed to a line farther down the page that read: *compromised, unreliable inside intelligence.* Mendez scrolled to the top of the page, highlighting the date. "Madison submitted this after we learned of her switching sides. That means she likely intended to divert our attention and rush our hand."

I scowled. I understood that Madison was not exactly well-liked around here, but discrediting a tip simply because she was the one to submit it?

Mendez palmed the back of his neck. "What I don't understand is why this was above our clearance. This is the first I'm seeing it. Chan?"

Chan shook his head. "Me too."

Mendez pursed his lips and narrowed his eyes, seemingly displeased with this answer. Meanwhile, I was just grateful Chan seemed cool with me hacking into the CIA database and accessing files beyond their clearance. Most other people probably would have turned me in by now.

"Not to look a gift horse in the mouth," I said, chewing my

lip lightly, "but how come I'm not in handcuffs for accessing the database?"

Chan chuckled and waved his hand, like he was dispelling a bad odor. "You weren't hurting anyone. And you haven't given me any reason not to trust you yet." He shrugged like I was making this into a bigger deal than it was. "Plus, the CIA doesn't make arrests. That's the FBI's jurisdiction. We gather intelligence."

Mendez put his hands on his knees, sighed, and stood up. "It's a moot point. It's not credible intel."

"So, you're just going to ignore it?" I asked, rising also. "The chief operating officer of the CIA could die, simply because you don't like the person who told you about it?"

Harsh. Sucked to be on the CIA's bad side. Or their good side, for that matter, since I was guessing the COO had probably received a few promotions to get to where he was.

Mendez turned to me and placed his hands on my shoulders. The weight of it stopped me in my tracks. "This could be exactly what she wants, Dove. To create false trails and spread us thin. It's literally something she took right out of the handbook. If we act, they'll already have their men in position to take ours out. She could be hoping to put all of the special task force we have for Holt in one location. It's a trap."

I refused to believe that. Okay, maybe my sister was working for the bad guys, but that didn't mean she herself had truly gone over to the dark side. They could be blackmailing her, or she could simply be pretending for some reason we couldn't understand. We owed her the benefit of the doubt.

"Has she ever given you bad information before?" I pressed, really, really hoping the answer to that question was no. Because if Madison *had* given the CIA misinformation, I wasn't entirely sure I wanted to know about it.

Now I made Mendez pause. His eyes narrowed ever so slightly, and he frowned like he'd eaten something sour. "No," he said, curtly.

"So, don't you think someone should at least look into it?" I asked.

I didn't know the COO guy. But that didn't mean I wanted him dead. And more important, I didn't want anyone to blame Madison for anything else. If she was trying to do the right thing here, I at least wanted her to get credit. Plus, it'd be great to help the guy to . . . well . . . not die. That was a bonus.

Mendez crossed his arms, making his shirt pull taut across his shoulders. I momentarily forgot what I was talking about, transported into a daydream where Mendez was shirtless and we were alone. Chan brought me back to reality.

"I think the fact that she's your sister is clouding your judgment on this one, Dove." Chan stood by the table, sifting through papers while he talked.

Maybe that was true. But he didn't know my sister, and I didn't think she'd want an innocent man to die if she could help it. Of course, she had killed the man in the station, but he was one of the bad guys. Not the chief operating officer of the CIA.

"You say I haven't given you any reason not to trust me yet." I turned to Chan. "Well, neither has my sister." I hastily amended my statement, because I'd seen the evidence myself. "At least not in her official communication with the CIA. She hasn't outright lied."

Lies of omission and withholding information were another thing entirely, but I was hoping he wouldn't go there.

"You've been undercover," I said. "Isn't there *some* chance she has honorable reasons for her choices?" I looked between

Mendez and Chan, judging their expressions. Mendez gave in first.

"Okay, we can at least determine the location and time of the inaugural CIA patrons gala. I don't like that this was above our clearance. Something seems off."

Chan conceded, following the lead of his senior officer. I resisted the urge to pump my fist with the victory. Because even though it felt like it, I hadn't won yet. He was looking into it. That didn't mean he thought Madison was innocent.

Mendez returned to the computer on the couch, opening it up and navigating to an internal page on the CIA database. I tried not to look impatient as I ran my fingers through my hair. Mendez clicked a few things, the lines on his forehead creasing with each new tab he opened.

He sat back and chewed on his lower lip. After a minute of thinking, he sighed. "I hate to say it, but I think Dove is right."

Normally, I'd have felt vindicated by someone telling me that. Now I just felt scared. Someone's life was in danger, and he didn't even know it.

Mendez handed the computer over to Chan, who began scanning the page Mendez had left up.

"The COO wasn't even scheduled to attend the gala," Mendez said, standing. "But the officer previously assigned was just admitted to the hospital because of a heart attack. I know our line of work can be stressful, but he was only forty-five, so the chances of that being a natural occurrence are fairly slim." He started to pace. "Add that to the fact that the caterers were changed last minute, and there are too many coincidences for me to ignore."

I furrowed my brows. "What do the caterers have to do with anything?" I looked to Mendez, but it was Chan who answered.

"The easiest way to smuggle in an assassin is through wait-staff and caterers. Their staff has such high turnover that no one notices a new face, and they don't need to pass a background check. If they do, it's easily faked because no one pays them much attention."

"Even at something hosted by the Central Intelligence Agency?" I asked. My breakfast was beginning to turn sour in my stomach and I could hear my pulse pounding in my ears. "Won't they do background checks and have security and all that?"

Chan smiled weakly. "This is a patrons gala, meant to honor retired officers. Because most of the attendees won't be on active duty, it won't have the same kind of security required at most CIA functions."

In other words, no. "Remind me again why no one believed Madison when she tipped them off about all this?" I asked.

Mendez rubbed the stubble along his jaw. "She's persona non grata. She submitted her tip after going rogue, which means the agency isn't going to give credence to anything she says, especially as all this *could* still be a trap." He shook his head. "But it could also be that someone at the CIA buried her tip so no one on our operation would see it. Either Madison is the double agent, or someone else is framing her to take the fall. Even I don't know what to believe anymore."

I should have been happy that Mendez was—maybe—coming around. Instead, I twisted the hem of my shirt and tried really hard not to think of worst-case scenarios. Of course, the more I tried not to think about them, the more those ideas popped up in my head. Images of Madison sent to execute the chief operating officer of the CIA because Holt had some kind of dirt on her. Of her broken body bleeding out on the floor because Mendez took the first flight home and shot her before she could shoot anyone else. Sure, it was possible the assassin was some-body I didn't know, an unknown player in this deadly game. But in my nightmares (daymares?), it was Madison's face I saw.

"How could we have missed all this?" Mendez asked. "What if this is part of Holt's attempt at taking over the CIA? Taking out the COO would leave a key position open for him to fill with an inside man." Mendez strode over to the window and stared out, hands on his hips. His jaw was set, his eyes determined as he looked over the Prague skyline.

"There's got to be somebody handling this, right?" I asked. "I mean, yes, the tip was discredited, but surely there's someone who noticed the caterers being switched out, or the original officer having a heart attack. Someone had to find those things odd."

I was holding on to hope, but Mendez was already shaking his head. "It's normal enough that they wouldn't give it a second thought. *I* wouldn't have. If it weren't for the tip that you uncovered. A tip you weren't even supposed to find. It's everything together that makes the picture."

Mendez brought one hand up to his jaw, rubbing the stubble there. "How far up the chain do you think the tip has gone?" he asked. "We can't alert the COO without credible intel, but what about the positions directly beneath him? Do you think Tobias Matthews or Alexis Claire would be receptive to a theory?"

I vaguely recognized Tobias's name. He was Mendez's superior he'd been in contact with throughout the entire operation, and I'd heard Mendez talk with him on the phone. As for this Alexis Claire person, I didn't know who she was, but it was clear from the way Chan widened his eyes that he thought Mendez had officially lost it, and then some.

Chan regrouped, shaking his head. "A theory from a documented turned agent?" He scoffed. "If we contact Alexis Claire without verifying everything personally," he continued, giving Mendez a significant look, "and I mean crossing every t and dotting every single i, *in person*, we could be blacklisted forever. Even Tobias Matthews—he's lower on the totem pole, but he doesn't strike me as the type of person who likes people wasting his time. He'd be just as likely to hand us our resignation papers as hand us any kind of accolades for thinking outside the box."

Chan paused, palming the back of his neck. "I don't know about you, but I don't want to work at McDonald's. Been there, done that. And that's if we don't end up in jail somehow for 'assisting' a turned agent's agenda. Besides, if it *was* a credible tip that was buried, how do we know who buried it without alerting them that we're onto them?"

Everyone was silent as we digested this.

The fact remained, if Madison wasn't the double agent, we didn't know who else in the CIA we could trust.

When I could finally stand the quiet no longer, I spoke up. "So, what are we going to do about it?"

Mendez turned to face the room, looking between Chan and me. "We're going to stop Holt once and for all, and we're going to have to do it fast. Ourselves."

Chan placed the laptop on the table. "How long do we have?" he asked.

Mendez took a deep breath. "Three days," he said. "Holt plans to assassinate the chief operating officer of the CIA in three days."

Chapter Nineteen

· · · · · · · · · ·

OUR PLAN WAS STRAIGHTFORWARD. THREE DAYS DIDN'T give us a lot of time to fly back to the United States and catch Holt, especially if he sent someone else to do his dirty work while he stayed in Prague. Plus, it wasn't exactly smart to waltz blindly into the gala when it could very likely be a trap, so we had to stop Holt here, now. Okay, simple enough. We just had to figure out where Holt's base of operations was. Which was . . . not so simple enough.

The men that Mendez had taken care of outside Madison's house had finally given Chan's team one piece of information we hoped to use to our advantage. Holt had an abandoned warehouse he no longer used.

That was where I came in. I'd hack the CCTV cameras at the warehouse location to track the comings and goings of Holt's employees from the last time they'd used it. With any luck we could track them to Holt's main base. Finding them within the city had never been an option before since Prague was one of the top tourist destinations in all of Europe, plus the city's cameras were too far from here to hack anyway. But now that we had a starting point at a less busy location—well, we had our fingers and toes crossed.

Once at the base, we'd find the files we needed to back up Madison's claims that Holt planned to assassinate the COO, which would prove someone was setting her up as the double agent and save the guy from walking into a really bad situation, to put it mildly.

The real problem was what would happen once we found Holt's base. No matter what I said, I couldn't make Mendez see sense. It was like talking to a brick wall. A really handsome, muscular brick wall.

"If you want records of his entire operation," I said, getting a drink from the kitchen, "you'll need to take me with you. You'll need someone who can access their database and decrypt their files. Otherwise, didn't you say you'd run the risk of someone else picking up the pieces and taking over Holt's operation?"

Mendez didn't seem happy with my logic, but I could tell from the set of his shoulders that he couldn't dispute it.

"Holt's system couldn't be accessed remotely?" Mendez asked me, his eyes clouded with an emotion I couldn't name.

I shook my head. Someone in Holt's line of work would definitely maintain a closed system, probably with some of the best firewalls and security money could buy. Even I wasn't sure I could break it. I swallowed and clamped my teeth together, determined not to let Mendez see my doubt.

But Mendez wasn't looking at me anymore. He turned to Chan and crossed his arms. "You've been stationed here a year. Know of any hackers near Prague?"

Chan looked between Mendez and me, clearly uncomfortable with playing the middleman. Slowly, he nodded. "He's not the most . . ." Chan paused and considered his words carefully.

"He's not the most *ethical* of people. Hangs out with some pretty unsavory characters. But he's the only one who could do it."

I was expecting to feel relief at this pronouncement. Instead, resentment reared its ugly head. This was my one real chance to help my sister, and Mendez was taking it away. I wanted to see this through. I wanted them to see me as competent. Talented. And as far as Mendez was concerned, sexy. Right now, I'd settle for him just wanting me along for the ride, but sexy was definitely becoming increasingly important to me.

Still, I didn't say anything. Because as much as I wanted to help, I wanted to stay alive more. Who said you couldn't teach an old dog new tricks? I could keep my nose out of things after all.

Mendez gave a short nod. "Once we figure out the location of Holt's base with Dove's help, you and I will break in with this hacker. He can get us the files from the database to bring down Holt's operation once and for all. Get in, get out. Holt won't even know we've been there."

Mendez walked to the kitchen counter, picked up the keys there, and tossed them to Chan. "We'll need to recruit the hacker and gather supplies. Get the van ready and pull it out front. Dove and I will be down in a minute."

"Can't I stay here?" I asked. Maybe the safe house didn't feel as secure as I'd like, but at least it seemed safer than the streets of Prague with an arms dealer and his thugs on the loose. And if I stayed here, I'd have Wi-Fi and all the resources I needed to start accessing the CCTV cameras near the warehouse.

Plus, more homemade Oreos.

Chan stashed the keys in his pocket and was out the door with a wave, always quick to follow instructions. I was the only one who had a hard time accepting orders.

Mendez stepped around the kitchen island and came to where I leaned against the counter. He placed one hand on either side of me so my back was flush against the counter and he was directly in front of me. Against my will, my pulse picked up and I felt my cheeks go hot.

"The last time I let you out of my sight, you listened to an enemy operative and tried running away. And you still think I'd let you stay here alone?"

"I don't know," I said, voice only slightly breathy. "You're the one who brought in another person. Maybe you're trying to tell me I should get used to space."

His low growl cut me off as he pushed me against the counter and silenced my mouth with his. Instinctively, my arms wrapped around his waist and pulled him even closer. After a minute he broke off the kiss and I immediately was filled with disappointment—until I realized he had a different target in mind, and he began kissing my neck instead. His lips worked their way along my collarbone and my breath became ragged.

"Bringing in Chan wasn't my idea," he said, lips still at my throat. "The director thought I needed more backup." He scattered more kisses along my neck. "Or a babysitter. I'm not sure which."

Knowing this lifted a burden I didn't even know I'd been carrying. Mendez hadn't been the one to call in a buffer; not only that, he wanted to make sure I knew it hadn't been his idea. Relief washed over me and I let out a breath, which only made Mendez double his efforts. His lips traced along my jaw and the tips of my fingers dug into his waist.

Then he was kissing me again, pulling my bottom lip in between his and coaxing my mouth open. I eagerly reciprocated, moving one hand to his hair where I could feel the strands between my fingertips. The other hand I placed on his chest, the strong beat of his heart fast beneath my palm. My own mimicked the pace, thrumming like a hummingbird.

Last night hadn't been my imagination, then. Mendez was kissing me, and not because he was ordered to reciprocate if I fell victim to his honeypot ways or because I'd been so pathetic he pitied me. Because he was kissing me now, when I wasn't emotional, and when Chan couldn't see. If he'd been under orders, kissing in front of Chan would practically have been expected.

Still. Some doubt crept in despite my effort to shove it away. "Last night," I said, breaking away slightly, "I was the one who kissed you. I don't want you to feel obligated because—"

He covered my mouth with his, stalling me from saying anything else and telling me with his actions rather than his words just what he thought of my comment. For a moment, all I could focus on was the way his lips moved against mine and the feel of his chest under my hand. It wasn't fair, that this man could be so good at everything he did. How was I supposed to stay objective when my skin felt electrified by his touch?

He kissed the sensitive spot beneath my ear, and I bit my lip to keep from letting out any embarrassing sounds. My fingers curled into his hair and Mendez's hands traced the hem of my shirt, his thumbs touching my skin and making me light-headed.

"You still don't do commitment?" I had to say it before I lost all ability to think straight.

Ah, who was I kidding? My time for thinking had come and gone.

Mendez nuzzled my neck, then kissed a line along my jaw to my lips.

"I've changed my mind." His voice was low and gravelly, and

I shivered in response. Then he kissed me again and I was a goner.

He grasped my waist and lifted me onto the counter, bringing my height closer to his. I wrapped my legs around him and pulled him closer again, never breaking our contact. I was heady with it, this intoxicating feeling of need and want. Of realizing Mendez wanted me too. Knowing my feelings weren't as one-sided as I'd once believed. Because he felt it too. Or he wouldn't be crashing into me with the same kind of desperation that raced through every nerve ending I had.

The clock was ticking on some poor unknowing man's life, but the only place I felt its crunch was here and now, knowing we didn't have long before Chan expected us down at the van. Of course, Chan had to have his suspicions, but seeing them confirmed like this would be another matter entirely. Mendez's hands roamed up the back of my shirt and I arched my back to bring myself even closer.

I'd been fooling myself when I'd thought I could remain impartial. It was laughable really, because there was no way I could ignore the pull of this man in front of me. The way he was kissing me was practically criminal, and I didn't ever want it to stop. There were so many bigger things to take my attention right then, but all I could focus on was how his fingers felt against the skin of my back and the way his teeth lightly nibbled my lower lip.

His kisses grew less hungry and urgent, but they were still slow and deep. I felt it from my toes to my fingertips. We fell into a languid rhythm, as if we had all the time in the world, when I knew for a fact we did not. Mendez held me like I was something precious, one hand cradling my face while the other rested on my lower back. My head was fuzzy from all the dopamine, but somehow, it still wasn't enough. I wasn't sure if it ever would be. Now that I knew what it was like to kiss Mendez—to *really* kiss Mendez—I knew I'd never be able to pretend indifference again.

And it seemed like he felt the same way. Because as he drew back to kiss my temple, his breath caught and his lips almost trembled when they touched my skin. I knew it was too much to hope for, but the need for him to reciprocate my feelings burned through me all the same. Because I couldn't be this far gone if he wasn't simultaneously affected. I'd probably do anything for this man, whether he asked me to or not, and if he didn't feel at least a fraction of what I felt? I wasn't sure I'd be able to bear that.

Was I being dramatic? Yes. Was I being honest? Also yes.

"I hate to say it," Mendez said, breathing heavily, "but we should probably stop." He brushed a light kiss on my forehead, and I melted even more. "I wouldn't want Chan to get tired of waiting and come up to see what's taking so long."

"I don't know." I pretended to consider. "That'd be one way to make him run for the hills."

Mendez laughed and placed his hands on my hips, pulling me off the counter so I stood in front of him once again. I didn't really want to leave the apartment, but if I got to be with Mendez, I guess I couldn't complain. Especially when he wove his fingers between mine and looked at me the way he was looking at me now.

"Let's go." Mendez kissed me lightly on the lips, then tugged me forward with our hands clasped. "We have a lot to do if we're going to save the world in three days."

Chapter Twenty

. . . .

I'D SAY THIS MUCH FOR IT—PRAGUE HAD SOME REALLY good food. Especially this . . . what had Chan called it again? *Palačinky?* He'd gotten it from a street vendor while we were out and about buying supplies, and I'd almost had an orgasm the moment it touched my lips. Yes, Prague had bad guys, but feed me, throw in some kissing with Mendez, and it was enough to make me forget all that.

Now I was in my happy place, sitting in front of a computer, analyzing code in the van while Mendez and Chan met with the hacker they hoped to recruit to their cause. They were in some industrial complex, and I was parked out front, with enough passersby that I felt safe alone, though it helped knowing they were close.

Plus, Mendez had given me a panic button, and he was literally only seconds away. We'd already done all the shopping, including buying all the items I thought the hacker would need once he got on-site at Holt's headquarters. I was surrounded by adapters, dongles, and enough cords to knit an exceptionally long scarf should the desire hit me. All we had left to do was get the hacker on our side and find out where Holt's headquarters were.

Which meant it was my turn.

My IP scanner told me there were five CCTV cameras attached to the warehouse that Holt once used in his operations. I input the most common ports and configured my scanner, tapping my fingers on the keyboard while I waited for the fetchers to display the manufacturer information. There it was. Hikvision. I googled the default password and crossed my fingers, but no dice. Whoever had installed these cameras had been smart enough to change the default passwords. Well, I hadn't thought this would be easy. I'd have to use the exploit tool and hope they hadn't updated their software recently. I'd get the IP camera internal user list and set a new password that way. But I could only do that if their cameras were a specific model, and first I needed to know what models these ones were.

I typed the string of code and hit enter, briefly wondering how things were going with Mendez and Chan. Would Chan's hacker agree to help? Did I want that? If my unsettled stomach was any sign, I still wasn't sure. I took another bite of my *palačinky* to soothe it, but even crepes with chocolate and cream couldn't make my worries disappear. It did make me think of Mendez though. And kissing. And kissing Mendez.

He'd forever ruined chocolate for me, and I wasn't even mad.

Then something else made my stomach swoop, but not in a good way. The code populated on my screen, and the model numbers were too new for the security breach to work. I scrunched my forehead, trying to think of any other possible solution, but the truth of it was staring me in the face. I didn't think I could hack this.

I tried the hack I knew anyway, typing the camera IP port

followed by a string of commands, inputting the newer model number at the end. It didn't take a screenshot like it was supposed to, or grant me access to the video logs, or display anything in my web browser at all besides my own code. The cursor blinked slowly at me, my brain struggling to catch up with this new reality. It wasn't working.

"No." I spoke out loud, even though I was the only one in the van. I started to sweat along my hairline and my fingers shook on the keyboard. I wiped them on my pants and clasped them together, trying to still them. My brain buzzed, feeling a pressure I didn't normally have with any of my corporate jobs. *Lives* were at stake here. That was brand-new territory for me, and I wasn't about to go down without a fight.

I placed my hands back on the keyboard and forced my stomach bile down. *Think, Dove.* There had to be another way. I chewed on my lower lip. A possibility hovered at the corner of my brain, but it wasn't one I wanted to acknowledge. Because if I failed in a brute force attack . . . that was it. There were no second chances. Zilch. Nada.

I'd be locked out forever and I wouldn't get another stab at it. Some newer models had protocols against attacks like that, and if they noticed too many failed password attempts, they shut everything down. Normally I could wait out something like that. But now? Not so much. Time wasn't exactly on our side.

I didn't know what else to do. My fingers tapped on the edge of the laptop as I tried to think of other options.

But there weren't any.

Slowly, I booted up the software. Then I started it running and began the brute force attack, holding my breath the whole time. Either it would work or it wouldn't, and there wasn't anything else I could do now besides wait.

The code ran across my screen, lighting up the interior of the van where I sat in the back. My *palačinky* sat forgotten on the seat beside me. The numbers paused in their scrolling and my breath hitched. They resumed and I choked back a strangled laugh. Then they stopped moving altogether and I stopped breathing.

I had failed. Really, truly. Failed.

It was a foreign concept to me. Normally I could hack anything. I'd even been able to access restricted files on the CIA database, for crying out loud. Sure, I'd had a boost with Mendez's login, but it wasn't right that I'd been bested by a few CCTV cameras. Though, it made sense that Holt's security would be top-notch. And true, this wasn't my usual thing. I was used to computers, not cameras. Also true, if I'd had enough time, I could have researched something else to try once the system unlocked. But that still didn't help us now when I didn't have forty-eight hours to wait. That was the real rub. Besides, those were just excuses. I shouldn't have failed this miserably, and I shouldn't have needed more time in the first place.

I was trying to do the noble thing here. Didn't the universe know that?

I sucked in a shaky breath and placed my head between my knees. What was I supposed to do now? How was I going to tell Mendez and Chan what I'd done? Mendez had counted on me. A man's *life* was literally at stake, and I hadn't been able to do my part.

Even worse, Chan's hacker wouldn't be able to do it either, because my brute force attack would have shut down the systems to everyone, even Holt's internal administrators. If they were watching their systems, they'd also know someone had tried to access them. If nothing else, they'd know someone was trying something, so we'd lose the element of surprise.

I sat back up and stared dully out the window. I watched as people walked by, oblivious to the crisis happening only feet away from them. My eyes started to burn, and I pressed the palms of my hands into them, willing myself not to cry.

I'd messed up. So very badly.

Of course, that was when I heard Mendez and Chan come back, fumbling loudly with the door. I turned my back to it, hastily swiping under my eyes in case any tears had managed to escape and willing myself to regain some composure. I heard the side door open, and I sucked in a deep breath.

I turned around, expecting to see Mendez or Chan. But it wasn't either of them who stood framed in the doorway.

It was Madison.

Chapter Twenty-One

....

I'D ENVISIONED THIS MOMENT. WHAT I WOULD DO AND say to get my sister to come back with me when I came face-to-face with her. But now that she was in front of me, my mind was blank, and I'd forgotten how to do words.

So, I fell back on my manners.

"*Palačinky?*" I held out my half-eaten plate covered in chocolate and powdered sugar.

Madison stood backlit in the open frame of the van, her hand on the door like she might turn and run at any moment. But her eyes were fixed on me, unwavering in their focus. She tilted her head and one corner of her mouth quirked up in a grin like I'd just said the one thing that would make her pause.

"Um." She scanned the interior of the van, likely checking to make sure we were alone. "No thanks. Lactose intolerant, remember?" She grinned again. "Unless that's the CIA's plan to take me out?"

I saw the *palačinky* from her point of view, the oozing chocolate and cream, and placed it back on my lap. She nodded.

"Glad to see we haven't gotten to that point." She chuckled under her breath. "Yet."

With that, she climbed into the van and closed the door behind her, settling into the seat to my right.

"If I asked, would you come back with me?" I eyed the panic button, all steel and plastic, devoid of anything soft or giving. I pushed it under the seat, unused. "I think we can convince Mendez to hear you out."

Madison shook her head. "You know I can't do that. It doesn't matter what Mendez thinks. I'm not safe with the CIA. Not yet."

"Then you shouldn't be here." I looked around the van. "Mendez and Chan will be back any second."

Madison snorted. "They won't be back anytime soon." Her expression, combined with her fiery hair, made her look decidedly devious. I knew that look. I didn't like that look.

"What's that supposed to mean?" Laptop now forgotten, I placed it and my *palačinky* on the driver's seat in front of me so I could turn and give Madison my full attention.

"Forget about it," she said. She already had, obviously. She tossed the edge of her braid over one shoulder and casually checked the time on her watch, like she hadn't just caused me to go into cardiac arrest.

With a start I realized I was more scared now, in this instant, than I had been when Mendez told me he was supposed to kill her on sight. I could convince Mendez to change his course of action. But Madison? Well, it was a truth universally acknowledged that older sisters never listened to their younger sisters. About anything. And it seemed like *her* course of action was already in motion. Still, I had to try.

"Come on," Madison said. "We need to go. The less you know, the better."

"It's too late for that and you know it," I said. "Mendez already tried using that line on me back when I first got caught up in this mess. I deserve to know what your part in all this is and how Holt has his hooks in you. Now tell me what's going on." I narrowed my eyes at her. She didn't look like she was going to budge, so I tried another tactic. "Mendez keeps me in the loop, you know."

"Mendez is going to get you killed. You're not a CIA officer and you shouldn't be involved. We need to get you out of here."

Okay, so that attempt had failed, just like my hacking attempt earlier. The thought brought a pang with it. Desperation clawed its way up my throat. If I didn't fix my mess with the CCTV cameras and Madison pulled me out of here now, who would help Mendez? I needed to make Madison see the value I was adding or she'd have me out of here before I could say anything about it. I had no doubt she could force me out of the van. I'd seen her in a fitness class, and she'd quite literally kicked butt. My own skills, on the other hand, left a lot to be desired. The fact that I'd needed a nose job after one boxing class was exhibit A.

Madison was already scoping out the windows, one hand on the interior door handle, the other reaching for my wrist. I pulled back before she could make contact. If it came to physical force, I didn't stand a chance.

"Mendez needs me. If I go now, that will put him in danger."

She grunted, then grabbed my wrist anyway. Welp, I'd lasted a grand total of three seconds.

"I don't care about Mendez; I care about you." She pulled my arm, practically lifting me from my seat while I resisted.

"Well, I care about Mendez."

There must have been something in my voice because Madison stopped, finally turning to look at me.

She swore and let go of my arm. I sank back into my seat with a grateful thump.

"You do, don't you?" Her voice rose a full octave. "Dove, what were you thinking?" She released the door, sat back in her seat with a defeated sigh, and rubbed at her temples. This was the stance she'd adopted whenever we'd fought over my grades, or when she'd complained that I'd never taken anything seriously in life. Most recently, it was the pose she'd struck whenever we'd discussed Everett or my love life in general, so it looked like we were back to square one. The world might be ending, but here we were arguing over my relationship status. Some things never changed.

I blushed and looked anywhere but at my sister.

"Right," she muttered. "Probably wasn't much thinking involved. That's your problem."

"Hey," I objected. "You're the one who told me to move on from Everett. And it's not my fault I'm in this situation, you know."

This seemed to deflate her, and her face instantly became contrite. "I know." Her voice sounded haunted, and I knew with complete certainty I'd forgive her. No matter what her story ended up being.

"Look," Madison said. "I just want you to be safe, and right now, teaming up with the dynamic duo isn't doing you any favors."

"I don't know," I hedged. "Seems like better odds than throwing my lot in with an international arms dealer."

I looked pointedly at my sister and raised my eyebrows, daring her to explain herself. She still didn't take the bait. Instead, she leaned in close and lowered her voice. "That hacker they're trying to recruit? He's in Holt's pocket. He alerted Holt the minute he understood what Mendez was proposing, then he kept them talking long enough to get the full details of their plan. How do you think I even knew to come here?"

Ice poured down my spine as the full implications of what Madison was saying sank in.

All the supplies we'd bought, everything we'd planned—it was all going to fail. Not only that, but Holt knew we were coming, so future plans would fail too. There was literally nothing we could do now that wasn't bound to get us all killed.

I took in a shaky breath and tried unsuccessfully to slow down my racing heart. My shirt chafed at my neck, and I pulled at it, as if that somehow would make the air in the van less stale. Outside a car horn blared and I jumped. Madison, meanwhile, didn't even blink. If I needed a reminder that she was a veteran of this world and I was merely a visitor, this little trip confirmed it. All my worst fears were laid out before me, and Madison wasn't even concerned. She touched something at her ear.

"Don't kill them," she said.

If I thought I was scared before, it was nothing like the terror that was now coursing through my veins at her little command.

"Who are you talking to?" I gripped her chin and turned her face so I could see the ear that was partly covered by her braid, and sure enough, there was an earpiece. She hadn't come alone. I brought my shaking hand back to my mouth and retreated farther into my chair, but there wasn't anywhere for me to go. Even if I left the van, I knew Madison probably had it surrounded. How many of Holt's men were out there? How many encircled the van, and how many were going after Mendez and Chan?

Don't kill them, she'd said, which meant she fully believed that the people she was talking to *could*. She knew Mendez personally. Knew his strengths and training. And if she thought these men could overpower him and Chan together, then my odds were about as good as a corgi running a marathon. Actually, the corgi probably had better odds.

My muscles felt stiff from tensing for too long, and I forced myself to release my death grip on the seat belt clamp.

Madison placed a hand on my knee. "I know it might not seem like it, but I'm trying to keep you alive."

"And Mendez?"

She pursed her lips and I took a deep breath through my nose.

I swallowed, then asked the one question that was taking up all the space between us. "So, what happens next?"

Madison was already in motion, checking pockets and typing something in a digital device that I didn't even recognize. It was sleek and rounded, like a phone but smaller and less boxy. I glanced at it curiously, because it was rare for me to find an electronic device that was unfamiliar. But it made sense for Holt to use a closed-circuit communicator that wasn't manufactured by any of the leading developers. My curiosity only lasted for so long before the fear came spiking back.

"I'm going to take you with me and explain how your *involvement*"—her mouth twisted on the word—"with Mendez was my fault and not your doing. Then you're going to take the first flight back to DC and forget any of this ever happened."

I would have laughed at her, if her expression hadn't made it clear that she was dead serious.

I placed a hand gently on her arm. "If I pretend like none of this ever happened, an innocent man is going to die."

She didn't even flinch.

"His life is important." She nodded. "It's true. But given the choice, I'd choose you every time."

I looked her in the eyes. "But it's not just a choice between him or me. There are national ramifications here that will last decades into the future if Holt manages to replace the COO with one of his yes-men. So it's a choice between me and countless other people's lives. It's literally a matter of our country's security."

Mendez had said Holt was trying to take over the CIA. Madison didn't refute it.

There was something in her expression that only I could read. It was the way her forehead scrunched ever so slightly without crinkling around her eyes. It probably wouldn't have set off a polygraph test, but I'd spent years with her and knew my sister's tells. She was the one who'd taught me poker. I'd always known there was something about her situation that wasn't as black-and-white as the CIA wanted me to believe, and now it was written clearly on her face, just like when she tried bluffing in a game of cards.

"Listen," I continued, "I don't know everything that you've gotten yourself into, or why you're working for Holt now. I'm hoping that when this is all over you can explain everything and we can laugh about that time you worked for an international arms dealer." I shook my head. "But I know there's more to the story because I know you, and you wouldn't just turn your back on the CIA. And you know if the COO dies, it's a domino effect. He's the chief operating officer of the Central Intelligence Agency, and if Holt takes him out, he's one step closer to gaining control of the CIA. And if he gains control of the CIA, that's a whole world at his fingertips, just ripe for the taking. Tell me I'm wrong."

I didn't break eye contact, but Madison didn't answer me. Silence enveloped the van, like we were underwater except for the muted sounds of the cars and pedestrians around us. Eventually she looked away and placed her communicator back in her pocket.

"Mendez can't stop this," Madison said softly. "Not alone. If the CIA had sent an entire task force, or—"

"He can't stop it if you keep getting in his way," I interrupted. "But if you help, or—I don't know—if you trust him—" I paused. "If you trust *me* . . ." My voice broke, and I could barely bring myself to look at my sister. To my surprise, she actually looked like she might cry. My big sister. The one who literally battled bad guys and took her coffee blacker than night. The one who laughed whenever she got a new tattoo because she said it tickled.

"Let me help you." My hand was still on her arm, and she gently placed hers on top of mine. I'd made the offer without even being sure how I could keep it, but I desperately wanted to. I wanted to be that person my sister could depend on. The person who could get her out of a bad situation and who she could call even when it was three a.m. and bad life choices had been made. Because that was who she was to me, and she deserved someone like that too.

Her lower lip wobbled a little when she spoke. "If you stay, I can't promise your safety."

"I know."

She shook her head. "You don't understand. I. Can't. Keep. You. Safe." Her face crumpled. "You're all I have left, Dove."

I wasn't sure how I did it, but I smiled, and then I leaned over to kiss her on the cheek, all without even a hitch in my breath.

"It's going to be okay," I said. I didn't know how it was possible, not with everything falling apart. But Madison needed me to be the strong one right now. She'd done it so often for me in the past that I took up the mantle without even knowing how it happened.

"I'm the flint and you're the steel," I said. "Remember?"

Her smile was hesitant, just a slight upturn at the corners before it disappeared again.

But it was enough for now.

She sucked in a breath and all her composure was back again, like a rubber band that had snapped back into place. "You're sure?" She raised an eyebrow. "About Mendez?"

I nodded.

She raised her hand to her earpiece again. "Time to go," she said. But not to me. "Leave them."

A lump formed in my throat. This might be the last time I saw Madison. For all my bravado, I didn't know how Mendez, Chan, and I were going to stop Holt from assassinating the chief operating officer of the CIA. At least not without getting killed in the process. Madison seemed to be in deep, so I couldn't rely on her for help, and she was right that we needed more than three people to take on an international arms dealer.

I might not see her again, and here I was lying to her. Sister of the year award, right here. Our plan hadn't worked, Holt knew we were coming for him, I'd failed at hacking the CCTV cameras, and I was lying to my own sister about just how bad the situation was. My chin wobbled, but before Madison could see, I plastered a mask back on.

Madison leaned over and gave me a tight hug, the pockets of her jacket digging into me with all their sharp corners and jagged edges.

We didn't say "I love you," because that would be too much like saying goodbye. Our years in the foster system taught us that. Everyone reacted differently to trauma, and we now saved "I love yous" the way a hoarder collected newspaper clippings.

Instead, she just squeezed me fiercely, holding on a little longer than was strictly necessary, before tearing herself away and throwing herself at the door. She wrenched it open and disappeared around a corner, leaving me wondering if the entire encounter had all been a fever dream.

Until a minute later, when Mendez and Chan rushed to the van, bloodied and limping, arms poised like they were prepared for a full-scale attack, which—well—fair.

Mendez's face relaxed infinitesimally when he saw me, but his eyes immediately roved my body like he was searching for injuries. Of course, he wouldn't find any, which only made me feel an intense shame for what he'd obviously gone through. Blood dripped down the sleeve of his shirt where he held his left arm loosely to his chest. His shoulder was torn and bloodied, a horrible gash reaching across his chest.

Chan looked to have taken the worst beating. Half his face was swollen like he'd been attacked by bees. He physically had to pull his right leg into the van with his arms instead of stepping inside of his own accord, and when he slumped into the chair that Madison had been in only moments before, he clutched at his stomach and groaned like he was about to give birth.

I hovered over him uncertainly, my hands reaching out but not touching anything because I didn't want to hurt him any more than he already had been. Mendez closed the door and walked around to the driver's side of the van, moving my laptop and *palačinky* to the passenger seat so he could slide behind the wheel.

His eyes appraised me in the rearview mirror, taking in my lack of bruises. "Madison was here?" he asked, his gaze skipping to the panic button that I'd kicked beneath his seat and that now rested by the gas pedal.

I bit my lip but nodded.

"She leave any trackers?" Mendez turned the van on and pulled into the street, cutting off a group of people and causing a man to swear at him in Czech.

"I don't think so."

His mouth formed a tight line. "We'll trade vehicles just in case."

I already felt guilty about not being able to help, but this was the icing on the three-tiered cake. Because I'd been the one to let her in the van. I hadn't used the panic button, and now he and Chan had suffered the consequences. They'd literally paid the price with their blood. Now we had to trade vehicles when they were tired and injured. I rested my head against the window and closed my eyes so the blurred buildings wouldn't give me a headache. Well, a worse headache.

The CCTV cameras being blocked, the plan backfiring, and now Mendez and Chan being injured—it was all my fault. The reality of the situation began to sink in as we navigated the streets of Prague. It could have been car sickness, but I was pretty sure it was just good old-fashioned regret that made my stomach sour with each turn we took.

Chan moaned and Mendez stayed silent. We drove away, our spirits—and plan—completely broken.

Chapter Twenty-Two

· · · · · · · · · ·

TWO CAR CHANGES AND THREE HOURS LATER, MENDEZ pronounced us "clean," and we made it back to the apartment. We'd seen a medic and tried to procure new hearing aids for Chan since his were broken beyond repair. That recovery mission had been unsuccessful, so every three minutes Chan said "What?" really loudly and we had to repeat whatever we'd just said, which wasn't exactly helping anyone's temper. When I asked why the CIA didn't require him to keep backup hearing aids, he muttered something about how this was why he was assigned desk duty and how the CIA typically had rules against letting "people like him" work in the field. It sounded like a touchy subject, so I let the matter drop.

Mendez wore his left arm in a sling and paced the length of the living room. Chan wore a leg brace and had so much salve on his face that it reflected the lights of the apartment like a decked-out disco ball. Mendez kept muttering about how we were out of time if we wanted to come up with another plan. But all I could think about was the way Madison had hugged me and how, despite everything, I still didn't think she'd gone bad, even though she hadn't answered my questions. She had some kind of ulterior motive—if only I could figure out what it was.

"It's too bad we didn't have any trackers you could have put on Madison," Mendez said, coming to stand behind my chair. "Then we would know where Holt's base is."

I nodded in agreement, even though I knew any kind of tracker would have collected dust like the panic button had. Madison was my Achilles heel, and even if Mendez didn't call me out on it, he likely felt this truth in his bones, which was why he couldn't bring himself to chastise me for not using it. I still didn't know where we stood with each other after that. Mendez hadn't exactly been affectionate since returning to the apartment, but it wasn't like we'd had the proper moment either. Chan had been with us the entire time, like an annoying Regency-era chaperone, even though he couldn't always hear what we were saying.

I got up from the table and walked to the kitchen, getting myself a glass of water while I watched Mendez resume his pacing. Something was niggling at the corner of my brain, but I couldn't quite put my finger on it: a thought about how they'd originally intended to locate Holt's base by following the guy who was supposed to meet me at the tram depot.

If they could set up something like that again . . . which wouldn't work because Holt now knew I was here, and Madison would put a stop to anything like that. Even if she hadn't gone bad, she still had to act like she was on Holt's side so that he wouldn't get suspicious. Like how she'd gone after Mendez and Chan at the hacker's. She had her role to play, so whatever we figured out here at the apartment had to fit into that. She might not want me killed, but she couldn't shield me from everything. She could only do so much from the shadows, and she wouldn't let me impersonate her again. But there was something else—a puzzle piece that I knew had to fit if I turned it around enough times. Like a string of code that kept bouncing because one letter was out of sequence, even though the framework was all there on the page.

And suddenly, I knew what it was.

"The airport," I blurted, loud enough that even Chan heard that I'd spoken.

Both men turned to face me with matching expressions of confusion. I focused on Mendez.

"You said Holt killed a CIA team as soon as they landed at the airport." I walked closer and laid a hand on Mendez's arm before remembering Chan was there and hastily pulling it back. "And when we flew in, we took all kinds of precautions to make sure we weren't on any records that Holt could access, yes?"

Mendez nodded, but his eyebrows still dipped in confusion. I grew more animated, waving my hands as I explained.

"So, then you were going to follow the guy at the tram depot so he could lead you to Holt." I waited a beat for them to catch up with me, but neither appeared to see where I was going with this. Chan looked like he was trying to read my lips, but I was probably talking too fast for him to keep up. Mendez just looked like I was speaking a foreign language, and this wasn't one of the four he already spoke. I let out a breath in exasperation. "So couldn't you set up some kind of fake flight that would intentionally alert Holt, then follow his men from the airport to Holt's base of operations?"

Mendez was moving before I finished my explanation, striding to the table and opening the laptop, his fingers from one hand flying across the keyboard.

Judging by the way he tilted his head, Chan hadn't caught

our entire conversation, or even half of it, but he waited patiently while Mendez worked on the computer.

"We make it look like I requested backup yesterday." Mendez turned to me. "You can do that in the system, right?"

I nodded, but Mendez was still talking.

"And make it seem like they sent a team as soon as possible, then account nine hours for a private flight for the travel, and we could have a phantom flight touching down in as little as an hour from now." He tapped his fingers on the table and started muttering to himself. "Hmm, but does that give Holt enough time to send someone to the airport?" He turned back to me. "Better make the flight arrive in two hours, then make sure the air traffic tower gets the alert."

It was like my earlier misstep with the CCTV cameras was completely forgotten and Mendez had the utmost faith that I could do everything he was asking without a single hiccup. It was simultaneously gratifying and terrifying. My palms started to sweat as he pushed the laptop in my direction.

"There are two runways at Václav Havel." Mendez shoved back from the table and stood up. "If Chan's old team helps with the stakeout and we leave now, we'll have enough numbers to cover every exit and we can be in place in time."

Mendez clapped Chan on the shoulder and he glanced up.

"What?" Chan asked, looking embarrassed.

Mendez found a piece of paper and started writing everything down for Chan while I focused on the computer. Creating a fake private flight wasn't hard, and I had everything finished by the time Mendez had brought Chan up to speed.

"What are you going to do once you've located Holt's base?" I asked. Mendez was packing equipment into a bag one-handed since his other was still strapped to his chest. He didn't give many outward signs of discomfort, but I caught him rubbing his shoulder a few times when he thought I wasn't looking.

Mendez's eyes cut to Chan, whose leg was propped up on a chair while he worked on the computer. Mendez lowered his voice. "Chan will stay here at the apartment. With his injured leg he won't be able to move quickly if Holt's men come in hot. And without his hearing aids he won't be able to help from the outside either."

"That didn't answer my question," I said, crossing my arms. I didn't look away even when Mendez did, staring up at the ceiling like he was trying to figure out what lie would be the most believable. Eventually his shoulders sagged, he winced, and he sighed.

"Then I'm going to break into Holt's base. Tonight. Before Holt thinks I could easily recover from what happened this afternoon. The plan hasn't changed just because Holt knows about it. He certainly won't think we'll break in now that we've lost the element of surprise. I might not be able to get all the files from the database to take down his operation, but I can at least find the files I need to prove Holt is planning to assassinate the chief operating officer of the CIA. So after we find his headquarters, I'll make my way there. Hopefully with Chan's team if I can convince them to go against their commanding officer's orders, but if not, I'll go alone."

I was so stunned that for a moment I couldn't find the words.

"Alone?" I finally whispered, careful not to draw Chan's attention. I shook my head at Mendez. "You might think you're Superman, but you're not. Do you have a death wish?"

We both looked at Chan to make sure we weren't speaking too loudly. His dark brows were furrowed as he read something on the laptop. He was communicating with his team there, coordinating who would handle which vantage point and when they'd need to check in with various coded phrases. Knowing how many people Holt had killed at that very airport, Chan was taking the operation very seriously and had barely glanced up since he'd been tasked with the assignment.

Mendez still hadn't answered me, so I pressed him further. "You're injured," I pointed out, motioning to his arm sling. "And what happened to the whole"—I used air quotes to emphasize my point—"'if you don't get all the data to incriminate Holt now, you won't actually be able to stop Holt's whole organization' thing?"

Mendez's mouth was a thin line, but he didn't argue with me. Eventually he shrugged, eyes pained, then quickly smoothed his face like he hoped I wouldn't notice.

"After I break in and get the information about the assassination attempt," he said, "Holt will likely move his operations, which will set us back several months, if not more. But I don't see an alternative if we're to save the COO. I need to gather enough evidence to force the CIA to see the threat as credible, which doesn't leave us a lot of time to also take down Holt's entire operation."

I knew I had to tread lightly here, and a pit was forming in my stomach at the mere thought of what I was about to propose. I swallowed and laid a shaky hand on Mendez's good arm.

"You could take me with you," I said, trying to keep my voice light so it wouldn't betray the absolute terror that was now shooting through my veins like a semitruck skidding on black ice. My feet were rooted to the spot, and I pressed my elbows against my sides so Mendez wouldn't be able to see them shake. Of course, I forgot that my hand was still on his arm, so he could feel it through my fingertips anyway.

If anything, Mendez's lips compressed even further until they practically disappeared. "You're not coming with me."

When I first met Mendez, I'd thought he was monosyllabic... well, when he wasn't pretending to be a journalist, because he'd actually been flirty then. But afterward, he'd been so gruff and tense while he was putting together the pieces of this case that I'd barely gotten him to string two words together in a sentence.

I'd thought we'd grown past that. Grown together.

I guess not.

Because now, his face was tight and his voice was clipped, leaving no room for discussion. He took a step back so my hand fell from his arm, awkwardly swinging in the distance between us.

"But I can get the data from the closed system," I said, voice small.

At least, I hoped I could. I kept talking so I didn't have to focus on any of my insecurities, because the truth of the matter was, I was only about 50 percent confident I could get the encrypted data.

"Look," I said. "I don't want to put myself in danger, but I don't want you to be in danger either, and—"

"Is that why you're doing this?" he interrupted. "Because you're worried about me?" He ran a hand through his hair and shook his head. I hated to admit it, but even when he was frustrated, he was gorgeous. It was all kinds of unfair.

I snuck a glance in Chan's direction to make sure his attention was directed at the computer. His skin practically glowed from all the ointment, but his gaze was still firmly on his screen, thank goodness.

"Dove, you're a civilian. It's not your responsibility—"

"Maybe it's not, but are you saying you aren't my responsibility either?"

He only waited a beat, but when he answered, his voice was strangely flat. "No. I'm not your responsibility." He took in a steady breath, his expression never wavering. While my hands fluttered unsure at my sides, Mendez was as solid and determined as ever. Like the Lincoln Memorial statue that silently judged me every time my friends wanted to meet for lunch by the National Mall, Mendez was cold, imposing, and resolute. He exhaled, his eyebrows furrowing ever so slightly.

He studied my face and his mouth turned down at the edges. When he spoke again, his words were measured, his voice detached and low.

"I'm not your responsibility because we aren't anything to each other," he said.

My heart hammered in its rib cage. What was he saying? The tips of my fingers went numb, and I suddenly couldn't remember how to breathe.

He shook his head. "Dove, I told you before that I was acting on orders when I was instructed to get close to you. You should've been paying more attention then." Mendez didn't break eye contact, though I desperately wanted to look away. He took a step closer and lowered his voice. "My orders never changed. And if you came with me tonight out of some sense of relationship or feelings, you'd only be putting yourself in danger for something that *isn't real*."

The entire time he'd spoken, my thoughts had spun faster and faster until I was almost dizzy simply from trying to understand what was happening. Something inside me had broken, and I couldn't find the pathways that would make my brain function the way it was supposed to anymore. I felt downright stupid for missing all the signs.

Because the worst part about all of it was, *I wasn't even sur-*

prised. Of *course* Mendez didn't want me. He didn't have feelings for me. He was only using me. Because why would someone like him want someone like me?

It had felt like sunlight, whenever he touched me or kissed me. But sunlight only lasted for so long before being swallowed up by the night. The familiar gut punch of rejection hit me hard, just like it did whenever a foster family said they couldn't be our forever home after all. Of course, they'd all acted sorry. But no one ever wanted me in the end. I'd gotten so used to the feeling, I'd preemptively acted out at each new home, anticipating that they'd call our social worker and say they couldn't take it anymore. Couldn't handle *me* anymore. Because if I did it on purpose, then *I* was in control. I was the one rejecting them. *I'd* made the choice to be alone. I'd controlled the situation the best way my teenage self had known how.

But I wasn't in control now. As much as I hated to admit it, I'd let those protective walls down with Mendez. I'd finally allowed someone in, and once again I was the one paying the price.

Sure, it had hurt when past boyfriends had broken up with me. But none of them had ever made me feel safe the way Mendez did. They had never *seen* me the way he saw me—like he knew my faults but didn't care. Mendez dealt with the real scary monsters of the world; how could he care about mine?

Except . . . apparently, I'd been wrong. About so many things.

I stumbled back and tried to keep my chin from trembling. Mendez reached out to steady me, placing a hand on my arm as he softened his tone.

"So you can stay here—"

"No." My voice was firm. I broke contact, flinging my arm away from his as I kept a foot of distance between us. His gaze darted to Chan, but his face was turned toward his screen as if Mendez and I weren't combusting before his eyes.

"Dove, stay here," Mendez repeated.

I shook my head.

Maybe Mendez didn't want me, but Madison needed me. I'd told her she could trust me, and even if it felt like my heart was shattering into jagged shards at Mendez's feet, I was going to get all the data from Holt's database so she could be free of him once and for all. Because if there was one thing I'd learned from tonight, it was that my sister was the only person on the face of this earth who wanted me in her life, and I was going to fight for that with every ounce of strength I had.

"Dove."

I couldn't interpret Mendez's voice and I wasn't about to look at his face. Not when he said my name like that, all soft and caressing. The way he was probably trained to say it.

I still didn't know what to say, so I watched Chan instead, his back hunched over the computer as he worked out the details of the airport surveillance with his team. He shifted in his chair and winced as the movement jostled the leg that was in the brace. He'd already given so much. Mendez was willing to risk his life. If there was something I could do to help, even if it put me in danger, how could I not do it?

I took a deep breath and hoped my voice wouldn't shake. "I'm coming with you because it's the right thing to do, and I won't desert Madison now. I don't care if you only got close to me because of orders."

The lie burned on my tongue, twisting my stomach and making my insides wither and decay. Too bad acting confident on the outside didn't stop the roiling emotions going on inside me.

"Dove," Mendez repeated, voice still meltingly soft and pleading.

"I don't want to talk about it," I said, swallowing hard.

His chest rose and fell. "Fine. We won't talk about it. But you're not coming with me. I won't allow it."

I scoffed and raised my eyebrows. "You won't *allow* it?"

For the first time since I met him, Mendez looked a bit uncertain. His mouth opened, but no words came out. Then he seemed to regain himself and he crossed his arms.

"I'm still the commanding case officer of this operation."

The pain was so intense I almost couldn't handle it, but I could channel it into anger. I put a finger to his chest.

"As you so kindly reminded me, *officer*, I'm a civilian." My finger pushed hard into his chest and Mendez stumbled back. "Which means I don't have to take orders from you. Do I also have to remind you that I can access all the airport CCTV cameras and communication devices you'll use with Chan's team? That means I can find out Holt's location one way or another. So, you either let me come with you or I follow on my own." I raised my eyebrows in a challenge. "Then you'd have an inexperienced civilian bumbling along, possibly alerting Holt's men to your whereabouts." I paused, breathing heavily and praying that the burning in my eyes wouldn't turn into tears, or it would ruin my whole speech.

I desperately needed a minute, or days and months, to process everything that Mendez had revealed tonight, but right now I needed to get through the next thirty seconds. After everything else that had happened over the last couple of weeks it seemed laughably absurd that the thing bringing me close to tears now was rejection by a man, but I'd been strong for so long, and I could feel myself crumbling as the weight of this last straw was added to my back. *Just focus on the next thirty seconds.*

A muscle in Mendez's jaw clenched and an expression I couldn't name crossed his features. I studied his eyes, hoping to puzzle out some kind of remorse or longing, but anything I saw quickly shifted back to blank. I deflated then, not even bothering to hide it, because that would take more energy than I had to give.

"Fine," Mendez said, voice clipped. "Grab your things, plus the supplies we bought today." He leaned in, his entire body tense and strung tight like a live wire. His breath was hot near my ear, and I desperately tried not to notice the way he felt next to me, wondering if this might be the last time he ever got this close. The thought was sharp and achingly painful, and I pushed it aside.

"You *never* leave my side. Got it?" The steel edge to his tone was harsher than anything he'd directed at me before, and I shivered under his gaze.

Eventually it became clear he expected an answer, so I nodded. Without another word, Mendez spun on his heel and left the room, not once looking back. The silence said more than his words did, echoing in the room while the entire conversation played on repeat in my mind.

I had won.

So why did it feel like I'd lost everything?

Chapter Twenty-Three

· · · · · · · · ·

I THOUGHT I KNEW AWKWARD. BUT THAT WAS BEFORE I was stuck inside a tactical control van with a man who'd admitted he'd only made out with me because he'd been ordered to. How pathetic did I have to be for someone to literally be *ordered* to kiss me? *Desperate, party of one, your table is ready.*

The only good thing about the evening was that it was dark outside, so Mendez couldn't easily see the red that stained my cheeks or the way my breath hitched whenever I remembered how he'd pushed me up against the kitchen counter. And oh, I remembered it.

Then again, Mendez did have night vision goggles. Maybe my shame was broadcast for all the world to see. Or at least all the agents. So, that was great.

We didn't say anything. Mendez wore an earpiece and mic, so anything we said would be heard by the four other operatives stationed across the airport tarmac. We sat without saying anything, the sound of each movement amplified in the silence.

Fine by me. I didn't want to talk anyway.

I'd always considered myself an intelligent person, but now I sat in an unmarked surveillance van and wondered how I could be so stupid. All the signs had been there. He'd even told me to my face that he'd been ordered to get close to me. Why hadn't I listened? The man was trained in deception, and I'd chosen to believe I was the exception to every rule. Stupid.

I tapped my fingers on the door handle and looked out across the two runways. Our van was sandwiched between four similar-looking airport vehicles. Most of the other operatives were on foot, though one had a motorcycle stashed somewhere. Two of them were disguised as airport personnel while the others were keeping out of sight.

A slight drizzle made patterns on the windshield, blurring the red lights of the airport control tower. We didn't turn on the van or use the wipers, instead taking advantage of the rainfall to better camouflage our presence.

Mendez still wore his left arm in a sling, driving here only with his right, which he now used to hold up the night vision goggles. Some past instinct made me want to smooth out the tense line of his shoulders, but I reminded myself that (1) now probably wasn't the best time, and (2) Mendez didn't want me.

I winced and loosened my hair from its bun, attempting to hide my face from prying eyes by draping my hair forward. I slouched in my seat and pulled one leg up, turning my head so Mendez could only see the back of it. But a tap on my shoulder made me turn back around.

"You hungry?"

It was the first thing Mendez had said to me since admitting his feelings weren't real. He held out a burrito that he'd grabbed from the back seat, taken earlier from the apartment.

I turned back to the window streaked with rain. "No."

He nudged me with the burrito again. "We don't know when we'll get another chance to eat. You should take it."

Maybe it was spite, or just the same stupidity that had caused me to overlook all the signs of Mendez's betrayal, but in that moment in time I would have rather stepped on a thousand LEGO bricks than eat a single bite of anything Mendez offered me.

I fixed him with a glare, and he had the audacity to smirk in response.

"Suit yourself," he said, placing it on the floor between us. He took a burrito for himself and painstakingly tried to unwrap it singlehandedly. I watched him struggle for a minute before giving an exaggerated sigh and swiping it from his hands to do the task myself. This only made him grin wider, so I shoved it back with more force than was strictly necessary once I'd unwrapped it halfway. But he didn't take it.

"Can you, uh"—he cleared his throat—"make sure the tinfoil is covered completely? So it doesn't reflect the lights of the airport towers?" At least this time he sounded chagrined, ducking his chin ever so slightly.

I glared, then made sure the fold went all the way, so only the white interior paper was showing. He took it, then slowly began eating. Without looking at me, he offered the night vision goggles, and I hated that he still had the nerve to be considerate when I was intent on hating him.

But I took the goggles anyway, bringing them up to my face and blinking as the world around me changed to green. According to Mendez they were thermal infrared as well, allowing them to detect the body heat of targets. Our hidden agents wore thermal protective suits, in case Holt's men had similar equipment, and our van was also protected, in addition to being soundproof.

If Mendez did bring up our relationship—or lack thereof—in conversation again, at least it'd only be the CIA who would be privy to my heartbreak. Yay me.

I shook my head and focused on looking for Holt's men. The fake flight was scheduled to arrive twenty minutes from now, and we'd still seen no sign of movement. If this didn't work, I was all out of ideas on how to find Holt's base of operations. The airport didn't keep video records longer than three months, and I had a sneaking suspicion that even if we were able to access older records, anything with footage of Holt's men would have been scrubbed almost immediately.

When Mendez finished eating, I passed the binoculars back and begrudgingly picked up the other burrito, giving Mendez one last glare in case he even thought about saying something. He didn't, because if there was one thing he was good at, it was knowing when a situation was life or death.

My burrito was almost gone when Mendez sat forward and breathed in sharply.

"What is it?" I whispered, momentarily forgetting no one could hear us outside the van.

The rain had picked up, along with wind that pushed against the doors and made the people outside lean forward like they were worried about a different kind of takeoff. One of the members of Chan's team was a woman, and she seemed to be having the hardest time, bracing her legs far apart for stability while holding up her arm to keep the rain from her eyes. In that moment I was glad to be in the van, even if it meant I was stuck with Mendez.

"A car." He gestured with his chin, pointing to the darkness beyond our rain-splattered windshield. With the lights from the airport, I could barely see as it pulled in.

In every respect it looked like a stereotypical vehicle an arms dealer might own. It was a black SUV with darkly tinted windows, but I didn't know enough about cars to identify the make or model. It drove slowly, keeping to the outer edges of the tarmac as it made its way forward. Because this was a private airport, cars were allowed on the premises, so it could be anyone. We had to be sure these were our guys.

The woman on our team stepped forward, talking with the driver when the car reached the "employees." I knew that was part of the plan. She'd seem the least threatening. The least likely to garner suspicion.

I leaned forward in my seat as if that'd help me read her lips, but the rain was too strong to make out more than her vague shape. Of course, I couldn't hear anything either because I didn't have an earpiece. Mendez motioned for me to move to the back of the van and my pulse skittered in response. I climbed over the seat, settling in front of an assortment of computer screens. Mendez followed, closing the divider between the driver's box and the back of the van, plunging us into total darkness.

"Umm," I said, awkwardness creeping over my skin like a sunburn. Being alone with Mendez was bad enough, but being alone with him in the dark? I didn't think my nerves could handle it.

Correction: I knew they couldn't.

Without a word, Mendez reached across me and pushed a button on a monitor, bringing the screen to life. Suddenly I could see a live feed from a camera somewhere on the female operative's body. Mendez clicked something else and then there was audio. It didn't help at all though, because they were speaking in Czech.

Through the screen, I watched as the operative leaned a casual arm at the top of the car window, chatting unconcernedly with the two men in the car.

"That's your cue." Mendez typed something on the keyboard, bringing up an additional window. Finally, he sat back, leaving space between us so I could breathe again. I hadn't even realized I'd been holding my breath, but at Mendez's small smile, I knew he'd caught it.

"Already?" I spun in my chair, giving Mendez my full attention for the first time since he'd admitted he'd been using me. The corners of his eyes softened, and I pretended not to be affected. Even that expression was a tool of his trade. The man used his smoldering eyes the way a substitute teacher relied on educational documentaries.

When they'd been discussing the plan and my part in it, Chan had been the one to go over everything with me because I'd refused to speak with Mendez. Now that I'd given him my attention, Mendez was obviously trying to appear unaffected. The slight relaxing of his eyes was the only outward sign I'd noticed, but the way he angled his body toward me told me he didn't like my cold shoulder any more than I liked his admission of guilt.

Mendez pointed at the screen, bringing himself close again. I stiffened and stared straight ahead.

"See her arm? That's where she planted the tracker on the car. These are definitely Holt's men."

I squinted at the screen, unconvinced. One of these days, I was going to have to learn Czech. My bet was that she'd given some verbal cue I'd missed, and Mendez wasn't saying anything so he'd appear smart.

I pulled the keyboard toward me and opened the airport systems, pausing when a thought hit me.

"Canceling the flight entirely like we'd planned might make them suspicious," I said, tapping my fingers on the edge of the desk. "But if I take advantage of the weather and redirect it—"

Mendez nodded. "Holt's men would still leave the airport, leading us to his base. Holt might have allies in the other location, but by the time he sends men there I would already be in and out of his operations here. Good plan."

I narrowed my eyes. "We," I said.

"What?" Mendez tilted his head like an innocent puppy, but from the slight clench of his jaw I had no doubt he knew exactly what I meant.

"*We*," I repeated. "You said *I*, but both of us are going into Holt's operations here."

Neither of us said anything for a full thirty seconds, the silence stretching uncomfortably between us in the dark van. I glanced at the screen and saw the men had rolled up their window against the rain. The female operative returned to her fake duties with the other "employee."

Eventually Mendez nodded, a terse dip of his head that didn't show acceptance so much as an unwillingness to put the operation at risk by delaying any longer. He nudged the keyboard toward me.

"Redirect the flight to Dresden, Germany."

I did so silently, Mendez watching over my shoulder the whole time. Not that I noticed or anything.

Before tonight, I'd had fantasies of Mendez handcuffing me. Now I wondered if I should be worried he'd actually do it, only not in a kinky way. More like a "stuff her in the back of a van and she'll be lucky to see the sun the next day" kind of way.

It was obvious the minute Holt's men received news of the diverted flight. They rolled down their window and waved down

our operative, who checked something on her phone and nodded to them, all sympathetic apologies and customer service
smiles.

They wasted no time, driving away from her without so
much as a goodbye.

"Shouldn't we follow them?" I asked.

"Not yet." Mendez minimized the airport window on the
screen, pulling up a map of the city instead. A small red dot
moved across the monitor, blinking as it made its way out of the
airport. Two blue dots from either side moved in the same direction, keeping a much greater distance between them than I
would have thought prudent.

"What if the tracker malfunctions because of the rain?" My
fingers hovered uncertainly over the keyboard, itching to do
something. I knew more than most how often technology could
fail, and we were *so close*.

Mendez placed his hand over mine to still its twitching. I
stiffened, my back going ramrod straight in my chair. For a guy
who knew fifty ways to kill someone, he'd forgotten the top way
to die—annoy a girl one too many times.

"Trust the plan." His voice was low and gravelly in the darkness of the van, reminding me of other moments we'd been
alone. He paused, choosing his words carefully. Then he sighed.
"People make mistakes when they get nervous."

What was that supposed to mean? Something caught in my
throat, and I stared straight ahead. I wouldn't read into his statement about mistakes. That's what he wanted, and I was not
about to give Mendez *anything* that he wanted ever again.

He pulled his hand away and I breathed again, not daring to
meet his eyes. Instead, I watched the dots on the screen, counting the seconds as the red one traveled farther and farther from

our location. The blue dots never closed the gap, and sometimes even widened it, going left or right when the target traveled in the opposite direction. Each time this happened I chewed on a nail, waiting for the fateful moment the red dot would glitch and disappear from our screen.

I expected it to move toward the outskirts of the city, toward fewer prying eyes and nosy neighbors, but it traveled farther toward the city center, past the historical churches and inward to business towers and skyscrapers. As usual, Mendez was closed off, giving nothing away except a slight tightening of his jaw to indicate whether this was to be expected. But I'd been around him long enough to know it wasn't.

When ten minutes had passed, Mendez opened the divider and slipped into the driver's seat, finally starting the van and our pursuit of the target. I stayed in the back, watching the dots and bouncing my knee under the table, relieved that our dot was finally on the move.

See Spot, I chanted to myself. *See Spot run from the law.*

Then the red dot stopped moving, and I stopped breathing.

Mendez brought a hand to his ear. "Copy," he said, pulling over and parking at the side of the road.

I moved to the front of the van, leaving the computers behind in favor of more up-to-date intelligence.

Mendez stared straight ahead.

"Well?" I asked impatiently.

A corner of his mouth twitched up and I hated that I still thought he was attractive. By now, my body should have gotten with the program, and I should have found him repulsive. Like people who find out their significant other puts the toilet paper roll on backward, or worse, doesn't use headphones while watching YouTube videos on public transport.

"The SUV is parked in an underground garage. Our operatives are casing the building now to make sure it's not a satellite. We'll wait here to give them time."

A satellite building. My heart sank at the thought. I'd never even considered that Holt might send men from a location that wasn't his main base of operations. But he did have his old warehouse, after all. How many other buildings did he have?

I hit my head on the headrest with a thunk.

"Relax," Mendez said, putting a hand on my thigh. "It's not likely a satellite. He has locations closer to the airport, I'm sure, and those would have been easier for him to send men from. The only reason we're this far away is because he sent people that he trusted. That typically implies an important location."

I stared daggers at his hand until Mendez removed it with a chuckle. The heat was still there though, burning through my clothes where his fingers had been. I stared out the window, refusing to let him win this game. If he weren't wearing an earpiece, I'd have let him have a piece of my mind. But instead, I guessed at his motives and replayed our argument from earlier and how he'd said, *My orders never changed.*

If he was really so set on following orders, did that mean he'd follow the command to kill Madison? His promise to me was obviously worth nothing.

Rain still beat down on the windows, keeping a steady rhythm despite the faltering beat of my heart.

When the silence became too much, I asked, "Can't we help them case the building? Why are we waiting here?"

I needed to do something. Something like warn my sister.

Mendez sighed. "Too many unfamiliar vehicles in the area could tip them off. We don't even know if this is the right place. Now isn't the time to rush."

I hated that he was right. Hated that he was handsome. Hated that he still made my breath catch simply by existing. If there was any justice in the world, Mendez would get a receding hairline and lose his six-pack for what he did to me.

Twenty minutes later Mendez straightened in his seat and I glanced over, instantly alert. He gestured for me to stay silent, holding a finger up while he listened to something on his earpiece. I held my breath while the officers relayed their information.

Mendez finally spoke. "Affirmative," he said, a gleam in his eye. He looked over at me, grinned and nodded.

We'd finally found Holt's base.

Chapter Twenty-Four

. . . .

I THOUGHT HE'D BE HAPPY AT THIS NEWS, BUT AS QUICKLY as he showed excitement, his face darkened, a storm clouding over his features.

"Understood," he said, voice grim.

I knew better than to ask what had happened. Asking meant getting answers, and lately I'd been learning firsthand that those weren't always in my favor.

I picked at my nails while I waited for Mendez to finish his conversation.

"Thank you," he said. Not to me. To the invisible person on the other end of the line.

Mendez pulled the earpiece out and threw it in the cup holder. Running his hand through his hair, he breathed slowly in, still facing the windshield. He placed his right hand on the steering wheel, the skin pulling taut across his knuckles as he flexed with tension. We were still parked on the side of the road, but without explaining anything, Mendez put the car in drive and eased back into traffic. I clicked my seat belt on and focused on the rain, but my stomach did gymnastics.

"Holt's there." Mendez practically spat the words. "Along with perhaps fifteen or so associates, which means it's definitely where he's primarily operating from."

I chewed on my lower lip while I debated how best to answer. I figured it was probably like a Band-Aid. Best to rip it off. I sucked in a breath.

"Then why do you sound like the chocolate chip in your cookie turned out to be a raisin?" I snuck a glance in his direction. Mendez chuckled.

At first, I glowed with pleasure that *I'd* made that happen. *I'd* made him smile when only moments before he'd looked like someone had force-fed him vinegar. But then everything came crashing back and I turned away, hating myself for falling so easily for his tricks. Again.

Mendez turned down a street lined with more close-set buildings and even closer cars. The traffic here was worse than back in DC, and I found myself hit with a sudden burst of homesickness. When this was all over, I was never going to leave my apartment again. Well, after those promised self-defense classes. But if Madison thought I was a homebody before, she hadn't seen anything yet. I wasn't going to date for a year. Better yet, I'd become a monk. Or a nun, rather. I'd seriously consider converting to Catholicism if it meant I could avoid the dating scene for a while. Or forever.

"Chan's team hasn't received leave to continue working our case. Their involvement ends here. Surveillance is one thing, but they're not willing to disobey direct orders because of Chan's or my say-so. If we go in, we go in without cover or backup. In CIA terms, we're naked." Mendez took the next turn a little sharply, and momentum brought my shoulder into the doorframe, but I didn't feel it. I was numb.

"So, we're . . . on our own?" I heard myself say it like I was outside my body.

Now I understood why he'd removed his earpiece. There was no point communicating with someone who wasn't there.

A muscle in Mendez's jaw twitched—the only outward indication he'd even heard me. His eyes remained on the slick road, ever focused on his target. I admired his unshaken determination, even if it made me feel like a chicken with its head chopped off by comparison.

The silence that fell upon the van was different now. Instead of being charged with anger and hurt, it was fueled by fear. Maybe not for his part—Mendez was likely quiet because he was planning and strategizing. But I was spiraling with what-ifs, my tongue frozen and immobile.

I'd known it might come to this, of course. But knowing and experiencing were two different beasts. Coming face-to-face with this fanged reality was taking me a bit to process, that was all.

"They didn't see any sign of Madison," he said. "So that's one less hurdle for us to get past. We don't have to fool her. Plus, I know you worry about her safety, and if it comes down to a shoot-out, you wouldn't want her there."

No, I would not. But mostly because I needed to keep Madison as far away from Mendez as possible.

Five minutes later, we pulled to a stop in front of a coffee shop, and I raised an eyebrow. "You need some caffeine?"

I guess I couldn't blame him. If we were going to take down fifteen baddies by ourselves it wouldn't hurt to have a little boost, but we might need something a touch stronger than coffee. That's all I was saying.

He nodded farther down the street. "The building with the glass and metal doors, about six up from here? That's the one."

It looked so innocent. Like a regular business sandwiched between a consulting firm and an accounting building. Not like the harbinger of doom that I knew it to be. Dramatic maybe, but what else do you call the seven-story base of an international weapons dealer intent on worldwide domination?

"Their front is manned by guards," Mendez said. "But the side door is only wired by an alarm, which I can disable. That's our in." He turned to face me, and in the dim light of the van his face looked somber. Lines creased his forehead and his eyes softened at the edges. He placed a hand on my knee.

"You don't have to go."

I wasn't going to fall for it this time. I shoved his hand from my leg and crossed my arms. "Stop." I glared, but so much fear was mixing with the anger that it probably wasn't coming out right. "Just stop it. I'm coming."

Mendez was silent for a moment. He closed his eyes and breathed, but when he opened them, he nodded once, face tight. "Fine. Get your things."

He grabbed his backpack from the back seat and was out his door without another word. I hurried to catch up, slinging mine over my shoulder and coming around the front of the van to stand by his side. The rain had stopped, but the wind hadn't, pushing my hair in every direction until I pulled it back in a hurried ponytail. Just what I needed. To walk into the devil's den looking like death warmed over.

Mendez barely waited for me to finish before striding off in the direction of the building. I supposed I should be glad he at least waited that long, and that he hadn't tied me up in the van.

But I wasn't sure if I should call it a victory either. I was walking toward danger and possibly death, after all.

When we were two buildings away, Mendez stopped abruptly and turned to face me. I'd been so focused on keeping up I didn't notice until I'd already barreled into him, my hand, like it had when we'd first met, landing in an intimate area. I stumbled back and shook my head, a low chuckle escaping despite what we were about to face.

I covered my mouth and tried not to think about how just a day ago, touching him there would have had very different consequences. I'd wanted to then—if we'd had more time in the kitchen, things might have progressed that far. I could still feel the heat of his hand on my back and his lips at my throat. My stomach swooped in response and my cheeks burned with the memory.

If I was going to die, I didn't want my last conversation with Mendez to be full of anger and bitterness. I wanted some of that tenderness back, even if he'd been faking.

It'd been real to me.

He'd only been doing a job. Sure, it hurt now, but I could pull my big-girl panties up and be polite. It wouldn't kill me to be nice, would it? Well. At least not literally.

Mendez looked at my hand that I'd snatched back, and one side of his mouth quirked up in a grin.

I laughed. I couldn't help it. "Just like old times?" I said.

He reached out his one working hand and gently pulled the hood of my sweatshirt up, his fingers tracing the skin of my cheek and leaving a trail of fire in their wake. It was probably the reason he'd stopped in the first place. To hide our identity from any cameras, but I couldn't help but read more into the gesture.

I wanted him to want to touch me—it was as simple as that. And as complicated.

"Not quite like old times." His voice was soft in the darkness.

Perhaps it was because the rain had only just stopped or because of the late hour, but we were all alone on a street in Prague, like we owned the night, just the two of us against the world. With a start, I realized that was exactly what we were up against, and despite everything, there wasn't anyone else I'd rather face the odds with.

He pulled his own hood up, and it was like we were in a cocoon against the wind. A wisp of hair had escaped my ponytail and Mendez brought his hand back up to tuck it behind my ear. I bit my lip, suddenly unsure how to react.

"Stay safe," he said, liquid brown eyes boring into mine. "Please. Don't do anything impulsive. Stay with me."

I nodded in response, the motion dragging the tips of his fingers against my skin. Goose bumps erupted on my arms, but I didn't step away.

I wanted to lean forward and kiss him. Wanted Mendez to wrap his arm around my waist and tug me against his body. I wanted it so fiercely I could feel the magnetism of the moment, throbbing in the air like a hypnotic pull. I could imagine the way it'd feel to have his lips move against mine, to taste him and forget about the dangers we were about to encounter. I could focus on his muscles under my hands and the heat of his skin against mine. I could forget it was all a lie because sometimes I needed to believe in magic. Like the fairy tale that someone like him could love someone like me.

Against my will, my lips parted and my skin flushed. It might have been my imagination, but I could have sworn Mendez's hand trembled slightly and his Adam's apple bobbed as he swallowed. I didn't breathe. But that didn't stop my heart from pounding faster in my chest. My fingers ached with the need to reach out and touch him, but I kept my hands at my sides, light-headed from the effort it took.

Any minute now, I was going to cave. I was going to close the distance between us and give in to the desire crowding out all other thoughts. The other thoughts were scary. But these ones were warm and pleasurable. They didn't require anything from me except to fulfill my own wants. It would be easy.

I thought I recognized the same hungry expression in Mendez, but then he blinked, nodded, and dropped his hand, instantly leaving my face feeling cold without his touch.

He was a good actor, but no one was that good. I had to mean more to him than he let on. Still, I stayed where I was, my feet planted to the ground like cement. I was not about to make a fool of myself again.

"Follow my movement and stick close to the wall," he said. "And we can avoid the cameras."

I nodded, a different emotion creeping over my skin and capturing my tongue.

Fear.

This was real.

Chapter Twenty-Five

. . . .

ONCE HE'D DISABLED THE ALARMS AND WE'D MADE IT through the doors, Mendez didn't waste any time.

"Servers will likely be this way," he said, heading down the hall past a water fountain that was foaming so much I wondered if it had rabies. I didn't answer because I'd been in enough business buildings to know he was probably right.

At least Madison wasn't here. It was the one silver lining to what was already a cloud-filled sky.

The building itself was seven stories, and we'd entered at the basement level. Knowing there were at least fifteen people stashed somewhere on those floors kept my heartbeat firmly in my throat.

My head swiveled from side to side like a GIF stuck on a loop. Then I noticed something. "No cameras? That's odd, right?"

Mendez snorted. "Typical of an illegal operation, actually. They'd want video surveillance on the exterior to warn them of authorities. But they wouldn't want video evidence of what happens inside."

I shuddered at the thought. I could imagine a lot of scary scenarios. Drug deals. Torture. Weapons trafficking. Money laundering. Along with a lot of other illegal activities I definitely didn't want to know about, especially if my sister was somehow involved with any of it.

Mendez pushed open a door that led to a stairwell, quickly darting his head in to make sure it was safe before motioning me inside. I felt less exposed here, but every moment that passed without us seeing another person made my hackles rise. That, combined with the clang our boots made against the metal stairs, left my nerves frayed beyond hope of recovery. The stairwell made me feel like a fish in a barrel, easily trapped and cornered. Well, if barrels had corners.

The stairway had one of those maps that let you know where to exit in case of a fire, which, in addition to helpfully pointing out YOU ARE HERE, also showed the fire department that the electrical room was on the fifth floor. We dutifully made our way there, and I tried to keep my burrito from coming up.

Activity seemed to bustle on the opposite side of this door, so we waited in the stairwell, barely daring to breathe. Mendez kept his one hand on the gun holstered at his belt. I kept out of the way in case he had to use it.

When the noise had died down some, he cracked the door open and listened. There were still more sounds than I would have liked, this floor clearly being more heavily populated than the previous ones we'd passed. Mendez let the door drift closed again and chewed on his lower lip. Eventually he nodded.

"We can't avoid people," he said. "Which means we have no choice but to face them." He squared his shoulders and swung his bag around so that he could root through the contents. He pulled out a black leather jacket and thrust it into my arms. A red wig came next, and it was like a weight slammed into my gut. I took a step back and gasped, despite trying my hardest to stay quiet.

That shade of red—a deep burgundy with cherry highlights—was instantly familiar. It helped that it was braided in a way that I'd only ever seen on my sister. I squeezed my eyes shut as memories came crashing to the surface. My sister in the bathroom at the tram depot. My sister surprising me in the van while Chan and Mendez met with the hacker who secretly worked for Holt. Both times her hair had been this shade of red, braided this way.

"We're out of options, Dove." Mendez kept his voice low and soothing, like one might when approaching a wild animal.

I held the wig with two fingers and felt Madison's disapproving glare from wherever she was, like a psychic sisterly bond. "But what if someone knows she's not supposed to be here," I said, "and they ask me why she—I mean I—came back?"

Yeah, I wasn't going to be able to pull this off. Sitting on a bench was one thing. This was walking into the lion's den with a steak around my neck.

"We'll have to chance it." He glanced down the stairwell. "Someone is going to see us, and I can't take out everyone on this floor. Not with one arm."

"Are you saying you could do it with two?" I asked under my breath, still holding the wig away from me like it was contagious.

If Holt didn't kill me, Madison was going to. I had a sneaking suspicion this wasn't what she meant when she gave permission for Mendez and me to handle things. She knew her line of work was dangerous, and she wouldn't take kindly to me stepping into her shoes. Literally. Mendez had just pulled shoes out of his bag and placed them on the floor, motioning for me to get started.

"Even the shoes?" I hissed, wondering when he'd bought all

these supplies. Probably while I'd been busy salivating over my *palačinky*. Just throw some sugar my way and I was blissfully ignorant of my surroundings.

"Madison wore shoes like this in the videos from the van," he replied. "And she's not the type to own multiple styles. It's the details that matter."

I whimpered, but then something else he said caught my attention. "Videos from the van?" I repeated slowly. "You . . . you had cameras there? You recorded our whole conversation?"

It made sense. Because how else would he know that Madison had dyed her hair? He hadn't seen her at the tram depot. He'd admitted as much. But now that I was remembering the conversation from the van . . . I groaned.

I'd told Madison I *cared* for Mendez. And now I had to find some ground to swallow me whole because Mendez had simply been acting under orders this whole time. My cheeks burned and I kicked my shoes off, shoving my feet into the new ones Mendez had laid out so that I could keep my face turned down.

Mendez put a hand on my arm, tilting his head in an attempt to see into my eyes.

"We'll talk about it later," he said, voice meltingly soft. It was the kind of tone that got me into trouble. Like putting on Madison's clothes and surrounding myself with enemy spies.

"No, we won't," I countered. We'd never speak of it again if I had anything to say about it.

Mendez sighed and released my arm so I could focus on donning the clothes. When it came time for the wig, Mendez made the final adjustments, the fingers of his right hand trailing along my cheekbones until I felt like I was on fire.

"What if someone tries to talk to me?" I asked, dying to change the subject.

Mendez shook his head. "Pretend you came back for something and don't have time to talk with anyone. Don't let anyone get a good look at you. People won't question me if they see I'm with you. Get in, get out."

My hands were clammy as I dragged on the leather jacket with all its pockets, pulling the tail of the braid out from the collar and placing it over my shoulder. My wig wasn't going to fool anyone. These people worked with her every day. They knew the slope of her nose and stride of her walk. They'd sniff me out in a heartbeat.

I felt ridiculous. Like a toddler wearing her mother's heels and calling herself Cinderella, only this was some next-level high-stakes cosplay game that could end up with me going home in a body bag.

Mendez stared steadily into my eyes. "You remember what room we're going to?"

I nodded. All I had to do was walk from point A to point B. Without getting caught. Or killed. Or, or, or . . . I swallowed hard as my brain came up with a thousand and one possible ways for this to all go wrong. Mendez put his hand on my shoulder, the weight of it heavy and solid.

"Don't think of the future. Think of this moment, right now."

How he knew I was spiraling I'd never know, but I tried to take his pep talk to heart, sucking in deep breaths like I was in some kind of Lamaze class instead of a dingy stairwell five thousand miles away from home. A light overhead flickered, and Mendez removed his hand, signaling my time for freaking out was coming to a close. He picked up his bag and slung it over his shoulder.

"You ready?"

I wasn't, but I nodded anyway.

Chapter Twenty-Six

· · · · · · · · · ·

MENDEZ PULLED OPEN THE DOOR WITH AUTHORITY AND I marched through it, hood down, shoulders back. Before, we'd been skulking around corners and speed walking down hallways. Now we moved like we belonged here, practically daring people to look in our direction.

I was exposed. My hands curled into fists at my sides, and I stared straight ahead, counting the doors as we strode down the hall. A handful of people went about their business, moving from one room to another. A few of them glanced in our direction before hastily returning their gazes to the floor. I refused to dwell on that. If they were scared of Madison, it was because she was acting around them. She wasn't acting around me.

One man called out to us in Czech and my stomach turned over with acid. Did Madison speak Czech? Why didn't I know that about my own sister? And what was I supposed to do now? Thankfully Mendez answered, placing his hand at the small of my back, pushing me to continue forward.

"*Není čas. Promiň,*" he said to the man with a curt tone that left no room for negotiation. I kept my gaze forward, my eyes now locked on the door in question.

Ten feet.

Five feet.

One.

Locked.

Mendez swore under his breath.

I panicked. Sure, maybe Mendez could pick the lock, but with me dressed as Madison, that wouldn't exactly make me look like I was really my sister, now would it? A few people still moved around the hallway, eyeing us with curiosity. Their gazes effectively prevented us from either picking the lock or moving on without explaining ourselves, which meant we were sitting ducks with a ticking clock.

The man who had called out earlier caught up to us, his long legs erasing the distance between us easily. This time he spoke in English, thankfully, so if he was going to kill us, at least I'd understand why. Life's little blessings.

"Your plans changed, eh?" he asked, his accent heavy as he crossed his arms.

I nodded, then faked a coughing fit, bringing my hand up to cover as much of my face as possible. Mendez angled his body in front of mine, answering for me.

"She received word about a possible security breach and came to investigate. But in her hurry forgot the keys."

Fingers crossed Madison would be high enough on the chain to actually *have* keys to the server room so Mendez's statement would make sense. But one thing at a time.

"And you are?" the man asked, turning his full attention to Mendez and eyeing him from head to toe. If it came to a fight,

I'd put my money on Mendez, even with his arm in a sling. But that was probably because I was biased. This man looked impressive in his own right, and he carried himself like he knew how to deliver a punch.

I really hoped it wouldn't come to that.

Especially now that another man was coming to join us in the hall. I didn't like those odds. But Mendez didn't seem ruffled. He casually widened his stance, putting his weight on his back leg while keeping his good arm free.

"That's on a need-to-know basis," I cut in, doing my best impression of Madison when she was impatient. "Do you have the keys or not? I'm in a hurry." I turned back to the door, so I was once again facing away from them. Still, I thought I'd detected a ghost of a smile on Mendez's face. It'd disappeared as quickly as it had come, but I'd seen it.

"Of course, Steel," the man replied in his heavy accent.

Hopefully he wasn't waiting for me to acknowledge him by name, because I didn't know it. Instead, I nodded as he reached around me and unlocked the server room, pushing open the door to reveal the towers of computers and cords we'd hoped were there. My shoulders sagged in relief for a moment before remembering two of Holt's men stood behind me. I straightened my spine.

"We'll take it from here," I said, not bothering to thank them. Madison wouldn't have. Not that she was rude, but—well, okay, sometimes my sister was rude. It was part of her . . . charm.

We stepped into the server room and Mendez closed the door after us. I could only hope the men would go about their business and forget they'd ever seen us. Although knowing my luck, we wouldn't be that fortunate.

"How long did you say it will take you to hack the system again?" Mendez asked, voice barely above a whisper.

"Four minutes." I'd already removed the flash drive from my pocket and stepped toward the towers of blinking lights.

"We might not have that long." Mendez paced the small opening between the computer towers.

So much was riding on me right now, the pressure was enough to make even a diamond crack. I'd never been one to get heart palpitations before, and frankly, I was insulted that my body had decided now was the time to start. I was only twenty-seven. My body wasn't supposed to fall apart until I was in my thirties, thank you very much.

My eyes scanned the towers until I found the port I was looking for and inserted the USB drive. Back at the safe house I'd preloaded it with automated programming to save as much time as possible. Now I was simply grateful for the forethought, because my brain was like shredded cheese. And not the gourmet kind served in fancy restaurants—no, mine was the prepackaged plastic stuff that barely even deserved the name.

It took two tries to pull my laptop from the bag because my hands were shaking so much, and my palms were slick with sweat. I sat cross-legged on the floor, hoping the familiar position would help, because I'd heard muscle memory was a thing. For all I knew, scientists were full of it, but I was willing to try if it'd get me out of this situation any faster.

I shook my fingers out and placed them on the keyboard, watching as it booted up. Code began to populate on my screen from the synced flash drive.

A knock sounded on the door.

Mendez and I exchanged a worried glance. It had only been

one minute. If that. I shook my head, telling him what he had to already know. I needed more time.

His eyes roved around the room, settling on a metal chair two feet away.

The knock came again. Someone tested the handle from the outside and found it locked, but I knew they had the key. It wasn't like these interior rooms had dead bolts, so Mendez and I were done for. I bent over my laptop while Mendez dragged the chair over to the door and positioned it under the handle, creating one more barrier to entry.

Sure, he could pop his head out and pretend nothing was wrong, but that wasn't going to fool anyone. Not if they were already checking on us after only a minute, and not if I was sitting on the floor with a computer on my lap.

Mendez stationed himself by the door, drawing his gun for the first time since entering the building. Goose bumps erupted along my arms, and I shuddered, my movements becoming jerky. Thankfully I didn't have to do much because I'd preprogrammed the drive, but staring at the screen and urging the numbers to scroll faster wasn't helping matters either.

The door handle shook, turning as someone inserted the key. My program had sniffed the traffic and grabbed the session token, already brute-forcing the password list to create a fake admin account. I now had a back door into the system, mirrored onto my virtual account.

Unlike when I did work for my paying customers, I didn't need to record my every move, which saved time. But unlike when I worked for my paying customers, I also had to *hide* my every move so Holt couldn't track where I was storing his data, which . . . well . . . took extra time. Really, it was a wash as far as time went. I wiped my brow and placed my shaking fingers back on the keyboard, trying to measure the elapsed time without Taylor Swift playing in my ear. The rattling doorknob just wasn't the same.

The door slammed into the chair, making me jump. Mendez motioned for me to move, away from the line of fire should there be any. I swallowed and scuttled out of the way, clutching my laptop like a life preserver.

A minute and a half down. It wasn't enough.

Shouting erupted on the other side of the door and something slammed into it, making the chair slide an inch. Gunfire exploded across the frame, popping out the handle so that it clattered to the floor a foot from where I huddled against a computer tower. There was more shouting, and this time, a voice I recognized rose above the others.

"Stop!" It was Madison. "You'll damage the servers."

Blood drained from my face as I pushed farther into the cords, hugging my laptop to my chest as if it somehow could stop a bullet.

Madison was *here*. She'd always been here. We'd received faulty intelligence and our plan had been bound to fail before we'd even started.

I couldn't save her, and now we were both in the middle of live gunfire with nowhere to run, nowhere to hide.

Worst of all, I had no idea what Mendez would do once he saw Madison.

Or what she'd do when she saw him.

Or me.

She shouted some more about damage to the servers, but the real damage had already been done. A hand from outside reached through the hole and shoved the chair farther into the room, effectively undoing the makeshift lock Mendez had set.

The door burst open, and Mendez hit the first person through it. The second one went down like the first, but the third was able to step inside and grapple with him, knocking the gun from his hands in the process.

It was only then that I realized I'd never truly seen Mendez in action before. Not live and in person. A little recording from a doorbell camera didn't do him justice. Sure, he was good at strategizing, and I'd had my suspicions that the CIA kept him around for his skills as a honeypot. But hand-to-hand combat? The man was like a Marvel superhero. He moved with skill and precision. No motion was wasted or unnecessary. One man barely made it into the room before being thrown back out, taking another two with him.

Madison once made me watch all the *Bourne* movies in one weekend. She said it was because Matt Damon was hot, but now that I knew she was a spy, I wondered whether she just liked the covert ops of it all. That was what Mendez reminded me of now. Matt Damon taking somebody out with only a rolled-up newspaper.

In one fluid motion Mendez whipped the sling from his shoulder and wrapped it around a stocky man's neck. A woman grasped his wounded arm, practically wrenching it from its socket, and Mendez grunted. Still, he acted like his shoulder was never hurt in the first place, moving it regardless of his injury.

He pivoted, using the man's weight that he held and flinging him against the woman, knocking her to the ground. In the same motion, he threw his elbow back and hit another assailant square in his face, blood squirting from the man's now broken nose.

I urged my computer to work faster, even though there was literally nothing more I could do. I couldn't type faster than the programming itself, and already it was hot on my lap, its processor overheating from doing too much at once. What had it been? Two minutes? Two and a half?

More people came through the door, probably five in all, and my mouth went dry. At least another seven still stood in the hall, all of them armed and muscled. Madison stood in the doorway, hands on her hips, eyes blazing.

When one man started in my direction, she shoved him toward Mendez. "Who do you think is the bigger threat?" she shouted. "Use your head. I can take care of her."

Okay, I loved my sister and all. I knew she was trying to protect me. But Mendez was only one man. He couldn't handle these numbers. I clambered to my feet and clenched my hands into fists, knowing it was only a matter of time before some of them made it to me, even if they were trying to clear a way for Madison to get to me first. There was zero possibility I'd be able to stand up to any of them—I had vivid flashbacks to that boxing class I'd taken with Madison and how I'd needed actual surgery after only one punch. But what else was I supposed to do? Sit here like a good little girl?

My heart hammered so rapidly it drowned out all common sense, and I backed into the computer tower behind me. My wig tangled in something, and I looked up.

The man who had let us into the room was watching me. His eyes followed mine to the flash drive, the edge of it blinking as it stuck out from the back of the computer tower and into my wig.

I flung my arms to the side and tried to make myself as tall as possible, but it was no use. Despite Madison's orders, the man was past her and Mendez in a blink, ducking low while Mendez grappled with two other assailants. He stood in front of me, and I braced myself for a blow, but his attention was on the drive.

He yanked it out, taking my wig with it, ripping it from my

head and leaving my hair in a tangled mess. The internal timer in my head stopped counting at only three minutes.

Three minutes.

It wasn't enough.

After creating a back door to get in, my program's first task was to find any files pertaining to the chief operating officer and his ordered assassination so we could turn that data on the flash drive over to the CIA. Then I'd manually transfer everything else from Holt's servers to the cloud so we could take down his entire operation. But my program hadn't even finished finding the files about the assassination.

At the very least, I was supposed to clear my sister's name, and I'd failed.

A shout from Madison brought my attention back to the fighting at the door. Mendez took a nasty crack to his jaw and his head snapped back, slamming into the wall. I stepped forward, but the man who'd let us into the room, and who'd taken the drive, grabbed my arm and twisted it behind my back, yanking me to my knees. A crack of pain reverberated up my body from where my knees hit the linoleum floor, making me cry out. I could barely see Mendez, outnumbered and tired, struggling to hold his head up as another man pummeled him in the stomach, before my arm was twisted even further, forcing me to turn away from the gut-wrenching sight.

Well, this day kept getting better and better.

My captor threw the flash drive onto the floor in front of me, crushing it under the heel of his boot. I flinched, more for Mendez than for the drive, but the way my arm was twisted made it impossible for me to turn and see how he fared. All I could focus on were the pieces of the drive, smashed on the floor before me like all our hopes and dreams.

I vaguely heard Madison telling her men to move Mendez, but there were too many competing noises for me to make sense of anything else.

A thud sounded behind me and a voice I recognized as Mendez's groaned. I cried out and thrashed against the arms that bound me, only succeeding at making my muscles burn and my shoulder feel like I was going to tear my arm from its socket. Still, I had to try. I threw my head back and felt my skull connect with the face of the man who held me. His nose crunched under the force of my attack.

He cursed, but he didn't release his hold. His fingers only dug in more, cutting off any circulation past my elbow. His other hand came around my chest and clasped my twisted bicep, trapping my once-free arm at my side and pulling me tight to his body.

I stopped struggling and sagged in defeat. Two feet away, my laptop sat undisturbed and forgotten, its cursor blinking in the dim light of the server room, waiting for someone to input a command now that the drive had been disconnected from the tower. The man dragged me to the computer, my shoulder screaming in protest with every jerky move. We reached it and the man bent to see the screen better, wrenching my arm until tears blurred my vision. He chuckled, low and hard, the edges of it sending spikes of panic down my spine.

"You have been naughty, haven't you?" His breath was hot on my ear in a way that made me sick to my stomach.

I only needed one more minute. If I could just get this man off me, I could at least get to the computer to—

He called out to someone in Czech and I heard footsteps approach from behind. The room was quiet now that Mendez had stopped fighting, with only the hushed movements of shuffled feet and muffled groans as Holt's men struggled to stand. I strained to hear any sign of Mendez—his voice, his cough, anything. But if he made a sound, it was indistinguishable from those around him.

A young, stocky white man entered my field of vision and crouched in front of the computer, his black hair falling in front of his eyes as he scanned the monitor.

A voice spoke up from behind me.

"Holt's hacker."

I should have been dismayed at this pronouncement, but instead, relief surged through my veins. Because even though his voice was hoarse and weak, I recognized it immediately as Mendez's. Mendez was still alive.

Who cared whether there was another hacker here as long as Mendez was still alive?

My captor misinterpreted the tears of relief coursing down my cheeks and laughed, yanking my arm again as if I'd forgotten who was in control of the situation. "Worried, little pet?" he whispered in my ear. "Soon, we will know all your secrets."

I wasn't. Worried, that is. I knew what I was doing enough to cover all my tracks. There was no way Holt's hacker could see what I'd been doing, no matter what methods he tried. The worst he could do was execute a kill command . . . which he did almost immediately after looking at the screen. Grunting, he closed the laptop lid with a nod and stood up, brushing his hands on his pants as he did so.

"She's done here," he said, pointing to me with his chin. I was shocked to discover he spoke with an American accent. He looked at the broken thumb drive on the ground and grinned. His smile was oily and condescending. "With the flash drive destroyed, the information is still safe on the servers. You kill her, the information dies with her."

Well, there was a pleasant thought. Thanks for that, random stranger. So much for "hackers before backers"—our unofficial code not to let money turn us against a fellow practitioner of our trade. I hoped his socks were always wet and whoever he ended up marrying suffered from back acne.

"You can leave now," Madison told him, sounding unnaturally cold.

Finally, the man holding me turned so I could get a better look at the room. More people had filed in, each holding a weapon, or in some cases two. Overkill, in my opinion, but maybe they were compensating for something.

Mendez lay facedown on the floor, the barrel of an automatic rifle pressed to his temple. His arms were twisted behind his back. Another man stood between his legs with an additional gun pointed between his shoulder blades, waiting for any sign of movement.

Madison had her arms crossed, surveying the chaos that had been created in only a few short minutes. It was clear from her stance and the way everyone orbited around her that she was the one in charge.

She wouldn't hurt me. But she was surrounded by a lot of people who would, and she couldn't protect me from all of them.

"Hey, Mads," I said, smiling weakly.

She didn't smile back. Her face was as cold as the day our dad had left and Child Protective Services showed up at our door. My heart sank.

There'd be no talking our way out of this.

"Take them to interrogation room B," she said, hardly glancing in my direction. I barely had time to register the fact that they had more than one interrogation room before her next words washed over me like ice, freezing the blood in my veins and causing black spots to appear at the edges of my vision.

She turned from the room, flipping her braid over one shoulder.

"I'll go get Holt."

Chapter Twenty-Seven

. . . .

MENDEZ AND I SAT BACK-TO-BACK IN HARD METAL chairs in a room that had way too many scary-looking objects I couldn't identify hanging from the walls. Our arms were bound behind us with zip ties that dug into my skin and cut off the blood circulation to my fingertips, while our ankles were fastened to the legs of the chairs. All in all, it was very intimidating. I had to give them ten points for authenticity.

Once we were secured, the men doing the tying left the room and I looked around in confusion before realizing the chairs themselves were literally cemented into the floor. No wonder they weren't worried about leaving us alone with our thoughts.

Despite knowing Madison was somewhere in the building, I didn't have high hopes she'd come to our rescue. Too many people were watching her every move. If we were to have any chance of escape, we'd have to figure it out ourselves. Now—before Holt got here.

Our chairs were close enough together that I felt it when Mendez's shoulders moved. My hands were tied behind my back, with Mendez's only an inch away in the same position, our chairs facing opposite walls. Our hands kept bumping into each other, but it wasn't like I could shift out of the way. At the same time, it wasn't like I wanted to. Right now, I needed all the comfort I could get, and putting all my hopes of escape on Mendez was the only thing keeping me from hyperventilating like a squeaky toy.

The room reminded me of my high school biology lab, with metal slab tables lined up around the exterior and two enormous sinks near the door. Plus a drain underneath our feet. That didn't bode well. I couldn't see any other exit. That didn't bode well either.

"You okay?" Mendez's voice was low, carrying only in the space between us.

My knees still hurt, but I wasn't about to mention it. Not when he'd taken a literal beating only minutes before.

"Yes," I said, surprised when my voice came out wispy and scared. It wasn't like I'd been in a situation like this before, but I had Mendez with me, so my odds of survival had to be at least fifty-fifty. Right? For some reason, my stomach didn't agree and was doing somersaults like it was competing in the Olympics.

"I . . ." Mendez cleared his throat. "I have a confession."

If there was anything in the world that would take my attention off the pliers and knives hanging on the walls, it was those four words. I turned my neck to try and see his expression but could only see the back of his head.

"I lied." He paused, swallowing. The silence was almost too much, here in this disturbing room. I wanted to shake Mendez and force the story out of him, but something told me he needed space to tell it on his own terms. So, I waited, barely daring to breathe as the circulation drained from my toes. If I made it out alive, I promised to never complain about high heels hurting my feet again.

"When I told you my orders were to get close to you," he said, voice wavering slightly. "I mean, what I said earlier tonight. That wasn't true. Those orders stopped the minute you agreed to the mission in Prague. I only said that because I didn't want you to come here tonight. I was worried . . ." he trailed off, and sighed. "I was worried about something like this. And I thought if you weren't trying to protect me, you might stay at the safe house."

"So you lied?" I was still trying to wrap my brain around it to be honest. Was he saying he *did* have feelings for me, then? Now was a great time to tell me. That meant he probably thought we were going to die, and this was his deathbed confession. Rather than make me feel better, his statement only made me sweat harder. Was there no hope, then?

My silence must have made Mendez nervous, because he hurried to fill it. "Remember when I told you I'd lost someone close to me?"

I nodded. With our chairs backed up against each other, I was sure he could feel the movement. He didn't speak for a minute and I wondered whether he'd reached his daily word limit. He'd always been a man of few words. But then he took in a shuddering breath.

"Three years ago, I was dating a civilian who didn't know I was an officer in the CIA. Her name was Gabriella. We'd only been together eight months, but . . ." He paused, and his next words came out in a rush. "I loved her, and things were going really well. Or so I thought."

A sinking feeling in my gut told me the story was about to take a turn.

"I couldn't tell Gabby about my job," Mendez said, shaking

his head. "And I guess all my unplanned trips and late-night calls made her think I was having an affair." He sighed. "One night she followed me."

Oh no. At least I'd knowingly gotten myself into this situation, but Gabby didn't have any idea what risk she'd been taking. The hairs rose on the backs of my arms as I waited for Mendez to continue speaking.

"I was undercover at a sex-trafficking sting when Gabby waltzed in, nearly blowing everything. The only thing I could think to do was to bring her in on it, promising to tell her everything once the night was over. I thought if I sent her away, they'd have tailed her for sure, and I couldn't guarantee her safety if I wasn't with her. But Gabby didn't fully understand the situation and things went sideways and—" Mendez's voice caught, the emotion behind his words forcing him to take a deep breath.

I didn't say anything in the silence. By now, I knew where the story was headed, and I was pretty sure there wasn't anything I could say that would make it better. I could feel every shaky breath Mendez took as his shoulders rose up and down.

"There's a reason the CIA doesn't want you to have relationships," he said finally. His voice was low and quiet, barely audible in the already still room. My fingers bumped into his, and this time, I didn't pull away.

"Gabby died from a bullet wound," Mendez said. "A bullet wound she never would have gotten if I'd made the right call and sent her home. I put my own feelings before the mission, and it cost Gabby her life."

"You couldn't have known what would happen—"

"You live and you learn." Mendez's voice was gruff with emotion. "Which was why I tried to keep you out of this. I thought that lying might make you stay at the safe house, where you'd be—you know—safe." He chuckled. One short, low laugh that was obviously directed more at himself than at me.

"Tobias—the deputy director—" Mendez said, picking up the story where he left off. He paused a lot though, like he was choosing his words carefully. "He took me off duty for months before I was fit to even be around people. He called me every day, just to check up on me." Mendez's voice took on a different tone when he talked about his superior, and it was clear that he respected the man—that he credited him with bringing him back from the dark.

"I haven't dated since then," he said. "Not seriously. I thought I'd made the right choice. Putting my career first and thinking of the good I was doing for my country."

He cleared his throat. "I never considered what I was giving up. Until I met you."

It probably—okay, definitely—wasn't the right time for it, but I could have sworn my heart grew three sizes, like the Grinch's on Christmas Day. Yes, I was surrounded by scary-looking torture devices and my hands were tied behind my back, but the man I'd fallen for had just confessed to . . . well, to lying to me. Admittedly, that also didn't sound good, but under the circumstances, it really was exactly what I needed to hear. Even if it did make me think our lives were in imminent danger.

I nudged my elbow into his, knocking our arms together lightly.

"If you were lying to me then, who's to say you're not lying to me now?" I asked in a teasing voice. "You know, just to make me feel better."

Mendez intertwined his fingers with mine . . . as much as was possible, considering we were both hog-tied and had limited movement.

"Think of it this way," he said. "If my orders were to get close to you, why would I try to hide our relationship from Chan?"

Our relationship.

I shouldn't have felt so warm and glowy if I was about to die.

"To be fair," I said, relishing the feeling of his fingers in mine, "I'm pretty sure Chan had his suspicions."

Mendez chuckled, the warm sound of it doing more to ease the tension in my shoulders than a really good massage, which I could also have used right about now. The list of things I needed to do when all this was over was a mile long, including taking self-defense classes and learning Mendez's first name. I repeated the list to myself, because if I kept a running tally, that meant I was going to make it out alive.

Dead women didn't need to-do lists.

Mendez squeezed my fingers, bringing a little feeling back into the tips where they'd gone numb. He'd done a good job distracting me from my surroundings, even if the fact of the matter was, things weren't looking good. I was grateful they hadn't killed us yet, but the delay was making me nervous. What was taking so long? Why leave us alone?

Maybe it was an intimidation thing. We were supposed to see all the shiny metal scalpels and leather straps and our mouths were supposed to go dry at the thought of them using the tools on us. Well, good job, bad guys. Mission accomplished.

"I'm sorry I lied," Mendez said, bringing my thoughts back to our conversation. "Having to act around you, even for a few minutes, was the hardest thing I've ever done. It killed me that you even bought it in the first place. I'd take it all back if it meant you didn't spend the night mad at me."

As if anyone could stay mad at Mendez for long. I almost rolled my eyes, even though he couldn't see it.

"I'd say you're cute when you're mad," Mendez continued, "but truthfully I thought you might try to kill me in my sleep, and from here on out I think it's best if I just stay on your good side."

"Is that so?" A smile tugged at the corners of my lips. It was ridiculous, really. How I could smile right now was beyond me, and it was a testament to Mendez's abundance of charm. It wasn't fair. I mean, leave some for the other guys, come on.

"Yes," he said. "And I know this may be a promise I come to regret, especially in my line of work, but I swear I'm never going to lie to you again. About anything. Because I never want you to look at me the way you did when I—" He broke off, voice shaking.

"You're forgiven," I whispered. I tightened my fingers around his, squeezing once. "Do you have a plan?"

As far as I could tell, there wasn't a way out of this situation. Maybe Mendez had some ninja stars in his pocket or something though.

I felt his head bob against mine as he nodded. "But every plan involves the use of my hands." His fingers shifted ever so slightly. "Zip ties are easy enough to break if they let us move our hands. You just raise your arms up high with the connection point in the middle, then bring your arms down hard and pull out to the sides simultaneously. They'll probably bring our hands out front once they try to extract information from us."

Extract information. If I had to guess, that was a polite way of saying *torture*, and if they wanted to bring our hands out for it, that meant our hands would most likely be . . . involved. I shuddered. I was quite attached to my thumbs—literally—and wanted them to remain where they were, please and thank you.

"I'll admit," Mendez said, "most of my plans don't give me a clean escape. So, if you see a way out, even if I'm not with you, I want you to take it." His voice sounded grim. Determined. His fingers around mine had gone still.

"What?" I asked in disbelief, turning my neck to catch his expression. Mendez didn't budge and I let out a frustrated sigh at only seeing the back of his head. "I'm not leaving you here, Mendez, and that's that. End of discussion."

I wasn't sure what I could do to help, but running away with my tail between my legs wasn't an option. Maybe I could contact Chan for backup, but that might be too little, too late. Madison had confiscated all our electronics when they'd taken us to this room, so I'd have to return to the van and wait for Chan and his team to meet me there. Who knew how long that would take, or if they'd even show up. Considering how Chan's team had responded to Mendez earlier, I was guessing that was going to be a big, fat no.

I was all Mendez had. I wasn't going to desert him.

We didn't get a chance to discuss things further, because at that moment, the door to interrogation room B opened and Madison strolled in.

Holt was a step behind her.

Chapter Twenty-Eight

· · · · · · · · ·

I RECOGNIZED HOLT IMMEDIATELY FROM THE PICTURES in his file. His flat features made his face somehow expressionless, except for the thick eyebrows that verged dangerously close to a unibrow. He stood a good foot and a half taller than Madison, looming over her with arms crossed. With his sandy hair and thick neck, he was the spitting image of a blond rhinoceros.

What the pictures didn't convey was the way he took up space. His presence was domineering and deadly, at once making me feel insignificant. I didn't know how Madison could stand next to him and not be cowed. Maybe that was why he liked her. She never was one to back down from a fight. Once she set her sights on something, she stayed the course. I could only hope that included working for the United States government.

Of course, the second Holt opened his mouth, he tried to convince me that was no longer the case.

"Does it make you sad, seeing your sister working for someone like me?" His voice was a deep bass but distinctly American.

"I'm not all bad, you know," he continued. "It's the government and politicians that have created a system so broken that people like me have to step in and force order out of the chaos. If you want something done, you can't wait a decade to make it happen. People only listen to power, guns, and money."

His thoughts were so disjointed and crazed, I didn't think he expected me to answer. But when I looked up, his blue eyes were fixed on mine, and his gaze was insistent, like he needed me to agree with him. The guy really needed to bring the conspiracy theories down a notch.

"That's a sad way of looking at things." I didn't know what possessed me to be so bold. Maybe all my brushes with death lately had been building to this moment, right now, when I could talk to Holt and not pee my pants.

Ah, who was I kidding? My bladder control was hanging on by a thread.

Holt only chuckled. It wasn't a pleasant sound. It raised the hair on my arms and made my skin crawl. "You've got guts, I'll give you that much. I see the family resemblance doesn't stop at your appearance." He smiled at Madison and placed a possessive hand on her shoulder. I stared at that hand, wishing the daggers in my eyes were as sharp as the ones on the walls. But Holt's smile only grew wider as he took in my expression.

"I'm afraid your sister doesn't hold the same ideals as you. That's all it took, you know. To turn her. More money." Holt squeezed Madison's shoulder, then returned to the wall, his gaze running up and down its lengths. "Someone as talented as her, and I can ensure she's mine just by being the highest bidder."

He turned and rested his weight against the counter, crossing his arms as he brought his gaze back to me. "That's how I knew I could trust her, that we spoke the same language. The other agents the CIA tried to plant? They tried to promise me power, play on my emotions, to claim they weren't actually operatives. Not your sister. No, she told me she was an agent the first time we met, and that she could work for me if I played my cards right. Or she'd walk. She didn't need me; I needed her." He tapped his temple. "See? Smart. That's why she took the money."

"I'll admit she can beat me in an arm-wrestling match," I said. "But I don't know, I always thought I had an edge in the brains department. No offense, sis." Neither Holt nor Madison was looking at me now. Madison stood by the door, one hand on her hip as she looked at the watch on her wrist. Holt watched my sister, as if her actions reminded him of something. He nodded.

"I think I would have liked you, Dove Barkley. It's a shame you kept getting in my way." He turned to Madison again. "Check their bonds." He gestured to Mendez and me with his chin.

Holt inspected the items on the wall like he was greeting old friends. He picked up an electric drill, weighing it in his hands before replacing it on the wall. Occasionally his hand would rest on one object, caressing it and lingering for a moment before moving to another. His focus was absolute, not even sparing Mendez and me a glance. I had been dismissed. My worth had never before been reduced to less than that of an inanimate object, and I'd tried online dating, so that was saying something.

Madison walked forward, her back to Holt. When she caught my eyes, she smiled reassuringly, and it was so unexpected, I simply stared back, eyes wide and questioning. Mendez turned his head, and we watched her approach in silence, both of us wary. She crouched down at our sides and separated our hands.

"Shh," she hissed, barely loud enough for us to hear.

Something plastic and cylindrical passed by my fingertips

and into Mendez's palm. I glanced down and watched as Madison hid the tip of the syringe up the edge of Mendez's sleeve. Instantly, he folded his hands in such a way that I wouldn't have suspected a thing had I not seen it only a moment before.

"I'm going to break your ties," Madison whispered to Mendez. "When I do, hit me. Hard."

I shot my sister an incredulous look, but she only held her hand up, warning me not to say anything. Her gaze darted over to Holt, who had picked up a serrated knife and was running his finger along the edge of the blade.

"Use the syringe on Holt," Madison said. "I can't help until he's out. Got it?"

Mendez didn't say anything for a moment, likely calculating how much he trusted my sister and whether this could all be a setup. If he used the syringe and nothing happened—then what? And if Madison was telling the truth? Mendez had an injured arm. Could he take on Holt by himself?

"Got it?" Madison said again, more urgently this time, throwing a glance over her shoulder with a worried frown.

Mendez nodded once, and Madison pulled a pocketknife from her boot, going to work on his bonds. She began with his ankles, the tiny click of the plastic zip ties falling to the floor the only sound of her betrayal. She hid her motions with her body, but she worked fast anyway, leaving nothing to chance. When she moved to his wrists, I felt the cold metal of the blade bite into my own ties ever so slightly as she sawed back and forth. But Mendez's fell loose and mine stayed firmly where they were.

The second Mendez was free he burst from his chair, knocking Madison back a foot. She staggered to her feet, but before she had regained her balance, he swung his fist in a tight arc that connected with her jaw, snapping her chin back with a crack that was so loud I could almost physically feel it. She hit the wall behind her and crumpled to the ground, not moving, arms and legs bent beneath her in a painfully abnormal way.

I stared, barely breathing. Knowing it was going to happen and seeing it play out before my eyes were two very different things. Especially when I wasn't even sure my sister was faking being knocked out. Madison had taken me with her to her boxing class and I'd seen her take hard hits before. She always came back swinging.

But something told me Mendez wasn't sure he could trust Madison, and he hadn't held anything back. Either that or he was still mad at her for giving him the slip the last couple of weeks. It was hard to tell. All I knew for certain was Madison wasn't moving.

A roar behind me made me turn my neck as Holt came charging at Mendez. In his hand he still held the serrated knife, its six-inch blade gleaming. He swung it toward Mendez's face.

I knew Mendez could handle himself. I'd seen him outnumbered and cornered in the server room, fighting with nothing but his fists. But now he was injured *and* tired, facing a man who had twice his muscle mass and five times his rage . . . also, a deadly looking weapon that would make any serial killer jealous.

Mendez dodged the attack and twisted his torso out of reach, grabbing for the wall of weapons. But Holt kicked his knee and swept his leg out from under him, knocking Mendez onto his back. With his right arm, Mendez gripped the front of Holt's shirt, bringing him down with him, so the two grappled on the floor.

From the corner of my eye, I watched as the syringe slipped from Mendez's sleeve and rolled across the floor, landing well out of reach of either man. Mendez stretched his fingers, but with his already injured arm, all Holt had to do was dig his fingers into his shoulder and Mendez lurched back in pain. I bit my lip and tried to keep my heartbeat from exploding out of my chest. Already I felt dizzy and all I was doing was sitting in a chair.

Holt adjusted his grasp on the knife, angling it toward Mendez's unprotected side, but Mendez managed to get on top of him and grab his wrist, pinning his arm to the floor and pounding the veins of Holt's wrist with his elbow until Holt loosened his grip on the weapon. Mendez kicked it away and it landed a few inches from my foot, but with my arms still tied behind my back, it was about as useful to me as a computer virus.

A shout brought my wide-eyed stare away from the knife, back to Holt and Mendez. Holt was positioned above Mendez, and he was using his weight to twist Mendez's injured arm back at an unnatural angle. Sweat trickled down my back and I hurled curses at Holt, hoping to break his concentration for even a second. But it was no use. Holt knew I wasn't a threat, tied up as I was.

I strained at my bonds, the plastic digging into my skin. It may have been my imagination, but I could have sworn the plastic gave just a little. Probably from when Madison had accidentally cut into it while freeing Mendez from his zip ties. I pulled harder, but it only cut me, mocking my efforts.

Holt flung Mendez around and backed up against the wall, using it for stability while he wrapped a beefy arm around Mendez's neck. He tightened his choke hold, and I curled my hands into fists. What had Mendez said about breaking zip ties? It was easier to do with the hands out front, but surely now that my restraints were weakened, I could accomplish the same thing.

I pulled my arms back as far as my shoulders would allow

and yanked them forward, trying to separate them at the same time. Nothing happened except that I banged my wrists against the metal frame of my chair. I bit back a cry and braced myself for another attempt, black dots speckling my vision. At the last minute, I decided to stand up—as much as possible—hoping that the added height might give me more leverage. At the very least it'd prevent me from hitting my wrists on the chair again and allow me more room away from the other chair.

With my feet still tied, my balance was tricky, but I pulled my arms back anyway and yanked them forward once more. Again, nothing. Frustrated tears leaked from the corners of my eyes. If I made it out alive, I promised myself that I was going to hit the gym more. Like, actually go. Not just pay for a membership.

Then I remembered Mendez had said the connector had to be in the center of my wrists and I shuffled it around, using my pinkies until it was positioned correctly.

Squeezing my eyes closed, I tried again, and this time I gave it absolutely everything that was in me. I shoved my hands so far back my shoulders screamed in protest, and when I yanked them forward I had so much momentum I couldn't help but fall face forward to the floor.

Luckily, I had my hands to catch me.

The ties broke, and my hands flung out wildly to my sides, barely coming forward in time to break my fall. Because my feet were still tied, my knees hit the ground first with a crack. I stifled a moan. My knees were never going to be the same after this. I was going to be a twenty-seven-year-old who needed knee replacement surgery.

My cheek rested against the floor, my tears making my face stick to the ground like a bad craft project. When I opened my eyes I saw Holt's knife, its serrated edge only inches from where I fell. I reached out a shaky hand and grasped its handle, pulling it to me. My fingers curled around the rubberized grip. A gurgle from behind told me I had to move fast, and I forced my quaking limbs to cooperate, pushing up from my palms to a kneeling position until I could sit back on the chair. Using the knife, I sawed at the ties around my ankles, finally freeing myself from my restraints.

Then I looked at Mendez.

His feet scrambled for purchase against the floor as Holt strangled him in a choke hold. His elbow repeatedly slammed back into Holt's gut, but Holt's grip never faltered.

A feral scream ripped from my throat. I launched myself at Holt, knife clutched in my fist.

I didn't have a game plan. I acted on impulse, sinking the knife hilt-deep into Holt's thigh when I reached their struggling bodies. Holt roared and kicked me in the face, his heavy boots likely laced with metal, judging by the way I was flung back, jaw aching from the strike.

But it worked.

His hold on Mendez loosened just enough for Mendez to wrench himself free, thrusting his head back into Holt's face and knocking the back of Holt's skull into the wall behind them. With that, Mendez lunged forward, and Holt was left clutching air.

I expected Holt to focus his attention on Mendez. Mendez was the greater threat.

But the thing I didn't consider?

I was the weak, wounded gazelle.

Chapter Twenty-Nine

· · · · · · · · · ·

HOLT LEFT THE KNIFE IN HIS LEG AND LURCHED FOR-
ward, his rabid eyes fixing on me. Crimson blood dripped
from his leg onto the floor and I stared at it, my breath coming
in ragged gulps. I scrambled back on hands and knees, my movements slow and jerky. I didn't have time to blink before Holt was
on me, the impact stealing the remaining air from my lungs and
smacking me into the metal chair I'd escaped from only seconds
before. Stars overtook my vision and I tried to make sense of the
black spots and disjointed flashes of the room. My face was half
pushed into the ground while Holt violently pulled me by my
ankle.

I think I screamed. My throat was raw from the sound that
burst out of me. But the panic was so blinding I physically lost
control of my limbs and I seized up, which—hello—now was
not a good time for that. It was like I could see myself from afar,
my leg in Holt's grasp, the rest of me curled up in a fetal position
around the chair. I wanted to fight. I wanted to claw Holt's eyes
out. But instead, I did nothing as Holt's enormous body crashed

on top of mine and wrestled me away from the chair. If people had a fight-or-flight response, I guess mine was broken.

I couldn't see. I couldn't breathe. The weight of him was suffocating and all-encompassing.

Then it somehow got worse, as Holt became a deadweight on top of me.

But that also meant he'd stopped moving.

Then the weight was gone as Holt's body was rolled off me and Mendez was there, his concerned expression filling my vision. "Dove, can you hear me?"

I coughed. Then whimpered, curling my fingers around Mendez's arm in case he tried to pull away. His face swam in front of me, his brown eyes wide and worried. I was impressed that even after everything that had happened, his face was mostly unscathed. Most of his bruises had to be on his body.

Then he too was gone, ripped from my grasp as Madison yanked him to his feet by the collar of his jacket.

"You almost got my sister killed!" Her face was inches from his, hair escaping from her braid as she yelled.

Mendez didn't even try to argue. He closed his eyes like whatever she'd said was no less than what he deserved. A line creased his forehead and he let out a breath.

"Madison, stop." I pulled myself to my aching knees.

"And you." She whirled on me. "What were you thinking getting involved like that?"

She pulled me to my feet and wrapped me in a hug so fierce my ribs creaked. With her lips close to my ear she whispered, "One more millisecond and I was coming to the rescue. If I didn't see that Mendez had the syringe, I swear—"

"It's okay," I cut in. I turned to address them both. "I'm okay."

Madison released me and I swayed on my feet. Mendez immediately swooped in, placing his hand at the small of my back, his brows crinkled with worry.

"Help me get Holt onto one of these gurneys," Madison instructed Mendez, already striding to the edge of the room where three metal tables were pushed up against the wall.

Mendez had been inspecting my face, cataloging every injury and tracing them with his fingertips, but he looked up when Madison spoke. "Why?" he asked, voice sharp. "What's the plan?"

Madison pushed a stray lock of hair behind her ear as she wheeled a gurney to where Holt was lying on the ground. She snuck a glance over at me.

"Holt's hacker said if we killed Dove, the information would die with her. I take that to mean you can still get the data from the servers somehow, right?"

I grinned, the stress in my shoulders finally relaxing. I hadn't wanted to rely on this method, but if Madison was asking . . .

"I wasn't able to transfer everything we needed to the flash drive. But I created a backdoor access point and can continue the download from another computer once I get out of here."

She nodded. "Get that data to the CIA as soon as possible. It has information that can clear my name." Her eyes cut to Mendez. "But the official inquiry will take weeks. You know how they are. Until then, Holt's team has to think I'm loyal. He's already set explosives to go off around this building to destroy evidence, and his partners are going to set up operations elsewhere. The CIA needs me inside for everything not on the servers. They'll need to know where to go once all the smoke clears."

"Explosives?" Mendez repeated. "How long do we have?"

"Forty-five minutes. It might seem like a long time, because Holt wanted to . . . play with you before he left, but I promise, you'll need it to transfer everything, not just the files on the COO you came for. Even then, you might not have enough time."

Mendez swore under his breath and gestured to Holt. "What was in the syringe and how long will he be out?"

Madison pulled on Holt's arm, turning him onto his back. "Ketamine." She grunted. "Probably a couple of hours. I'll have some men take Holt to the hospital where you can have a team waiting to take him in. That way you get Holt in custody, I'll still be in the good graces of Holt's operation, and we can take this thing down from the inside."

"You've given this a lot of thought." Mendez stepped over Holt's legs to stand behind his head. He grasped Holt under his armpits while Madison moved down to his waist. "And if Holt's men ask you why you risked sending him to a hospital when you knew I might escape and alert the authorities?"

She grunted as they lifted Holt onto the gurney. "I'll claim I didn't know what was in the syringe and I didn't want him to die. Plus this knife wound in his leg will make him bleed out if he doesn't get medical attention quickly. When I woke up you were planning your escape. I subdued you and secured you to the chairs again before getting help for Holt. I'll tell them you probably died in the explosion. If you did manage to escape, how would you guess we'd send him to Unicare Medical under the alias of Marcus Benner, let alone get out in time to contact your team?" They slid Holt onto the table, his body skidding as it moved toward the center.

"After all," Madison said, panting, wiping her hands on her legs with a smirk, "there's also no way you could have known this interrogation room had a secret exit where you wouldn't have to risk the hallways with their possible exposure."

Mendez shook his head and grinned. "It's good to have you back on the team, Madison."

"I never left," she replied, already wrapping something around Holt's leg and the knife still stuck in it, to slow the bleeding.

I held up a hand. "If evidence of your true loyalty exists on Holt's servers," I interrupted, "how come he thinks you're loyal to him?"

As tempting as it was, I resisted the urge to gloat. I'd known all along Madison could never betray her country, but I was happy to hear the CIA wouldn't have to take my word for it anymore—not if I could get the data from the servers. No pressure.

They both turned to me like they'd forgotten I was in the room.

"Holt knew I was an operative for the CIA all along," Madison said. "So, when he decided he wanted me all to himself because he recently acquired higher sources in the CIA—"

Mendez swore. Madison held up her hand to stop him from interrupting. "I don't know who, and we're running out of time. Forty-three minutes, and you'll need every one of those to download the data." She turned to me. "Holt approached me about cutting ties with the CIA. There's video evidence that I was coerced and that the only way to keep my cover intact here would be to make the CIA believe I'd gone rogue. Holt likes to keep those kinds of confrontations on file to remind us of what he's capable of. What he could do if I changed my mind. But the CIA will recognize what I had to do to maintain my cover. The operative I put in the hospital? That was a test from Holt to prove my loyalty. But I made sure I didn't hit any arteries so the operative would make it to the ER and survive. I'd never turn my back on my country. Or my sister."

It took a moment for me to grasp the meaning behind her words, prior to the whole "test" thing, but when I did, I had to take a steadying breath.

"You mean Holt tortured you? And recorded it?"

She barely even blinked. "I tried to make him see that I was valuable as a double agent, and that they'd send operatives after me if I went rogue. But Holt doesn't take other viewpoints into consideration. So, yes, when I argued, he made sure I was put in my place."

"And he didn't worry you'd find employment elsewhere?" Mendez asked. "That you were only interested in the money and that his actions would make you leave?" He shoved Holt's shoulder roughly.

"Holt views money as the primary motivator. But it can't be the only tool in his arsenal. Fear is his second favorite trick."

"He sounds like such a great guy," I quipped. "It's a wonder he's single."

One side of Madison's mouth tilted up in a tight grin. "It might surprise you to learn that Holt currently has three girlfriends, none of whom are the mother of his child."

I thought back to what I'd seen on the CIA database.

"Since his daughter is around my age, I guess it makes sense he can't keep a woman that long." I felt bad for his daughter, who didn't have a choice being related to the man. With a father like that, who needed enemies? Unless, of course, the apple didn't fall far from the tree, in which case, I didn't feel bad for her at all.

Madison checked her watch. "Forty-two minutes. We need

to get you both out of here. This whole building is going to blow, and Dove needs to get the data." She strapped Holt to the stretcher and adjusted the legs of the gurney so they were no longer stationary.

"Won't Holt suspect you released my bonds originally?" Mendez asked, helping Madison wheel the stretcher around so it lined up with the door. "He was here for that part."

Madison shook her head, grasping Mendez's wrist so she could sync his watch with hers.

"The man who tied you up—his name is Vilem. He's also the one who let you into the server room. It won't be hard to shift blame onto him. He's made too many mistakes lately."

I kind of felt bad for Vilem. Then I remembered the way he'd twisted my shoulder and manhandled me back in the server room and I didn't feel so bad anymore.

"Where's the hidden exit?" Mendez rose from his hunched position over the stretcher. His eyes scanned the room. Madison sped to the wall of tools like there was no time to waste. With a start, I realized there wasn't. I needed to download the data before it disappeared, and I only had forty-one-ish minutes to do so. That included going down five flights of stairs and over two blocks before reaching the van, then downloading everything to the computers there.

Madison reached into a drawer attached to the wall, pulling something I couldn't see. Across the room, I heard a click. I turned and saw a square lift out of the floor where previously there'd been no hint of anything out of the ordinary.

"The stairs lead all the way to the basement, which is where the parking garage is. Most of Holt's employees have been evacuated, which is what took Holt so long in coming here . . . clearing out the building, his equipment, and electronics. But some employees might still be in the basement, so you'll want to exit on the main floor. Don't be seen."

I rolled my eyes. "I'll take 'Things We Didn't Need to Be Told' for one hundred, Alex."

Madison ignored me and kept talking.

"With any luck, Holt and his men will think you've died in the explosion. But after you return to the States, Dove, you need to get off-grid until this entire operation is scrubbed. I'm so sorry."

She looked it too. Her shoulders fell as she wiped a hand over her face. She opened her mouth like she was going to say something else but closed it with a shake of her head.

Here she was apologizing, but I was just grateful to be alive.

"Don't worry about it." I waved my hand. "I don't have a life, remember?"

Madison stepped forward, her eyes wet as she placed a hand on my shoulder. "See, that's where I steered you wrong." Her voice was low, for my ears only. "A normal life? One filled with laughter, and friends, and doing the things *you* love? That's a life worth protecting." Her eyes darted to Mendez, who was pulling open the trapdoor and inspecting the stairs leading down from it. "And I guess Mendez isn't so bad. I'm glad you have someone like him looking out for you when I can't be there."

She pulled me into a hug so tight it physically hurt. I was battered and bruised across 90 percent of my body, but there was no way I'd be the one to tap out first. I squeezed Madison back, not knowing when I'd next get the chance to hug my sister.

"Forty minutes," she whispered into my ear. "Move fast."

Then Madison said the one thing that actually shocked me. "Love you, sis."

She let go, gently pushing me toward the trapdoor, where Mendez was waiting. I stumbled backward, keeping my gaze locked on Madison. Mendez caught me, his hands at my waist as he kept me from falling in. Madison was wheeling Holt out the door, but I made sure she heard me.

"Love you too," I called out.

She smiled.

Then she was gone.

Chapter Thirty

. . . .

THE METAL STAIRS CLANGED AS WE RAN DOWN THEM. Because they weren't accessible from any other floors besides the ground level and basement, we opted for speed over stealth, but Mendez still insisted on going first in case anyone happened to be lying in wait. I thought it unlikely, but given how twisted Holt's mind was, I guessed anything was possible. Stranger things had happened. He did have three girlfriends, after all.

By the time we made it to the ground floor I already had a stitch in my side. Mendez wasn't even breathing heavily, but then again, he was literally trained for this kind of thing. *My* kind of training was more like . . . resistance training. And by that, I mean I was good at resisting it.

We reached the door and Mendez listened while looking out the window, keeping me behind him. It would have been a nice gesture—if we weren't on a huge time crunch. Since I was the only one able to access the data, and therefore the only one running against the time constraint, I pushed past his arm and against the door, sprinting into the night.

I heard Mendez curse behind me, but it didn't take him long to catch up. He tugged on my elbow, directing me toward a back alley that ran parallel to the street we were on. I changed course, my lungs burning as I pumped my arms harder.

No one came after us. There weren't any shouts or shots fired. Just my own labored breathing loud in my ears.

I should have been grateful Madison hadn't lied and that most of Holt's men had evacuated already. Instead, I mentally tallied up all the ways she owed me and planned how I'd make her pay when we were safely back in the United States. Because we *would* make it through this, and Madison was going to come back home. Sooner rather than later. And when she did, she owed me a spa day. Plus tickets to whatever concerts I wanted to see for the next year. Good tickets. Not nosebleed seats. Sure, she'd saved my life, but she'd also gotten me into this mess, so it was only fair.

The van was up ahead, practically glowing in the moonlight. I'd never run this fast in my entire life, and that was counting the time we had to run the mile for school, and everyone had to make it in under a certain time or we'd get a failing grade in PE. I only prayed there wouldn't be vomit involved this time. I didn't think Mendez and I were at the point in our relationship where he could watch me throw up and still find me physically attractive.

We reached the van and Mendez had to open the doors because I was braced against the side, wheezing like an asthmatic donkey.

"In you go." Mendez lifted me into the van with little effort, as if I needed another reminder to hit the gym. But once I stopped moving, my limbs refused to cooperate and I collapsed in a heap on the floor. My legs shook and I gulped air like it was going out of style. Mendez climbed in beside me and closed the door, surrounding us in the safety of the van. He placed a computer on my lap.

"What else do you need?" His voice was edged with concern as he hovered over me. I was still splayed out on the floor of the van, my shoulder pressed against a seat and my arm stuck in something sticky.

I forced myself to my elbows. "All the computers," I rasped.

"All of them?" He looked over his shoulder for the others plugged into the setup around the perimeter of the van. There were three I could remember from when we'd used this as a type of command center for staking out the airport. Hopefully there were more I didn't know about as well.

I struggled to a sitting position, booting up the laptop as I did so. I was sweating so hard I could have formed my own swimming pool, but I wiped my shaky fingers on my pants and placed them on the keyboard.

"Originally I brought just the flash drive," I explained, still breathing hard, "but that was when I thought we'd only need the file to pin the fault on Holt. We just needed the COO not to attend the gala. I was going to upload everything else to the cloud."

I opened the digital back door I'd created to Holt's system.

"But now Holt is destroying everything on his database, and I'm guessing the CIA wants all the files, right?" I didn't bother waiting for Mendez to respond. I simply barreled ahead while I reopened all the channels that had been severed back in the server room.

"There's not enough storage on this laptop for everything Holt is trying to destroy," I said. "And I'm not about to upload the files to the cloud now unless absolutely necessary, in case

Holt's hacker has a tracer on them. Before, he didn't know we were coming tonight. Now, if he's smart, he'll be on the lookout for the files so he can delete them before we can get the information. So I need all the computers. Get them started, then line them up for me."

I realized I was sounding rather bossy, so I tacked on a meek "please and thank you," for good measure.

Mendez moved around the van with way more energy than I could muster, while I urged my fingers not to give up on me now. My heartbeat still acted like I was dying, but at least my stomach had returned to its normal position and was no longer trying to force its way up my throat. Maybe I should have had Mendez carry me, like some heroine in a movie. Then my fingers wouldn't be shaking so much, and I would have been able to breathe without sounding like Darth Vader.

My eyes zeroed in on the screen in front of me, everything else muted to a low buzz. I was dimly aware of Mendez placing three more laptops at my feet, but the only thing I saw was the string of code playing out on my monitor.

"That won't be enough," I said, brushing a strand of hair behind my ear.

I wasn't sure where he'd get more computers at this hour, but that was his problem. Mine was downloading the data before it all went up in a goodness gracious great ball of fire.

A second later, Mendez got behind the wheel and I felt the van move.

I wasn't worried about our connection. This van was equipped like a mobile control center—slash—battering ram. What I was worried about was time.

The download started on the first computer, the progress bar creeping across my screen at a snail's pace. There wasn't anything else I could do besides wait. While that worked, I pulled up the second computer and got it prepped, careful not to overlap the two systems. I chewed my nail and tried not to get sick from the motion of the van. We careered around a corner and the laptops slid into my leg.

"Sorry," Mendez called over his shoulder. I barely heard him. My entire world was focused on watching that progress bar inch slowly to the right. Finally, an alert popped up on the screen saying the storage on the computer was full, and I pulled over the next one, starting the process again.

A knot formed in my stomach the size of a bowling ball. I wouldn't be surprised if everyone in the CIA secretly had ulcers. How else did they deal with this kind of stress on a daily basis? Yoga certainly wasn't going to cut it.

Mendez was on the phone with Chan, asking about computers. And by asking, I mean yelling. Because Chan still didn't have his hearing aids. Mendez gave Chan the information about the hospital where Holt would be, instructing him on the name and how to handle the takedown.

That was when the first bullet hit the side of our tactical van and Mendez swore under his breath. I was too exhausted to cry out when another one hit the window above my head. Luckily this van was built like a tank, so nothing happened beyond the noise, but it meant we hadn't escaped unnoticed.

"Hold on," Mendez said, taking a corner so tight I slid across the floor of the van.

I was getting really tired of gunfire. It probably should have worried me that I was considering it more of an inconvenience than an actual threat to my life at this point.

"Keep your head down," Mendez instructed as he rolled down his window.

Oh goodie. He was going to return fire. He no longer wore the sling, but that didn't mean his shoulder wasn't injured. So that meant he was driving, and shooting, with one good arm.

Solid plan. What could go wrong?

I carefully closed the first laptop and secured it in a drawer. With all this careering about, I didn't want it to get damaged and lose the files we'd already transferred. The second computer finished downloading as Mendez yanked the steering wheel, bringing us about so hard we were practically perpendicular to whoever was shooting at us. I tried not to calculate how much time this was taking away from getting more laptops, or how much we had left before the servers literally blew up and the data was lost forever.

No pressure.

Our van jerked to the left and Mendez fired out the window. "Dove, come up front." He shouted to be heard above the noise.

I started the download on the third computer, cradling it to my chest as I crawled to the front of the van and hunched between the seats. I placed it on the passenger seat, watching the impossibly slow progress bar transition across the screen, at odds with the rapid pace of everything else around me.

Mendez unbuckled his seat belt and looked over his shoulder, barely glancing at me as he spoke. "Take the wheel."

I had to yell to be heard over the noise around me. "You're kidding me, right?"

"Take the wheel now."

He twisted his upper body out the window, relinquishing the steering wheel as he did so. He didn't specify that he'd need me to take control of the pedals too, but seeing as how half his body wasn't even in the vehicle anymore, I took that as a given and slid into the driver's seat with a white-knuckled grip. He sat on the window frame, his knees blocking my view as I tried unsuccessfully to see the road ahead.

"I think there's something you should know," I yelled.

Mendez didn't answer. Maybe because he was too busy shooting.

Our tire hit the curb and the steering wheel jerked in the opposite direction. Mendez cursed and scrambled for a grip along the top of the van as one of his legs flew from the window.

"I don't know how to drive," I yelled, clutching the steering wheel with a death grip. I smashed my foot down on the pedal, unsure if that was the correct thing to do. The only experience I'd had prior to this was when our foster home had taken us go-karting once. That and a few video games, which I was coming to realize weren't the same. At. All.

I was going to survive Holt only to die by my own driving.

"What?" Mendez's incredulous tone made it clear he wasn't asking me to repeat myself. I heard a few thumps on the hood of the van and his foot scrambled for purchase in the window frame. I'd have helped him place his boot, but my hands might as well have been glued to that wheel—only a miracle would remove them now.

If I played Carrie Underwood's "Jesus, Take the Wheel" the next time we did Name That Tune, would Mendez find it funny? Something told me, probably not.

"You couldn't have mentioned that earlier?" Mendez called out when I hit a bike rack.

"You didn't exactly give me time," I called back. "Be grateful it's the middle of the night and there aren't any pedestrians."

"How do you not know how to drive?" He fired at a black

SUV, aiming for what I assumed was the gas tank, because a second later it was engulfed in flames.

"I live in a big city, and I ride public transport," I shouted. "It's good for the environment. Don't judge me."

"That's no excuse." He finally found a solid grip on the side of the car and grunted as my swerve pulled on his injured shoulder.

"Who was going to teach me?" I asked. "My nonexistent father?"

Mendez finally let the subject drop after that, either from guilt or because he was too busy shooting out the tires of a motorcycle that had come up alongside us. I ducked out of the way when a bullet hit the rearview mirror, causing glass to cascade into my lap.

"Turn right," Mendez called, swinging around to face the opposite direction. The fact of the matter was, having his toned body half blocking the window wasn't doing anything to help my concentration. He looked entirely too good, muscles bulging as he hung on to the frame of the van, and I wished I had a moment to appreciate the view.

I turned the wheel, a little too far, and ended up on the curb again. From the corner of my eye, I saw the data had finished downloading to the computer. There was still more information to be downloaded, and only a few feet away on the floor of the van, the last laptop sat unused. I wasn't sure how much time had passed, but I knew there wasn't much left.

I glanced at the road, then back at the laptop. If I kept my hands on the wheel, I should be able to use my leg to drag the computer to me.

I tried this, sliding my right leg out like a pole dancer until the tip of my boot reached the edge of the laptop and I could slide the case my way.

What I wasn't counting on was the inertia of the van slowing down so much once I released my foot from the pedal.

Something rammed into us from behind and I was thrown forward in my seat. The airbags exploded in my face and knocked my head back, all of it happening so fast I couldn't even register what was going on.

The car lurched forward, the force from behind carrying us past the dividing line on the road and into opposing traffic. We jerked to a halt and I tried to process what exactly had happened. A few cars were out, even at this absurd hour and in this random alley. They swerved out of the way to avoid a collision and I silently prayed all the innocent bystanders would be all right. It was bad enough we were involved—

"Mendez!" He wasn't hanging on to the outside of our van anymore. I pushed open the driver's door and stumbled onto the road. My neck hurt from the whiplash, but I swung it around, searching for any sign of Mendez.

One man stood in the middle of the road, leather jacket so dark it practically blended in with the night.

His shoulders relaxed and he turned to face me. "Risky maneuver," Mendez said, "but I think it paid off."

Around us, the rubble from the accident littered the road. By my count there'd been a motorcycle and two cars, but no one was left to follow us now. Mendez checked each of the cars anyway, and I finally allowed myself to breathe. I made a conscious decision *not* to look in the other cars at the men who must be dead or knocked out in those vehicles.

"Because I totally did it on purpose," I drawled, pushing hair out of my face. He grinned.

"Let's grab the computers and get out of here," Mendez said. "I've set up a CPU with Chan's team about two streets over."

"A CPU?"

The only CPU I knew about was a central processing unit of a computer, and something told me that wasn't what Mendez was talking about.

"A car pick up. They'll bring more laptops, and they'll have a secure connection to continue the download. Think you can run?"

I grimaced, then nodded.

Mendez jogged to the van, shaking his head ruefully at the wreckage.

"I guess you can't be good at everything," he said, bracing one leg against the bumper as he pried open the back doors of the van and pulled.

I placed my hands on my hips. "We're alive, aren't we?"

He chuckled as he disappeared inside.

"Next time," his muffled voice came back, "I'm driving."

Chapter Thirty-One

· · · · · · · · ·

J UST THINK, I MUSED, *SOME PEOPLE ACTUALLY* LIKE *running*.

Mendez had shoved the laptops into a bag and slung them over his good shoulder. Now he led the way, navigating the dark streets of Prague while I stumbled behind like a drunken tourist. I had no idea what time it was, or how many minutes we had left before Holt's base went up in flames. All I knew was I desperately needed sleep. And a shower. Apparently my body only had so much adrenaline to spend, and I was, quite literally, running out of it.

"Almost there." Mendez grabbed my hand and pulled me along.

We reached a deserted corner and looked around. Presumably Mendez, or Chan's team, had chosen it as a rendezvous point because it was far removed from the city center, but there wasn't anyone here. Mendez checked his watch, worry lines creasing his forehead.

"Come on," he muttered, his gaze bouncing between the shadows, one hand resting protectively on the gun holstered at his hip.

Tires squealed to our left and another tactical van rounded

the corner. I was still on high alert, but a grin broke out on Mendez's face when he saw who sat behind the wheel.

"Let's go." He grabbed my hand again, bringing me around to the side of the van where a door was already opening. I recognized the white woman who leaned out as the same one who'd been at the airport tarmac.

"Run countersurveillance." Mendez pulled himself up. "We're coming in dirty. Left a mess about two blocks back."

The woman's mouth was set in a firm line. "So we saw." She reached down, helped me into the van, and closed the door as soon as I was in.

"Go." She motioned to the driver, another man I recognized from the airport.

The woman crossed her arms, staring down Mendez. "You said this was a routine CPU because you needed more laptops. No risk."

"Well, it started that way."

Mendez unzipped the bag holding the computers and passed me the last one from our van. I immediately got to work and muted their argument to a corner of my brain. I didn't care what Mendez had said to get them here. Frankly, I was still upset they hadn't come with us in the first place. Then maybe we wouldn't have needed to resort to such drastic measures.

The download started and I checked the remaining capacity of Holt's servers. By my estimate, I'd transferred about half of the data.

"How many computers do you have?" I interrupted their bickering to ask.

The woman blinked at me. "Uh, three, I think." She twisted her torso, looking over her shoulder at the command center behind her.

Disappointment bloomed in my chest.

It wasn't going to be enough. Not if it'd taken four to make it halfway.

"What's their storage capacity?" I asked. Were all CIA laptops issued with the same number of gigabytes? I hadn't checked the previous ones to know how even the data spread was.

The woman only stared at me blankly before handing me one of the laptops from the command center.

The van took another corner and we all leaned with the movement.

I booted it up, prepping it for the download while I analyzed its available specs. The hollow feeling in my gut only got bigger.

"Get the others ready, please." My voice shook. Math wasn't my strong suit, but even I knew the numbers weren't adding up in my favor. Mendez did it without a word, lining the computers up like dominos on the floor of the van.

"We don't have a tail," the driver called back. "I'll stick to back roads and weave my way back to your safe house if you give me the coordinates."

Mendez moved to the front of the van, leaving me with the woman who did not seem at all pleased by this turn of events. Then again, she hadn't seemed happy since we'd entered the van, so maybe that was just her demeanor.

I focused on the laptop instead. Computers, I understood. People, not so much. The progress bar finally made it to one hundred. I set it aside and grabbed the next in the lineup. My movements were so frantic and hurried that the first laptop skidded across the floor, only to be caught by the woman with a disapproving glare.

Take one down, pass it around, only three laptops to save us all now.

True, I had a lot of data. But I needed all of it. I didn't know which part might vindicate Madison.

I completed the next download, all the while chewing on a nail and calculating the remaining storage like I was doing quantum mechanics or attempting to launch a space shuttle into orbit.

I heard Mendez on the phone with Chan, yelling something.

His loudest exclamation of all came a short time later when he pumped his fist in the air and shouted, "We've got him. We've got Holt."

The surrounding agents celebrated, cheers erupting all around me, but my work wasn't over yet. I zeroed in on the computer in front of me. By the time I was halfway through the second laptop, I knew for sure it wasn't going to be enough.

"Dove, I hate to pressure you," Mendez called from the front, voice sounding very pressuring, "but there are only four minutes left on the timer."

Four minutes.

Four minutes to figure out the solution to an impossible problem.

Unbeknownst to me, the familiar time constraint was exactly what I needed.

Like an athlete relying on muscle memory, my body shifted into a trained rhythm. My breathing settled and my brain quieted, focusing on the dilemma in front of me. I didn't want any data to be lost. Even one piece of information could be critical if it saved someone's life. More important, if it cleared Madison's name.

So, I did what I had to do. I figured it out.

Taylor Swift's "I Did Something Bad" started playing in my head, quieting my nerves. The progress bar on the third computer reached one hundred and I quickly pivoted to the final laptop, my fingers flying across the keyboard.

"Give me your phones," I said to the passengers of the van. "Now."

They didn't argue, and a second later, a collection of cell phones landed at my feet. One skidded under the command center and Mendez reached back to fish it out, passing it to the woman to add to the pile.

"Adapter cord," I barked out, sounding like a surgeon, one heartbeat away from a flatlining patient.

I didn't want to think about my options if they didn't have an adapter in the van. I already had so few options.

They searched frantically around me while I set up the transfer. The woman passed me a cord and I looked at it, then glanced at the phones.

I had to hand it to the CIA—they were efficient. Getting all their operatives on the same phone plan had its benefits. Like me not needing multiple adapters for different makes and models of Android and Apple phones.

I ripped the cord from her hands and plugged it into the nearest phone, getting it ready for when the laptop was finished.

"Passcode?" I asked. I had no idea whose phone I held. There was no identifying picture on the lock screen. But the operatives looked at the case, and the driver of the van called out his passcode over his shoulder.

We turned another corner and I typed in the passcode, light illuminating the screen. As soon as the computer finished, I plugged the phone into it, transferring whatever files I could to the free space there. It wasn't a lot. Phones weren't a substitute for computers in that sense. But five phones . . .

The van was silent as we all counted down the minutes. Every time one phone's storage was full, I grabbed another, and someone yelled out the passcode.

Then Mendez was yelling out different numbers. I knew the significance because Taylor Swift's song in my head was coming to a close.

"Ten, nine, eight," Mendez started counting down, his eyes on his watch. Mine were on the last phone, which I held in my sweaty palm, the wheel slowly spinning as it transferred data into its storage.

"Seven, six, five," he continued.

I held my breath as the wheel stopped, only one megabyte of available storage left unused.

All the data from Holt's servers transferred.

I let out my breath in a whoosh, my heartbeat finally picking up again.

"Four, three, two, one."

A message popped up on my screen.

CONNECTION LOST.

The woman who'd stayed in the back of the van with me held her hand up to her ear, listening to something on her earpiece. "Our eyes on the ground just reported that an explosion engulfed Holt's building," she said.

They all turned to me, their faces asking the question none of them dared ask out loud.

"We got it," I said, slumping back against the side of the van. "All of it. Every piece of data is on the computers and these phones."

I didn't understand why I felt like crying and laughing at the same time. I brought a shaky hand to my forehead and brushed back a piece of hair that had escaped my ponytail. The gravity of the moment hit me at the same time my adrenaline finally ran out. I was left trembling in the back of the van while everyone celebrated around me. Still, the relief washed over me and I found myself smiling.

The driver let out a hoot and Mendez clapped him on the back with his bad arm, wincing as the movement pulled at his shoulder.

The other operatives in the van relaxed and the woman beside me actually smiled. And here I was beginning to think she wasn't capable of the action.

The operatives went about removing the passcodes from their phones so the CIA wouldn't have to contact them once they received the technology.

There were still two laptops back at the safe house—the one I'd used to access the CIA database, and Mendez's computer, to which I'd added the Remote Access Trojan. But I didn't exactly want that back in CIA custody until I'd had a chance to remove the Trojan, and I wasn't sure of the best way to go about doing that without telling Mendez what I'd done. So, the phones were definitely the better of my options for now, even if it inconvenienced the operatives for a bit. Best to have the agents remove their passcodes, and I could go about my life without, well, going to jail.

When the phones were ready, one of the operatives stacked them and the computers in a padded case with wheels that reminded me of luggage. All that information in one container, easily stored and transported, as if it hadn't caused a world of trouble to obtain.

Mendez must have finished giving directions to the driver,

because he came back to sit at my side while the woman took his place in the front of the van. The other case officers busied themselves in a conversation and I lowered my voice so only Mendez could hear.

"The next time something explodes," I said, "I want to be there. That way I can walk away without looking back while everything bursts into flames behind me, like James Bond. Otherwise, what's the point?"

Mendez shook his head. "You'll never be that close to an explosion if I can help it," he said, and I pouted.

He chuckled. "When we get inside," he said, "I'll schedule a flight back to the US so we can get these off our hands."

He motioned to the case of computers, then sent me a wicked grin as he tucked a piece of hair behind my ear. "And then," he said, "I'm going to kiss you."

Despite the fact that I'd made it in and out of Holt's base, driven a car for the first time, survived being shot at, obtained critical data of national importance, seen with my own eyes that my sister was safe and sound, and was still alive to tell the tale—*that* was the best news I'd heard all day.

After all, a girl had to have her priorities straight.

I was still thinking about it when we pulled up to the safe house. A warm, secure feeling took up permanent residence in my gut now that we were finally home free—like I'd drunk a whole gallon of hot chocolate, prepared at just the right temperature with the creamiest whipped cream on top, and now I could curl up with a blanket and sleep for a hundred years.

Fitting, since it felt like I hadn't slept in at least that long.

Still, I was in a dreamlike state as Mendez helped me from the van, his fingers trailing along my hip and lingering for a bit longer than was probably necessary. Maybe it was the adrenaline finally wearing off, because my knees buckled a little. My legs felt shaky as the reality that everything was over finally started to sink in.

Mendez caught me with a grin, holding me close while the other operatives checked on the van and milled about.

"I haven't even kissed you yet," he said, seeing my smile.

He paused, his chest moving as he breathed. Something in his expression changed.

"You know," he said, "the CIA has a protocol for whenever an operative starts dating someone exclusively. Paperwork, an external contact form, that kind of thing, to get approval."

He ducked his head and a loose piece of hair fell across his eyes. It was the sexiest thing I'd ever seen.

"I'm not saying it'd be easy." He cleared his throat. "Dating an operative can be lonely, and I wouldn't be able to tell you some things, and—"

"Are you asking me to be your girlfriend?" I asked in a teasing tone, pulling him closer and placing my hands on his arms once more since he had created too much space for my liking. Sure, there were other people around, but after everything I'd been through that day and night, I really couldn't care less.

Mendez smiled and leaned in so I was pressed against the tactical van, his forearms flexing under my fingertips. His lips were only inches away from mine and if I stood on my tiptoes, I'd be able to close that distance.

"That's what I'm asking, yes." His voice was low and husky, setting every nerve ending in me on fire. Forget fire, I was molten lava, my insides nothing but liquid heat.

Then he kissed me, his fingers curling into my hair as his body pressed against mine. His kiss was hungry and desperate, a reminder that we were lucky to be alive. It was a kiss that didn't care whether anyone was watching or if we might get in trouble for not reporting our relationship to his superiors first. I thought I might melt into a puddle right then and there.

By the time he pulled away, I was out of breath and more than a little frazzled, smoothing my hair with my hands, like that would somehow take away all evidence of the kiss. As if my swollen lips and red cheeks weren't a dead giveaway.

If the other agents witnessed anything, they didn't mention it. I was sure I'd read about it in some report later, because CIA operatives were trained to be observant. But maybe they were allowing us special leeway, considering we *had* just single-handedly taken down an international arms dealer intent on destroying the CIA from the inside.

I caught one of the agents smirking though, so maybe not.

Mendez ran a hand through his hair and stepped away, chest heaving.

Finally, the other agents left and we were alone, standing on an empty corner clutching a case with seven computers and a handful of phones, chock-full of top secret information people would literally kill for.

I only hoped we wouldn't be next.

Chapter Thirty-Two

. . . .

CALL ME CYNICAL, BUT CONSIDERING ALL THE REST of the CIA's secrets, I was surprised to learn we wouldn't be touching down directly on top of Langley itself or something similarly impressive, like skydiving or rappelling from the belly of the plane. Instead, we had to drive from the airport, and even when we'd made it to Langley, we had to take a shuttle from the west parking lot. Who has a shuttle from the parking lot? The CIA, apparently, that's who. Granted, the lot itself was enormous, so I was grateful we didn't have to make the trek, especially after all we'd just been through. My legs already felt like wet noodles.

They did have a doctor for us on the plane though, so at least there was that.

When Mendez, Chan, and I walked through the doors, a small team of people were waiting for us, literally clapping like we were heroes. I wasn't going to lie—it felt great.

I didn't recognize any of them, though it was obvious most of them had at least heard of Madison from the way they studied me. Open curiosity overtook their expressions, with a few of them outright staring. I figured those must be the analysts, since they weren't exactly trained in the art of being subtle.

One face was vaguely familiar, like when you have a dream and try to remember it once you've woken up. It was only after he introduced himself as Tobias Matthews that I realized he was Mendez's superior. The one Mendez had talked so fondly about, who'd checked in on him every day when his girlfriend had passed.

I'd seen his file when I'd hacked the CIA database, but had no reason to expect I'd ever meet him in person. He was white, looked to be in his early fifties, was graying at the temples, and had an overly enthusiastic handshake, but otherwise there was nothing to make him stand out from a crowd. He gave off such a fatherly vibe I was overcome by a sudden, irrational need to impress this man—like by doing so, I'd be worthy of Mendez's affections and Tobias might give me away at an altar in some hypothetical wedding at some future date. Way, way, way in the future, I reminded myself.

Ridiculous. He wasn't even Mendez's father. But it was clear from the way he clapped Mendez on the shoulder—his good shoulder—that the two of them had a special bond.

Clearly I needed more sleep. This whole thing made me feel like I was sleepwalking. Here I was, inside the CIA headquarters, and I was daydreaming about marrying Mendez, surrounded by special agents and armed security officers wearing bulletproof vests, all of them clapping and congratulating us for taking down Holt. This kind of thing didn't happen in real life.

I shook my head and looked around, taking in the impressive columns and wide-open floors. It was exactly how I'd imagined it. There was even the CIA seal on the floor, with the eagle head on top of the shield, the words CENTRAL INTELLIGENCE

AGENCY—UNITED STATES OF AMERICA written in bold letters encircling the compass star. It was enormous—easily fifteen feet across, inlaid in the granite.

Tobias gestured to a Black woman on his right who stepped forward, holding a small box.

"Team," Tobias said, "this is Kiara from communications. Together with a few other departments, they've been developing these special hearing aids. They're still prototypes, but they've configured them to Chan's specifications. So how about we let him put them in so he can be a part of our conversation?"

Chan's eyes lit up when Kiara opened the box to reveal the hearing aids. He'd been politely and professionally keeping up appearances since landing in Virginia, but he hadn't been his usual witty self. Since making it to the parking lot, he hadn't said *what* once, but he hadn't said anything else either. I didn't know how much of anything he'd actually heard. Probably nothing, which, frankly, I couldn't even imagine.

"The CIA is manufacturing hearing aids now?" I peered over Chan's shoulder to get a better look at the little electronic pieces nestled in the box. Technology always intrigued me, especially when it was top-of-the-line, not-something-you-could-get-anywhere-else technology. Chan fit the hearing aids into his ears and turned them on.

"These are Bluetooth-enabled, meaning they can act as earpieces as well." Kiara practically bounced on her heels. "Chan and other hard of hearing operatives could conceivably work in the field without sacrificing the integrity of the mission."

Tobias cleared his throat. "Let's not get ahead of ourselves. We all agree that'd be great, but there's still a lot to consider."

Everyone stared at their shoes or the ceiling, but I stole a glance at Chan. His eyes shone with an emotion I couldn't identify. Determination? Hope? Shame? It flashed too quickly, then it was gone, replaced by a carefully controlled blank expression. The one thing that was clear: the hearing aids worked.

Tobias gestured to two of the other men in the group and introduced them. "These are two agents of the Federal Bureau of Investigation that will be working with our agency. When Mendez alerted us to a possible double agent, the director of internal affairs enlisted their help. They'd like to be present for an internal audit of all agents assigned to Holt's case. They'll be with us for the debriefing with case officers Mendez and Chan."

If Mendez hadn't told me this might happen and that they'd be investigating all of his actions, I'd probably be anxious. As it was, my stomach still swooped in response, and I looked for the nearest trash can, just in case I needed to throw up. I didn't want to vomit all over the CIA seal in the lobby of Langley headquarters in front of Mendez's boss.

The CIA gathered intelligence. The FBI handled arrests. And everyone was working together to get rid of any double agents. Because there was still someone out there who'd tried to pin everything on Madison. Hopefully the data in Holt's files would sort everything out. All I knew was it wasn't my problem anymore. *I* had a date with a bubble bath that was long overdue.

On the plane, Mendez had made it seem like it was routine to call in the FBI. But Chan's compressed lips and clenched jaw told me no one was safe from their scrutiny. Not even them.

Still, I smiled and nodded as they shook my hand, hoping they wouldn't send me to jail for having sweaty palms.

Tobias didn't introduce the other members of the group, leading me to believe my security clearance didn't go that high. Honestly, that wasn't that surprising, because despite all I'd been through, I had to remind myself I didn't *have* any security clearance.

"Kiara will get you checked in as a visitor," Tobias told me. "If you hand over the computers from Prague, our team can get started on that while I debrief Mendez and Chan. I'm afraid it might take some time. I hope you don't mind waiting a few hours."

Mendez had warned me about this too. I would get my turn, but all the top secret stuff would have to be discussed first, without me present. Even though I already knew more than most people here, which was all kinds of ironic.

Mendez wheeled the suitcase containing the laptops over to the other people in the group, and I held on to mine with a death grip. Because those computers only had *most* of the information. This laptop had something special. Something secret.

"This was an extra laptop that was already cleared by the agency." My knuckles were turning white, and the FBI agents had turned to look because of the weird way my voice had raised in pitch. "I was hoping I could catch up on work while everyone else is in the debriefing? Since I'll be waiting for a while?"

I'd heard rumors that CIA agents were trained to be walking human lie detectors. They probably didn't need a polygraph test to see the bead of sweat running from my temple into my ponytail. But I was also hoping nervousness in a situation like this was a common enough thing that they'd give my odd behavior a pass. Expecting otherwise would be like asking a chicken to act normal in a fox den.

"Sure, sure," Tobias said. "It was one of the laptops from the safe house?"

I nodded, and he shrugged.

"You'll need to turn it in before leaving, but I see no reason why you can't work on it while you wait."

My shoulders slumped in relief, and then I quickly looked around to see if anyone had noticed. Thankfully they'd all resumed their normal activities as soon as Tobias had given his okay. The two FBI agents were conferring in low voices, and Kiara was talking to Chan about the hearing aids. The other men were wheeling the laptops down a corridor, already several feet away from our group. Mendez was the only one watching me with a quizzical expression. He didn't say anything though, and I was grateful that while he'd promised never to lie to me, I hadn't made the same vow.

"Oh, but Dove," Tobias added, clapping a hand on my shoulder and making me jump, "I understand you originally found the threat to our COO by hacking into the CIA database after cloning Mendez's account and granting it additional privileges."

I wasn't sure if I was supposed to actually answer that. Wasn't there the whole "innocent until proven guilty" thing? So I stayed silent and Tobias grinned.

"We did have to reset Mendez's account and wipe all your access points to the CIA database. Your assistance with this case has been invaluable, but it's a risk the CIA simply can't afford to take. I hope you understand. Good job though. Seriously, I'm impressed. Don't be surprised when our recruiters come knocking on your door."

He let go of my shoulder and I remembered to breathe. I was pretty sure I'd have a lot of questions to answer about *that* when it came time for me to meet with the board, or whoever it was that'd be judging me for my crimes, but that was a problem for future me. I could only handle so much at once. So, I laughed with him and hoped I didn't sound too much like the Joker.

If I hadn't been internally cataloging every way this could all go wrong, I might have taken a second to bask in his praise. But as it was, his compliment barely blipped on my radar before I went back to analyzing the body language of everyone around me. Mendez looked suspicious of my behavior, but that could almost be considered his default expression, so I tried to pay it no mind.

"Well." Tobias put a hand in his pocket, removed his phone, and checked the time. "We'd best get on with it. Nice to meet you, Dove. I'm sure I'll be seeing you later."

Chan gave me a reassuring smile before hobbling away on his crutches. Mendez tried to communicate something with his eyes, but I wasn't exactly clear on the message. Since leaving the plane, we'd gone back to a polite distance, pretending we hadn't crossed any personal boundaries while holed up in Prague until he could fill out the paperwork.

Tobias joined the FBI agents and herded them down the hall. With a tilt of his chin, he motioned for Mendez to follow. I stood next to Kiara, only releasing one hand from the laptop long enough to wave at Mendez's retreating figure.

A nervous feeling settled in the pit of my stomach as I said goodbye. Here we were in one of the safest buildings in America, but with Mendez and me being separated and a double agent still on the loose, I couldn't shake the feeling we were anything but safe.

Chapter Thirty-Three

· · · · · · · · · ·

GETTING CHECKED IN AS A GUEST TOOK SO LONG, I half expected the debriefing to be over by the time Kiara said I was clear. She took me to her office, where approximately ten different cell phones, five smartwatches, a handful of earpieces, and a collection of electronic bugs littered her desk. I was half tempted to ask for one of the phones to replace mine, which Mendez had taken apart in the parking garage back when all this had started, but I was also pretty sure the ones on her desk all came with tracking devices preinstalled, so I'd be better off with . . . well, anything else. Not that the United States government wouldn't already be tracking my every move from here on out, but at least then I'd have the illusion of privacy.

I motioned to the assortment of gadgets on her desk. "So, you're in communications, right?"

Kiara made a half-hearted effort to clean up her desk but gave up when she realized there wasn't anywhere else to put the items. "Yep, and these, uh, these aren't bugs. The CIA doesn't, umm, do that."

She shoved the not-bugs in a drawer, and I laughed, grateful

I'd spent most of my time with someone like Mendez who didn't mince words. Eventually Kiara grinned too, shrugging as she walked me over to an empty desk a few feet away from hers. "The person I share this office with is away on vacation. You can work here while you wait. Can I get you anything?"

I placed my laptop on the desk, angling it in such a way that she wouldn't be able to see my screen from her desk.

"Nope." I motioned to the copy machine across the room, more to get her away from me than anything else. The woman was sweet, but I could feel my time slipping away. "You left your copy machine open though."

She waved her hand dismissively, still not moving from my side. "Oh, that's policy. In our line of work, we leave the lid open to make sure no sensitive documents are ever left behind."

"Ah." I pulled out the chair and settled into it. Kiara finally took the hint.

"Well, holler if you need anything. I'm happy to help."

"Thanks." I was still waiting for her to leave. She gave an awkward wave, then returned to her desk, only a few feet away. I opened the lid of my laptop and navigated to the hidden folder of files that I'd transferred off Holt's servers. Everything else was on the laptops we'd delivered to the CIA.

Everything else, *except* this.

This folder had been labeled FLINT, and I knew Madison had left it just for me. I'd found it on the plane ride home when we'd been sorting through everything for easier cataloging for the CIA. I'd transferred it as soon as Mendez's back was turned.

The fact that Madison hadn't brought it up, even to Mendez, let me know I couldn't trust anyone else with the information. I would have looked at it earlier, but everything in the folder had been encrypted and I didn't have the time to break it with Mendez and Chan breathing down my neck. Soon, I wouldn't have any time at all, because Tobias would expect me to return this laptop to the CIA, and my chance would be gone for good. Unless I wanted to transfer the files to the cloud, which seemed risky at best. It might be my only option, but it wasn't a great one if I wanted to get to the bottom of things while I was still at CIA headquarters.

I studiously ignored the one file that wasn't encrypted—Madison's torture video, which I'd made sure was also in the files the CIA had—and set about breaking the encryption on the others. It made sense that Madison had included that one here. She wanted to make sure I'd get it to whoever needed to clear her name. But I wasn't about to give myself nightmares if I could help it. The other files were harder to explain. There was no way Madison had encrypted them. She didn't have the resources or know-how.

What was more likely was that Madison had found the files elsewhere and knew they were important. If Holt was hiding things from his own team, he had to be up to no good.

I looked at the API calls, but Holt used a custom-written encryption algorithm. Because of course he did. It was symmetric, so I set my algorithm accordingly, adjusting for the flavor of the AES and key size.

It took several loops, but there it was, a weakness in his implementation. I exploited it and the files populated on my screen. I glanced at Kiara, who was busily tapping something on her computer. Then I looked at the clock. How long would the debriefing take?

I clicked into the first file, muting my laptop in case there was sound. I needn't have worried. It looked like some sort of wire money transfer, but I knew the names would be fake. The money would be real, but it'd be washed through several different banks and accounts. By the time I tracked down the numbers, the accounts would be long gone, and the owners, whether real or not, would probably be none the wiser to the nefarious dealings that had taken place. I took note of the account numbers and dates, then moved on to the next file.

Another wire transfer opened, this one in the amount of $500,000. My eyes bugged out of my head as I mentally calculated what I could do with that kind of money. Retire, probably. Well, maybe not, because inflation was no joke, but it'd be a good start.

This one also had a postscript detailing the purpose of the payment, and I leaned in close so I could read it better. Then I quickly closed out of it as I realized this was blood money. Payment for taking out the COO of the CIA. Except the COO was still alive, so maybe this was just a down payment, like an advance on services to be rendered. Would this hitman have to pay it back? And why was Holt paying someone off when Holt, or one of his men, was the one doing the killing?

Unless . . . maybe Holt was paying them to create the window of opportunity. The chief operating officer of the Central Intelligence Agency had to be a pretty well-protected man. It wasn't like he regularly attended things like the inaugural CIA patrons gala. Didn't Mendez say the original officer assigned to the task was in the hospital because of a heart attack? Then the caterers were changed last minute. Had Holt paid someone to make those things happen?

The code name attached to all the shady dealings was the Wolf, and so far there hadn't been any real names at all. But with each file I opened, it was becoming increasingly obvious that this Wolf person was the CIA double agent everyone was so concerned about.

The real threat within the CIA. Someone higher up or with enough access that they could change outcomes and fudge reports. Suddenly, it made sense that Holt would show his hand to Madison if he had someone like the Wolf in his pocket.

The reason Holt kept these files encrypted, and why Madison had worked so hard to get them to me, was because even Madison didn't know the Wolf's real identity.

Kiara could be the Wolf and I could be all alone in the room with her, not even knowing my life had a time limit on it. If she found out what I was doing, she'd kill me in a heartbeat. Shoot first, ask questions later. Wasn't that the CIA motto?

I snuck a glance at the woman, wondering what kinds of secrets she could be hiding. Sure, she seemed nice enough, but that was probably all a front.

Perhaps sensing my scrutiny, she looked up and caught me staring.

"Oh, sorry." My blush crept down my neckline and I quickly closed all my opened files. "I was just zoning out."

Please don't kill me, I chanted in my mind, suddenly aware that while Kiara was only an inch or two taller than me, she had zero percent body fat and could probably squash me with her pinky finger. She smiled, but it seemed more forced than before.

I waited to open anything else until Kiara returned to her work, glancing over my computer screen every so often to make sure she hadn't pulled out any knives I should be concerned about. By the look of things, the Wolf had begun working for Holt recently, but they'd already proven to be a valuable asset. Someone with this kind of pull had to be one of the higher-ups.

So, probably not Kiara, who seemed more like a cog in the machine.

Then again, communications employees would have access to every office, every employee file, every phone, and every email or digital piece of, well, communication. If you wanted to know anything about anyone, perhaps someone like Kiara would be the perfect mole.

The perfect mole, yes, but not the perfect puppeteer. And it was obvious the Wolf was that. Someone able to orchestrate things without drawing suspicion, even from halfway around the world. Madison got into Holt's good graces by meeting with him face-to-face. Judging from the documented emails, the Wolf was someone Holt had recruited himself, but they never met in person. Holt would target someone with power over his investigation. Someone who maybe got too close to putting him behind bars. Chan?

No. It couldn't be him. I refused to believe it.

The hair on the back of my neck rose and a feeling of dread settled in my stomach. I opened one file after another, looking for a name, a photo, or anything that might settle my fears once and for all. There were dozens of files in the folder. Things Holt kept on hand as blackmail in case the Wolf ever attempted to cut ties with him.

And there it was. An audio file.

"Kiara?" I asked, voice a little breathless. "I hate to bother you, but is there a vending machine or something nearby you could grab me a soda from?"

The file was only a minute long and the CIA headquarters was enormous. Surely it'd take her longer than a minute to run the errand. But she shook her head. "Not in this wing, sorry. Because they need to be restocked, they can only be in specific locations due to the security concerns. And our Starbucks is clear on the other side."

The CIA had their own Starbucks? This place was what I imagined Apple headquarters to be like, only with more metal detectors and polyester suits.

Maybe I could send her there by claiming I desperately needed caffeine. Would that be too obvious? Before I could come up with a game plan, Kiara riffled through the bag she'd placed near the foot of her desk, distracting me from my thoughts. "But I did bring an extra water bottle, if you'd like that?" She stood up and brought it over, holding it out with a smile. I accepted it, because what else was I supposed to do? This woman clearly couldn't take a hint. Either that or she was under orders to never leave me alone, which was probably closer to the truth. I'd already hacked the CIA once. They weren't going to trust me to roam the halls of Langley without an escort.

She glanced at my computer screen, and I froze, my breath caught in my throat. The audio file was still up, front and center for all the world—or specifically, Kiara—to see.

"Oh." Her eyebrows dipped down, and she put a hand on her hip. "You should have said something."

Uh, no, I was pretty sure I shouldn't have. Kiara walked back to her desk and rummaged through the drawers, muttering to herself. Sweat beaded down my back and I eyed the exit. Was there some kind of panic button hidden in Kiara's desk? She'd alert some guards and they'd take me away in handcuffs, confiscate this computer, and my suspicions over the Wolf's identity would always be a giant question mark in my mind.

Kiara gave a shout and straightened from her crouched position over her desk. I eyed her warily. She clutched something in her hand and a spike of fear shot through me.

I pushed my chair back, looking around for a possible weapon to defend myself, but Kiara made it back to my desk in just two strides. Before I could move, she'd opened her hand and dropped a pair of earbuds on the desk.

Earbuds.

My hands shook as I placed them on my knees. I'd been frightened of an electronic accessory.

"I *am* in communications, you know," Kiara said. "So, if you'd prefer the over-the-ear headphones or wired earbuds rather than Bluetooth—"

"No, these are great," I interrupted. "Thanks so much."

She beamed, a hop in her step as she returned to her computer. How could I think this woman was evil when she was clearly too sweet for this world, let alone this line of work?

I connected the earbuds to my laptop, testing the wireless connection with a random song first. I didn't want to hit play on the file only to discover I hadn't paired them correctly. But the song played perfectly, so I muted that and brought up Holt's audio file once again.

At first there was silence. Then a click sounded, like someone picking up a phone call.

"What is it this time?" a male voice said in my ear.

I recognized that voice.

It was tired, and more annoyed than I'd heard it before, but it had the same ever-so-slightly-southern accent that gave off that fatherly vibe and made me feel comfortable and safe.

Not so safe anymore.

Of course, there had to be other people with southern accents in the CIA. I'd only met the man once, so I couldn't exactly accuse him after hearing one sentence on a voice recording. I needed more proof.

"Well, if it isn't Tobias Matthews," Holt said, his voice causing my entire body to lock up like a deer caught in the headlights of an approaching vehicle. Even knowing Holt was in CIA custody somewhere, thousands of miles and an ocean between us, I could still feel the weight of him on top of me. I could smell his breath on my face and hear his labored breathing as he struggled to keep me pinned against the floor. My reaction was so visceral, I almost missed Tobias's answering hiss of anger.

"Call signs, Tank. Only ever use my call sign."

Holt only laughed. "There's nothing in writing here, and no one's recording this."

Liar. Holt recorded this. He'd purposefully used Tobias's full name, then saved it for potential blackmail on an encrypted drive Madison happened to find first.

But part of me still held out hope that Tobias might have another reason for being on this call. Maybe Holt called to recruit him, then Tobias shut him down and Holt kept this recording as proof that everyone at the CIA was squeaky clean and not worth the effort.

Or maybe Holt was calling to rat out one of Tobias's operatives, and Tobias didn't want to hear it.

I didn't want to hear it either.

"Fine." Holt sighed. "Wolf. There, you happy?"

Tobias grunted. "What do you want?"

The audio recording went dead, along with all the hope I'd had that Mendez's superior was a decent person.

Tobias Matthews was the real double agent. And Chan and Mendez were alone with him right now.

Chapter Thirty-Four

· · · · · · · · · ·

THE RECORDING ON ITS OWN WASN'T INCRIMINATING. But when I put it together with everything else in Madison's folder, I couldn't deny it anymore. The real question was, what was I going to do with this information?

Option one: I could tell someone, and they could take it out of my hands. That's probably what the CIA would want me to do, and probably what I *should* do.

But there were several problems with this plan. Namely, I didn't know if anyone would believe me. Also, Mendez and Chan were with Tobias *right now*. What if Tobias took away this computer and its evidence, wiped the other encrypted files before anyone else ever saw them, and tried to shift the blame onto Mendez and Chan? My sister? Or . . . me?

Sending the files to someone wouldn't take care of the immediate danger we all were in right now.

The CIA took an eternity sorting through things. Madison had mentioned this before. And without the evidence to back me up, Tobias might pin everything on Madison, and I could be stuck in jail for a very long time for aiding my sister. I wasn't the sort of girl who could survive in jail. I didn't have those kinds of skills. I didn't know how to make a shiv out of an ordinary kitchen utensil. And sure, maybe I was making mountains out of molehills. Maybe Tobias wouldn't do anything like what I'd imagined, and I had time to tell Mendez after his meeting.

But maybe I didn't.

The fact was, I didn't know. If I were Tobias, I wouldn't wait. I didn't even know who to send this information to.

With everyone back in the United States, Tobias had to know his back was against the wall. He'd already have a plan in place, just waiting for the right time to put it into action. Mendez and Chan could be walking into a trap without even knowing it. In fact, I was pretty confident they were.

Mendez and Chan were in law enforcement. Jail for them wasn't the same as jail for me. I'd heard horror stories of what prison inmates did to cops and other people who'd put them there. It could literally be a death sentence for two CIA officers.

Option two: I could do . . . something.

But what? I wasn't a trained operative. I was a penetration tester, with limited resources. Tobias had already cut off my access to the CIA database. I didn't even have a phone.

But . . . I had this laptop. And Mendez had his. His laptop that still had that Remote Access Trojan I'd installed back at the safe house in Prague.

I snuck a glance at Kiara to make sure her attention was elsewhere, then I pulled up the RAT credentials to see if Mendez had his computer open.

When I saw he did, my sigh of relief could have sent a ship to Spain. Kiara glanced up and I unconvincingly turned my sigh into a cough. This was where Mendez's acting abilities would have come in handy, because Kiara raised her eyebrows, obviously skeptical, but didn't comment.

I thanked my lucky stars that she was too polite to meddle, then I went about my business. I didn't have any time to waste. I took control of his webcam first. If Mendez was observant, he might notice a light turn on at the top of his screen. But the code to hide that would take too long, and I was already bringing up the dialogue box to send him a message. I just had to see through his camera to make sure he'd be the only one reading it.

Through the webcam I saw Mendez sitting in a nondescript room, leaning back in an office chair, his attention on something in the distance. The CIA could really use an interior decorator. Put some color on their walls. The tan was a bit depressing. Even Mendez looked sallow in that lighting.

A muscle in his jaw twitched, the only sign of tension, but I'd been around him enough that I could recognize it now. A pair of crutches was perched against the wall behind him, and once in a while Chan's face floated into view when he adjusted in his seat.

I could deal with Chan seeing the messages I'd send. It was Tobias I was worried about. With a few more keystrokes, I took over the audio from the webcam so I could hear what was happening in the room. Mendez was practically on a conference call with me and he didn't even know it. I could see and hear him, but I was a silent bystander.

Tobias was talking somewhere in the distance with that light southern drawl of his. Something about . . .

Me.

I sat up.

Tobias was talking about me. All about how Mendez had broken protocol by getting me so involved and how there'd be a disciplinary hearing for his actions. It hit me that Tobias was already laying the groundwork for Mendez to take the fall.

There were also other voices that I didn't recognize. Two men who spoke with authority, even more so than Tobias.

With a start, I realized they were the FBI agents. They were there in the room, listening to Tobias spout his lies, and they were buying it.

I put my head on the desk and focused on breathing evenly. Blood rushed through my ears and drowned out the other noise of the room. Heat flushed all over me, to the point where I thought I must be having hot flashes. Too young for that—I was just boiling over with rage.

Then I remembered Kiara was in the room, likely watching everything I was doing. So I raised my head and stared at my computer. The embers of a fire were burning inside me. I hadn't gone through everything else only to fail now. I would not be bested by a mediocre man who cared more about money and politics than he did about loyalty, family, or doing the right thing.

I wasn't sure how I was going to do it, but I was the flint, and I was about to bring down a raging wildfire on this entire organization if I had to.

No time for beating around the bush. I typed a message in the dialogue box that would appear on Mendez's computer.

MENDEZ, THIS IS DOVE. TOBIAS IS THE DOUBLE
AGENT.

I hit enter and waited for him to notice it.
And waited.
And waited.

It was Chan who reached over and nudged Mendez to look at his screen.

Mendez's expression didn't change for even a second.

Can't read my, can't read my, no he can't read my poker face, I silently sang to myself, vowing to play Lady Gaga's song for Mendez the next time we played Name That Tune. I was building up quite the playlist.

Mendez kept his eyes on the board or whatever it was in the distance, then moved one hand to the keyboard and typed one word.

PROOF?

I leaned forward and typed quickly.

I HAVE IT ALL. CODE NAMES, DOCUMENTATION OF HIM RECEIVING PAYMENT, AND AN AUDIO FILE OF TOBIAS ON THE PHONE WITH HOLT.

I chewed on a nail while I watched Mendez read my message. In my own room, at her desk a few feet away, Kiara opened a package of chips. She chomped down on one so aggressively I worried she might crack a tooth. Normally, this would bother me. But now, I counted it as a blessing that she was in her own little bubble.

Mendez typed an email address into the dialogue box and I stared at it. I was not a mind reader. He had to give me a little more to go on. He said something out loud to Tobias and I realized he was having two conversations at once. One with the people in his room, and one with me. I'd have to be a little patient while he sorted things out.

A second later, he sent another message.

SEND ALL YOUR FILES THERE. USE MY EMAIL
ADDRESS BECAUSE THE CIA HAS FIREWALLS TO BLOCK
OUTSIDE ADDRESSES. WAIT FOR MY SIGNAL, THEN PLAY
YOUR AUDIO RECORDING THROUGH THIS COMPUTER'S
SPEAKERS.

I noticed he didn't ask whether I could do that. I mean, I could. But still. Would it have killed him to ask?

I did as he instructed, emailing the files to the address he'd provided and marking the message as urgent and time sensitive. Then there wasn't anything for me to do besides wait, finger poised on the audio file, ready to play it for the room Mendez was in.

I knew I shouldn't be worried. I'd seen Mendez in far worse scrapes than this one. If things got physical here, Tobias wasn't the wolf he thought himself to be. But it was three against two, and Chan was injured. Plus, there was the little fact that assaulting FBI agents wouldn't exactly make Mendez look innocent.

Tobias was listing every time the operation went sideways and finding a way to blame it on Mendez. "Officer Mendez let Dove know his plans," he said. "Through her, Madison Barkley was able to learn key details of the mission and sabotage the CIA's efforts. When she saw an opportunity, she tried to make it appear like she hadn't turned her back on the CIA, but that was easy to do with the help of Officer Mendez as her inside man. Then he let her escape."

I didn't think he could stoop any lower. But there was low, and then there was Mariana Trench low, and somehow Tobias had managed to dig a hole in it. How did he think I'd contacted Madison when I never even knew where she was? Tobias really was trying to take out everyone who could implicate him—Mendez, Madison, and now me. We'd cleared Madison's name and he was trying to drag her back in, claiming she'd only helped out to save face when the kitchen got too hot. Surely the FBI agents could see the holes in Tobias's argument.

But no. The FBI agents murmured their agreement, and panic crept in around the edges of my vision.

Still, Mendez didn't have me play the recording.

What was he waiting for? Me to have a heart attack?

Mendez leaned back in his chair, the picture of casual confidence, a glint in his eye as he smiled smugly at Tobias somewhere off-screen.

That was so the opposite of me, rocking in place and hyperventilating like breathing was going out of style.

Apparently, Tobias wasn't expecting his calm demeanor either, because he paused in his explanation. "Find something humorous, Officer Mendez?"

Mendez shrugged. "You. Grasping at straws. From what I hear, you're the one we need to launch an investigation into, Tobias."

The room went silent. I rubbed my hand on my pant leg while my stomach roiled. Tobias didn't say anything. I couldn't see him either, so I had only Mendez's solid expression as an indication that Tobias was still there. In my own room, a clock ticked by the seconds.

Finally, Tobias cleared his throat. "You're out of line."

My heartbeat pounded double-time and I couldn't help the whimper that escaped. The FBI had already heard Tobias's argument. Would they even listen to Mendez?

Mendez stood up and moved out of range of my screen. I was left with a view of a tan wall and crutches.

Great. That was great. The least he could have done was turn the laptop so I could watch what was happening. Now I was tuned to a channel with nothing but sound.

Until something else came into my field of view. My real view, here in this room.

Kiara stood just to the side of the computer, hands on her hips. "What's going on here?"

I gaped at her. "N-nothing," I stammered.

She was nonplussed. Before I could stop her, she'd reached out and pulled the earbud from my left ear, inserting it into her own. I couldn't mute the sound. I needed to hear Mendez so he could give me the signal. There wasn't anything I could do besides let Kiara hear too. If I snatched it back, there was a chance I'd leave this room with my mission a failure.

She pushed my chair far to the side and my feet skittered along the linoleum to gain purchase. I'd thought she was too sweet for this world, but I'd been wrong in believing she wasn't cut out for this line of work. Sweet as she might be, she obviously took her job seriously.

She leaned over the computer, watching the screen.

The video feed showed nothing except the wall, but Mendez's voice played through my remaining earbud. "Don't try to spin this," Mendez said to Tobias. "You were orchestrating things all along, weren't you? That's the real reason you were scared to let Dove access the database and why you never authorized Chan's team to act as backup in Prague once we found Holt's base. You wanted this operation to fail."

"Oh please," Tobias said in his slow southern drawl. "Would you listen to yourself? I'm sorry it's come to this. You know I've always thought of you like a son."

At that, a pang went through me, remembering everything

Mendez had told me about his past with Tobias. How Tobias had helped him after his girlfriend Gabby's death. And yet, Mendez still chose to believe me, even without seeing all the evidence first.

A bloom of warmth spread in my chest and I swallowed a lump in my throat.

Slowly, so I wouldn't startle Kiara, who was now watching the computer monitor, I started to roll my chair back to the desk.

Tobias made a disappointed sound. "What do you have to say for yourself?"

"This," Mendez said. "Dove, play the recording."

Finally.

I reached around Kiara to hit the button, but she blocked my arm. "I don't know what's happening," she said, "but it's clear to me that you're interfering with CIA matters. We never should have given you access to a laptop. There's a reason you're not in that debriefing, and I'm sure they'll get to the bottom of things without you. Sorry, Dove."

She moved like she was going to take away the computer.

My vision went blank with terror and blood rushed through my ears. Then I did the unthinkable.

I assaulted a CIA officer.

Forming my hands into claws, I lurched up and grabbed Kiara's shoulders, shoving her out of the way. Her mouth formed a small O of surprise as she fell to the side.

My finger slammed down on the key and I heard the audio file for the second time.

"*Well, if it isn't Tobias Matthews,*" Holt said, the conversation playing out exactly as I remembered.

"*Call signs, Tank. Only ever use my call sign.*"

The sound of Holt's laugh came through a little tinny on the speakers. I could only hope everything sounded normal in the room.

"*There's nothing in writing here, and no one's recording this,*" Holt said.

As if anticipating Tobias trying to close the laptop, Chan moved the computer onto his lap. Now my view was a close-up of Chan's blue shirt.

Well, at least it wasn't something else.

"*Fine,*" Holt said with a sigh. "*Wolf. There, you happy?*"

"*What do you want?*" the audio recording of Tobias asked.

It clicked off and there was silence in the room.

Kiara pushed herself to her elbows, mouth pinched.

Tobias finally spoke. "That doesn't prove anything. Except that you gave Dove unauthorized access to a government-issued laptop."

One of the voices I didn't recognize, an FBI agent, spoke up. "The deputy director said you might try to pull something like this, Officer Mendez. I'll have to take you into custody if you don't cooperate."

My heart dropped. It wasn't enough. Even a phone call with Tobias's voice wasn't enough to convince the FBI they had the wrong man.

Chan seemed to agree with me. "But the recording?" he asked. He flipped the computer around so I could see the room, like he was holding the computer out as evidence.

Kiara was getting up. If she took away the laptop now, I wouldn't know what happened with Mendez. I couldn't show the other files to the FBI agents if he asked. Desperation pooled in my stomach and I picked up the laptop. I backed away from the desk, putting as much distance between Kiara and me as possible.

"Please, just wait." My voice shook. "Give me one minute."

I returned my attention to the screen, careful to keep one eye on Kiara.

"Audio recordings are easily faked," the other FBI agent said. It was the first time I could see him, and I almost wished I couldn't. He stood with his legs shoulder-width apart, like he was poised for a takedown, and the expression on his face was enough to make a grizzly bear pause. But the thing that made me break out in a cold sweat was the gleam of silver from the handcuffs he held.

"I'd like to show you something on this computer first," Mendez said. "There's other evidence."

With harried strokes, I pulled it up in another window so it would display on Mendez's screen. Just in case anyone happened to look. Even though I knew they wouldn't.

"I'm sure there is." The sarcasm in the FBI agent's voice made it clear he'd already chosen his side.

But I'd been too invested in pulling up the documents to notice how close Kiara had gotten. Faster than I would have thought possible, she'd yanked the computer from my hands and dropped it back on the desk.

"It's over, Dove." She held out her hand. "Earbuds."

There wasn't a point in fighting. The FBI agents wouldn't listen, and it would only make things worse for me. Besides, there wasn't anything else I could do. Reluctantly, I pulled the remaining earbud out and handed it to her. She returned it to the case with hers and the audio disconnected from the Bluetooth. It started playing through the laptop's speakers instead.

"Officer Mendez," one of the FBI officers said, "please come with us. We'll get this sorted."

I didn't buy that for a second. If Mendez went with them,

this would be the last time I saw him without prison bars between us.

My heartbeat was thumping so loudly in my ears I almost couldn't hear what they were saying. If I had to guess, this was why people had to pass such rigorous physicals to become CIA agents. Because my blood pressure was through the roof simply from listening to a conversation.

He put Mendez in handcuffs and I winced like I was the one feeling the cold metal snapping around my wrists. Part of me was surprised Kiara hadn't powered down the computer yet, but then I caught her glancing at the screen, clearly trying to hide her interest.

Something told me this was above her security clearance.

She shook her head and motioned for me to follow. "Come with me." She grabbed my arm, already steering me toward the door.

My nails dug tiny half-moons into the palms of my hands. Numbness spread from my chest to my fingers, and I had to blink back the heat that I felt building behind my eyelids.

This wasn't supposed to happen. We weren't supposed to lose when we had the winning hand.

Kiara reached back for the laptop, hand hovering over the lid, about to close it.

I took a final glance at the computer screen. At that moment, the door to their room opened again. A woman I didn't recognize strode in.

Everyone else recognized her immediately though.

It was clear from the way they straightened their posture. This was a woman who commanded respect. Honestly? She was who I wanted to be when I grew up and I didn't even know her.

She was older, perhaps in her fifties, with light brown skin, her dark hair pulled back in a sleek low bun.

Kiara stopped, watching the computer with an awed expression.

"Good," the woman said, looking around. "Everyone's here, including the FBI."

She gestured to the two agents in question. "Gentlemen, I'm going to need you to take Tobias Matthews into custody for treason."

When they didn't move immediately, she snapped her fingers. Then they moved.

When Chan placed the computer on the table, I couldn't tell if it was the screen moving or my own head spinning from this sudden change of events. One second I was planning accessories for an orange jumpsuit, and the next I was saved by a mysterious woman in sensible heels. My angle on the room had shifted, just like my outlook on life. Mendez nodded his head, shoulders back, like he'd never been worried for a second. Show-off.

"Ms. Alexis Claire, thank you for coming," he said.

I recognized the name from Mendez and Chan talking, and from when I'd poked around on the CIA database. She was the assistant director of the CIA—aka, I could count the number of people higher up the chain with only one hand.

Mendez cleared his throat.

"I see you got my email."

Chapter Thirty-Five

. . . .

One week later

IT WAS THE FIRST TIME I'D BEEN ALONE WITH MENDEZ
since we'd returned to the States, and from the way he kept
touching me—a hand on my back, fingers playing in my hair,
pads of his fingertips tracing along my arm as he walked me up
the stairs to my new apartment—I could tell he'd missed me too.

As for my new apartment, I got all the benefits of a better,
bigger place without the trouble of having to pack up my things
myself. It was all done under the cover of darkness, as CIA operatives first combed my old apartment for bugs, then packed
everything and set it all up for me here, in a new location that
was unknown to any of Holt's associates. In the meantime, I'd
been staying at a hotel but practically living at Langley as I spent
hours answering questions and filling out paperwork.

Holt and Tobias were under arrest, true, but they still had to
be tried for their crimes, which, knowing our criminal justice
system, could take a while. The CIA wanted me to testify against
them, which meant placing me in a modified witness-protection
program. Because of my skill set as a penetration tester, they

wanted to keep me close rather than send me off to some unknown barely-a-town in Montana. For which I was grateful.

I'd have to lie low, but for a social introvert like me, giving
me permission to stay home at night was just the icing on an already delicious cake. Mendez already lived off-the-grid because
of his occupation, so he wouldn't have to do much different.

"You ready to see it?" Mendez stood in front of a door with
the number 24 written in matte black. He bounced on the balls
of his feet, the keys to my new apartment swinging from his
fingers. When I tried to snatch them, he held them out of reach,
wrapping an arm around my back and pulling me close.

I'll admit it, that was kind of my goal all along.

His arm wasn't in a sling anymore. Originally the doctors
had been worried he'd torn his rotator cuff, which might require
surgery. But it had just been a sprain. And now that it'd been a
week, they wanted him to use it more so he wouldn't get a frozen
shoulder. I was coming to find I really liked Mendez with both
arms.

"Show me." I leaned in and brushed a kiss across his lips.

"Oh, I'll show you." He flipped us around so I was pinned
against the door as he deepened the kiss. It was a good five
minutes later that he inserted the key in the lock and turned the
handle. I stumbled backward into my apartment, still locked together with Mendez. My shoes sunk into plush carpet, and I
tripped, breaking us apart, which allowed me to get a good look
around.

This apartment was in Richmond, Virginia, which meant my
rent stretched a lot further than it did in Washington, DC, but it
was still close to CIA headquarters and all the things I was familiar with. Because it was located farther out, public transport

wasn't quite as good. I'd probably have to learn to drive, which was all right by me, as long as Mendez was willing to teach me.

Gorgeous bay windows took up most of the living room, with views of a green belt stretching behind it. The kitchen was twice the size of my old one, and newly remodeled to boot. Plus, best of all, off to the side I had my very own office, complete with a desk and everything. No more working from my couch, though I was sure I'd probably wind up there more often than not. The point was, I now had options.

It was weird to have all my things set up in an apartment I'd never even seen, but now that I had my own washer and dryer, plus central air, I wasn't about to look the gift apartment in the mouth. There were a few boxes they'd left for me to unpack, but overall, the CIA had been very efficient. So efficient I wondered whether they did this for everyone, or whether Mendez had pulled some strings to make sure this move had been as painless as possible.

"No one traced the moving van here?" I asked. A moving van was kind of hard to hide, after all, but Mendez shook his head with a smile, coming over to rest his hands on my shoulders.

"I took care of everything myself."

Overkill? Maybe. But I loved that he was so protective. There were a lot of things I loved about Mendez, and I was getting a sneaking suspicion it wasn't just things *about* him I loved either. But that was a conversation for another day.

"Even people within the CIA can't trace me here?" I asked.

"Only Ms. Claire. And Chan, since I thought you might want to see a friendly face. But Holt and Tobias have no way of finding you, even if they still have informants in the CIA."

My shoulders dropped in relief, but that might also have

been a result of the way Mendez's thumbs were tracing small, lazy circles along the skin there. It had a way of making me feel relaxed. Soothed. Like I was ready to strip off all my clothes and take him to bed with me.

Mendez chuckled. "You know, Tobias had even more evidence against him on his own computer?"

I'd been in meetings for a week, but this was news to me. Mostly they'd wanted *me* to talk, rather than tell me anything. Go figure. I looked up and cocked my head to the side. "Really?"

Mendez nodded. "I've been completely exonerated and Tobias is in a hole so deep there's no way he'll be able to crawl out. I can't believe I actually thought he was looking out for me all this time." He shook his head, then turned me around and hooked his fingers into my belt loops, tugging me closer. He bent down and started nuzzling my neck in a way that made everything else he was saying rather fuzzy in my mind. "You're sure you like it?"

"Mm-hmm." I leaned in so he could have easier access.

"Your apartment." Mendez laughed, nibbling on my ear. His breath was warm, sending shivers across my body. My hands reached for the hem of his shirt almost against my will. I couldn't control them. It was all the waiting that was making them move.

"Yes," I said. "But you know what room I haven't seen yet?" I started pulling him in the direction where I thought the bedroom was. There was only one hall branching off the living room, so I was pretty sure I was going the right way. But Mendez planted his feet and brought me back, his arm snaking around my waist and up the back of my shirt. Heat wound its way down my stomach until my legs felt like jelly.

"You've hardly even looked at the rest of it." Mendez grinned.

"Don't you want to look at the kitchen? There's an automatic faucet."

"You think I care about an automatic faucet right now?" My voice came out all wispy, but I didn't care. He already knew the effect he had on me. My lips parted, needing him to kiss me. I was acutely aware of my own heartbeat, thumping like a sub-woofer.

Mendez pulled a strand of my hair between his fingers, play-ing with the ends as he looked around us. "But you like it?"

I groaned. I didn't think it'd be this difficult to get Mendez naked. "Yes, I love it. Why are you so concerned?" Unless he cared because he was planning on spending a lot of time here . . . then I was okay with it.

He sighed, pulling back so I could look him in the eyes. "Because"—he paused, palming the back of his neck—"I feel re-sponsible for you having to move. For you getting involved in the first place. I . . . I bought you new plants. To replace the ones that died. I know it's not much, but I'll spend every day making it up to you—"

I rolled my eyes and placed a hand on his arm, pulling it back so it was around my waist once more. "It wasn't you who got me involved—it was my sister." And the fact that we looked too much alike. My sister, who I still hadn't heard from since we'd cleared her name with the CIA. So much for gratitude.

"Oh, speaking of Madison." His eyes twinkled as he reached into his pocket and pulled out a phone. "I've taken the liberty of preprogramming a few numbers into it for you."

I gasped and pulled the phone from his grip. I hadn't had my own phone for weeks, and sometimes it actually felt like I'd been missing a limb. I'd had a lot going on, but in the moments of boredom, when I hadn't had meetings or paperwork to fill out, when I'd been waiting on important CIA people to acknowledge my existence, I'd often wished I had my phone back.

This wasn't the same one—it was shiny and new, with its front glass still intact, unlike my old one, which Mendez had disassembled back in the parking garage forever ago. That felt like a different life. This was a new beginning, complete with a seven-inch OLED screen and a whole terabyte of storage space.

But best of all, it had my sister's phone number. I scrolled to the *M*'s and was surprised to see Mendez's number wasn't in there. I'd have to ask him about that later.

I hit call on Madison's name and brought the receiver up to my ear, hoping Mendez wouldn't mind this little delay in our evening's plans. Then again, he had only himself to blame.

I wasn't sure she'd answer. She might be off saving the world right now. Or on the flip side, pretending to be a bad guy. But she picked up on the third ring, her familiar voice making me sag against Mendez in relief.

"Hey, sis," she said. "They only gave me your number an hour ago. I'm surprised you have it already."

"Apparently, the government *can* work quickly," I replied. "Who would have thought."

"Ah." She laughed, the sound of it making me feel lighter than I had in days. "You're beginning to see how things really work. The red tape, the endless paperwork, the meetings that go on for days . . ."

"Do you know when you'll get to come home?" I cut in. She'd said it might take a while, but I already missed her more than I'd thought possible. I wanted her here, safe, where she could criticize my clothing choices, and I could gloat that I finally had a boyfriend.

"Soon," she said. "We're tying up loose ends now. They're

planning a few simultaneous takedowns that will hopefully wrap everything up nice and neat in a bow."

I gnawed on a fingernail. Mendez gently pulled my hand from my face, taking it in his and leading me to the couch. We sat down and he pulled my legs across his lap. I rested my head against his shoulder, holding the phone against my other ear. His hands traced along the skin at my waist, applying just enough pressure that it didn't tickle.

"You'll be safe?" I asked.

"You know I will be," Madison's voice came through the line.

I didn't think I'd felt this content . . . ever. I curled up against Mendez and let it wash over me, relishing the way it felt simply to be held. Cherished. Like I was something that mattered.

"I have to go, Dove. But I'll see you soon, okay? That's a promise. I love you."

I smiled. I liked this new tradition. Letting go of old fears and embracing better habits. Healthier ones.

"I love you too," I said. "Bye, Mads."

We hung up and I sighed, cradling the phone against my chest like it was something precious.

"Was that a good surprise?" Mendez's voice rumbled against my ear, and I sat up a little.

"You know what would have made it better?"

He tilted his head, so I continued. "If your number was in my phone too." I tried to give it to him, but he pushed my hand back.

"It's already in there," he replied, smiling.

I shook my head.

He leaned over and began nibbling on my ear. When he spoke, it sent shivers along my arms.

"It's sorted by first name. You need to look in the *N*'s."

I'd been inside the CIA's database but still hadn't looked up Mendez's profile. It wasn't the type of information one sought out uninvited. His first name had to be earned. Even the CIA paperwork referred to him as Officer Mendez.

I opened the contacts and scrolled to the *N*'s, pausing when my finger hovered over his name. His full name.

Nick Mendez.

My eyes shot back to his and he grinned.

"Now you know what to call out in the bedroom." He caught my bottom lip with his in a kiss. A familiar heat swirled in my stomach, traveling lower as I sunk my hands into his hair. When that wasn't enough, I brought them to his chest, pulling on his shirt until he was on top of me.

When he broke off the kiss, I raised my eyebrows. "Cocky, aren't we?" I asked. "That I'll be calling out your name?"

He shook his head. "Confident."

He began trailing kisses along my neck, down to my clavicle. The phone clattered to the floor, forgotten as I pulled Mendez even closer. I wrapped one leg around him, holding him there in case he had any ideas of pulling away.

"Nick," I breathed.

He smiled against my lips. "I like the way my name sounds when you say it."

There was nothing between us now. No secrets or deadly operations. No lives on the line or hidden agendas.

Nothing.

Except clothes.

Acknowledgments

Just like every good spy needs a team to be successful, this book never would have happened without the incredible group of people I have supporting me.

A big shout-out goes to my editor, Kristine Swartz, who is brilliant at seeing the forest for the trees. Not only did she help make this book what it is, but she was always so understanding and made sure my voice was heard throughout the process. I couldn't be more grateful.

Other amazing people at Berkley who deserve recognition: editorial assistant Mary Baker, managing editor Christine Legon, production editor Megha Jain, marketer Jessica Plummer, and publicist Dache' Rogers—who all took care of me, made this book shine, and helped get it to as many readers as possible. Special thanks go to cover designer Colleen Reinhart and cover artist Jekaterina Budryte, without whom this stunning cover would not have been possible.

I'm so lucky to have my agent, Eric Smith, in my corner. He supported me 100 percent when I told him I wanted to switch gears and write an adult spy rom-com, and he's always been one of my biggest cheerleaders.

To Janette Rallison and Brandon Chambers, who read my book prior to final edits, you are too good for this world. Thank you from the bottom of my heart. And to the people who read parts of it while I was still working on the first draft: Kelly Lyman, Robin King, Brielle Porter, and Aashna Avachat—you are all rock stars. To the authors who have read and blurbed my book—words can't express how much that means to me.

Sending hugs to my brother Scott for answering my medical questions about ketamine. If it weren't for you, this book would have been stuck at the end. Thank you, Andrew Rosen, for providing me with resources on ethical hackers. If there are any mistakes, they come from my own research, and I hope that hackers everywhere can forgive me.

The Berkletes—you are such a warm, encouraging group of authors, and I'm fortunate to have stumbled into this community and have you all in my camp.

Major love to my family, who put up with so much while I was writing and on deadlines. Thanks, Mom and Dad, for understanding whenever I disappeared for weeks without a call, and thank you to my siblings for being okay with it when I bowed out of family events. (Truth was, I just didn't want to lose another game of Hand and Foot, but I have too much pride to say so.) My mother-in-law was great about watching my son whenever my poor time-management skills got the better of me, so thank you for the Grandma Days. Speaking of my son, he was incredibly understanding of my deadlines and played countless hours on the Nintendo Switch—for which I'm sure he was heartbroken. Thanks, kiddo, for taking one for the team.

But the real MVP was my husband, Brad. He made sure the house didn't burn down, we were all fed, and the dishes didn't pile up in the sink. Brad, I love you more every day, and I have no idea how I got so lucky. I could write an entire acknowledgments section devoted entirely to you, but the fact of the matter is, you're the whole reason I write love stories. So in that sense, every book is an acknowledgment to you. You're my favorite.

Lastly, thank *you* for picking up my book. I know there's a lot of other things you could have done with your time, so the fact that you read my book means the world to me. Thank you, thank you!

Keep reading for an excerpt from

Mr. Nice Spy

Coming soon!

I'VE ALWAYS HAD A KNACK FOR BLOWING STUFF UP.
My friends' phones. My temper. My love life.

But where I really excel is explosive pyrotechnics of a physical nature. On an epic scale. When things start looking dim, that's when I like to light up the darkness with things that go boom.

I double-checked my calculations, then triple-checked them just because I didn't feel like losing any fingers today. When I was completely sure I'd mixed the right quantities of sulfur, potassium nitrate, and the other combustible chemicals for the shells I'd been putting together in secret for the last month, I put on my protective gear.

Of course, I'd started planning this all at the paper stage. Then the computer. Now it was finally time to see whether all my planning amounted to anything. Whether it'd be the stuff dreams were made of . . . or whether it'd quite literally blow up in my face.

By the time I'd finished putting on my conductive shoes to

limit sparks, I couldn't remember why I'd thought any of this was a good idea.

I could lose my job because of this.

My shirt chafed at my neck, and I wasn't sure whether my knees could support my weight. Sure, I liked the idea of being a rebel. Until the time came to light the fuse.

If I were in a heist movie, I'd be the crew member who planned the whole thing but stayed back behind the curtain, eager for the bad guy to get what was coming to them, but ultimately unable to physically stand up to them in any way. Actually, never mind. I'd obviously be the detonation expert, called in to blow stuff up. They never had to confront the bad guy either.

The point was, I didn't like it when it was *my* reputation on the line. I didn't want to get in trouble. I just wanted to watch the night sky light up.

Eventually I couldn't put it off any longer. I killed the lights, so darkness enveloped the room. Silence wrapped around me— the suffocating kind that made all my internal thoughts too loud. Before I could think about it, I hit the button that signaled the machine to light the cake fuse. I was safely behind a clear fire-proof window, along with my audience of coworkers, who would get to watch my attempt live to see whether it was a success or failure.

As a pyrotechnic engineer, aka fireworks designer, I'd had my fair share of both. The phrase "crash and burn" got pretty literal around here. But I rarely took on a project in secret and *never* against the express order of my boss.

Today was full of firsts for me.

The cake fuse—a single fuse that lit several fireworks in a se-quence—was out of my control now. Everyone behind the glass would now see the entirety of the design I'd been working on, albeit on a much smaller scale. Our testing facility in Virginia was large, but it wasn't like we produced full-scale fireworks for everyone in the vicinity to get a free fireworks show every night. Could you imagine the noise complaints? No, we worked in an enclosed protective bunker that let us record things like the decibel noise level, the smoke whiteout levels, and more. But because we could calculate the apex and hang without needing to physically produce it, we could make smaller fireworks here in the bunker that still gave us an accurate idea of how they'd react in the wild.

I held my breath as the spark lit up the fuse, its neon orange flare winding along the cord like the bead of sweat going down my spine.

Please work, please work.

The spark hit the base of the first shell and my gaze shot up, away from the wrappings into the empty air above it. I'd started with a brocade waterfall, but what made my firework special was adding the newer ghost color changing effect.

I stood so close that my nose was pressed against the glass. When the firework went off, the lights and sounds hit me almost simultaneously, my whole body taking in everything at once.

It. Was. Glorious.

For once in my life, everything happened exactly like I'd planned it. At the peak of the apex, the waterfall unfurled like a blanket, the delicate streamers cresting over the edge, its colors starting to shift from red to blue and incandescent white. The top corner crackled as it shifted with red and white bursts, the rest extending out in even lines that stretched toward the ground—displaying a perfect American flag unfurling as they went.

And they'd said it couldn't be done. That there wasn't enough time before the president's inauguration and we'd need to figure something else out for the finale *so, Andee, would you just drop it already?*

I turned, expecting to see the congratulatory faces of my co-workers.

What I got instead were sour attitudes and pinched expressions.

Okay, so maybe I'd gone behind everyone's backs to work on this. And maybe the creative director had told me in no uncertain terms that we needed to focus our attention elsewhere. But couldn't they see that this was better than our original plan? That this was the type of firework display that made history and was worth working a few extra hours for, even if we had to change a few things for the finale?

They started stripping their protective wear in silence, a few of them muttering "Congratulations, Superstar" as they passed me on the way to one of the many doors. First rule of fire safety—always make sure there are multiple exits in case of an explosion.

I ignored the jabs because I refused to take the bait, looking past their faces for my creative director's.

Just once, I wished they'd call me by my name, especially when I was really doing them a favor, if you thought about it. No one wanted to watch a subpar fireworks show at something as important as a presidential inauguration. But I knew that was asking too much from people who had called me "Superstar" nonstop ever since I let it slip I was related to one. Add that to the fact that they considered me to be an overachiever, and, well . . . honestly, I didn't think half of them even knew my real name. Sometimes I felt like shouting "It's Andee Paxton, by the way" after their retreating forms, but then they'd know their bullying got to me. I wasn't about to give them the satisfaction.

My creative director shuffled over while I was removing my conductive shoes, hands in his pockets.

"Well," Rob said, "looks like you did it."

It wasn't a reprimand, but it wasn't a compliment either. It *should* have been a compliment. I'd just pulled off the impossible. Something that had never been done before and would bring notoriety and credibility to the firm. Well, even more credibility. We were already the premier firework designer company in the nation, hence why we worked prestigious events like presidential inaugurations and New Year's Eve ball drops televised worldwide.

If I had to guess, maybe Rob didn't like a junior designer stepping on his toes. Because why else was he acting like such a wet blanket?

"It's late and I want to go home." Rob scrubbed a hand across his face. "We'll talk about this on Monday."

He walked away without another word, leaving me to wonder whether I'd still have a job after the weekend. Everyone else followed soon after him, until it was only Karina and me left in the bunker. I started walking back to my office, hoping she'd take the hint.

She didn't.

Karina matched me stride for stride, keeping up with my pace even as I rounded a corner so fast, I practically gave myself whiplash coming around the other side.

"Nice job, Superstar," she said.

She wasn't even breaking a sweat. Curse her long legs.

"You know, I saw an article about your *dad* on Celebrity Gossip this morning." She walked into my office with me, seemingly oblivious to my death stare that should have burned a hole in her forehead.

I switched tactics, hoping indifference might work instead. I glanced at my fingernails, inspecting a hangnail on my pinky.

"Not surprising," I said. "He's kind of a big deal, so . . ."

My dad was Keith Huxley-Beck, the famous actor with four Oscar wins and three Emmy nominations. And no, I'd never actually met him, which was why everyone gave me such a hard time about it. Why would my mom never ask for child support or insist on me meeting my father when he'd been voted *People* magazine's sexiest man alive on two separate occasions?

Answer: because we'd done just fine on our own and didn't need that kind of drama in our lives, that's why. Plus, it was none of their business, thank you very much. It was a fun tidbit I shared with people during get-to-know-you games, like Two Truths and a Lie, but it wasn't exactly something I wanted dominating my life. That was why my mom never shared my pictures online growing up and I didn't have social media accounts even now.

Most of the time, people found this fact about my life fascinating. But then I started my new job here and no one believed me. Which was great. Was I pushing myself so hard to achieve greatness because I had to prove myself every single day?

Well, I wasn't saying it *wasn't* true.

Karina continued like I hadn't said anything.

"Word on the street is he knocked up an intern from a late-night talk show interview he did a few months back. You might have a half sibling running around come Christmastime. You know, if you're telling the truth."

I resisted the urge to sigh. This was exactly the type of drama I didn't need but that came hand in hand with having a celebrity for a parent.

Back when I was a naive teenager, I'd set up Google alerts for his name, because I wanted to know everything that came up.

What a mistake that had been.

Now I purposefully kept myself in the dark, only learning of his . . . adventures . . . when he was trending or someone like Karina backed me into a corner.

"I'll be sure to invite the baby over for the holidays," I dead-panned, hoping she'd drop it. Thankfully, she did, leaving my office with a bounce, her mission accomplished.

As soon as she left, I pulled out my phone and opened the internet, typing in my father's name and clicking on the first YouTube video that came up relating to the new scandal. The thumbnail for this one looked like someone actually interviewed him, rather than regurgitating the same headlines as everyone else. So, on that promising note, I closed my office door and sat down at my desk to watch it.

The news anchor for *Good Morning America* sat across from him, her pressed collared shirt making her look a bit like a floating head because it matched too well with the background.

"We're here with Keith Huxley-Beck, who is busy promoting his newest film, *Traitors Never Die*. Keith, thank you for joining us today."

He murmured something polite and the host waited approximately two milliseconds before pouncing.

"Lately you've been more in the news for a possible baby-daddy scandal than your acting work. The mother recently announced it's a girl. Keith, is there anything you'd like to share with our audience?"

My father chuckled and shifted on his chair, running a hand through his golden curls. His fans loved whenever he did that, but I was pretty sure his hair and makeup person probably felt the opposite.

"The claims are baseless," Keith said. "We had a brief, mutually consensual relationship and took every precaution to prevent against unwanted pregnancy."

I rolled my eyes. He sounded like a robot. Usually he oozed charisma, so it was easy to tell when he was following a script written by his publicity team. This was exhibit A.

The host spread her arms, palms up to the ceiling. "Accidents happen."

Keith shook his head and pulled a paper out of his back pocket, shifting on his chair to do so. He handed the paper to the host.

"I know," he said. "Which is why I did a DNA test through DNA and Me to prove it."

I leaned forward in my chair, as if I could somehow read the paper through the tiny screen of my phone if I could only get close enough.

The host raised her eyebrows as she accepted the paper, then she unfolded it slowly and dramatically for the cameras. Three whole seconds passed without her saying anything. She read the paper silently, pursing her lips that were obviously overfilled and overlined.

"So, you're not the father after all," she finally announced.

I sat back with a grunt.

This. *This* was why I didn't pay attention to the drama. Because nine times out of ten, it never amounted to anything. Except when it did, and those times I wished I didn't know. All in all, it was better to remain in blissful ignorance.

My father smiled for the cameras and I mentally calculated how much his veneers had cost.

"I'm not," he stated. "Though I wish the baby and her mother all the success in life."

Author Photo by Pepperfox Photos

Tiana Smith is a web designer turned novelist who grew up in the Rocky Mountains. She graduated from Westminster University with double degrees in Honors and English with a focus in creative writing. In her spare time she's learning sign language with her hard of hearing husband, and she volunteers with special needs individuals attending the biweekly activities for Utah County's SNAP program.

VISIT TIANA SMITH ONLINE

TianaSmith.com

TianaSmithBooks

Ready to find
your next great read?

Let us help.

Visit prh.com/nextread

Penguin
Random
House